If God
Wills It

ROB MCLAREN

If God Wills It

Rob McLaren

This edition was published in 2025.
Printed by Amazon — KDP Printing
Copyright © 2017 Dylan Trust

Robert McLaren asserts the moral right
to be identified as the author of this work.

This novel is a work of fiction. The incidents and some of the characters
portrayed in it, while based on real historical events and figures,
are the work of the author's imagination.

A CiP record for this book is available from the National Library
of Australia and the State Library of Queensland.

Text and illustration copyright © 2023 Rob McLaren
Graphic design, typesetting and map illustrations by Matthew Lin
www.matthewlin.com.au

Paperback   ISBN 978-1-7635-392-1-1
E-book   ISBN 978-1-7635-392-2-8

Typeset in Bembo Semi-bold 12 pt

If God Wills It

Acknowledgements

I sincerely thank the following people who generously supported the publishing of this book:

Martin Boycott-Brown

Gail Cartwright

Victor Eiser

Lauren Elise Daniels

Michael Hunzel

Matthew Lin

Sophie Walker

If God Wills It
Maps

If God Wills It
Appendices

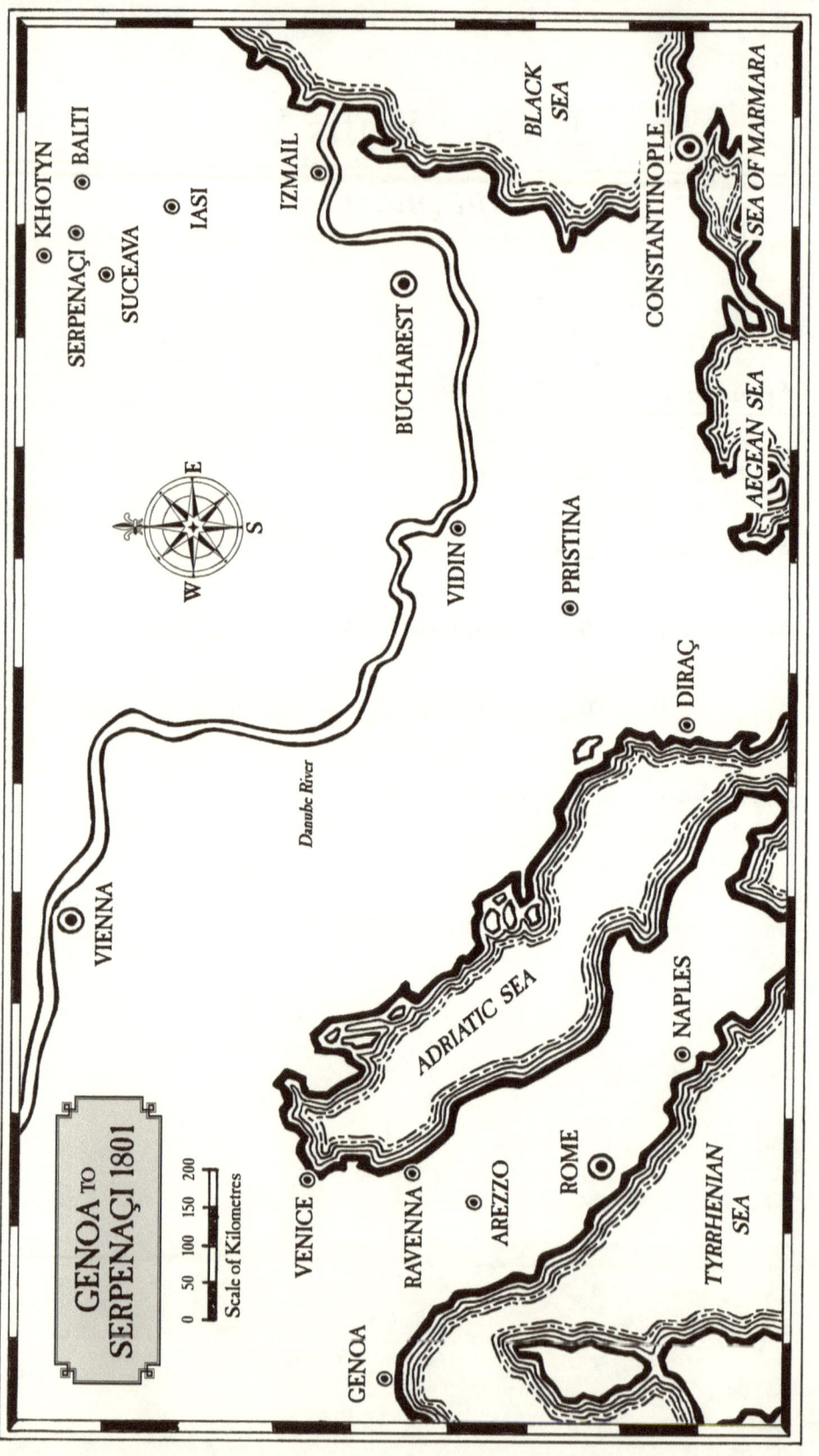

GENOA TO
SERPENAÇI 1801

Scale of Kilometres
0   50 100 150 200

KHOTYN
BALTI
SERPENAÇI
SUCEAVA
IASI
IZMAIL
BLACK SEA
CONSTANTINOPLE
SEA OF MARMARA
BUCHAREST
AEGEAN SEA
VIDIN
PRISTINA
DIRAÇ
Danube River
VIENNA
ADRIATIC SEA
NAPLES
VENICE
RAVENNA
AREZZO
ROME
TYRRHENIAN SEA
GENOA

Prologue
September 1801, Serpenaçi, Moldavia

Lieutenant Colonel André Jobert's extended sabre locked everyone's attention.

The nervous eyes that surrounded Jobert and his companions did not blink. Men's eyes. Women's eyes. Some flickered, betraying their thoughts of escape.

Even the tethered horses rolled their eyes and swivelled their ears towards the silent confrontation, their nostrils square as they scented the panic around them.

Hundreds of such eyes drilled into the three raised, unwavering blades. Peering over their hilts, three steely faces assessed the surrounding crowd. Outnumbered over one hundred to one, Jobert needed to act to break the trance of fear. Before the eyes twinkled with possibility of revenge, where every past sin, every moment of suffering these people had endured would be expunged if they could only rip this tiny, but lethal, group of sabreurs apart.

In the shadow of the battlement's arch and with their backs to the barred fortress gate, Jobert's friends' faces started to lower. Their sabre tips dipped with their wavering spirit.

I have failed, he thought. *They have won.*

Jobert believed he could have held if Koschak had remained at his side.

But Koschak was gone.

Not only had he lost Koschak, he had lost everything.

All the gold.

All the horses.

All he had was his life.

And the lives of his friends beside him.

And the lives of the terrified people who confronted him.

These angry eyes caused Jobert little concern. What he dreaded was the steady, unblinking gaze of Begnzarov.

For beyond the thick timber gate behind him, on the steppe beyond, Jobert knew something truly terrible was thundering towards them all. Tonight, or tomorrow morning, this barbaric savagery would arrive and inflict excruciating misery upon each soul.

Tomorrow, everyone present in front of Serpenaçi's Iasi Gate would be flayed, screaming meat. All these eyeballs would be torn from their skulls.

It cannot end this way. Jobert lowered his blade. *These people are not my enemies.*

The two men beside him twitched at his capitulation.

With flowing smoothness, Jobert sheathed his sabre.

The crowd hissed with exhaled relief.

With shoulders heavy with sadness, Jobert turned his back on the crowd. He willed his leaden knees to bend as he walked towards the brooding gate.

He heaved to lift the locking bar. He strained to pivot one of the gates inwards. Ash eddied on the steppe beyond the walls.

How had it unravelled so badly?

Jobert's voice rasped with failure.

'We go home today.'

Chapter One
August 1800, Auvergne, France

Over a year before …

Lieutenant Colonel André Jobert leaned back against the steady rise and fall of the horse's sun-warmed ribcage. No sooner had he closed his eyes, than a woman's scream tore the air.

'André!'

Just beyond his outstretched arm stood a young woman. Despite her hair piled with combs, curls fell across her lowered face as she inspected a wound in her belly. Wearing an oversized *chasseur's* tailcoat, her fingers barely emerged from the long sleeves to staunch the bleeding.

Jobert's heart punched against his ribs. His chest was crushed by such an intense longing for the girl that he could only hiss her name. 'Gianna!'

Drumming hooves pounded his senses.

She pointed a dripping finger from a soaked cuff. 'Behind you!'

Cossacks? he thought. Jobert could not see the source of

the thunderous hoof falls. He could not control his feet as he turned. An empty meadow under a bright blue sky swirled in his vision. He groped at the air. *Where is she?*

Jobert's bumbling movement startled a horse lying at his feet. He recognised his warhorse, Rouge, thrashing to stand. His sabre was trapped in Rouge's throat. Rouge's eyes rolled in panic. Jobert's hand and forearm stung with the heat of Rouge's blood. Jobert lurched, struggling to extract his hand from the sabre's sword knot.

'André!' A familiar voice called.

Jobert swivelled once more.

Gianna considered him with a grey-white face. Mottled blue lips curled in disdain.

She extended a pistol's muzzle towards Jobert.

A puff of smoke bloomed from the barrel. No sound of the shot.

The ball shoved Jobert as it struck.

He choked as blood filled his mouth.

Jobert was buffeted awake from his nightmare, as the warhorse against whom he napped, Bleu, lurched in the process of standing.

Facedown on his elbows and knees beside Bleu's hooves, Jobert shuddered from the emotions of the dream. His strangled cough twisted the word 'Gianna.' Jobert gripped tight to the meadow's clover and steadied his reeling senses. Mountain grass, yellowing under an August sun, yielded to a cool breeze. Wildflowers nodded their petals to pollen-laden bees. Warblers poked for beetles amongst the horse dung.

'André?' The same voice.

Jobert's head jerked at the call. Jobert blinked at the legs of two horses, and beyond Bleu's belly at the stirrupped feet of their riders.

One horseman dismounted and passed his reins to the other.

At an unseen signal, Bleu dropped his great head and stepped backwards.

Duque stepped around Bleu's nose and helped Jobert to kneel. 'Bad dreams?'

As he calmed his breathing, Jobert's gaze flickered from his boyhood friend's drooping, speckled moustache to his missing right ear. Jobert spat blood from his mouth.

Duque's thick forearms and solid chest bulged through his jacket as he lifted Jobert to stand. 'Did Bleu knock you as he rose?'

Jobert sought surety by gripping Bleu's neck. 'My dentures.' Jobert's fingers, still quivering from his confusion, scraped a row of three false teeth from his lower left jaw. 'I usually remove them when I ... I found Bleu sleeping here in the sun. I thought I would steal a quick nap.'

The second horseman leaned from his saddle to stroke Bleu's neck. 'A good day for a snooze with an old mate.' As Moench, Jobert's trumpeter, sat upright, a handsome smile curved one twisted end of his mouse-brown moustache. He patted an Austrian fusilier's satchel slung across his chest. 'An even better day for a picnic in the shade.'

Moench walked his grey, and led Duque's chestnut, towards boulders beneath the forest's branches.

Jobert and Duque followed and took their places on a fallen log. From his satchel, Moench produced a bottle of *Marc d'Auvergne* and a round of *fouchtra*.

'Rinse your mouth.' The remaining three fingers of Duque's right hand curled around the offered cup. 'How are you feeling?'

Jobert winced as the smoky brandy stung the cuts in his gum. 'Better.'

'Duque and I are to accompany a convoy to Paris,' Moench mumbled through a mouthful of cheese. 'Why not come with us?'

'I am barely home a week from Italy,' Jobert said.

Moench swept hair strands, errant from his long brown queue, behind his ear. 'We have washed the sweat and blood from our skin.' A gulp of slightly amber liquor cleansed his mouth. 'We have drunk the dust and smoke from our throats. We have eaten and shat the ammunition bread from our guts.' He raised the mouldy rind with a flourish. 'We are home.'

Duque shared the last wedge of silky soft cheese with Jobert. 'And we have buried and grieved for Tulloc.'

Moench's steady hazel eyes watched Jobert from above his cup rim. 'Marengo is in our past, sir. Italy is behind us. Our friend is at peace. Come to Paris.'

'Marengo is only two months in our past.' Jobert blinked at memories of brick dust and vine trellises. 'It is not Marengo that confounds me. I am still posted to headquarters in Milan,' Jobert said as he hung his head, 'and I must return.'

'The Army of Italy can wait, sir. Paris is what we all need.' Moench dribbled the flask's dregs into the three cups. 'Paris in summer — music, wine and women.' Moench offered an encouraging grin. 'Your brother and De Chabenac enjoy the Parisian season. Why not us?'

'Go to Paris. Enjoy her pleasures.' Jobert drained his cup and passed it to Moench, as Moench packed his satchel. 'I will remain here with my uncle. There is much to do.'

'Bullshit,' Duque said, leading his horse from under the branches to which it was hitched. 'What is there to do?'

Jobert lowered his face. 'I will ...'

Moench ran his reins over his horse's ears then paused before placing his foot in the stirrup. He glanced at Jobert. 'It is not like you to be indecisive, sir.'

Duque gripped Jobert's upper arm and squeezed. The remaining fingers of his combat-mutilated hand were as tight as forge tongs. 'We will speak of her when I return.'

With a furtive glance, Jobert's eyes swept the meadow for Gianna.

Just in case.

Two months later, with an October sunset far beyond the western ridges, Jobert squelched up the path from the stables to the Chauvel family's farmhouse. A blue-grey light hung in the spaces between the interlocking stone walls of pigsty, milking yard and vegetable garden. Jobert felt his grandfather's presence as smoke from the farm's many chimneys swirled like a passing cloak.

Kitchen warmth and the smell of soap greeted Jobert as he passed through the back door. Maria, his dead groom's widow, scrubbed shirts on a washboard at the other end of the laundry. Her son, three-year-old Andrea, Jobert's namesake, whimpered and wiped his snotty nose with his pudgy hand. Jobert's vision drifted to his first encounter with Tulloc, the child's strapping father. Tulloc sobbed as he was informed that he was not good enough a rider to serve in Jobert's chasseur company. Duque had suggested Tulloc become an apprentice farrier. Jobert's vision slid to his last memory of his groom. Tulloc's face dusted white from the broken walls of Marengo. His crushed chest seeping brown through his tunic.

He put toe to heel to remove his muddy stable clogs. As he set them towards the wall, so he placed down Tulloc's bespattered memory.

In his stockings, he padded along the cold flagstones and entered the internal hall. His uncle sat at a long teak dining room table, his back to a fire in the hearth, surrounded by books of account, candles and ink pots.

Yann arched his eyebrows above his wire spectacles as he followed Jobert's progress across the room. 'Did you visit them again?' As was the family tradition, Yann spoke German whilst in the house.

Jobert stopped beside an engraved sideboard. He filled a thick green glass with *Saint-Porçain* white wine from a ceramic jug. Jobert gave an affirmative grunt before draining his glass. 'Just grandfather.' Jobert responded in German. 'Want one?'

Yann nodded. 'Did they ... he have anything different to say than last time?'

Jobert shrugged as he refilled his glass and Yann's, then made his way to a spare chair at the table. With a fingertip, he pivoted a news broadsheet to read the headlines.

Yann jabbed his silver pen at the newspaper. 'Despite the flogging you gave them in Italy, the Austrians refuse to submit to a new peace. Bonaparte has ordered Moreau to cross the Rhine and finish the bastards off.'

The humidity of the June day four months ago pulsed at Jobert from the glass cup close to his face. Grime-matted bearfur helmets, both French and Austrian, lay dead-still in the spiky wheat stubble. He swallowed deeply to sluice Marengo's dust and blood from his throat.

With his left hand, Yann adjusted the stump of his right arm amputated at the elbow, that had rested on a pillow on his lap, before flipping over the newspaper to reveal a letter. 'For you.'

Jobert checked both sides of the envelope, before cracking open the wax seal. 'It is from Raive.' As his eyes slid down the page, so his shoulders drooped. 'I am to report for duty in Genoa on the first of March.'

Yann creaked back in his wooden chair and considered his

dead sister's son. 'Then I can squeeze three more months of work out of you.'

'Before returning to Italy?' Jobert's fingers flicked the letter onto the table. 'Maybe not.'

Yann's brow creased with irritation. 'By God's whiskers, do orders not apply to officers? Fuck the Revolution, eh? You have not changed from the arrogant pricks we had before. Who is caring for your soldiers?'

'I do not command. I am a staff officer.'

'Another idle bastard staff officer. Then who is organising bread and meat for the men?'

Jobert levelled his stare at his uncle. 'Would you like me to stay or return?'

'I want you to return, but not to Italy. To us.' The intensity of Yann's eyes was magnified through his spectacles' lenses. 'I served for twenty-five years. I fought for seven. I have my wounds.' The fingers of Yann's left hand extended towards Jobert. Then they retracted under his palm. 'I see yours.'

Jobert sat very still. His breath slid through his nostrils. The scent of the prey he sought was in the moment. He just could not determine its form.

'Not that I am complaining,' Yann said. 'I am very happy you are here.'

Jobert's phantom darted from his coursing mind.

'Horses are what you are good at, André. You ought to stay. Your contributions from Italy over the last six years have grown your ownership to thirty per cent.'

Jobert's face twitched in calculation. 'Is the farm in financial difficulty?'

'No, not at all. Five years of the Directory's chaos gone. New century. New consulate. A window of opportunity opens with the stability that Bonaparte brings.' His left fist punched the table. 'By God's whiskers, seize it!'

Faced by Jobert's wooden silence, Yann's exuberance wilted, and his concern regrew. 'Tell me, André. What dread awaits you in Milan?'

'My time is wasted there.' Jobert shrugged. 'I feel ... lost.'

'Then find yourself, man. Here. Italy. Anywhere. But, for God's teeth, act!'

Jobert glanced up from the nervous colt he was handling at a flurry of Christmas snow whipping into the cloying warmth of the small indoor round yard. A groom, arms threaded through harness collars, shouted with frustration as he struggled to close the barn door.

Jobert's bay colt tensed. Its swivelling ears searched for threat.

Jobert slid his finger into the young horse's mouth and tickled its sticky tongue. The colt softened its lower jaw at Jobert's intrusive touch and relaxed its taut neck muscles.

'I know your future, little man ...' Jobert's caress slowed at the memory of a Chauvel horse harnessed to a gun limber. The vision stood patiently with the rest of the artillery horse team. Trapped in the stalled wagon traffic in the rout from Novi. *Probably ... hopefully ... serving now in the Austrian or Russian army.* Jobert shook off the miserable recollection and returned to his own predicament. 'But do you know mine?'

The young horse rolled his closest eye with uncertainty.

Jobert traced his fingertips along the colt's back, loins and down towards its hocks. The horse lifted it rear hoof to the signal. Jobert bent, cupped the pastern to support the raised foot, and rubbed the obedient leg.

'Having flogged the Austrians at Hohenlinden,' said a voice behind Jobert's folded posture. 'Moreau has pursued them tothe gates of Vienna. That will surely force a peace on the emperor.'

Jobert twisted to see Duque shuffling through the arena dust scanning a newssheet. Feeling the colt's leg muscles tense at the crinkling page, Jobert placed the colt's foot back down, stood and rubbed the horse's rump with long, slow strokes.

'And in Egypt ...' Duque's eyes flicked from the pages to the colt's clamped tail and startled eyes. 'Sorry.' Duque stepped back and lowered the pages.

Jobert tickled the dock of the horse's tail. By raising the tail, the colt relaxed again.

'Did you ever see any of our horses during the campaigns?' Duque asked.

'Every now and then.' Jobert pushed the Novi memory away with a welcoming smile. 'How was Christmas in Paris?'

'You were missed,' said Duque. 'Everyone sends their fondest regards.'

'You are returning?'

'Yes. Another order demands our immediate return. A quick trip before Genoa. Come back to Paris with me. There is only so long you can subsist on cuddling a horse.'

'No.'

'Come to Paris and buy as many sweet embraces —'

'No!' The colt perked alert at Jobert's shift in tension.

'André, Paris is not Italy.' Duque's square jaw clenched. 'She is not in Paris.'

'I will not find ... I have these colts ...'

'What happened?'

'About what?'

'You know what. Gianna.'

Jobert's face pinched with sadness. A ghost wrapped in a gore-stained canvas horse rug lay across the back of the twitching colt.

'After Marengo, I took her brother's body back to her family. I was too slow.'

'Moench said you and Koschak pushed hard for Mantua on the eve we held the field.'

'Still, I was too late. She had not waited.'

'So, where —'

'She had married a man from her past.'

'In a matter of weeks?' Duque recoiled in disbelief. 'You were together in April, and she was married by June?'

With his wrists resting on the colt's rump, Jobert extended his fingers. 'She said that while I held sabre and reins, I was unable to hold her.' He wiggled his fingertips. The curls on her slender neck dissipated in the steam of his breath. 'It is simple, Duque.' Jobert shrugged. 'Gianna is gone.'

'Very well. It is not the girl.' Duque raised his palms. 'I ask because ... I see your fire extinguished by these ill humours. I do not recognise you. If it is not Gianna, what is it about returning to Italy that fills you with despair? The Italian chasseurs? The headquarters in Milan?'

'It is none of that.' Jobert shuddered. 'My assignment with the chasseurs has, thankfully, ended. Yes, I dread Milan ... her father, any of them around the headquarters ... no, what I want ...'

'You want what?'

'I want ... I feel lost.' Jobert's palms anchored in the horse's winter coat. 'I want to find ... my place.'

Duque gripped Jobert's shoulder. 'When we return from Paris, we will prepare for Genoa. André, you have four weeks. Currently, you cannot find your arse with both hands.' Duque gave Jobert a rough shake. 'Find yourself.'

The valley's clouds rose through powder-laden branches. The blanket of February snow muted any sound. As Jobert adjusted his seat on his grandfather's grave, the stacked rocks clicked with frosty sharpness. It was Bleu's snort, and the crunch from his hooves as he shifted his weight, that alerted Jobert to an approaching rider.

De Chabenac entered the grove around the graves and tethered his charger beside Bleu. 'Yann told me you would be up here.' De Chabenac's long polished riding boots disappeared into the snow at each step, the hem of his well-tailored riding cloak skimmed the icy surface, and, hanging beneath the coat, the steel tip of a scabbard scored a rut in his wake.

Jobert stood and gripped his friend in a tight hug. 'What news from Paris?'

'Peace with Austria has been signed at Lunéville. Egypt remains quiet. Bonaparte's new consulate brings confidence to this new century. You never know what is around the corner.'

'That is true. You do not know what lies around the corner. It is usually an ambush.' Jobert indicated for De Chabenac to sit upon the grave. 'Join me.'

De Chabenac hesitated. 'Is this your father?'

'No.' Jobert jerked his chin towards a mossy cairn further away. 'This is my grandfather. I am reflecting upon his words.'

'And they are?'

'They say, young man, you have all the time in the world. They are wrong. You do not have a moment to lose.'

'And you reflect upon his wisdom because ...'

'I am afraid I am losing such moments.'

De Chabenac extended his long legs and nodded in agreement. 'Are you ready for your return to Italy?'

Jobert's posture folded, his elbows on his knees, his head hung. 'I suppose so.'

'Will it not be good to see Koschak again?'

'Yes, it will.'

'And Raive and Marguerite in Genoa?'

Jobert winced and looked away.

'What? Did you leave Raive on poor terms? No misgivings about him, surely?'

Certainly no concerns about the husband, Jobert thought. 'Yes, it will be good to see Koschak again.'

'Is that a renewed commitment to return to duty?'

Jobert scoffed and threw up his hands.

De Chabenac's eyebrows raised to the sullen clouds. 'I will take that as a yes.'

Chapter Two
March 1801, Genoa, Italy

As he stepped back from his embrace with Colonel Raive, Jobert sensed a trap.

Jobert masked his suspicions by turning to the room's aspect over the sea. Light rain speckled the glassed panelled doors. Jobert had not seen the Mediterranean for over a year since last with Raive. Viewed over the stone balustrade encircling the patio, the wave-dappled surface warped as the ocean breathed.

'A year, my friend. Too long.' Raive patted Jobert's shoulder. 'And Marengo? A desperate affair, I hear.'

Jobert's lips crimped in a grim smile as he avoided looking at the marked shift in Raive's receding hairline. 'Slightly better than enduring the deprivations of a six-week siege, as you did here.'

'Such moments have passed.' As a maid set down a coffee service, Raive indicated a plush, embroidered armchair. 'Please, Jobert, sit.' Raive poured rich, black coffee from the silver pot.

The fire in the wrought-iron hearth crackled.

'Spring has brought opportunity. A chance that would suit

you well.' A sense of delight wrinkled Raive's eyes. 'Tall black horses.' As Raive extended a porcelain cup and saucer to Jobert, his jacket's velvet sleeve glistened and revealed the delicate lace of his cuff.

'Tall black horses?'

'For Bonaparte's Consular Guard. I read that they performed rather well at Marengo. Did you see them go in?'

'I was on the other side of the field.' Jobert grimaced. 'Black horses, you say?'

'A recent attempt to supply the required remounts found them relatively rare. Prices as high as three thousand francs per horse.' Raive's moustache wiggled as he sipped. 'A consortium of investors is looking to establish a horse-breeding enterprise to supply the army. We have secured the land and a number of fine stallions.' Raive's clear eyes locked on Jobert. 'We now need brood mares.'

Jobert twitched a polite smile. *Of course, another scheme.* 'Into which branch of service are your foals destined? To be trained under saddle or in harness? Or are you focused only on black horse for the Guard?'

'Not draught stock,' Raive said. 'The market for Percheron and Norman crossbreds is well supplied. No, we are interested in producing cavalry remounts. Nothing speculative. A solid return from a consistent market.'

'How many remounts do you intend to supply? How large a breeding herd?'

Raive lowered his eyes and his smile widened. 'We hope to maintain contracts by being viewed as a dependable source. Perhaps one hundred mares and grow from there.' Raive offered a plate of oblong wafers. '*Cantuccio?*'

'To sell one hundred four-year olds would need,' Jobert's thumb calculated on his fingertips, 'a herd of around five hundred, based on one hundred and twenty mares.'

'One hundred and twenty mares? Is that so?' Raive's eyebrows arched in surprise.

Jobert twirled a cantuccio across the surface of his coffee. 'To turn off a crop of one hundred four-year-olds, one must allow a percentage of wastage per annum.' Jobert savoured the biscuit's citrus and coconut flavours. 'It will take five years to turn off your first crop of foals. Are your investors able to cover the expenses until your first sale?'

'They are aware of the period until first revenue.' said Raive. 'Budgeting on purchasing mares at one thousand five hundred francs per head—'

'Our purse stands at two hundred thousand francs.'

Jobert emitted an impressed grunt. 'Where would you base the herd?'

'In the Loire. Near Tours.'

'The Loire? That valley country would easily stock one horse per two hectares. Your intended herd would require around one thousand hectares. Do you have access to such an area?'

Raive cocked his head in search of a memory. 'Over double that, I believe, but I shall check.' Raive jotted a note on a pad by his elbow.

'Double? Sufficient for two hundred and fifty brood mares?' Jobert sipped at his coffee. 'You have the land available to produce two hundred saleable four-year-olds?'

'Double the mares to be purchased? Interesting.' Raive put his fingertip to his chin. 'At one thousand five hundred francs per horse would require ... a pot of four hundred thousand francs should cover it.' Raive's eyes narrowed on Jobert. 'Very interesting.'

'Are your investors expecting their seed capital to double?'

'The shareholders are quite diverse, each with deep pockets and stable incomes.' The coffee pot exhaled aromatic steam as Raive refilled Jobert's cup. 'Parisians, who are open to speculation in all manner of circumstances, welcome my local insight.'

Jobert accepted his returned cup and saucer with gloved fingers. 'Have you invested in this venture?'

Raive shrugged. 'A little.'

Jobert contemplated Raive. 'How many potential stallions do you intend to stand?'

'Currently, four.'

'Based on four stallions for crossbreeding and keeping your two-year-old fillies for breeding stock ...' Jobert took a pencil and notebook from within his chasseur-green tailcoat. 'Then you could quadruple your brood mare herd in eight years. You would increase your sale ...'

Raive settled back into his chair and his mouth closed on a coffee-infused wafer.

Jobert continued to scribble. 'You still meet your original outcome, but your situation is improved. You shift from one hundred horses for sale within four years, to one hundred geldings within four years and one hundred fillies join your brood mare herd in two years, all within your first crop of—.'

Raive reached out a hand and stopped Jobert. 'Can you hear yourself, Jobert? Can you see how such an undertaking is ideal for you? You were born for an enterprise like this.'

Jobert stiffened in his chair and eyed Raive warily.

'That is why you are needed.' Raive watched Jobert over the rim of his cup as he drank the last of his coffee. 'You can think in the scale required. Would you consider joining the affair?'

Jobert flinched. 'Investing?'

'No,' said Raive. 'Managing.'

Jobert frowned as fragments of previous advice swirled.

His uncle's views on opportunity.

His grandfather's views on time.

'Moments with the new peace are fleeting.' Raive waggled a fingertip. 'For a young man unsure of his path, there have never been so many signs indicating his way. No wonder your uncle wants to keep you in the Auvergne.'

Leaning back, Jobert intertwined his fingers in his lap. 'Where would I start? Your venture has no mares.'

'Perhaps that is somewhere for you to start.' Raive grinned. 'With the new peace, acquire mares here in Italy. Koschak reports—'

'Italy! Are our Italian … friends involved? Will there be a need to return to …?'

'Rizzoli in Milan? Bernasconi in Mantua? Why? Is there a problem?'

Jobert exhaled deeply. 'My assignment to the Cisalpine Chasseurs was not …'

'Since Marengo,' Raive opened his palms upwards, 'I have heard nothing but praise from those in high office. The First Consul, Berthier, Masséna and Lannes all spoke well of your conduct with the Cisalpine Chasseurs.'

'I would like to avoid … I would feel most uncomfortable encountering Prefetto Bernasconi again.'

'Ah … the daughter Gianna.' Raive pursed his lips. 'Perhaps here on the Army of Italy's Genoan staff we might keep you occupied in western and southern Italy. Allow De Chabenac to enjoy Milan.'

'I would appreciate that, sir.' Jobert nodded. 'You spoke of Koschak. Where is he?'

'Italians dominate the horse trade in the Po valley. I sent Koschak off to investigate the availability of mares in Piedmont and Lombardy. I am expecting him back any day now. He reports potential leads around Ravenna.'

'You have ensnared Koschak in your scheme?'

'No, no, just engaged his talents during the winter months to establish a network.' Raive turned to stoke the fire. The logs crumbled to embers. Raive placed two wedges of timber on the bright orange coals. 'So, your new role … a procurer of horses for the army, yes?'

'If I must remain a staff officer then …' Jobert's fingers twisted in their interlocking grip. 'Yes, I suppose … that might suit me best.'

'Then that is settled.' Raive moved to the sideboard upon which a Venetian decanter sat. 'I shall have letters of introduction prepared. A toast.' Raive poured two glasses of *grappa di prugna* and handed one to Jobert. 'To buying horses with someone else's money.'

Jobert stood and raised his glass. 'Two hundred and fifty brood mares with four hundred thousand francs, no less.'

Jobert rolled the grappa over his tongue and let the flavours of honeyed fruit and gentle spices excite his imagination.

Raive beamed and refilled their glasses. 'The ladies are excited that you and De Chabenac will join us for dinner tonight. The boys will be keen to see their uncles.'

Jobert shivered. *How will Marguerite receive me now?*

Jobert juggled his *vermentino* as he attempted to sit less awkwardly on the edge of the divan.

Backlit by the sizzling coals, Raive's two little sons danced on the salon's hearth rug. Cheered by Raive's clapping beat, the children, one five years old and the other three, wobbled and swayed to a lively tune that Moench played on his violin.

Awaiting the signal to return the children to their nursery, Anissa, the maid, also kept time with her fingertips tapping her palm.

Anissa. Had eight years really passed since the de Rossi ball? thought Jobert. He remembered dance lessons with Anissa and her fellow Avignon prostitutes. At the ball, his friend Fergnes badgered him to dance with the cousin Camille so Fergnes could engage the beautiful Marguerite.

Fergnes eventually married Marguerite. She bore him a son. Fergnes was impaled by an uhlan's lance at Caldiero. Raive married the widow Marguerite and now clapped encouragement to a prancing five-year-old stepson.

Marguerite sat erect on her upholstered chair. Jobert savoured her gown trapped tight around her long thighs. Her upraised chin extended her neck. Her pulsing veins were mauve under her porcelain skin. Her lips quivered as if she desired to bestow a kiss. Her dark eyes were attentive on Moench.

As Moench's fingers danced along his fingerboard, so his eyes flitted from Margeurite to the children. To Raive. To Jobert.

A memory of Marguerite rocking above his straining waist caused a flare of heat through Jobert's loins. The younger child was his. An evening together with Marguerite immediately prior to Raive's marriage proposal. The resemblance to Jobert's uncle and brother was obvious. Nothing had ever been said.

Jobert averted a scowl. The implications of a son were still to be processed. As the child grew, then that clarity was pressing.

The rural melody ended. The five-year-old bowed. The three-year-old parodied his big brother. Their audience applauded. Anissa's firm grip guided the children from the room. Childish protestations were muted with affectionate pats.

Following the maid and the boys, Moench passed the back of Jobert's divan.

Jobert smiled. 'Do not, Moench.'

'Do not, sir?'

Knowing Moench's midnight intentions, Jobert's eyes hardened above his smile. 'Do not!'

De Chabenac stretched his stockinged calves and buckled court shoes towards the fire. 'Colonel Raive, what news of our army stranded in Egypt?'

'Trapped, I am afraid.' Raive stepped his toasted thighs away from the hearth's intensity. 'Our fleet is incapable of defeating the British squadron in the Mediterranean and returning our men. Apart from contesting Egypt, our war with Britain remains inconclusive.'

'Politics. How dull.' The folded lace fan of Marguerite's cousin, Camille, tapped Jobert's forearm. 'You would not have seen the boys since we evacuated Genoa before the siege.' Camille's view followed the departing children and staff. Dark curls in the Grecian style swept her neck behind her earlobe. 'Does the baby not look like his father?' A faint smile creased her soft cheek. She returned her attention to Jobert, inclining forward onto a crimson cushion between them. 'When will we be entertained by your children, Jobert?'

Jobert fought the temptation of admiring her deliberately placed decolletage. 'Did you not ask that last time we dined?'

Marguerite tipped her head towards Jobert and Camille. 'Last year, dear Jobert, we had hoped to be introduced to Signorina Bernasconi.'

'I believe Jobert's signorina married an Austrian officer?' Camille affected a theatrical melancholy.

'It was not to be.' Jobert forced a smile. 'Gianna has found companionship with an old friend of her brother's.' Jobert shrugged. 'They had known each other for many years. He lost his arm at Rivoli and no longer serves. I imagine her family well satisfied at the arrangement and her most content.'

'Her happiness must cause you great delight?' Marguerite twisted a ruby-set wedding band on her left hand.

'I am ... am happy for her.' Engaged from both sides, Jobert was unsure of whom to parry. 'Although our friendship

28

was strong, my service to France would cause Gianna such discomfort I could not bear her to suffer.' Jobert shot a look of desperation at De Chabenac.

With his charming smile, De Chabenac gave Jobert an imperceptible dip of his head. 'A shopping expedition, I hear, Colonel. For brood mares, no less.'

'Quite so.' Raive bounced upon his toes. 'One must pluck the hopes that are blossoming with this new peace. I have enlisted Jobert's skills in this regard.'

De Chabenac considered Jobert with an amused expression. 'Fine horsemanship is but one of Jobert's many accomplishments.'

Camille ran her fingertips along Jobert's forearm. 'If anyone can identify the fertile, Jobert is your man.'

With a quiver of conspiratorial eyelashes towards her cousin, Marguerite repressed her amusement. 'As firm as dear Jobert's competence for breeding may be, when we seek pleasure, he wilts. Darling De Chabenac, do not deny us the latest pleasures of Paris.'

'Your mother and sister are quite well?' Raive asked.

De Chabenac bowed his head. 'They are—'

'Your gorgeous sister is sure to be sporting the latest style,' Camille said. 'We are going up to Paris for the season. Without another dreary war to interrupt us.'

'Yes, darling Raive,' Marguerite's slim finger aimed at her husband, 'you promised no more wars.' The finger then cut to Camille. 'Mother will know the fashion once we are together in Avignon.'

'And, did you hear, cousin,' Camille nodded, 'darling De Chabenac will attend headquarters in Milan?'

'Ooh!' Marguerite's curls bobbed as she smiled. 'A reliable source for this year's Milanese scandals.'

De Chabenac's smile broadened as his attempts to re-enter the fray were thwarted.

Thankful for the shift in the attack towards De Chabenac, Jobert's gaze swept the salon. Multiple candle flames pulsed on splayed silver arms. The finely wrought candelabra, with matching courtly figures entwined around the stem, stood on dark polished surfaces around the room. Each piece of elegant furniture floated above the embroidered carpets on intricate legs. Broad antique tapestries buttressed the wall's upper shadows.

If I had married Gianna, would this be me?

Through the patterned detail in the crystal wine glass in Jobert's fingertips, the room's light flowered tiny rainbows. Although he appreciated the beauty of each item, and how pleasant the room felt, Jobert could only see the cost. The cost to buy. The cost of the staff to polish. The cost to move upon each change of posting. *No, this is not who I am.*

'Oh, Jobert!'

Jobert jerked back into the conversation.

De Chabenac smiled. 'I saw our friend Zenari in Paris on occasion.'

'Zenari?' Jobert coughed on his sweet wine. *At Novi, the prick went for a walk in the middle of a battle.* 'Zenari is certainly not my friend.'

'Was he well?' Raive asked.

'He appeared most energised.' De Chabenac nodded. 'Promoted colonel, no less.'

Jobert's face crimped with impending calamity. 'Surely not regimental command?'

'Not yet,' Raive said. 'On the staff of the Cisalpine Legion. I thought it was resolved between you two?'

'Did he not come through at Marengo?' De Chabenac asked.

'It took too many empty saddles for him to be convinced of his appalling judgement.' Jobert clenched his jaw. 'I can only imagine he would revert to type.'

Anissa appeared at the salon door.

'No more such talk. Dinner is ready.' Marguerite stood and took De Chabenac's arm. 'What theatre did you attend in Paris, darling?'

The gentlemen escorted the ladies into the dining room.

Later that evening after dinner, as Jobert removed his jacket and waistcoat, a polite knock sounded on his bedchamber door.

Marguerite? A year ago, with his passion for Gianna roaring, Jobert had rebuffed Marguerite's approach. *I thought Moench might be on this evening's menu.*

Jobert opened the door.

Anissa, the maid, carried a tray on which she balanced a lit candle, a frosted pitcher and a squat glass. 'Madame felt you may require cold water, sir.'

Jobert smiled and accepted the tray.

Retaining the candle, Anissa curtsied and turned.

'Anissa, have your duties concluded for the evening?'

Anissa blinked in confusion. 'Yes, sir.'

Jobert turned a gold louis coin in his fingers.

'Might you stay a while?'

Chapter Three

A few days later, by the light of a single candle on a battered wooden table, Jobert flicked through one of Duque's equine anatomy texts. In the private room above a Genoese tavern, the raucous noise surged, like a swell beneath the deck, from the taproom below.

Moench sat with his back to the table, feet to the lit hearth, and strummed his violin strings in accompaniment to the musicians beneath.

At the table beside Jobert, Duque studied a text on medicinal compounds. He flicked back and forth between pages breathing the words he read.

Jobert tapped a page in the veterinary book that held his interest, a fold-out image of the bones of the horse's tail. 'Is it not of interest we use all of a horse, except these little bones in the tail?'

'Soup?' Moench strummed an ascending scale.

Duque's sad eyes roamed his memory. 'The bones of the coccygeal vertebrae.'

'Are these your notes in the margin?' Jobert asked.

'No. Your uncle's.'

Jobert flicked to the imprint page on the reverse of the title page. 'When he studied at Alfort? This textbook is from the late sixties?'

Duque frowned. 'Horses have not changed that much in forty years.'

Jobert glanced up as the door squealed open on rusted hinges.

Koschak billowed into the room as if lifted by the gale of tavern merriment at the base of the stairs. He removed a sun-bleached bicorne to reveal his smooth blond queue and hussar braids. 'I could not imagine a greater concentration of such ugly bastards.' He dropped his cylindrical portmanteau and his bedroll of blankets and paillasse and opened his muscular arms wide. 'Is there nothing but tea to welcome me, you miserly old tarts?'

Placing down his violin with care, Moench yielded to Koschak's crushing embrace.

'Making love, lad, or making money?' Koschak shook Moench's shoulders. 'What is your latest conquest? Wagers or women?'

'In the last nine months, sir? A lot of money,' Moench's moustache curled with pride, 'and a lot of ...' A nervous glance to Jobert betrayed him.

'Welcome, brother.' Duque's barrel chest thumped into Koschak's at the collision of their hug. 'And you? Still fleecing Italian officers at cards?'

'These boys need to learn,' Koschak boomed with laughter, 'and who better than an old soldier to teach them. What of you, my learned veterinary friend,' Koschak tapped the textbooks on the table, 'still studying interesting ways to getting your bollocks kicked by extending your arm into smelly holes?'

'I must constantly refine my techniques.' Duque held up the three fingers of his battle-scarred right hand. 'Last time I palpated ovaries, I lost two of the bastards.'

Koschak turned to Jobert and beamed. 'Sir.'

Jobert clinched Koschak hard in greeting.

Both men had no words, but their eyes smarted with the emotion of being together once again.

Koschak blinked and looked around the room. 'Where is that tall streak of piss who evaded the guillotine?'

'De Chabenac has departed for Milan,' Jobert said.

'And you?' Koschak slapped Jobert's shoulder. 'Last time I saw you, that bitch had you gut shot. Are you sufficiently … healed?'

'Sufficiently?' Jobert grinned. 'I believe so.'

'Moench,' Koschak growled, 'has the colonel here been attending to all his needs? Two legged fillies, not four?'

Moench coughed a laugh. 'At least once. That we know of.'

Jobert hunched with a guilty shrug. 'But it is those four-legged fillies I now desire.'

They all sat around the small table's candle, cleared Duque's books and each man had his cup refilled with a splash of grappa.

'One hundred mares cannot be found for love nor money.' Koschak exhaled a liquored cough. 'The war has stripped Lombardy of her horses. Perhaps old brood mares. Maybe fillies, farm by farm.'

Jobert rapped his pottery cup on the table. 'I have convinced Raive he no longer needs one hundred mares.'

'Oh?' Koschak raised his eyebrows.

'No, he needs two hundred and fifty.'

'Oh!'

Moench poured another round of the local *eau de vie*. 'So where do we find two hundred and fifty in a land with no horses?'

Duque folded his arms. 'The slow process of visiting every village and buying fillies.'

'Touring Italy and collecting horses.' Jobert raised his cup in toast. 'Could you imagine a more pleasant way to spend the summer?'

Koschak slid a cautious look at Jobert. 'Does Raive have the cash for two hundred and fifty?'

'Four hundred thousand francs? Yes.'

Koschak whistled. 'More chance in Tuscany and the Roman Republic. Perhaps I suggest we travel south and learn who are the major players around Florence and Rome. Then travel north once more buying mares as the cooler months make selling more attractive. Ten horses in the twenty-five largest towns in Italy. Even if we only buy one hundred mares, we can return for the rest next year.'

'Naples?' Duque asked.

Koschak winced. 'I hesitate to travel to Naples or beyond. The Neapolitans hate us.'

Moench filled Jobert's cup. 'South for fillies, sir?'

Duque nudged Jobert with his elbow. 'Now, there is a light in your eyes, André, I have not seen in a long time.'

'Yes, something has shifted.' Jobert's cheek creased in a wide smile. 'Something good.' He raised his cup. 'Gentlemen, to Rome and beyond.'

The Arezzo horse sales were conducted on the Val di Chiana flood plain, at the intersection of the road to Florence and the Castro tributary running north to the Arno River. Crowning a steep hill nearby, the tower of Arezzo's Basilica rose above the walls of its medieval fortress.

On this cold mid-March morning with high cloud cover, Jobert noted steamed breath, the aroma of baked bread and local laughter rose above the canvas awnings clustered around, and the cackling and mooing from within, the sale grounds.

There was no laughter amongst Jobert's dragoon escort.

The dragoon captain had half of the dragoon platoon remain mounted in all-round defence of the horse-holders. 'Sergeant, sabres rest,' he ordered. The ten dragoons drew their sabres and lowered the pommels onto their right thighs, the blades against their shoulders.

Moench exhaled in despair at the precaution. As Jobert handed him Bleu's reins, he gave Moench's thigh a reassuring punch.

As Jobert advanced over the stalls' slanted guy ropes, the eight dismounted dragoons formed a V-formation behind their captain, Jobert, Koschak and Duque. The dragoon captain gave a morose grunt that caused his silver moustache to flare. The two dragoon corporals cocked their musket hammers.

'A little provocative, Captain?' Jobert said.

With his thumb, the captain lifted the hilt of his dragoon sword clear of the scabbard. 'We are not safe here, sir.'

'Why?' Jobert asked. 'Did we strip Arezzo in '98?' Jobert remembered staving off February's ice with roast chestnuts as he participated in the French Army's pillage of Lucca two hundred kilometres to the northwest.

The dragoon officer snorted. 'Where did we not strip in '98?' The officer shook his head. 'We are in the heart of the *Viva Maria* resistance.'

'Part of the *Sanfedismo* movement?' Koschak asked.

'Indeed. Hence my colonel's insistence on your escort being no less than twenty men.'

As Jobert and dragoon escort emerged amongst the peripheral stalls and moved between the lines of tethered horses and cattle, penned sheep and crated geese, the marketplace's human voices fell silent.

All eyes turned towards them.

Bells sounded from the basilica in the centre of Arezzo.

'A little early for Lauds, is it not?' Duque asked.

'It is not a call to prayer.' The dragoon scanned the city walls from under the peak of his brass helmet. 'It is a warning.'

'The threat?' Koschak asked.

'Us.'

'Let us maintain our confidence, gentlemen,' Jobert said, 'as here comes a priest.'

'Huh!' the dragoon captain grumbled. 'Here comes the partisans' commander.'

'*Buongiorno, Padre,*' Jobert greeted the austere cleric. 'I understand the emotion our presence brings, but I wish to make small amends.'

The priest gave a disparaging look to the dragoon officer.

They were familiar with each other, as the dragoon replied with a remorseful shrug.

Over a dozen local men moved from where horses and cattle were tied. They circled around the escort and those they protected. The Arezzo men were in their prime, mature and strong, their faces were hard, and their eyes assessed the dragoons' weapons. They were wise enough not to mock the dragoons, but sufficiently intimidating that the dragoons flexed their fingers around their muskets' waists.

'Father, might I seek your support in translation, please?' Jobert stepped towards a number of elderly peasant women sitting on woven mats. Before them, the women had laid out a number of simple wares, including slabs of focaccia and bunches of tiny flowers, with the intent of trade with those here to purchase animals. Jobert tipped a handful of coins from his purse into his palm. 'I wish to purchase from these ladies their focaccia for the children and the needy under your care, and these early blossoms of spring for your altar.'

The women's eyes shone with concern at the priest as Jobert placed only a few coins in each outstretched palm. To Jobert a pittance of payment, but close to ten times the value of the bread and the posies.

The priest twitched a grim smile to the women as a blessing on the exchange. 'You have come a long way to buy bread and wildflowers.'

Jobert smiled at the Italian's determined insolence. 'I am here to buy horses, Father. I am told Arezzo's are the finest.'

One or two men in the surrounding crowd stepped away.

Koschak observed in which direction they had retired.

Jobert strolled towards the horse lines, where grim grooms held horses.

'Sir!' growled the captain. The escort could not follow easily among the horses, so formed a line.

Jobert chose one man who stood central. The Italian's distinguished goatee was closely shaved. His jacket and velvet waistcoat finely sewn. '*Buongiorno, Signore*. I am seeking to purchase mares, and I am willing to pay a good price.'

'Good morning, Colonel.' The man's cold eyes slid from Jobert to the priest. A smile flickered on Jobert's cheek at the Italian's recognition of Jobert's rank on his tailcoat's sleeve. 'There are so few horses available. You may have to try further north.'

Behind the Italian, a tall bay tossed her head.

'This is a fine mare.' Jobert pointed. 'Is she yours? May I ask her price?'

'Unfortunately, she has just been sold.' The wealthy Italian swished his fingers at the mare, and spoke to a man close by, probably her groom. 'Thank you for your business, *Signore*.

Treat her well. Travel home safely.' The groom gave an obedient nod, untied the horse and led her away.

Jobert maintained his smile at the subterfuge. 'The Arezzo horse sales are renowned throughout Europe. Surely, I can buy one mare.'

'We have been ravaged for three years by the movement of French, Neapolitan, Austrian and British troops. All our best horses have been taken.' The Italian's eyes narrowed, testing Jobert to contradict him. 'Perhaps I know of one mare for sale. Come.'

The Italian led Jobert, Koschak, Duque, the captain and the priest through the stalls. He pointed to a cart-pony nibbling dried grass. The peasant unloading cane-baskets of chickens froze, his nervous look darting between the priest and the dragoons.

'*Grazie, Signore*,' Jobert said. 'This is not the style of horse I sought.'

'Sir!' Koschak coughed.

Around the sale area, all the horses and all the large, white draught cattle were being led away. Stall holders were hurriedly packing their goods.

Jobert turned to the priest. 'Everything sold so quickly? I am most certainly in a competitive market, am I not? How can I prove my commercial commitment?' As Jobert looked hard at the wealthy Italian, he tugged at his tailcoat lapels which caused a rattle of coins from within his purse. 'You know where the coins came from. How can I return them in good faith? Could I not be introduced to potential sellers?'

The Italian slouched back on one heel and regarded the priest. 'I am not from this region, Colonel. I could not say.'

Both the Italian and the priest looked towards Arezzo, where a column of townsfolk, their rumble of anger draped about them, surged down the slope towards the sale area. More burly men, some with their hands concealed within their jackets, had gathered around the few dragoons.

'Colonel Jobert,' the dragoon captain rumbled, 'we need to leave. Now, sir.'

'*Padre. Signore.*' Jobert bowed in farewell, then strode through the crowd to their waiting horses. 'Did either of you get a look at the horses before they were taken away?' he asked Koschak and Duque.

Koschak glanced over his shoulder to appraise the following risk. 'The saddle horses I did see warranted further inspection.'

'How do we regain their trust?' Duque asked.

'Return what we looted.' Koschak spat. 'Shit! In Lucca, we even stole their shoes.'

The dragoon snorted as he mounted. 'Return the corpse of the Pope we kidnapped.'

Duque gave a resigned shake of his head. 'Do we now press south into the Kingdom of Naples?'

'Hah! Naples!' The dragoon captain shot a derisive look. 'That we were not murdered here is because of the threat of our razing Arezzo as a reprisal. Once you step over the Neapolitan border — where you will not have an escort, mind — you will be flayed, salted and roasted by lunchtime.' He held out a pleading hand to Jobert. 'I know the army needs horses, sir, but you underestimate the hatred the Italians have for us.'

As the dragoon column headed north at a brisk walk, Koschak turned in the saddle to Jobert. 'There may be another way, sir.'

'And that is?' Jobert asked.

'I am aware of horses being brought across from Albania.'

'From the Ottomans?' Jobert scowled. 'Bosnian mountain ponies?'

'No,' Koschak said. 'Well-bred warhorses with the conformation we seek.'

'Why had you not said before?'

Koschak shrugged. 'Colonel Raive and yourself spoke only of securing Italian horses.'

'Very well,' Jobert tipped his head, 'we can report there are none in Italy, and our superiors will respond "I do not care where they are, just find them" and we will respond "Are you willing to seek horses in the Ottoman Empire, while we are at war with the Sultan in Egypt?".'

Koschak held up his hands. 'The Turks are selling their horses, and they are being landed here from across the Adriatic.'

'Who is buying these horses?'

'Colonel Zenari, of the Cisalpine Legion.'

Jobert's face creased with confusion. 'That weasel! Why is he dabbling in Albanian horses?'

'Not Albanian horses, sir. The Turks are bringing them from the Danube to Diraç.'

'Where?'

'Diraç,' Koschak said. 'An Ottoman port on the Albanian coast.'

'What is Zenari doing with Ottoman horses? Did you speak to him in Ravenna?'

'Hah! Zenari would no sooner speak to me than speak to dog shit on his boot. The Turks bring these horses in from the Danube. Zenari has a trading galley filled with about twenty geldings. Claiming experience against the Russians and the Austrians over the last few years, Zenari puts a few handles on these horses then sells them at a premium to Italian officers.'

'His experience, my arse!' Jobert shook his head. 'Zenari had an average seat at best, and he would not soil his dress gloves working horses. Someone must educate these horses before selling them on. Who is his agent?'

Koschak smiled. 'Now this will make you laugh.'

'Who?'

'Fazio.'

'Fazio!' Jobert's jaw hung slack. He remembered himself and Fazio in the stench and gloom of a morgue in Novi, their daggers a handspan from each other's bellies.

Koschak interrupted with a flutter of his thick gloved fingers. 'It seems Fazio speaks a little Turkish. He says the Ottomans have hundreds of horses on their Black Sea coast and are seeking buyers.'

'Have you seen any of this Danube stock?' Duque asked.

Koschak twisted in the saddle towards Duque. 'As they were unloaded in Ravenna, I did. I too was expecting Bosnian mountain ponies, like the Croatian uhlans rode against us in late '96. The horses Fazio was unloading were far superior. Broad withers, good air, legs were straight-boned and wide-hoofed. I checked their teeth and, for their age they had decent height. I would be very happy if my squadron was issued with them. Suitable for chasseur and dragoon remounts.'

'This is the purpose I have been seeking.' Jobert nodded with conviction. 'Lads, if we find Fazio and he confirms this lead of Ottoman horses, would you be willing to sail across the Adriatic?'

'I am interested to see these exotic horses.' Duque nodded with eagerness. 'Count me in.'

'It will take us a week to travel to Ravenna,' Koschak said, 'before sailing to Diraç. I shall accompany you as far as Ravenna. Moench, you can assist me with horses I have collected there. We will find action a plenty.'

'Easy women or easy money?' Moench narrowed his eyes as he sought clarification.

'Both.'

'You never know what lies around the corner, André.' Duque leaned out of his saddle and slapped Jobert's shoulder. 'And an Ottoman corner for all that?' Duque laughed. 'Then let us track down Fazio and have him show us the delights of Diraç.'

Jobert made the hand motion of drawing his sabre and giving point. 'Gentlemen, to Albania!'

Chapter Four
April 1801, Diraç, Albania

At dawn on the first morning out of Ravenna, Jobert leaned against a starboard rail. With the Dalmatian coast yet unseen, a golden sun lifted from a silver shimmer on the eastern horizon. The dark green Italian coast slumbered to the west.

A salty northerly filled Jobert's senses and the *xebec's* three lateen sails. The bow sizzled southeast through the gentle swell. For vast stretches around the merchant ship, the undulating Adriatic churned with lurking fish. Engorging on these surface schools, gulls, in their hundreds, swirled in a dizzying array.

Jobert's eyes darted as he sought to follow any individual bird darting to snatch unwary prey. His heart quickened in such an unfamiliar environment. Anxiety from crossing the Atlantic as a young chasseur drowned his trust of benign sunshine and swell. What dangers coiled beneath such a smooth surface?

Beside Jobert, Duque gripped a taut line to steady his unreliable stance. 'Zenari is now on deck.'

A young man, at the other end of the vessel, emerged from under an awning shading the poop deck and tugged at the front of his jacket.

Jobert snorted. 'As we are not in uniform, thankfully I will not have to salute the bastard.'

Similar to Jobert and Duque, Zenari wore civilian dress of a woollen tailcoat with matching waistcoat and tall hat in tones of sober tan, knee-length culottes and buckled shoes. Zenari's waistcoat and hatband were finely brocaded, and he wore a dress épée on his left hip and wielded a polished cane with a bronze tip in his right hand.

'Why does he need a dress épée whilst on board?' Duque asked.

'Because he is a pompous clot.'

Zenari stepped with care down the portside, ducking around rigging which threatened his hat. He recoiled from rubbing against sweaty sailors as they checked straining fishing lines. With an authoritative air, he inspected the open hold full of jute-wrapped bundles, bulging gunnysack bales and stacks of wooden crates. Within nestled Venetian windowpanes, spectacles, silk damask, disassembled brass chandeliers, tin-plated sheet iron, cauldrons, cinnabar and bells.

As Zenari's cane tapped a route of inspection along the length of the vessel and he turned at the starboard bow, Jobert rolled his eyes at the inevitable.

'Colonel Zenari, sir,' said Jobert, as he and Duque touched the brims of their felt hats.

Zenari touched his brim with the bronze tip of his cane. 'Lieutenant Colonel Jobert.' Zenari's combed moustache — thicker since they parted company at Marengo — betrayed a quiver as he emphasised Jobert's inferior rank.

'Congratulations on your promotion, sir,' Jobert said.

Tiny muscles around Zenari's eyes spasmed in betrayal. A slow blink attempted to conceal the spark of momentary pleasure. 'Thank you, Colonel Jobert.'

Duque saluted. 'Would you excuse me, gentlemen, as duty

calls.' Angling away from Zenari, Duque's lips twisted in a failing effort to keep a straight face.

'An unexpected … pleasure to have you sail with us. It must be ten months since we parted on the field of battle,' Zenari said. 'Are you well, sir?'

'I am well, thank you.' Jobert smiled at the offer of conciliation. 'And you, sir, are you no longer with the Cisalpine *Chasseurs à Cheval*?'

'No, I am posted to the headquarters of the Cisalpine Legion.'

'And that assignment requires Ottoman connections?'

'Ah, no … well, my family are connected commercially. And what of you, Jobert?'

'I remain on the staff of the Army of Italy.'

'Maintaining your connections to Milan?' Zenari's eyebrows arched toward the tight brown curls emerging under his brim. 'Or Mantua?'

'Neither, sir.' *Prick!* Jobert's mouth creased to a humourless smile. 'I am currently based at the Genoese headquarters.'

'May I ask of your interest in Diraç? Am I correct that you have an interest in Turkish horses?'

'Quite so, sir, I am tasked with purchasing horses for the army. Do you accompany each of your family's shipments from Diraç?'

'Ah, no, I am on official … have other business to attend to. From Diraç, I press on to Constantinople. Will you be travelling to the Sublime Porte?'

'With our disaster in Egypt, I doubt a Frenchman will be well received in Constantinople.'

'Not so, Jobert. I found myself constantly tripping over French officers. All of them designing fortresses or organising factories for artillery and muskets.'

'You have visited Constantinople before? Oh, I was unaware.'

'My duties require me to establish Turkish connections.

Once in Diraç, may I make introductions that might support your enquiries?'

'That would be most generous, sir, but I have no wish to disrupt your itinerary.'

'Not at all. My contact is a man such as us. A commander of light cavalry. His name is Otal Alaybey.'

'I would be in your debt, sir.'

Zenari's gaze shifted to over Jobert's shoulder. 'Ah, here is Sergeant Fazio. I shall let you both immerse yourselves in the details of horses.' With a nod, Zenari made his way back to the poop deck.

As Zenari lurched past him, Fazio stiffened in salute and grunted 'Sir'. With his path clear, Fazio's lithe figure moved with sure steps over coiled rope and around lashed chests towards Jobert. He chatted with men flipping flatbread on small iron stoves and made admiring comments of the landed fish to those gutting the breakfast catch.

Jobert's jaw clenched at his memories of Fazio. On assignment to the Cisalpine Chasseurs three years ago, Fazio had been insubordinate to Jobert to the point of discharging a pistol. Over the course of the relentless fighting in 1799, Jobert and Fazio had found an uneasy truce. After the crisis of battle at Marengo last year, the pair had parted on respectful terms.

Rock steady on the rolling deck, Fazio raised his right hand in a crisp salute to the leather peak of his soft fabric cap. From under his cap, his thick black hair swept back into a queue, and wide sideburns trailed from his temples to his blue jaw. His dense moustache, drooping to his chin, twisted as he said, 'Good morning, sir,' out of the side of his mouth.

'Good morning, Sergeant Fazio,' Jobert said. 'I admire the ease with which you move about the deck. But look at you, my old comrade.' Jobert gave Fazio's shoulder a friendly slap. 'One moment a horse-gunner in Austrian service, next an Italian chasseur in the French Army, and now international buyers' agent. Are you on secondment from the regiment to the legion's headquarters? Or is this a more private arrangement with the Zenari family?'

'As seasoned cavalrymen, sir, are we not ever seeking opportunity?' With a wink, Fazio's dark eyes under bristling eyebrows, blazed. 'In these days of hard-earned peace, now is the time to capitalise.'

'Yes, so it would seem. And what is your connection to Albania?'

'My family has traded across the Adriatic for generations. I speak a little Serbian, a little Turkish. Duque says you seek horses in Diraç? Did you bring your purse?'

'I am not shopping. Just browsing. Zenari tells me our Diraç connection is a cavalry officer.'

'Otal Alaybey? Yes, he is *sipahi*. Turkish light cavalry. His rank — alaybey — is equivalent to a regimental or brigade commander. Be warned, these Ottomans drive a hard bargain. Be ready to haggle.'

A wave of a hand caught Jobert's attention. Duque was holding up platters of grilled fish and *piadina* bread, and a gourd of wine.

'A day full of promise begins with a hearty breakfast. Join us, Fazio?'

Two mornings later, Jobert, Duque and Fazio stood on the starboard quarter-deck savouring the tang of salt and pine pressing along the Albanian shoreline. The xebec surged under their feet as the crew strained at fourteen oars and pulled for the port.

Above the rocks of a wave-washed cliff, the red tiles and whitewashed walls of Diraç crowned a small headland. Over the slap of waves on hull and under the squawking of gulls, came a long wailing song.

'Is it an alarm?' Duque asked.

'No,' Fazio said, 'it is the Muslim call to prayer, the equivalent of church bells. See those slim towers that sit above the mosques.' Fazio pointed. 'The minarets. It is from there the faithful are called to prayer five times a day.'

'How should we conduct ourselves in these lands?' Jobert asked.

'Simply be respectful, sir. You will be expected to eat only with your right hand, with either your fingers or a spoon. Avoid any gallantry with women. And they do not, generally, drink alcohol.'

'What do they drink in lieu of wine?'

'Some may offer a distilled liquor called *raki*. Otherwise, strong coffee or smoking.'

'Are there plentiful cigars?'

Fazio's cheek crimped with glee. 'Have you never smoked a *shisha*?'

'A shisha?'

'Then you are in for a treat.'

Fazio looked around and identified Zenari some distance away on the poop deck. 'If you ever need to have anything done, sir, just ask.' Fazio concluded his offer with a conspiratorial wink.

'Then might we start with comfortable lodgings.'

After midday on the day of their arrival, Jobert, with Duque and Fazio, entered the coffee house designated by Zenari. The large room effused the aromas of coffee and baked spiced meat.

Wafts of tobacco smoke were fragrant with cinnamon and apple. Latticed screens created enticing alcoves, festooned with exotic carpets. Cushions, embroidered red and green, lay jumbled on benches. Low tables were laid with brass cups, and pewter pots with long slender spouts like the arms of exotic dancers.

'Where is Zenari?' Jobert asked.

'He spoke of attending another meeting.' Fazio shrugged as he searched the room. 'Ah, there is Otal Alaybey.'

Fazio walked towards a man in a loose jacket and trousers and pointed red felt slippers. Otal's bare head was shaved bald with a long, oiled top knot that curled from his crown above his left ear and slid like a viper around his temple. His face was slim with prominent cheekbones above a thick drooping moustache. His hooded eyes read a newspaper, but he turned the pages as if reading from the front to the back.

Fazio and Otal exchanged greetings. The languid movement of Otal's long fingers, interlaced with a string of beads, implied Otal's tolerance of Fazio's lower standing.

'May I introduce Colonel Jobert,' Fazio said in French.

'Forgive me, sir, I do not speak Turkish,' Jobert said.

'It is not a problem, I speak French,' Otal's dismissive fingers indicated that Jobert might be seated upon cushions on a long bench against the wall. 'The honour is mine, sir.' He tapped a broadsheet newspaper and opened it backwards. Curly scribbles blew across the page like burnt straw in a storm. 'I was reading of the defeat of the French in Egypt.' Otal's look searched for reaction. 'Our British allies have now besieged your army within Alexandria.'

'Forgive me.' Jobert said. 'I am unaware of our ... the current situation in Egypt. Does the conflict between our nations make you and I enemies?'

Otal glanced at the hilt of Jobert's sabre. 'Not at all. Here you honour me as my guest.' With a swish of his fingers, small black coffees were placed by everyone's elbows.

'I appreciate this moment of your time, sir,' Jobert said.

'Let us hope our friendship is more than a moment of time. Where is our friend Colonel Zenari? Did he not travel with you? He arrived on the morning tide, yes?'

'Zenari spoke of attending other business.'

'Other business, indeed?' Otal's eyes widened with affront, before his moustache bent to a smile. 'You are all accommodated in the same lodgings? Comfortably, I hope? You must inform me immediately I can do anything in my power to make your stay more pleasant. Baclava?' Otal offered a copper tray of square cakes of filo pastry with crushed nuts and honey and smothered in syrup.

Jobert reached with his left hand.

Fazio coughed and offered a small porcelain dish. 'Dish in your left hand, sir, and take the food with your right.'

A brief smile whipped across Otal's face. 'How is your family? Is your father still with us?'

Jobert juggled the crumbly sweetness of the baclava and the unusual question. 'No, he passed many years ago.'

'*Alham-dulillah*. Your family was well when you left them? Your wife and children?'

Jobert sipped at the thick strong coffee to clear his palate. 'I am not married.'

With an arched eyebrow and a turned cheek Otal recoiled slightly, before his calm smile resettled on his face. 'How can I be of service?'

'I am in the market for cavalry horses,' Jobert said.

Otal blinked. 'Horses?'

'I was informed by Colonel Zenari that you sell horses. Have I been misinformed? My sincere apologies if I have inconvenienced you, sir.' Jobert's eyes tightened. 'Are you able to assist me?'

Inshallah. With a twist of his wrist, Otal splayed his fingers. Jobert looked to Fazio.

Fazio smiled. 'It is a common expression here. It means if God wills it, or if God wants it to happen, it will happen. Our equivalent expression might be "by the Grace of God".'

'So, is that a yes or no?' Jobert said.

Fazio smiled without conviction.

Otal spoke rapidly to Fazio, his tone authoritative and dismissive. Although Jobert did not understand, he did hear the word 'Zenari'.

Fazio shrugged and mumbled.

Jobert took another baclava and a sip of thick coffee.

Otal seemed irritated at the conversation. 'How many horses do you seek, Jobert?'

'Two hundred and fifty tall black brood mares,' Jobert said.

Otal's lips froze on the shisha mouthpiece he smoked. His hollow cheeks stretched his long face even longer. His eyes searched something in his memory. An internal conversation concluded as he released his smoke-hazed breath. Like a serpent seeking to strike, Otal tilted his head. 'Brood mares specifically?'

'I seek mares for the breeding of cavalry remounts,' Jobert said. 'The offspring need to stand fifteen-and-a-half hands high.'

Otal shrugged. 'I am aware of mares that will throw that height. Why do you want tall black horses?'

'The preferred mount of the bodyguard of the French Government. Does the Ottoman cavalry not value tall black horses?'

Otal's splayed fingers released a puff of indifference to the smoky ceiling. 'Such animals are accepted on the northern frontier, but not elsewhere in the empire. The colour of the coat and their weight is not ideal in Mediterranean warmth. Their weight and height is not ideal in the steep, poor-pastured country of Anatolia and the Caucasus.' Otal sucked on the shisha's mouthpiece. 'And you have the gold sufficient for such a purchase?'

Jobert repressed a snort of surprise. 'The gold, sir? I have neither seen the herd nor have we settled on a price.'

Otal raised a finger for service. 'More coffee? I have four hundred brood mares and fillies available for sale.'

'Four hundred? Then I will take the best two hundred and fifty.'

'No, my friend.' Otal's hooded eyes softened with disappointment. 'Unfortunately, I must sell them as one lot. For it is either four hundred mares, or I am unable to assist you.' Otal offered the plate of sweet cakes to Jobert. 'The baclava is very good. Have you tried it before?'

Jobert raised a cupped palm in polite decline. 'And you, sir, own these four hundred mares?'

'I represent the man who does.'

'And who is this gentleman?'

'His Majesty the Hospodar Constantine Ypsilantis,' Otal said, his chest swelling with the introduction, 'who governs Moldavia and Wallachia on behalf of the Commander of the Faithful, his Majesty Sultan Selim the Third.'

'Hospodar?'

'The Prince of Moldavia and Wallachia,' Fazio mumbled.

'Forgive my rudeness, Otal Alaybey,' Jobert asked, 'but what position do you hold within the Hospodar's staff?'

'The Hospodar honours me with the command of his Moldavian sipahi,' Otal rearranged the folds of his loose saffron jacket over a peacock blue silk waist sash.

'And where are the Hospodar's mares now?'

'In northern Moldavia.'

'Again, forgive me, sir,' Jobert said, 'I am unacquainted with the area. How far from Moldavia are we?'

'You seem most unprepared for your task, Colonel Jobert,' Otal said. 'One thousand five hundred kilometres from where we sit.'

A distance equivalent from Paris to Naples! Jobert leaned forward to place down his coffee cup. 'I beg your forgiveness. I suspect I have inconvenienced you greatly. Apart from sharing your delicious baclava, I feel we cannot do business. I would need to inspect these horses before I can negotiate.'

Otal waggled the shisha's mouthpiece and blew a stream smoke from his lungs to the ceiling. 'Perhaps you would like to inspect my horse. A gelding of these bloodlines.' Otal clicked his long fingers, and an attendant appeared at his elbow. Otal murmured a command over his shoulder and the man bowed and departed. 'I have arranged a demonstration outside.'

Otal led Jobert, Duque and Fazio outside, where the street smelled of grilled spiced meat. Crates of eggs and chicken were piled beside canvas awning-draped tables laden with vegetables. Women worked, with infants strapped to their backs by colourful scarves, stacking fish and fruit, arranging sacks of flour, spice and pots of oil. Swift hands exchanged weights on scales and coins in purses.

'Behold, the Cricket.' Otal swept his fingers by means of introduction.

In the centre of the market square, stood a saddled black gelding. A servant held the horse's reins. A white crescent-shaped star was embossed on his forehead under the parted fly veil. Two white socks adorned his front pasterns.

'That is the type of horse the Zenari family imports,' Fazio said.

'Your views, Duque?' Jobert asked.

'About sixteen hands high,' Duque said, his fingertips brushing the horse as he walked around it, 'broad chest and wide throat. Well conformed legs and joints from every angle.

Thick gaskins, slightly toe out behind.' Duque peeled open the horse's lips. 'Teeth even.'

Jobert smiled at the muscles of the hindquarters and the rippling tight abdomen. 'Are there more like you?'

'There are ... only one thousand five hundred kilometres away from here,' Duque said.

'Jobert, allow me to demonstrate his abilities.' Otal mounted the gelding and within a walking stride rocked the horse to a slow canter. The horse remained collected on a floating rein, as Otal wove small circles to change the canter leads. 'Is the horse not perfectly conformed for war?'

'Your personal mount is black and tall.' Jobert said. 'You value him, yet the Ottoman cavalry does not.'

'I serve my Sultan on the Moldavian steppe.' Otal shrugged at the obvious connection. 'This horse is bred for such country.'

'The Cricket. Why the name?' Jobert asked.

Otal beamed. 'Because he can jump.'

With a flick of commanding fingers, two vegetable barrows were pushed together to make a barrier in the street.

Otal took a wide circle at the canter, set the horse towards the jump and cleared it easily. The Cricket landed neatly, took two strides and halted.

'Why not try him, Jobert?' Otal invited with pride.

Jobert mounted the Cricket and wriggled in the saddle to adapt to the shortened stirrup leathers and the square-edged copper stirrups. Jobert put the horse through his gaits along the base of the curved walls of Diraç Castle.

Otal clicked his fingers. 'Put him over the barrows.'

Jobert winced at jumping such an obstacle on cobblestones. He squeezed the horse to a canter and set the horse at the jump. The Cricket cracked his rear hooves on the barrows edge as he passed over.

Otal threw up his hands. 'Why are you confounding his

action with such a rearward seat?'

Jobert stroked the horse's neck. 'I will admit to being confounded myself by your shorter stirrups.'

'But you need short stirrups to maintain a forward seat.'

'A forward seat?' Jobert frowned. 'Does that not endanger the front legs?'

'How does he jump if he had his preferences? Let me show you.'

Once Jobert had dismounted, a rope was draped over the Cricket's neck. Otal circled the horse at a slow canter then guided him towards and over the barrows. 'See the arc in his body? How his head is down? How would you jump if you had no reins?'

Remounted, and with breastplate straps in hand, Jobert felt both uncomfortable and intrigued leaning so far forward as he approached the jump.

The Cricket sailed over the barrows to the cheers of the appreciative crowd

Otal stood with his hands on his hips. 'How can any army not wish for the blessing of four hundred mares to produce regiments of horses such as these?'

'I am impressed, Otal Alaybey,' Jobert dismounted and rubbed the horse's neck and chest, 'but I seek only two hundred and fifty mares, not four hundred.'

Otal winced. 'But I have four hundred mares for sale, not two hundred and fifty.'

Jobert hissed through his teeth. 'I would have to travel to inspect them. If I accept the quality of the horses, then we can negotiate a price. Only then would I be able to send for the payment.'

Otal shook his head. 'What you describe would take many months. The herd might be gone by then.'

'To whom?'

'Other interested parties.'

'Then why not sell to them.'

Otal wiggled his fingers. 'It would not be the Hospodar's preference. I can see I am dealing with someone who appreciates fine horses.'

'I would need to return to Genoa to have the extra horses approved.'

Otal laid his hand on Jobert's forearm. 'Then, my friend, it is not to be. My time in Diraç is brief and I am unable to wait. Perhaps next year.'

Jobert smiled. 'Is the sale of this size not worth your time?'

'I have travelled far expecting to meet with Zenari this morning. I am dutybound to escort him to Constantinople without delay. Now,' Otal said and spread a searching hand, 'he appears waylaid.'

With his other hand, Jobert squeezed the hand that Otal had laid on Jobert's forearm. 'My friend, allow me to return to Genoa to ask. I shall return within one month. Might we meet again in one month?'

Otal's wrist twisted and splayed his fingers. '*Inshallah.*'

'Otal Alaybey!' An agitated messenger pushed through the crowd to mutter a message to Otal.

Otal stiffened and exclaimed loudly, then strode up the street, his robes billowing around his lean frame.

Fazio whispered a translation. 'Otal said, "He is what? Where?" Someone is here in Diraç that upsets him.'

'Is that the end of our meeting?' Duque asked.

Beyond the barrows that had been used as jumping obstacles, Otal turned back to Jobert, a calm smile smoothing his features. 'Perhaps I can introduce you to someone who will assist our negotiations.'

Chapter Five

Jobert followed Otal's brisk stride up a long street to enter another coffee house.

In the centre of the room, Zenari lounged upon tasselled cushions, his legs outstretched and crossed at the ankles. Zenari shared a shisha, which exuded melon-scented smoke, with a Turk. The Turk's red hair curled onto his neck from under a tall *fez*.

As Otal strode in, Zenari was overcome with a coughing fit.

Otal seethed. 'Perhaps a different variety of melon might suit you better, Zenari.' Otal focused his agitation on the Turk beside Zenari.

The Turk, a square-faced man with light red moustache, prodded his shisha mouthpiece. 'You dishonour our guests, my dear Otal Alaybey. Speak French, I beg of you.'

Otal hooked his thumbs into his sash. 'Dikaletus Pasha, what a pleasant surprise. I was unaware your eminence was traveling to Diraç. You did not speak of it when we last spoke in Bucharest.'

Dikaletus Pasha tugged at his long yellow coat with a fur collar, which he spread to cover his voluminous black pants and embroidered slippers. 'I am ever at the whim of the Hospodar, Otal Alaybey. He felt my services were needed here. I can report Wallachia's interests are well served here. And who are these gentlemen? More Italian friends? May I welcome you, sir, to the lands of the Commander of the Faithful.'

Otal stared down and clenched his jaw. 'Your eminence, may I introduce Lieutenant Colonel Jobert of the French Army. Colonel Jobert, this is Dikaletus Pasha, the dragoman of the Hospodar.'

'A senior aide to the Hospodar,' Fazio muttered at Jobert's elbow.

'Welcome, Jobert,' Dikaletus said. 'The Sultan — peace be upon him — favours the Hospodar with the governing of Moldavia and Wallachia. I am the son of the Hospodar's vizier.'

'The son of the prince's chief minister,' Fazio said.

Jobert gave a small bow. 'I am your service, sir.'

Dikaletus touched his forehead and heart. 'And I at yours, sir.' He patted the cushions beside him on the broad couch upon which he sat. 'Please join me. Your family was well when you left them? Your wife and children?'

Jobert smiled. 'I am not married.'

A stab of alarm shocked Dikaletus' features. In an effort to renew the conversation, he offered Jobert a brass platter of starched gel cubes that smelled of roses and were dusted with icing sugar. 'Have you tried the lokum?'

'And what of you, Zenari, where have you been?' Otal glowered, at which Zenari shrank. 'I did not know you gentlemen had been introduced.'

Zenari's eyes glazed and twitched. 'We met by happy coincidence in the bazaar this morning. We were just discussing the recent British victory over the French—'

Otal held up a stiff hand. 'Something to discuss at our leisure, my friend, once at sea. But now we must leave.'

'Now?' Dikaletus asked. 'We still have a little time. Colonel Jobert, you seek horses, am I correct?'

'I do, sir,' Jobert said. 'Two hundred and fifty brood mares.'

'As many as that?' Dikaletus looked at Otal. 'The Hospodar does indeed have a significant herd at his command.'

Otal rolled a cube of lokum in his fingertips. 'It would please his excellency if all four hundred mares were sold as one lot. As his excellency's dragoman, would you be authorised to negotiate on his behalf?'

'The sale of four hundred horses?' Dikaletus' nostrils sensed a wisp of opportunity. 'Yes, I am. Do you carry any references from Genoa, Colonel Jobert?'

'I do, sir. I have travelled to Diraç to determine such a possibility. I am not in a position to negotiate until I have seen the herd.'

Otal's jaws savoured the sugary treat. 'Jobert has just ridden the Cricket.'

'The Cricket.' Dikaletus' green eyes examined Jobert. 'An admirable creature. Perhaps we can discuss indicative prices on these unseen horses. At what price did we sell our last horses, Otal?'

'One thousand five hundred francs each.'

'As much as that?' Jobert said. 'Was the stock you sold trained warhorses?'

Otal nodded. 'Indeed.'

'Then I would expect a lot less for brood mares.'

Dikaletus' palm opened in a conciliatory sweep. 'As you have not seen them, let us agree on one thousand two hundred francs per horse.'

Jobert rocked his head in calculation. 'I will not agree to any price over five hundred francs per head.'

Dikaletus sucked his teeth. 'My dear Jobert, is that your best offer?'

Jobert shrugged. 'So many horses sight unseen.'

Dikaletus shook his head. 'I foresee difficulties. You will buy the herd and have no way to transport them home. What if we agree on one thousand two hundred francs per horse which includes their transport by sea to ... to where? Marseilles? Toulon?'

'Ravenna would be sufficient.'

'There we have it. Ravenna, it is.'

'France seeks only two hundred and fifty.' Jobert leaned back. 'An extra one hundred and fifty will be a burden. Yet France might grant this small favour to the Hospodar at one thousand francs per horse which includes transport to Ravenna.'

Otal looked askance at Dikaletus, his eyebrow raised in surprise at the offer.

'I can agree to one thousand francs per horse, which includes transport to Ravenna, if ...', Dikaletus raised a pudgy finger, 'if you bring the gold with you when you inspect the mares. In gold louis, my dear Jobert, not francs.' Dikaletus patted Otal's arm, then raised a bejewelled finger to Jobert. 'France will not be disappointed.'

'Four hundred thousand francs is twenty thousand gold louis.' Jobert said.

'*Alham-dulillah!* So much easier to transport.'

Jobert frowned at Fazio.

'*Alham-dulillah?*' Fazio said softly. 'Our thanks for God's blessing, or all is as God wishes it to be.'

'If our negotiations are successful, Dikaletus, how will the herd be transported?'

'If successful, *inshallah*, they would be shipped by galley from the mouth of the Danube. The port of Izmail. Are the terms sufficient?'

'There will be expenses,' Otal said. 'Bring a little more.'

'How much more?' Jobert said.

'Half as much again.' Otal said.

'Six hundred thousand francs? Hah!' Jobert leaned back with his arms folded. 'Again, we return to one thousand five hundred francs per horse. France would expect the Hospodar to meet all expenses for horses to land in Ravenna.'

'If the Cricket has disappointed you,' Dikaletus lay his hands on Jobert's thighs, 'today we can farewell each other as friends. But if you are sufficiently impressed, we can escort you and your gold safely to the court at Bucharest and the herd beyond. If the herd is not to your liking, we will escort you safely back to Diraç.'

Jobert worked to repress his discomfort from the hand on his leg.

'Now if the herd was to your liking, as I know it will be, *alham-dulillah*,' Dikaletus squeezed Jobert's thigh, 'we would then negotiate a price. But you would then need to return to Italy and bring the gold upon which we agreed.' Dikaletus raised his hand. 'If we settle on a price now, we could escort the gold and if it was not to be, *inshallah*, you and your gold would return.'

Jobert leaned forward for a cube of lokum which caused Dikaletus to retract his hand.

'Perhaps this is not for you,' Dikaletus said. 'Our trip to Diraç was not for long, as my dear friend Otal has indicated, and we must return. Perhaps next year? Our friend Zenari has a pressing engagement in Constantinople.'

The call to prayer wafted through the external curtains and lattice screens of the coffee house.

Dikaletus smiled. 'My dear Otal Alaybey, will you not answer the call of the Prophet — peace be upon him?'

Otal stood hesitantly, his eyes full of menace towards Zenari, then strode from the room.

Zenari looked nervous. Jobert recognised that Zenari has done something dumb. *But what?* 'Are you too, Dikaletus, not called to prayer?'

'I am not Muslim,' Dikaletus said. 'The Hospodar, his vizier and I are of the Eastern Christian faith.' Pudgy fingers popped another cube of sugared lokum under his red moustache. 'I can see I have not convinced you, my dear Jobert. I hope we can continue our conversation next year … if the horses are still there.'

'But the horses—' Jobert said.

'They will be gone.'

'To whom? The Austrians?'

'I must go now,' Dikaletus said. 'We have an urgent business in Constantinople, my dear Zenari, do we not?'

'Allow me a little time to reflect upon your … the Hospodar's generous offer.' Jobert said. 'Please?'

'The wishes of my sovereign press heavily upon me. Zenari and I must depart tomorrow. Perhaps we might dine together this evening, Jobert?'

'Then, sir, until this evening.'

Once outside Jobert turned to Duque and Fazio. 'Lads, I need to get my bearings on Moldavia. Buy any charts you can that describe the ports of the Black Sea coast.'

Fazio gave a nod. 'A local mariner would know coastal routes.' Jobert patted Fazio's upper arm. 'Even if he can provide a sketch.'

Zenari watched Fazio and Duque depart. 'What are you dawdling for, Jobert?'

'Military courtesy, sir.' Jobert rolled his eyes. 'Since you are the senior rank, I am waiting for you to take the lead so I might take post on your left.'

'Oh, of course.'

Jobert and Zenari pressed through the marketplace towards their tavern accommodation on the hill above the medieval castle. A pungent open sewer channel gurgled in the centre of the street. Tethered goats shook their bells and their buzz of flies. Men lunched on woven mats, consuming balls of steaming rice on flat bread, and scoffing small coffees from large brass pots. Conversations raged so fiercely as if they raised an alarm for fire.

The crowd shuffled apart.

Under the mouldy awnings, four armed Albanians faced Jobert and Zenari. Small felt caps topped their bald heads. Grimy waistcoats draped over their yellowing shirts. Dull waist sashes wrapped their bespattered loose pants.

The leading assailant held a drawn scimitar. Two others gripped short lances. A fourth man behind them kept his hand concealed within a heavy sash draped around his chest.

The man with the scimitar spoke in a consoling, placating manner, his face smiling with evil intent.

Jobert gripped his scabbard and swept out his sabre. 'Do not make this easy for them, Zenari.' Jobert sighed at Zenari's dress épée. 'Step to the wall. *En garde!*'

Jobert stepped to the left of the street drain, Zenari to the right. With their shoulders to the walls of the narrow lane, Jobert and Zenari ceded the freedom of the centre of the street to the attackers, who now had to negotiate the sewer channel.

A javelin jabbed at Jobert.

Jobert parried the tip against the wall, grabbed and pulled

the shaft as he riposted to cut his man just above the collarbone.

Jobert withdrew his blade.

The assailant dropped his lance to clutch at the gush of blood from his lower throat.

The other lance tip thrust at Zenari. 'Zenari, *en garde.*' Jobert twirled to his right and sliced down onto the other javelin. 'Thrust!'

Zenari's thrust sliced along the man's extended forearm and into his elbow.

The attacker wielding the scimitar yelled at someone behind Jobert.

Jobert glanced over his shoulder.

Four more assailants stood clear of the crowd, similarly armed.

Jobert spun to take an attack from the rear. 'Zenari, *en garde* front. I have our rear.'

An apple struck Jobert's face, knocking off his hat.

With a low right blade, Jobert swept up to parry wide an approaching javelin tip. Jobert whipped his blade back as he spun to his right, and with such momentum, stepped forward to grab the shaft.

A scimitar was thrust on his left.

Releasing the javelin, Jobert swept the scimitar back with his gloved left hand. In that moment, he twisted his wrist to change his riposte against the lance and thrust into the face beyond the lunging scimitar.

Despite the man wrenching his face back from Jobert's blade, Jobert sliced open his cheek and ear.

An apple struck Jobert's eye.

An apple struck between Jobert's shoulder blades. *Apples?*

Zenari held up his hilt and empty hand to block the apples.

Albanians gripped the front of Zenari's jacket.

Jobert jerked his blade backward against the neck of the

pinned javelin attacker, and then swept his blade down to sever a wrist that gripped Zenari's tailcoat lapel.

Both men screamed.

Zenari held his ground with the wounded lancer at his feet.

The leader could not advance to Zenari without tripping over his fallen comrade.

Jobert hopped the gutter to position himself behind Zenari blocking any advance of the final rear lancer. *This attack is to capture him and kill me.*

The street behind Jobert filled with bellowing and tramping.

The leader with the scimitar cried out.

In front and behind, those bearing javelins and apples turned and ran into the market crowd. Four wounded cringed against the walls.

Otal arrived with a squad of uniformed men. They wore blue jackets and soft red caps. A red sash about their waists held long daggers. Scimitars hung on each hip, and pistols were slung on their chests. Armed with engraved muskets, these soldiers pressed back the crowd.

Otal stared at the wounded.

They stared back at him contrite.

They recognise each other!

Otal gave a nod to his patrol commander.

The soldiers drew looped cords from their belts.

Despite their protestations, the four wounded assailants had loops bind their wrists behind their backs, while loops noosed their necks. Each man was forced to his knees and stretched as his arms were pulled out from behind while his head was drawn forward. Groaning from their wounds, the assailants contorted their faces against the biting cords to beseech Otal. '*Allahu Akbar!*'

Otal drew his scimitar.

Jobert held up his hand. 'Otal, no. Wait.'

67

In swift succession, Otal's scimitar scythed through the extended necks. He handed his dripping weapon to a soldier. 'My apologies to our guests. I am pleased to see you safe. *Alhamdulillah.*'

Jobert sought for anything which might clean his own blade. 'Why did you not want to interrogate them?'

'Whatever for? They are local brigands.'

'With scimitars and lances?' Jobert said. 'They are soldiers. Someone sent them to capture Colonel Zenari.'

'Oh, no, I do not think so.' Otal flicked his fingers as he sheathed his shining blade. 'Colonel Zenari is quite well.'

Jobert picked up one of the javelins, much shorter than a lance. He had last seen a Cossack weapon like this a few years ago when the Russians had invaded Lombardy.

Jobert swung the javelin tip at Zenari. 'Why did they want you?'

'What are you doing here, Zenari?' Jobert shook the Turkish javelin at Zenari, once they had returned to their tavern rooms. 'You are not buying horses. The attack in the marketplace was an attempt to capture you. Who wants you? And why?'

'I do not know.' Zenari shook in agitation. 'Do not be ridiculous, Jobert. Your imaginings are becoming too wild.'

'Those men recognised Otal. He executed them before they could speak. Does Otal seek to capture you?'

'Stop it, Jobert.'

'You want to introduce me to Otal, yet you do not show,' Jobert said. 'You appear with someone else. This Dikaletus,

Who is he to you? Will any other member of the court of Moldavia be engaging us, with either bargains or weapons?'

'You are being insubordinate—'

Jobert drove the butt of the javelin into the floor. 'Fuck you, Zenari! I am happy to play the deference to your senior rank while we bow and scrape in foreign parts, but I have known you long enough.'

'You do not know me, Jobert.' Zenari curled his fist at Jobert's face. 'You do not what know I am capable of.'

'I have seen you in the heat of battle, where everything is revealed. I have seen you clearly. I was not impressed.'

Zenari turned to the window and threw open the shutters.

A soft rap on the door.

Duque and Fazio shuffled in the corridor. 'May we …' Duque swept his hand into the room.

Jobert calmed his breathing. 'Yes, of course. What have you …'

'We found a merchant, sir.' Fazio held out a scroll. 'We paid a fee to view his charts. I have drawn a map of the eastern coast of the Black Sea.'

Duque ran his finger over the splotchy hand-drawn sketch. 'We would sail five days to Athens. Five days to Constantinople. Then five days to Izmail at the mouth of the Danube. Was it Otal or Dikaletus that spoke of sailing further west up the Danube to Bucharest?'

'Where is Moldavia?' Jobert asked.

Fazio pointed a hairy finger. 'North of Izmail.'

Jobert ran a finger from the Adriatic coast across country to Izmail. 'What lies between?'

Fazio shrugged. 'Mountains?'

Duque folded his arms and frowned. 'Were the Turks not at war with both Austria and Russia in that region some years ago? Just recently. In the last ten years?'

Fazio mirrored Duque's posture of doubt. 'Is this the best course, sir?'

'Raive has placed an initial pot of four hundred thousand francs on the table,' Jobert said. 'One question I have is what will it take to raise another two hundred thousand francs?'

Duque winced at the numbers involved. 'Why the extra?'

'Raive's money buys the mares and lands them in Ravenna. The extra is the cost of the expedition into Ottoman lands and any unforeseen requirements.'

'Six hundred thousand francs is thirty thousand gold louis,' Fazio's face creased with concern. 'How much is that to carry?'

Zenari spoke out the window. 'That much gold coin would weigh three hundred kilograms.'

'Six packhorses,' Duque said. 'Even if you raise this money, you need to arrive back in a very short time. So, where would you find that much gold that quickly?'

Jobert stared at the hasty strokes on the paper at his fingertips.

'I will provide it.' Zenari turned and leaned against the sill. 'If you raise the sureties that guarantee the funds, Jobert, my family will provide the gold to sail from Ravenna. But there is a price.'

'What exactly do you want?' Jobert asked.

With his hands clasped behind his back, Zenari took slow steps across the floorboards. 'I have decided it is best if I delay my business in Constantinople. I will return to Milan and arrange the coin you need for the purchase of your horses.' Zenari threw up his hands. 'That amount of money must move by sea via Constantinople. My non-negotiable terms, Jobert, are that you and I remain together to enhance the security of the gold, and you remain by my side in Constantinople until my business there is complete.'

'Your business in Constantinople?' Jobert scowled. 'Some affair that requires your capture and my death. My only purpose in this land is to return home with brood mares.'

Zenari held up a finger. 'Once my business is concluded, Jobert, I shall not hinder your travels into Moldavia.'

Jobert appraised Zenari with suspicion. 'Then I need to speak with Dikaletus tonight, and the return to Raive on the morning tide to confirm the details.'

Later that evening in a smoke and spice infused coffee house, Jobert and Zenari met with Dikaletus and Otal.

Jobert exhaled shisha smoke to the ceiling's gloom. 'Would you gentlemen be gracious to give me time to return with the money?'

Dikaletus twirled an extended finger. 'We must have the gold to cover all eventualities, and we must reach Bucharest with all possible speed.'

'Confirm the route, please?' Jobert placed down the sketch of the Black Sea coast. 'Is Bucharest accessed by the river port of Izmail?'

Otal's eyebrows arched at the poor-quality drawing. 'Izmail is the port at the mouth of the Danube. We would sail west up the Danube to Bucharest.'

'Is not Moldavia, and the horses, north, not west, of Izmail?' Jobert asked.

'You are correct,' Dikaletus dabbed crumbs from his red moustache with a serviette, 'but we must first gain the Hospodar's approval for the sale. Bucharest is our first stop. That is why we will not sail. From here, it is safer for your party,' Dikaletus winked at Zenari, 'to travel over the mountains and down the Danube to Bucharest.'

'Through Serbia?' Otal looked aghast. 'There is no quicker way to having your gold stolen.'

Zenari leaned forward from his nest of cushions. 'Jobert and I shall return in one month with the gold. In that time, you can both decide on the fastest route.'

Otal's face wrinkled to contain his displeasure. 'There is no need for you to return, Zenari. We can sail to Constantinople and return in time to meet Jobert next month.'

Dikaletus squeezed Otal's leg. 'April on the Adriatic coast will be restorative, my dear Otal Alaybey.' Dikaletus wiggled a ringed finger at Jobert and Zenari. 'But be quick, my friends. This time next year, the price of these horses will increase.'

Jobert sucked on the shisha's mouthpiece, and his nostrils and throat filled with rose and honey flavours. *Six hundred thousand francs for four hundred horses. How does everyone else spend their thirty-sixth birthday?*

'To us dining together next month.' Jobert raised his shisha hose in salute. 'With three hundred kilograms of gold.'

Chapter Six
May 1801, Genoa, Italy

Two weeks later ...

Jobert transferred his anxiety to his fingers clasped behind his back. He attempted to maintain a posture of calm assurance by watching the gulls wheeling over the swell of the glinting sea from Raive's open full-length windows.

'We want mares.' Raive studied the maps that were strewn across his desk. 'I can confirm that my associates have sufficient land to run the expanded breeding herd we propose. They have authorised the increase in funds to four hundred thousand francs, to enable the purchase of two hundred and fifty mares.' He craned his head at Fazio's quick sketch. 'Company papers have been drawn up and signed. An agency has been appointed and all funds placed in escrow with them, with all necessary authorisations for drawing down on those funds.'

As ever, De Chabenac's calm demeanour never wavered as he sipped his coffee. 'So much fuss for the Consular Guard to ride black horses.'

'Surely to buy mares at one thousand francs and sell their

foals for three thousand francs, why not a little fuss?' Raive's glance stabbed at Jobert. 'But we now face the purchase of four hundred horses, based on the inspection of one horse. Who else has seen this horse?'

Jobert raised his chin. 'Duque.'

'Then I am sure I will be unable to slide a silk thread between your opinions. Are you entirely satisfied this Turkish breed is worth pursuing?'

'The horse I rode was impressive.'

'Its breeding or its training?' Raive asked.

'This horse was well conformed and had character and physique that relished the demands made of it.'

'Then, based on the paucity of Italian horses, these Turkish mares are worth pursuing.' Raive steepled his fingers under his nose. 'So, who are we doing business with? The Hospodar of Moldavia and Wallachia.'

De Chabenac's finger twirled his cup handle on its saucer. 'Is this not an indelicate moment when France is at war with the Ottoman Empire?'

'Our stranded forces—' Raive said.

'Our abandoned forces,' Jobert said.

'— in Egypt, besieged by the Turks and the British, are on the point of collapse.' Raive's hand smoothed the air. 'I do not feel the Egyptian affair is an issue with Constantinople. And France's dilemma is of no consequence to the Hospodar's court in Bucharest. Yet the situation intrigues me. Moldavia has an area as wide as the Italian peninsula and half as long, an area, one might reasonably assume, that generates significant wealth. Why then apparent haste on the part of the Hospodar?'

'Moldavia and Wallachia are vassal states of the Sultan's,' De Chabenac said, seeming delighted with the conundrum. 'Perhaps the sale of the Hospodar's horses generates the gold needed as annual tribute to Constantinople.' De Chabenac swivelled the maps so he might study them. 'Moldavia is squeezed between the Russian and Austrian empires. Was there not a five-year war between Constantinople, Vienna and Saint Petersburg ten years ago?'

'Quite so,' Raive said, 'and with France having concluded peace with Austria, and Austria's loss of Lombardy, perhaps the Ottomans feel the Austrian emperor looks east. Perhaps there are stirrings along the border with Russia of which we are unaware.'

Jobert reflected on the last exchange in Diraç. 'We have a sense of why the horses are being sold, but why are such senior members of the Bucharest court selling horses out of an Albanian port?'

Raive's eyes twinkled with glee. 'I sense a game afoot between the Christians in Bucharest and the Muslims in Constantinople.'

'Perhaps something to exploit?' said De Chabenac. 'Or do you sense a fraud, Jobert? Are Otal and Dikaletus false? That the appearance of being at odds with each other is a ruse to obscure their collusion?'

'We have either two rogues attempting to steal gold,' Jobert said, 'or there is something else at play of which we are unaware.'

Raive rummaged under the skewed documents and fished out the scroll containing Dikaletus' credentials. 'My contacts within the Genoese Council confirm the validity of the seals on Dikaletus' credentials.' Raive picked up the agreement. 'Four hundred brood mares to be delivered to Ravenna at one thousand francs per head. That is … too good to be true.'

'And the dragoman Dikaletus specified gold,' Jobert said.

De Chabenac smiled. 'Gold?'

Raive nodded. 'The signed arrangement is for four hundred brood mares delivered to Ravenna for four hundred thousand francs in gold. Twenty thousand gold louis.' Raive cocked an eyebrow with concern. 'Such a sum would weigh two hundred kilograms.'

'How would two hundred kilograms of gold be moved through one thousand kilometres of foreign lands?' De Chabenac asked.

'The cavalry commander Otal insisted it is safer by sea.' Jobert said. 'Yet the Greek dragoman maintained it would be quicker over the mountains to the Danube.'

Raive frowned. 'I would not agree to any movement through Serbia. The Turks are faced with their own rebellions in Serbia and northern Greece.'

'And you are due back in Diraç in two weeks, Jobert, are you not?' De Chabenac asked. 'Where does one conjure two hundred kilograms of gold?

'Zenari has offered us a solution,' Jobert said.

Raive and De Chabenac exchanged a glance. 'Zenari?'

'Zenari stated his family would be able to source the gold against our Parisian sureties.'

'What is Zenari's involvement?' De Chabenac asked. 'He speaks of business there. Family business? Buying Moldavian geldings as remounts. Paris in the winter. Constantinople in the summer.'

'Not just Constantinople.' Jobert shrugged. 'Zenari spoke of attending the Sublime Porte.'

'The Sublime Porte, no less?' De Chabenac raised an amused eyebrow. 'I sense a subterfuge.'

Raive raised a taut finger. 'Zenari is presenting at the court of the Ottoman Sultan, but not as an accredited representative of France. Who does he represent? What official exchanges does he convey?'

'He was in Paris,' De Chabenac said. 'Perhaps consular business that impacts on Milan and Constantinople?'

'Curious,' Raive said. 'He is up to something, and it has very little to do with the provision of horses. What rate of interest does Zenari demand?'

'Zero.'

Raive leaned back and folded his arms. 'Why would anyone lend that amount of money without an expectation of being paid interest?'

'I asked Zenari the same question,' Jobert said. 'Upon presentation of our sureties, Zenari will expedite the provision of our funding needs in gold at the port of Ravenna, if I swore to accompany him whilst in Constantinople. He vacillates between wanting nothing to do with me, and ensuring I am his constant companion.'

'Do you have such an agreement in writing?' De Chabenac chuckled. 'You said Dikaletus spoke of expenses.'

Jobert lowered his face. 'Yes, he proposed half as much again.'

Raive stiffened. 'Six hundred thousand francs! That makes each horse, should it arrive, one thousand five hundred francs per head. At that price, I would want four-year-old mares, proven as dams the previous season, to land pregnant covered by one of the Sultan's own stallions. I feel an extra one hundred thousand francs would be more than sufficient.'

De Chabenac's smile broadened, as it always did when he was troubled. 'You are proposing taking two hundred and fifty kilograms of gold one thousand, five hundred kilometres into a land you do not know, dealing with people in a language you do not speak, and then returning alone with four hundred horses. That sounds ... impossible.'

'Do you truly believe there is opportunity, Jobert?' Raive asked.

The Cricket's long stride lifted Jobert's chest into the air over the vegetable barrows. 'I do.'

Raive turned to De Chabenac. 'This is not the Jobert in the days following Marengo and in light of Gianna's departure.'

'Indeed, a Jobert of his youth.' De Chabenac's eyes narrowed, as he looked from one to the other. 'The enterprise is short one hundred thousand francs.'

'Jobert,' Raive steepled his fingers under his nose, 'I have raised four hundred thousand francs from my associates for this venture. Their goodwill toward this investment is at an end. We are at an impasse. Unless this extra one hundred thousand francs can be found immediately, the moment cannot be seized. Perhaps as the Turks suggest, next year. In the meantime, allow us to digest the options at table this evening. May I invite you both to join the ladies and I?'

'Ah … no.' Jobert squirmed at the thought of dancing children. 'Excuse us, sir, not tonight, thank you. De Chabenac and I have an appointment at the theatre.'

'Do we?' De Chabenac smiled. 'Yes, of course, we do.'

'What are you seeing?' Raive asked.

Jobert nervously glanced at De Chabenac. 'What are we seeing?'

On one of Raive's borrowed charts, Jobert's fingers traced the coast of the Black Sea. 'The wheels have fallen off our plan for Ottoman mares. We are to look elsewhere for horses.'

'Thank goodness,' Duque said. 'How so many wise men believed travelling one thousand, five hundred kilometres with nearly three hundred kilograms of gold to buy four hundred horses was a good idea, I do not know.'

Koschak rapped the table with his knuckles. 'A fascinating debate for a winter's eve, no doubt. Of greater importance at this very moment, it is an occasion to be seized.'

'We have the authority to purchase,' Fazio said. 'We have the money to purchase. We have met the suppliers. They have what we want, and they are willing to sell. What is stopping us from buying?'

De Chabenac stretched out his legs and crossed his boots at the ankles. 'We are short of cash, dear fellows. We estimate another one hundred thousand francs is needed to cover our travel and any unexpected costs over the next few months.'

'Does Raive not have more hidden away?' Koschak asked.

'No,' De Chabenac said, 'he is already invested. I imagine quite heavily.'

'What did Zenari say he would cover?' Koschak asked.

Jobert held up his hands. 'He and his family are not investing. They are just arranging for the gold to be made immediately available, so that we do not need to raise it from Milan or Paris.'

'At what rate?' Duque asked.

'None.'

Duque folded his arms. 'What is the catch?'

'I am to travel with him to Constantinople.'

'He has travelled to Constantinople before,' Fazio said. 'He will be travelling under the protection of Otal Alaybey. What does he fear?'

Jobert shrugged. 'I do not know.'

Fazio slumped back in his seat. 'That Cricket you rode was impressive.'

Duque nodded with reluctance. 'It was.'

Koschak thumped the table with a bunched fist. 'Bugger! I was looking forward to travelling to Ottoman lands.'

De Chabenac smiled. 'As was I.'

Moench cleared his throat with a cough. 'I make a nice little earning running my books based on soldierly speculation.' Everyone at the table turned to Moench. 'As this is nothing more than that, I would have stumped up five thousand francs.'

Duque poked a stern finger across the table at Moench. 'Do not be a fool, lad. Keep your money safe.'

Fazio's right cheek creased his unshaven jowl as he spoke out of the side of his mouth. 'Would you put five thousand in the pot, Moench? You feel that confident?'

Moench shrugged. 'If wealthy Parisian businessmen and senior officers would invest in this enterprise, why would I not?'

'Fuck it!' Fazio punched Moench's shoulder. 'That is the spirit, lad. Deal me in for five thousand, too. Unless my money is no good amongst you lot?'

Duque threw up his hands. 'You are both idiots. The grappa is talking. The Turks still need another ninety thousand.'

'Eighty thousand!' Koschak drummed his fingers on the table. 'Count me in for ten thousand. After what we have done and seen, if pricks like us cannot achieve this, then no-one can. At war for seven years, I have saved most of my pay,' Koschak nodded to Jobert, 'and all the annuity dividends from Toulon. I have seen how much officers are willing to wager at cards. Hell, ten thousand francs. I could steal and resell ten horses easily enough to cover any loss.'

'When did you lose all reason, Koschak?' Duque slumped backwards. 'André, stop this bullshit.'

'Koschak,' Jobert grinned, 'I remember you scolding Tulloc for spending two francs on a ribbon for a girl.'

'Come now, sir,' Koschak spread his hands wide, 'this venture is money lying on the ground.'

De Chabenac swept up a long finger. 'I am reminded of the military adventurers in the New World once the *Reconquista* of Iberia had been achieved. I must strike while good fortune abounds, as my mother's and my sister's futures are at stake. I can offer no more than thirty thousand francs.'

'Sir, stop!' Duque was aghast. 'Thirty thousand francs is a ridiculous amount for one man to spend. That is ten years' salary for you, sir. Do not commit.'

Fazio crimped his lips. 'Only fifty thousand to go.'

'Who do we know?' Moench asked.

All eyes turned to Jobert.

Jobert placed his palms flat down on the table. 'There is not time to convince another investor.' Jobert looked up. 'Count me in for fifty thousand francs.'

Koschak, Moench and Fazio hooted, slapped the table and stomped their boots.

'Stop!' Duque shouted. 'You cannot be serious? You want to get rich by taking over two hundred kilograms of gold nearly two thousand kilometres to collect four hundred horses?'

'I am sure my brother will support the venture,' Jobert said. 'Between us we own forty per cent of the herd.'

Duque stood so fast his chair fell over behind him. He pushed at the excitement around the table. 'Yann will kick your arse, André. Your grandfather's legacy? Fifty thousand francs. Forty colts. One year of revenue. The risks are ridiculous. If this goes wrong, you lose forty per cent of your family's breeding herd. This will ruin the community that relies on that farm, the veterans who shelter and work there. It exposes my family to ruin.'

'Everyone speaks of the fleeting opportunities of the new peace.' Jobert raised his palms. 'If not a withdrawal from the farm, I have my annuity of one hundred thousand francs.'

'Your annuity from the prizes gained at Toulon? André, do not be so stupid. You risk your future here.'

Jobert locked a stern face on his childhood friend. 'I risk my life in battle, Duque. Am I not risking my future by hesitating? What is fifty thousand francs?'

Duque's arms drooped to his side as he turned away.

The others were silent.

Jobert stood and walked to Duque. 'I am going, Duque.' Jobert gripped Duque's shoulders with both hands. 'I was four, and you eight, when you showed me how to steal duck eggs.

I needed you then, and I need you now. Your veterinary skills are vital to the success of this enterprise. Teeth, lameness, pregnancy testing. If you invest your time in this affair, then I will reward your effort. Ten thousand francs of my share I allocate to you.'

'So, you, me and Zenari?' Duque slowly shook his head. 'Shit, we will have our heads on Ottoman flatbread before dinnertime.'

Koschak stood and gave Duque's shoulder a shake. 'Then, brother, you need a sharp eye to watch your back.' Koschak gave Jobert a nod. 'Count me in.'

'And I speak a little Serbian and Turkish,' Fazio said with a wink to Jobert. 'Count me in.'

'And me.' Moench said. Everyone looked at him. 'To safeguard my investment. Someone will be needed to hold the horses.'

'Hold four hundred horses, lad?' Koschak laughed. 'You can barely keep a grip on your cock.'

'Gentlemen, for the sake of administrative completeness,' De Chabenac said, smiling with delight, 'Raive will warrant I attend as far as Constantinople to ensure the exchange of monies is fully documented.'

'We could form our own consortium,' Fazio said.

'Why not?' Moench said. 'We will own one-fifth of the mares we deliver to the Loire.'

'Then lads, if not us, who?' Jobert raised his glass. 'To Moldavia.'

'Ah!' De Chabenac gave Jobert a wink. 'He has returned.'

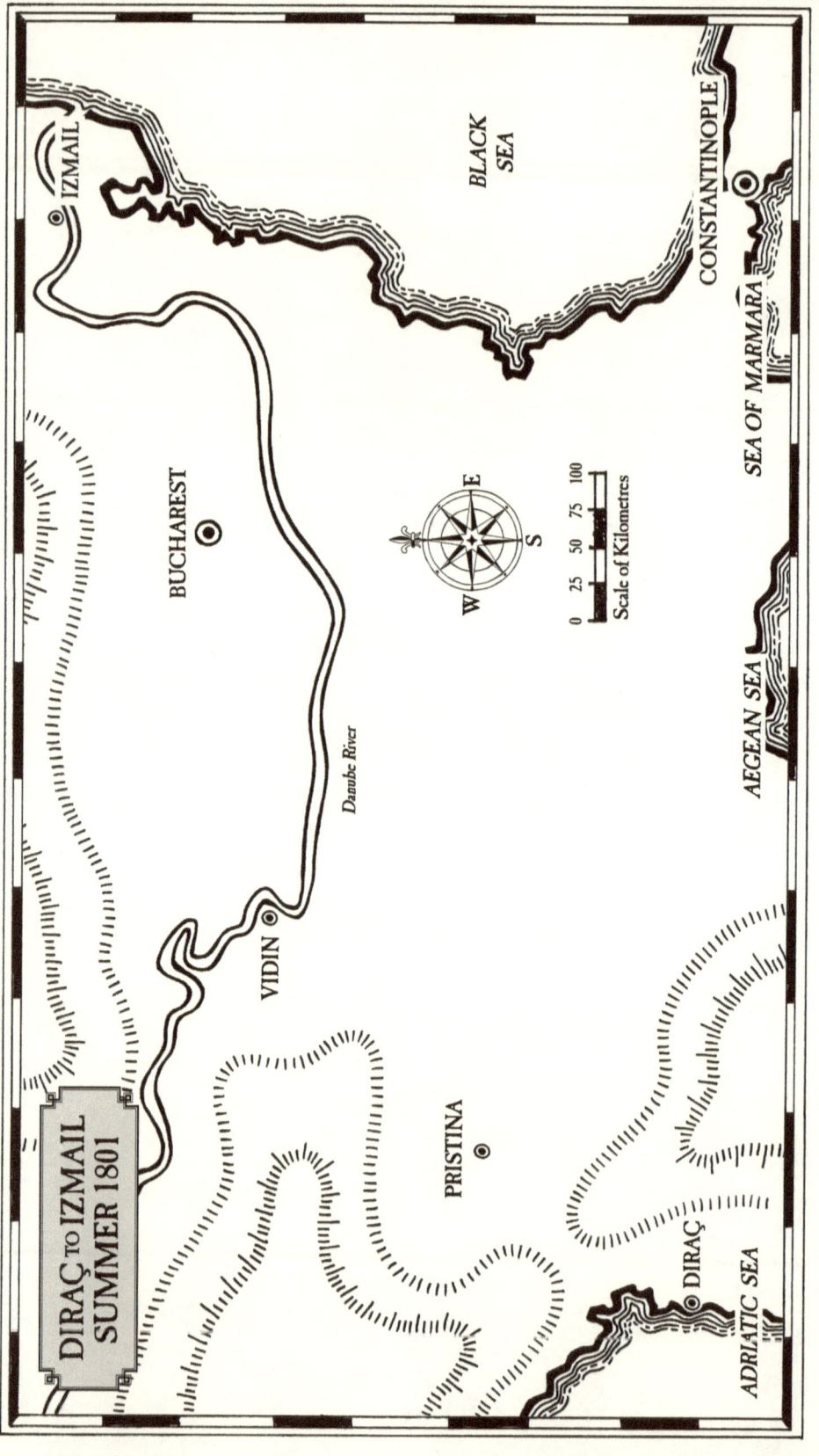

DIRAÇ TO IZMAIL
SUMMER 1801

IZMAIL

BLACK SEA

CONSTANTINOPLE

SEA OF MARMARA

BUCHAREST

Danube River

VIDIN

PRISTINA

AEGEAN SEA

DIRAÇ

ADRIATIC SEA

W E S N

Scale of Kilometres

0 25 50 75 100

Chapter Seven
May 1801, Diraç, Albania

The bowl of headland and sea that protected the port of Diraç amplified the squawking of gulls, the frustrated barks of labouring men and the morning's call to prayer. As the ship was moored alongside the dock, Jobert breathed in the Adriatic's salt. The morning's catch lay drying in the mid-May sun and the exotic spices grilled in stalls along the waterfront filled the air.

Zenari teetered down the gangplank with his cane. 'I shall seek Otal in the coffee house.'

'Very well.' Jobert turned to his fellow travellers. 'Koschak, stay on board with the gold. Have the ship anchor in the roads. I will send a boat out with fresh groceries. Duque and Fazio, please find accommodation and move our baggage.'

Moench scanned the foreign crowd of bald men with top-knots, wearing loose shirts and pants with waist sashes, lugging bales into the portside warehouses. 'And what do you wish me to bring with you, sir?'

'Leave the women alone, Moench,' Jobert said. 'I have seen firsthand how swift and harsh retribution is dealt in this land.

Maintain a watch on the gold. Allow me to meet with the Turks to appreciate the lie of the land. We will then arrange for your relief.'

Moench's jaw clenched with disappointment.

'Do you have our documents of authority?' Jobert asked.

'I do.' De Chabenac patted a satchel slung around his shoulder. 'Why is Zenari in such a rush? Would it not strengthen our hand to arrive together?'

'Who knows?' Jobert said as he and De Chabenac descended onto the wharf. 'The prick irritates me. He is rattled by this business in Constantinople.'

'I suspect he has entered into a difficult situation.'

Jobert's jaw rolled with anger. 'Then whatever it is better not impact on us.'

In the streets behind the port, the market bustled with daily purchasing by women in knee-length woollen skirts or billowing ankle-length trousers, with decorative veils and embroidered vests. The pungent fragrance in the spice market was mouth-watering. Cinnamon, cardamon and cumin. Peppercorns and paprika. Turmeric and thyme. Saffron, fenugreek, basil and mint.

Along one verandah of Diraç's Byzantine forum, Jobert and De Chabenac paused at the carved timber entrance to a coffee house into which Zenari had disappeared.

'Do our esteemed Turkish gentlemen speak French?' De Chabenac asked.

'They do, but watch for their oriental response of "*inshallah*" for it—'

De Chabenac's calm smile betrayed to Jobert his underlying concern. 'You are confident of the chosen path?'

'If we cannot do this, who can?'

Inside the labyrinth of lattice screens and carpets, Zenari was already availing himself of coffee. His fumbling agitation as he poured the thick black liquid into the tiny cup distracted

Otal and Dikaletus from Jobert's approach.

Jobert exchanged greetings with both Otal and Dikaletus, the touching of heads and hearts, before introducing De Chabenac.

Dikaletus rested his hand on De Chabenac's thigh. 'My dear De Chabenac, how is your family? Are they well?'

De Chabenac seemed at ease to what Jobert felt uncomfortable with, both the touch and the questioning. 'My mother is quite well, thank you, sir.'

'*Alham-dulillah.* And your wife and children?'

'I am not married, sir.'

Dikaletus withdrew his hand, and his bejewelled fingers wiggled as they sought something more seemly to grip.

Annoyance creased Otal's forehead. 'Why are we honoured with three colonels?'

With a nod from Jobert, De Chabenac produced documents from his satchel and placed them on the carved coffee table between their couches.

'France requires signatures that Moldavia has received twenty thousand gold louis,' Jobert said. 'Colonel De Chabenac is to return those signed documents to France. Can ink be arranged?'

'Since the horses are being purchased from the Hospodar of Moldavia,' Otal said, waving his shisha mouthpiece to his companion, 'then Dikaletus Pasha will sign.'

Dikaletus' pink finger poked in warning above a small porcelain coffee cup. 'Such documents will need to be translated into Turkish before being signed.' Dikaletus offered De Chabenac a brass platter of golden baklava. 'And where is the gold now?'

'My men and gold remain on board in the roads.' When offered, Jobert took a square of the sticky pastry. 'France's gold is not leaving my ship until I have signatures for its receipt.'

Otal's hooded eyes stared through his exhaled raspberry and honey-scented tobacco smoke. 'What vessel do you have?'

'A three-masted xebec.' Jobert flicked at pastry crumbs and crushed almonds from his tailcoat. 'The two hundred and fifty kilograms of gold is contained in six iron-bound chests.'

'Most excellent. Then we can proceed to Constantinople without delay.'

'Not at all, Otal Alaybey.' Dikaletus' red moustache quivered in horizontal tension. 'It is to Bucharest where we must proceed without delay. Jobert, since you purchase the Hospodar's horses, it is the Hospodar that must receive the gold and vouchsafe the amount to the Sultan — peace be upon him.'

'The Sultan? What is the Sultan's interest in this exchange?'

Otal scoffed. 'Keep the gold on your ship. We will sail with it.' Otal gave a twist of his head. 'We shall transfer to an imperial galley at Constantinople. We shall pass into the Black Sea and enter the mouth of the Danube at Izmail. We shall sail up the Danube to Bucharest.'

Dikaletus fluttered his fingers. 'If I sign for the gold, then I control how it moves. It will be brought ashore to move overland to Vidin.'

Otal jerked. 'Vidin! That nest of vipers?'

'Where is ... what is Vidin?' Jobert asked.

'A port of the Sultan's Danube fleet ruled by a bandit chief,' Otal said. 'Transport to Vidin would require the gold to constantly change hands. It cannot fail to be noticed and remarked upon. On board it can move swiftly without onlookers.'

'Once loaded onto packhorses, the gold will move just as swiftly,' Dikaletus said.

'Over the Serbian mountains?' Otal's face sneered in disbelief.

Dikaletus patted Otal's knee. 'This is of little concern. I have passports that will assure our safety to Vidin.' Dikaletus beamed his assurance at Jobert. 'Both warlords wish only for harmony with the Hospodar.'

'Both?' De Chabenac's smile widened.

Otal leant back on his cushions. 'And what of attacks by *hadjuk* who roam beyond the control of the warlords?'

De Chabenac smiled at Jobert. 'What are roaming hadjuk?'

Dikaletus picked at the baklava. 'Our combined escort of well over one hundred is sufficient. Corsairs between here and Izmail are of greater concern. If by sea is the preferred route, then why have both you and I travelled overland to Diraç?'

Jobert retrieved the documents and stared hard at Otal and Dikaletus. 'Gentlemen, which of you controls the horses I am buying?'

'The Pasha controls the sale,' Otal reclined on his cushions, 'and I control the horses.' Otal jabbed his shisha mouthpiece at the three Europeans. 'Which of you commands your delegation? Colonel Zenari or Lieutenant Colonel Jobert? Or our new friend, Lieutenant Colonel De Chabenac?'

'Certainly not myself.' De Chabenac raised his palms. 'Apart from the simple errand of returning with the signed documents, I am honoured to behold the delights of the Sultan's realm.'

Jobert looked at Zenari. 'Shall you answer, Zenari, or shall I?'

Zenari lowered his face and flapped his hands at an unseen pressure. 'In the matter of horses, Jobert leads. I am here on separate business.'

Dikaletus bent his ear towards Zenari. 'Business to be transacted where exactly, Zenari? What is your purpose here in the Sultan's land?'

Zenari appeared under pressure. 'I observe the purchase of the horses on behalf of vested interests.' Zenari looked at Otal. 'I am bound to move with Jobert.'

'If you are a representative of such interests,' Otal said, 'your views are of value. By sea or over mountains?'

Jobert glanced at Otal, Dikaletus and Zenari. *Four dogs. One scrap. Each wary of the next. But what exactly is the scrap?* 'As it is my gold France delivers to the Hospodar, I will not move without signatures. I say we travel by sea.'

Otal raised his hands to the heavens. '*Alham-dulillah.*'

'Then we all agree.' Dikaletus swished the crumbs from his fingers. 'We must receive such signatures of transaction in Bucharest. Yet the swiftest travel to Bucharest will be overland.' Dikaletus stood up and arranged the folds of his rose-pink coat. 'Since you are determined to travel by sea, my dear Otal Alaybey, then you shall be accountable to the Hospodar for the loss of the gold. Jobert, should your travels be safe as Otal assures you, I look forward to meeting with you in the court of our beloved prince.' Dikaletus bowed to Jobert. 'Gentlemen, I wish you God's peace.'

Dikaletus made his farewell bows with sweeping hand gestures.

Otal drew deeply on the shisha as he watched Dikaletus depart. 'Gentlemen, we sail at dawn. *Inshallah.*'

Outside the coffee house, Zenari, mumbling and shaking his fists, brushed past Duque.

Duque pointed in the opposite direction. 'Gentlemen, our accommodation is this way, uphill beyond the Venetian tower.'

De Chabenac looked at Zenari departing downhill. 'Where is he going?'

'The port, perhaps.' Jobert shrugged. 'Does he not remember we were attacked in the street?'

'What is going on, Jobert? Are you satisfied with that discussion?'

Jobert shook his scabbard with a rigid arm. 'No, I am not. My impression is that Otal and Dikaletus are in competition with each other. Over the gold, the horses, and something else.'

'This business with Zenari?'

'Possibly, Zenari himself. I felt they were testing him.' Jobert looked about the stalls they were between. 'It was here that Zenari and I were attacked by eight men. Four were executed by Otal.' Jobert looked to Duque. 'What if they try to assail Zenari again? Would you check on Zenari and escort him to the tavern, please?'

De Chabenac grinned encouragement as Duque trudged downhill once more. 'And what of two rival warlords? Did we not discuss this with Raive? Is this not a moment of possible concern?'

Jobert and De Chabenac walked the ascending lanes to their appointed tavern. Here Fazio sat in the sun looking southwest over the hazy blue sea and sipped a cloudy raki in a small glass. 'Gentlemen, I have placed your luggage in your rooms.'

De Chabenac poured a glass of raki. 'To Constantinople!' De Chabenac toasted the Adriatic below. 'I am genuinely thrilled.' His face blanched as he sipped the liquor.

Fazio reached across with a pottery jug. 'Add a dash of water, sir.'

'Down to business.' Jobert produced a pencil and notebook from within his tailcoat. 'Fazio, we are to sail for Constantinople. I want to consider what might be required for the voyage.'

Once Fazio's list was complete, and as Jobert was reaching for his purse, Zenari and Duque arrived outside the tavern. Zenari wheezed from his climb from the port. 'Where is our ship? Where is my baggage?'

Jobert stared sourly. 'Should you have the graciousness to—'

'Where is my baggage, Jobert!'

Duque held out his arm towards the tavern entrance. 'It has been taken to your room, sir.'

Zenari hissed in frustration. 'How dare you pack my trunks and move them without my express permission.' Zenari spun towards the entrance.

Fazio looked at Jobert with concern. 'I was unsure ... you will need this key, sir.'

'The Key! You have the Key?' Spluttering, Zenari stared at the door key Fazio held between his fingers. 'You imbecile.' Zenari snatched the room key and raced inside.

Jobert shook his head at De Chabenac and Duque as Fazio followed Zenari indoors.

A hoarse scream tore from the tavern's open shutters.

De Chabenac spilled his raki. 'Good gracious! Is that Zenari?'

Fazio burst from the entrance. 'Colonel Jobert, sir, come quickly.'

Zenari's room had been ransacked. Trunks had been prised open and clothing strewn. Bedding was thrown over and the bureau's drawers pulled out and upended.

'Everyone, check our rooms,' Jobert said.

Zenari hugged his tailcoat's lapels to his chest. Swollen with panic, he staggered from the room, only to collide with the door jamb.

Jobert grabbed at Zenari's upper arm to steady him. 'What has been stolen?'

Zenari buckled and retched a mush of honey. 'All is well.' He smeared pastry and chopped almonds from his lips to his sleeve. 'I must find Otal.'

Duque poked his head from a doorway further down the corridor. 'Our rooms are undisturbed, sir.'

Jobert ran his fingers over the battered peeling shutters. 'Were our shutters open or shut? Who did you engage at the wharves to carry our luggage?'

'I locked all the shutters, sir.' Fazio said. 'And local porters carted our luggage. But our chances of finding them ...'

'The room was locked,' Duque said. 'Servants are constantly moving along these corridors.'

'Our arrival was anticipated.' De Chabenac stepped with care over Zenari's belongings. 'We were informed where to meet Otal.' De Chabenac stopped and smiled. 'A mystery. My curiosity is piqued. First, Zenari's official duties, his time in Paris a few months ago, his need to arrive in Constantinople. Then an attack here in Diraç. Now a robbery. Otal's and Dikaletus' competing interest in our movement. Zenari carries something? Whatever has he got himself involved in?'

Jobert scowled. 'I am in no mood for mysteries. I am focused on gold and then horses.'

Thirty minutes later, Otal and Zenari arrived.

Otal Alaybey's eyes bulged from his livid expression as he surveyed the plundered luggage. His hand crushed the neck of his scabbard, as if ready to draw his scimitar. 'Are you sure?'

Zenari looked ashen.

'What is missing?' Jobert asked.

Zenari's lips trembled. 'My satchel.'

Fazio pointed at the toppled cases. 'Sir, I placed your satchel on the top of your hat boxes.'

Otal's eyes scoured the room, but his mind was envisioning something else. 'This was an unfortunate opportunity for local thieves. I am ashamed that my guests have been pillaged. Anything taken I will replace.' Otal turned to Jobert. 'But, of a graver matter, Jobert, I have received reports. There are brigands moving in the hills. I am concerned for Dikaletus' safety. We leave immediately. Dock your vessel, Jobert. Unload your gold and prepare to strike for the road to Vidin.'

'The hills!' Jobert recoiled in alarm. 'I am not taking my

gold into the hills. What has been stolen? What has changed?'

Otal flicked his fingers. 'There is no time to waste. Say your farewells, Zenari, and repack swiftly. You and I depart in one hour.'

'You sign for the gold,' Jobert said, 'then you can take it wherever you like.'

Zenari tugged at Jobert's sleeve. 'Bring our vessel alongside, Jobert. I must return on board to check if this moron Fazio left any of my effects onboard. I beg you to comply with our host's requests.' Zenari's knuckles pressed white through his clenched skin. 'You are bound to me, Jobert, if our path is overland to Vidin.'

Zenari staggered to navigate the corridor on his departure for the port.

Jobert sighed. 'Duque, please signal Koschak to re-enter port.'

Duque gave a slow despondent roll of his head as he shuffled to follow Zenari.

Jobert noted De Chabenac's apprehensive posture before turning to Otal. 'What was taken, Otal? Why are you now concerned for Dikaletus' safety?'

Otal was clearly vexed. 'It would be better if Dikaletus and I combined our strength.'

Jobert blocked the doorway. 'Two hours ago you were determined to avoid delivering my gold directly to the bandits within their mountain strongholds. What has changed?'

Otal gritted his teeth at the buttons on Jobert's tailcoat. 'I shall not haggle, Jobert. Your gold and your horses can wait until next year. Zenari and I are departing to protect Dikaletus.'

'Dikaletus is behind this robbery.' Jobert's finger jabbed at the mess behind Otal. 'When you showed me the Cricket, you were angry to find Dikaletus in Diraç and that Zenari was with him. It was Dikaletus who ordered Zenari to be taken in the street attack last time we were here. You realised Dikaletus' involvement and so executed our attackers to protect his identity. I will not move until the documents are signed ensuring the safety of French gold. What does he have that you want, Otal?'

'I do not answer to you, Jobert.'

Jobert leant close to Otal. 'You want that gold?' Otal's eyes confirmed as much. 'And I want those horses. Such a sale between our two nations demands your answer. What concern of Zenari's is of such importance to you and Dikaletus?'

Otal's rolled his eyes at some inferred tedium. 'I am entrusted to support Zenari's business. You, Jobert, merely intrude with this query around horses. I have waited a month in this town, not for you, but to accommodate Zenari's vacillation. I wait no longer. There are persons, who are not to be slighted, who expect Zenari to attend them. To that end, I am leaving. If you wish to see the horses this year, Jobert, then prepare to march.'

Jobert threw his hands wide. 'We are not equipped for an expedition. We need five packhorses at least for the gold, let alone our belongings. What is your escort's strength?'

'Why is that important? My escort is over sixty men. Sipahi, *djelli* and *panduk*. Over one hundred once combined with Dikaletus'.' Otal flicked his fingers into the air. 'Your packhorses will be arranged. We leave at dawn.'

Otal swirled from the room.

An hour later, Zenari returned from his investigation of their ship sweaty, without his hat and with his tied-back hair fraying into wisps. 'I need a candle.'

'Did you find your satchel?'

'No. Is it possible to fetch me a candle?'

'Where is Duque?' Jobert asked.

'At the port with the gold. Can I get a candle, please?'

'A candle for what? There is an oil lamp in your room.'

'I want a fucking candle, Jobert. To search my fucking room.

Get me a fucking candle. Now!' Zenari was on the verge of tears. 'Please, Jobert.'

'I have a candle in my portmanteau.' Jobert folded his arms. 'I shall fetch it once you have answered my questions.'

'I cannot. My errand requires me to travel with Otal. Jobert, I beg you, commit to this journey. You promised me. Come, the horses are of such importance. Travel with Otal.'

Jobert returned from his quarters rolling the candle in his fingers, scowling at both Zenari and De Chabenac. 'My two hundred and fifty kilograms of gold is less important than what has been taken from your room? What is more important? You are travelling with Otal to catch up with Dikaletus. What did your satchel contain?'

'Official documents.' Zenari plucked the candle from Jobert's fingers. 'I am embarrassed that they have been taken. They are of no value to common thieves. I beg you to come with me. This is a matter of the highest national importance. Trust me.'

De Chabenac rubbed his forehead. 'No less than national importance now.'

'I cannot speak of this.' Zenari scrutinised the candle. 'Please travel with me, Jobert.'

'I will accompany you to chase Dikaletus, if ...,' Jobert said. Zenari's glazed eyes quivered with hope. 'if you provide me a written guarantee your family will underwrite any loss of gold due to this overland diversion.'

'Yes, I will pen such a guarantee.'

Jobert bowed his head. 'Once I am satisfied, I will come with you.'

'Thank you. I ... bring me ink and paper once I emerge, but now I need to repack. Do not disturb me.'

Zenari entered his room. The door locked with a click.

Jobert turned to De Chabenac and Fazio standing in the corridor behind him. 'We have packed for a journey by sea.

We do not have the equipment to travel overland. We need to unload the galley and pack our baggage.'

'Why are you choosing to move the gold through the mountains, Jobert?' Trepidation tightened De Chabenac's eyes. 'We risk losing all that we have struggled to save.'

'Between Zenari, Otal and Dikaletus, we have an escort of over one hundred Turks, passports through the warlords' territories, and now a guarantee that we will not lose our contributions if Zenari loses his family's gold.' Jobert wrung his hands in frustration. 'I cannot wait another year to inspect these mares. Fazio, find us packhorses. Please.'

'Gentlemen, this is bullshit.' With bowed shoulders, Fazio swayed on the spot. 'If Koschak thought Arezzo or Naples was bad, wait until you disappear into Serbia.'

Chapter Eight
June 1801, Dinaric Mountains, Serbia

Jobert pulsed the reins on his hard-mouthed Bosnian pony to halt on the side of the mountain track beside Fazio. As the column of Otal's soldiers and attached caravans of merchants raised white dust on the road passing over the ridgeline, Fazio stared at the far western horizon. Beyond the steep dark green forests plunging away beneath them, the smudge of the Adriatic coast could just be discerned.

Beside Jobert, Fazio ground his jaw, which caused his thick black moustache to quiver. 'We should not be up here, sir. We are flopping our balls into a mince grinder.'

Amongst the grey boulders and spindly thorns on the flatter ground at the top of the pass Otal schooled Koschak in the use of the lance. Having discussed the relative merits of either couching the weapon under the arm for impact or holding it away from the body with the hand to stab, Koschak was keen to practise on his short-stepping pony.

Jobert rocked his resistant mount to join Otal's side. 'How long is our journey over the mountains?'

Otal's hand swept eastward. 'Our road follows the Drin River into the mountains. A week to Pristina, then a week to Vidin on the Danube. Dikaletus is a day or two's march ahead of us.'

'You were not expecting the Hospodar's dragoman in Diraç.'

Otal grimaced before inspecting Koschak's technique. 'His seat is very good.'

Jobert sneered at the obfuscation. 'It is interesting that Orthodox Greeks hold such powerful positions within the Sultan's empire.'

Otal sniffed with derision. 'His Sultanic Majesty — peace be upon him — graces many nations with his protection. His Greek subjects have been swayed by France's progressive shift away from sovereign and faith. I fear for Sultan Selim.'

'The Hospodar of Wallachia and Moldavia is Greek, and yet you serve him.'

Otal gathered the Cricket's reins. 'The Hospodar has my undying loyalty, as my Sultan directs, for which myself and the other sipahi are granted land and income from Moldavia.' Otal turned his mount and rejoined the column. 'Come, Jobert, we are many hours from camp.'

Otal's escort established their clean and orderly camps each afternoon. Merchants' caravans nestled within the imperial protection. Moving amongst the travellers, village hawkers sold vegetables, fresh bread and eggs. Moench, with his violin, accompanied other musicians as they wandered the camp playing the wide sixty-five string bandura and the long-necked, six-string *baglama* to the beat of a wide, shallow drum.

Jobert's companions set their small camp close to Otal's dozen sipahi. Under Duque's tight supervision, the five pack-ponies, each carrying fifty kilograms of gold, was central to their sleeping arrangement. Although Otal had organised saddle and pack-ponies before departing Diraç, Jobert felt vulnerable at being so ill-prepared for their journey. It had taken days, trading in the poor villages they passed, for them to accumulate sufficient blankets, knives and flints.

At the evening meal with Otal's sipahi, Jobert bit into grape leaves stuffed with fragrant vegetables and rice. Jobert had adapted to eating with only his right hand, until they finally purchased bowls and spoons. Yet, on the carpets spread for each meal, he remained unable to eat comfortably while either sitting cross-legged, squatting or kneeling. 'How serious is the threat of mountain bandits attacking a column of imperial troops?'

'Most people are wary of imperial columns, but ...' Otal scooped at a shared bowl of spiced grilled goat and lentils with a deft twist of a piece of hot flatbread, 'these hadjuk are ex-janissaries.'

Jobert dripped hummus from his unravelling flatbread. 'Janissaries?'

'Fierce ex-imperial soldiers. Well-drilled for battle.'

Jobert examined Otal's tufted horsehair standard, or tug, planted erect behind and above its commander. The thick wooden shaft was carved in geometric patterns and arrayed with dyed horsehair, either flowing green, tufted white and red or plaited black. 'These bandits do not provoke the local warlords?'

'These hadjuk are most likely in the warlords' employ.' Otal wiped his moustache and chin with a towel. 'Pasvanoglu, to our east in Vidin, and Ali Pasha, to our south, do not oppose each other. They are keen to establish their autonomy from the court in Constantinople. They act favourably towards Wallachia and Moldavia. And, indeed, France, so there is no need to worry.'

No need? Really? As he sipped his cup of raki, Jobert looked beyond the dozen sipahi around the widely spread dinner mats, to the further fifty-man encampment of horsemen. 'What is the difference between your sipahi and those djelli?'

Both groups of horsemen wore near identical clothing of jackets, loose trousers and leather boots, in an array of colours. Their sashes were stuffed with scimitars, knives and pistols. To Jobert, the difference appeared to be their hats and their horses. The sipahi wore tall red caps with intricate turban wraps and rode tall horses of similar breeding to the Cricket. The djelli wore black caps beneath their red turbans and rode the small hardy Bosnian ponies, as had been issued to Jobert and his men.

'My sipahi follow the true faith and are bound to our lands in Moldavia. The Bosnian djelli are irregulars assigned to me and Dikaletus in Vidin.'

'And your infantry?'

Beyond the horse lines of the djelli were set the panduk cooking fires from which smoke and songs arose. These infantry soldiers were clean shaven men with moustaches. They wore blue jackets with baggy sleeves, and red baggy pants that gathered at the knee. Each wore a soft red cap, some with brooches on the front. Although the clothing was unadorned, the leather work and timber work of the weapons were highly ornate. The soldiers took great care in oiling their engraved muskets. A sash about their waists held long daggers. Those on sentry duty had two pistols slung in a holster across the chest.

'The panduk are local militia.'

'Why do they not carry bayonets with their muskets?'

Otal snorted in disgust. 'The bayonet is not the weapon of a warrior. It is a toy for the weak.'

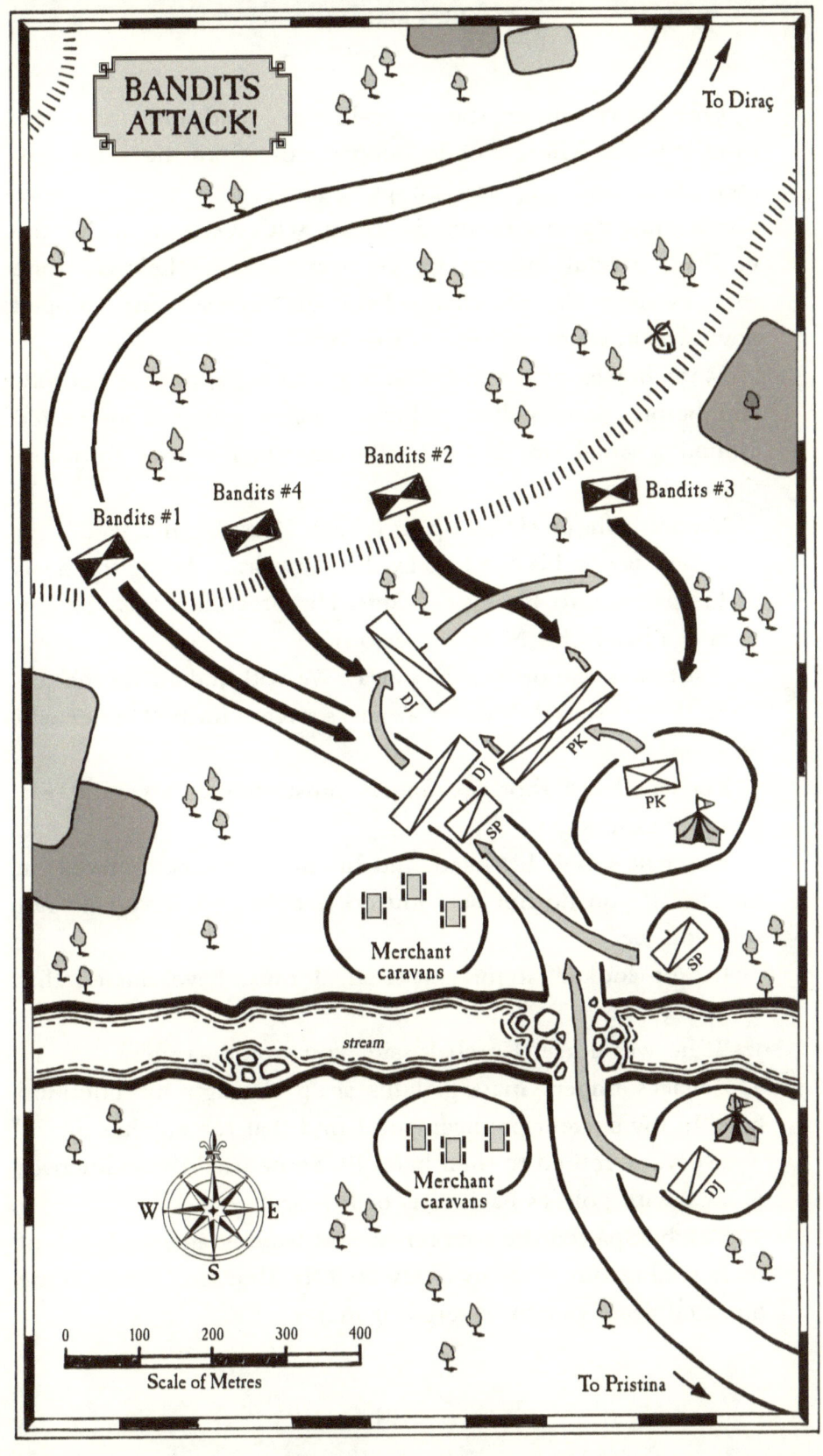

BANDITS
ATTACK!

To Diraç

Bandits #1
Bandits #4
Bandits #2
Bandits #3

DJ
DJ
PK
PK
SP

Merchant
caravans

SP

stream

Merchant
caravans

DJ

W   E
S

0   100   200   300   400
Scale of Metres

To Pristina

One afternoon on the Diraç-Pristina road, only two days from Pristina, where wooded slopes arose from the vale's lush meadows, Otal's imperial troops camped either side of a ford across a fast-flowing mountain stream with djelli cavalry on the far bank, panduk infantry on the near bank. As they had done each evening, the merchants led their caravans and camped downstream on either side of the ford.

With horses watered, fed and groomed, and with bedrolls laid before their saddle pillows, Jobert's companions rested around a small fire before collecting their dinner from the sipahis' kettles.

'André,' Duque sidled up to Jobert, 'Zenari is not well.'

Zenari lay on his blankets by the campfire, rubbing the heels of his palms into his eye sockets. His breathing was shallow. 'I have a headache. Nothing serious.'

'Pristina is one or two days away. We will find an apothecary there.' Jobert stared down at Zenari's sweaty form. 'Dinner will be soon.'

Zenari's hand shot up, fingers outstretched. 'I cannot eat. I simply cannot.'

Koschak shook his head, and his hussar plaits slithered on his jaw. 'If you do not eat, you do not shit, sir. If you do not shit, you die.'

Duque looked about surprised. 'I must have missed that lecture at Alfort.'

'If he was horse,' Koschak said, 'you would axe him.'

Zenari's fingers massaged his scalp through his unbound hair. 'In my current predicament, I find that remedy has merit.'

Everyone retired to their bedrolls. Some used the saddlebags packed with gold as back rests or low seats.

Koschak patted the pannier he was leaning against. 'Each of us is resting our scrawny arses on fifty thousand francs. One hundred years' pay for a sergeant major.'

Jobert sucked in his breath. 'Fifty thousand francs would yield an annuity income equivalent to the annual salary of a cavalry captain for life.'

Koschak grinned. 'What would each of us do with the money?'

'A town house.' Moench paused tuning his violin with his thumb. 'Where the ladies of the city are entertained by a chamber orchestra.' Moench leered. 'With sumptuous bedrooms upstairs ... for those desiring repose.'

Fazio clenched his pipestem in his mouth, so he growled out the right side of his mouth. 'If we survive ... maybe, a wine merchant with a private taproom. Ooh ... and card tables.'

'A farm.' By stirring the fire with a stick, Duque could visualise his hopes in the flames. 'Stables full of fat animals. Gardens full of ripe vegetables. A cosy house. A pretty ...' A rueful smile flitted across his lips.

'For me,' Koschak said, 'a sleek brig to travel to Africa, India and even China. From Constantinople to the gates of Persia.' Koschak swivelled his blond head to orient his mental compass on the sunset. 'India and China cannot be far beyond where we sit.'

De Chabenac reclined on his blankets, his arms folded behind his head on his saddle. 'My only desire is a safe home for my mother and sister.' He flashed a brief smile at Jobert. 'And you, Jobert.'

Jobert rocked his head as images swirled with the twisting smoke. Memories of Gianna's skin and curls blended with Raive's candelabras and tapestries. Jobert frowned. 'I think I would like—'

A shot was fired.

A yell, followed by two more shots.

Jobert and his companions stood and scanned the camp area.

The panduk infantry were pointing towards the tree-lined slopes and shouting.

'Stand to arms, lads.' Jobert scooped up his saddle. 'Koschak, mount!'

'Who?' Koschak rolled to his feet, his saddle over his forearm. 'How many?'

Wild cries rang from the wooded slopes.

A djelli sentry descended the road towards the ford, flapping his elbows to urge greater speed from his cantering pony.

The men around the merchants' fires crouched in panic. A shout broke their trance, and they raced for their lines of packhorses, mules, donkeys and oxen.

Otal yelled a command to his sipahi, picked up his lance and mounted the Cricket. Those sipahi who were already saddled mounted. Others flung their saddles onto their nervous horses. With his green and red tug held aloft behind him, Otal spun the Cricket towards Jobert. 'Hadjuk!' he cried. 'Bandits!'

From the saddle, Jobert looked down at the panniers. 'Lads, form a tight circle around the gold.'

De Chabenac, Zenari, Fazio and Moench took a corner each of a small square and presented *en garde*. Duque slung his veterinary satchel around his shoulders. 'Next time, André, pistols would be welcome.'

The panduk militia raced to form a fire line, then fired a volley.

Otal led his charging sipahi up the road.

With slightly increased height mounted on his pony, Jobert glimpsed rounded figures whooping and waving their lances and muskets as they darted from gun smoke to thornbush.

When the clatter of sipahi hooves and the crackle of panduk musketry dimmed, a truncated hiss sounded through the wild yelling. Something was moving through the air much slower than a musket ball. What it was Jobert could not see.

The militiamen in their fire line now gesticulated and bawled at a new threat.

Further along the slope on their half-right, a line of twenty sheepskin clad figures advanced. They stopped one hundred metres from the panduk line and drew back on bows. The air filled with the swift hiss of arrows.

'Fucking arrows!' Koschak scoffed and couched his lance against his ribs. 'We must be the first French soldiers to receive a volley of arrows since Jeanne d'Arc.'

The arrows rattled on the stones or thunked into flesh.

The panduks fired a second volley, dropped their muskets, drew their swords and long knives and charged the approaching bandits.

Behind Jobert, the djelli trotted across the stream and remained bunched on the road between the tents of the merchants and the sipahi campfires. Jobert watched the djelli commander. Was he unsure? Or was he waiting for the right moment to commit his horsemen?

Another howl of throats and hiss of arcing arrows. A third attack emerged along the river's banks from the full right of the panduks.

The panduks line buckled under the fresh assault.

Over the heads of the infantry, Jobert saw Otal's sipahi surge behind his flapping tug from the road on the left towards the flank attack on the right.

The djelli swung their attention towards the riverbank assault.

Howls of despair rose from the merchants' convoys.

Another twenty motley figures sprinted towards the loaded pack-animals.

'Fazio, get up behind,' Jobert cried, pulling his brown felt hat firmly down on his brow. 'Tell the djelli to follow me.'

Koschak dropped his lance head and cantered straight across the front of the crowded djelli.

Riding directly toward the incoming bandits' strike against the merchant's bales, Jobert urged his little horse to trot. Behind Jobert's saddle, Fazio yelled and yelled as they rode through the snarled group of Bosnian cavalry.

The djelli cheered in response and set their horses at a trot at the rush of oncoming bandits.

Arrows criss-crossed Jobert's vision. His pony would not yield to his leg pressure to bring him close enough to his elusive opponents. His sabre clattered on their upraised lance tips and bows.

Swishing his lance at the dodging hadjuk, Koschak coughed a maniacal laugh at the absurdity.

Yet the appearance of over twenty djelli was sufficient to disperse the twenty bandits back up the slope.

With a shriek of insane glee, Koschak spun his little warhorse towards the sipahi melee in front of the panduks.

Fazio yelled at the djelli leader as Jobert spurred his recalcitrant pony to follow Koschak.

Ahead in the dust cloud of furious hand-to-hand fighting, Otal's tug was central. Labouring men grunted and leaders choked hoarse commands. Scimitar and knife blades sizzled and clanged. Occasionally, the pop of a pistol. Lances clacked against leather shields and musket barrels. With a rattle of dropped weapons, the wounded hissed in agony and clutched at their wounds.

'Jobert!' Koschak thrust his lance into the back of a bandit. 'Otal's standard!' A second bandit swept the tug's staff to parry Koschak's unwieldy stabs.

'Fazio, take this fucking goat.' Jobert swung his leg forward over his pony's neck to dismount. Fazio slid over the cantle to take up the reins.

Running behind Koschak's nearside shoulder, Jobert sprang upon the banner thief and slid his blade through the man's belly, before being knocked to the ground by Koschak's horse's shoulder.

'I have it!' Koschak thrust the shaggy totem above his bright red face.

'Koschak, ride clear!' Jobert shouted as he espied the Cricket, with reins trailing, spooking at the violent actions around him. 'Otal is down.'

Jobert approached the unsure horse side on with his sabre low. He scooped the reins, rubbed the Cricket's neck, hopped to place his boot in the stirrup and mounted.

'Jobert!' Otal was cornered in a mess of downed horses amongst a swirl of bandits. Unable to vault over the backs of the heaving wounded animals, he parried with scimitar and knife at the thrusts of bandits' lances. Otal's mounted sipahi were unable to close the distance to protect their commander.

A courageous opponent leapt the thrashing hooves to collide with Otal.

Otal parried and stepped in close. In a swift levering movement, Otal grasped the bandit's scimitar pommel, pressed down on his blade and disarmed him, before running him through.

Two more bandits leapt across the bellies of the injured mounts.

Jobert lifted the Cricket onto a right canter lead and set the Cricket's shoulders towards two downed horses, one prostrate on its side, and the other hamstrung and struggling to stand. 'Otal Alaybey!'

Otal threw himself down amongst the ribs, hooves and saddles.

The Cricket sailed over the jump of two lying horses and crushed one assailant while Jobert cut down the other.

Cries of victory rose around them as bandits ran down the creek. The panduks sprinted to capture the slow and the wounded. The djelli pursued and roped those escapees retreating up the slopes.

As De Chabenac, Zenari, Koschak, Duque, Fazio and Moench gathered about him, Jobert dismounted and held out the Cricket's reins. 'Your horse, Otal Alaybey.'

Otal wiped his scimitar on the trouser leg of a groaning bandit at his feet, sheathed his weapon and removed his conical red hat. From its turban-woven brim, Otal unpinned an engraved pewter brooch. 'I was awarded this *çelenk* for saving a pasha's life during the war against the Russians.' Otal rubbed the brooch with his thumb, then indicated with his hand that he wished for Jobert's tall, crowned hat.

Jobert swept off his hat and passed it to Otal.

Otal pinned the award onto the brown-ribboned hat band. 'With my thanks to God, I award you this *çelenk* for your bravery.'

Jobert gave a solemn bow as he received back his hat in both hands. 'I am at your—'

A fierce sizzle.

A scream of terror.

A cloud of acrid smoke.

A cackle of nasty laughs.

The group of Frenchmen turned to witness two dozen bloodied prisoners, trussed and on their knees, surrounded by a crowd of leering panduk and djelli.

A group of around ten bearded bandits were having their long hair set alight. The flame flared and smoked as it engulfed their scalps and caught in their beards. Their skin twisted like paper on coals as they shrieked in pain, before falling face first into the stones.

'Pah! Serbians.' Otal flicked his fingers at the spectacle. 'I must arrange for the burial of our martyrs.'

'What of them?' Jobert pointed to the bound Muslim

prisoners whose shaved-bald heads sported sweat-plastered topknots, and who were being stripped to the waist.

'Ex-janissaries.' Otal turned on his heel and strode back towards his camp. 'They will receive the Sultan's deserved wrath, *alham-dulillah*.'

With a lance piercing the ropes binding their wrists, the bandits' hands were raised above their heads. The prisoners chanted '*Allahu Akbar!*' as they channelled their fear. Two djelli soldiers grabbed a fist full of the prisoner's abdominal skin each, then, with knives, slit a transverse cut from navel to spine and back to navel. The bandits wriggled and hissed at the slicing sensation. With their fingers under this flap, two djelli tore the tube of skin up to the bandit's armpits. This inside-out skin now engulfed the man's head and pinned him at his extended elbows.

Once all the prisoners had been flayed, the djelli wiped their knives, abandoned their captives and returned to camp.

The stranded victims whimpered and tottered. Blinded by agony and their wrappings, they tripped and fell into the thorns. With elbows trapped, the men's hands scrabbled up at the air. Nicked veins on their flensed ribs pulsed blood as they gulped for breath. Tickling flies crawled on the raw meat of their backs. Those who had lost the most blood, from either combat or punishment, wheezed to death first.

Jobert had seen all the gory ways the human body could be deformed on the battlefield, but he had never seen such deliberate brutality. He coughed to regain his voice. 'Return to camp, lads.' Jobert needed both hands to turn Moench's dumb-struck shoulders and get his feet moving.

Duque was pallid as he turned to Fazio. 'In your travels here … have you seen this before?'

Fazio's thick moustache warped in horror. 'I have heard of being "shirted" but have never seen it.'

De Chabenac's eyes were wide in his grey face. 'Into what depth of hell are we descending, Jobert?'

Chapter Nine
June 1801, Vidin, Wallachia

After a journey of ten days from Diraç, Jobert and Otal's column entered Pristina. The decapitated heads of over forty slain hajduks, displayed with great pride on djelli lances, were paraded through the tight lanes of the town and past the richly painted arches and dome of the city's Imperial Mosque.

Here the column met with a company of ex-janissaries in the employ of the regional warlord Pasvanoglu.

Jobert rolled his shoulders with unease. 'They look just like the bandits we fought in the mountains.'

'No, not at all. Very different.' Otal whisked his fingers into a dismissive flick. 'Very good fellows. There is nothing to worry about. What is more, good news. Dikaletus Pasha is only two days ahead of us.'

The onward journey to Vidin on the banks of the Danube took another ten days.

The river town of Vidin sheltered behind the great stone stronghold of Baba Vida. The stronghold's stone curtains amplified the soulful chime of church bells that emanated from the market squares. Within the arched tunnels that connected the upper bastions to the deeper magazines, smoke from kitchens and forges blended with clouds of river midges.

Otal had described to Jobert the ten-year peace between the Ottoman and Austrian Empires. Due to an Austrian garrison established only two hundred kilometres upstream, within the timber lanes of Vidin, a stream of industry now wove around the construction of a vast imperial barracks.

From Baba Vida's upper bastions, Ottoman artillery was laid across the hedge of galley masts and pelican-dotted water to the Danube's far treelined banks.

On the day of their arrival in mid-June, Jobert and Otal reunited with Dikaletus Pasha. Otal and Dikaletus exchanged greetings with much elegant sweeping of hands from heads and hearts. The duplicitous display irked Jobert due to its animated collusion.

Dikaletus beamed an effusive welcome towards Jobert and De Chabenac. 'My dear—'

Jobert parried the dragoman's gush with a back-handed brush. 'Otal, now that you have cornered Dikaletus, have you reclaimed what was stolen from Zenari?'

Otal soured at Jobert's abruptness. 'I am satisfied that the esteemed servant of my Hospodar is safe.'

'Dikaletus,' Jobert glared with menace, 'what did you steal from Zenari? Why have we endured three weeks traipsing brigand-infested mountains?'

'Steal, Jobert?' Dikaletus' bejewelled fingers froze suspended in mid-air, as if a harpsichord had been removed from beneath his wrists. 'Perhaps due to my limited grasp of your gracious language, I have misunderstood. Forgive me. Was it your intent to insult me?' His red moustache curled as he smiled. 'How is our dear friend, Colonel Zenari?'

Jobert held Dikaletus in stony contemplation. 'Zenari is ill. He needs attention and rest.'

Dikaletus' finger unfroze with a twist. 'We will take him to Marsden.'

'What is Marsden?'

'Marsden is not a place, my dear Jobert. He is my family's physician.'

Jobert exhaled the tension in his chest through his nose. 'Where next?'

Both Otal and Dikaletus answered. 'Bucharest.'

Jobert's eyes arched in disbelief at Otal. 'You now agree with Dikaletus?'

'We are closer to the court in Bucharest by river than overland to the Sublime Porte in Constantinople.'

'How, gentlemen, will we travel?' Jobert's mouth crimped as he forced courtesy back into his expressions. 'Esteemed hosts, forgive my sharpness. Near three hundred kilograms of gold weighs heavily on my mind.'

Dikaletus reached for Jobert's forearm and gave a rub with his thumb. 'My dear Jobert, your weariness will dissipate once safe aboard an imperial barge. With the current, we shall glide the five hundred kilometres in two days.'

'Colonel Jobert, sir,' Koschak called.

At the arched entry to one of Baba Vida's stone tunnels, a physical struggle erupted.

Koschak pinned a man in a choke hold with an arm twisted hard behind his back. Two sipahi grappled the arms of another. Two more sipahi wrestled to place a noose over the neck of a man who struggled in Fazio's grip. All three detainees wore loose, simple and clean clothes.

'Servants.' Otal twitched and his eyes slid towards Dikaletus.

'Another burglary.' Koschak hissed though clenched teeth as he exerted effort to restrain his struggling captive. 'They ratted through our portmanteaus. Nothing taken. The panniers untouched.'

'Again?' Jobert's malice sparked at Dikaletus. 'Duque? Moench?'

'With the gold,' Koschak said.

The men were driven to kneel at the feet of the sipahi. Nooses threaded their necks and ropes bound their hands tight behind their backs.

Otal spat brusque questions at their bowed heads.

The trembling men mumbled and shook their heads.

Otal turned to Dikaletus in silent confrontation.

Dikaletus raised his eyebrows and looked down his nose at those captured.

Standing back from the interrogation, Jobert raised an enquiring look at Fazio. 'Do you understand?'

Fazio shook his head in irritation.

'How will they be punished?'

'Thieves lose their right hands.'

Otal glanced at Jobert. 'Yes, amputation of the right hand is the customary punishment for their offence.' Otal drew his scimitar. 'But since such an affront has been perpetrated toward honoured foreign guests of the Sultan in the Hospodar's care, a more severe example must be made.' Otal offered his scimitar, handle foremost as the blade rested across his left forearm, to Jobert. 'You have been wronged. You have a right to dispense justice.'

Jobert recognised the same posture prior to beheading, witnessed previously after the failed assault in Diraç's marketplace. Nooses allowed the attendant sipahi to stretch the thieves' necks and hands. Overbalanced on their knees, the bound men choked the prayer, '*Allahu Akbar.*'

Jobert's rigid forefinger attempted to poke at understanding. 'A satchel is stolen in Diraç. Dikaletus races into the mountains. Against your own advice of the safe route by sea, Otal, you follow in great haste. No sooner are we reunited, we are subject to another intrusive search.' Jobert jabbed at Dikaletus. 'What else do you seek, Dikaletus?'

Dikaletus swished away Jobert's question with the river midges in front of his nose.

Jobert's hand balled into a fist. 'You barely questioned them, Otal, but are now swift to end their lives. What do they know that you conceal?'

'Enough, Jobert.' Otal shrugged, rolled his scimitar over his wrist, and then, in a series of muscular swirls, lopped through the three extended necks.

Faces first, the heads splatted onto the stone battlements.

The bodies slumped on their constraining ropes, hissing a release of urine, abdominal gas and arterial blood.

Dikaletus lifted the hem of his yellow silk robes, turned and departed.

Otal passed his scimitar to a sipahi, who wiped it clean on a dead man's shirt.

'To our rooms, lads.' Jobert spun on his heel.

Upon entering the shutter-darkened chamber allocated to them, Jobert crossed the room to the ten panniers. Their buckles were still wired shut and the leather bags had not been breached by blade.

They searched their personal belongings and found that their personal items had been disturbed but nothing taken.

On a stool in the corner, De Chabenac folded his long legs into a crouch, his elbows propped on his knees. 'If Dikaletus stole from Zenari, and Otal has pursued Dikaletus, why, yet again, does Otal silence the only witnesses? Why are our belongings still searched?'

'Otal and Dikaletus are at odds, but they seek the same thing.' Jobert paced the wide timber floorboards. 'And it remains unfound. You understood nothing of Otal's questions, Fazio?'

'No, they ...' Fazio winced. 'Perhaps jewellery?'

'Jewellery?' Jobert glared at Zenari.

Curled in a foetal ball on his blankets, Zenari faced the wall in a restless sleep.

Duque lay on his cot, propped on his bedroll. 'He is getting sicker. He needs rest.'

'He can rest on the Danube. What ails you, Zenari?' Jobert poked Zenari's blanket covered thighs with his toe. 'What did you see? What have you done, you stupid prick?'

Zenari groaned and flapped, too weak to be coherent.

With arms folded, Fazio leant against the door jamb. 'We must turn back, sir. We cannot get horses through the mountains of Serbia.'

Moench perched on the edge of his allocated timber and rope cot. 'This is bullshit. We are going deeper and deeper into the unknown. Further and further from home. We have made a mistake. I too vote for turning back. If that was the swiftest way in, then it must be our best way home.'

Duque ground the base of his palms into his eye sockets and exhaled his frustration. 'A little late, no?'

Koschak rubbed his knuckles with agitation and rolled his head as if he was limbering his shoulders to throw a punch. 'Fuck these foreigners and their fucking atrocities. Keep going. Just keep going.' His green eyes glowed with anger. 'All will be well.'

'And keep going we shall.' Jobert surveyed each man's dejected postures. 'Otal informs me we are two days by river from Bucharest, where the gold will be safe. From Bucharest, De Chabenac will sail, with Zenari and Otal I assume, for Constantinople, and then onto Ravenna. Any one of you can return with him. But I am staying the course.' Jobert glared at Zenari's shivering back. 'This is a distraction from me buying and returning with four hundred horses.'

Moench snorted with apprehension. '*Inshallah.*'

The imperial galliot from the Ottoman Danube fleet raced along the Danube's brown surface. Powered by oars and sail, the long flat-bottomed barge, with a crew of forty and four guns, dominated smaller fishing craft, cross-river ferries, submerged carcasses and islands of water weeds that crowded the gurgling course. Only great white pelicans on the wing maintained the pace alongside.

And the ever-present summer midges.

Jobert juggled a wedge of flat bread and baked pike and flapped oily fingers at a cloud of biting insects. Somehow the Danube's tiny insects were not swept away by the oar-driven breeze. This time last year, amongst similar tormentors on the reed-choked banks of the Po, Jobert bathed the corpse of her brother on the outskirts of Mantua. Could he wave away the bites of Gianna's memory? As the flaking fish filled his belly, would the hunger in his heart ever be sated?

'What draws your attention?' De Chabenac asked. 'Last summer on the Po?'

Jobert's smile never reached his eyes. 'The difference in the rooflines of the churches here. You?'

'I admit to being excited with our impending audience with the Hospodar.'

'With gold receipts signed, I imagine we will part company.'

'Do you feel Zenari will be in a fit state to travel with me to Constantinople? Are you still bound to travel with him and Otal Alaybey?'

Jobert swished his lunch-soiled fingers in a bucket. 'I am tired of Zenari's intrigues. I am adamant he will not interrupt Otal presenting these mares. If his humours persist, Zenari can wallow in Bucharest, and we can collect him on our return. I just want to see my horses.'

A few days later, Jobert and De Chabenac entered the court of Hospodar Constantine Ypsilantis within the palace of Curtea Noua on the heights above the city of Bucharest.

Central to the Hospodar's high vaulted throne hall, a golden high-backed throne, cushioned with red velvet, surmounted a central platform. Around a carpeted aisle leading to the throne stood rows of robed courtiers and petitioners. Their whispers were so faint that choral devotional music hummed through the long-latticed windows.

On a raised carpeted dais to the side of the throne, the Hospodar sat in a plush pink armchair. The Hospodar was a long-faced man in his forties, whose dark moustache carved a harsh line along his slim cheeks.

The Hospodar's vizier stood at his prince's right hand. The silent vizier — immediately recognisable as Dikaletus' father, but more solid than his son — wore draped expansive silks, and his russet eyebrows and moustache fairly bristled as his hooded eyes slid across the exchange.

Jobert and De Chabenac sat across from the Hospodar's armchair on a long wooden bench draped with velvet and gold tassels.

'Is your family well, Colonel Jobert?' the Hospodar asked with a slight Italian accent to his French.

Jobert bowed forward at the neck. *Why does this matter?* 'You are very kind to ask, my lord. My young wife is pregnant with our first child.'

Dikaletus looked at Jobert with bemusement, while De Chabenac beamed at such impending familial joy.

'With the Lord's blessing, let us pray it is a boy.' The Hospodar rearranged his forest green velour coat about his knees. 'We were disappointed by French aggression in Egypt, but we are delighted that has been resolved. The Mamluks were not favourites of the Sultan's — peace be upon him.' The Hospodar's cheeks barely creased to smile as he peered at Dikaletus. 'Dikaletus Pasha, how might we best welcome our French friends?'

Dikaletus bowed, his face showing delight at being addressed. 'Our dear friends have learnt of your excellent horses, sire, and hoped to view them, if that accorded with your desires.'

The Hospodar's eyes flashed steel. 'Horses? Not ...'

'That is a separate matter, sire.'

The Hospodar flinched. 'Which horses?'

'Serpenaçi, sire.' Dikaletus nearly whispered.

'Oh!' The Hospodar rolled his eyes towards his vizier. 'How much?'

'Two hundred kilograms of gold.'

The Hospodar slid his gaze back to Jobert and blinked in contemplation. 'Then, Dikaletus Pasha, place every amenity at our friends' disposal. When do they depart?'

'With your permission, sire, documents of receipt will be exchanged and the gold secured. Colonel De Chabenac, here,' Dikaletus said, wafting his fingers towards the attentively gracious De Chabenac, 'will then convey those documents back to the French court. From there, again with your permission, sire, Otal Alaybey will guide the French party north.'

The Hospodar twitched with irritation towards his vizier. 'Was Otal Alaybey not accompanying me to Constantinople?'

The vizier bowed. 'In light of this recent incursion across the Dniester, would your Highness not benefit from Otal Alaybey's service in the north?'

The Hospodar's calculating gaze returned to appraise Jobert. 'Are our French friends aware of this Cossack raid?'

'Otal Alaybey's sipahi report Begnzarov is far from Serpenaçi, sire.' Dikaletus pointed to the pewter çelenk on the hat cradled in Jobert's lap. 'Colonel Jobert's proven courage will not be daunted by such an inconvenience.'

The Hospodar appeared unconvinced.

'We beg your forgiveness, sire,' the vizier said, raising a bejewelled finger ever so slightly, 'one of our French friends is ill. His healthy participation is key to the success of the expedition. Might you excuse Dikaletus Pasha to attend to him personally.'

'The welfare of our friends is uppermost in my mind.' The Hospodar nodded in assent. 'Marsden?'

Dikaletus bowed. 'Yes, sire.'

'A most valued servant.' The Hospodar's eyes locked Dikaletus, his voice grim. 'You have pleased me, Dikaletus Pasha. You are excused.'

Chapter Ten
July 1801, Bucharest, Wallachia

Jobert, Dikaletus and Otal entered Zenari's bedchamber, followed by a train of servants. Awaiting them, Duque, with elbows leaning on the sill, gazed out the open window.

The room pulsed with devotional music from one of the two monastery complexes that spread either side of the timber watermills on the Dâmboviṭa River. Deep, undulating voices of a Byzantine choir, accompanied by high, wavering tones of horns and the throbbing of drums filled the air.

Dikaletus and Otal moved to a table upon which sat the shisha and a bowl of fruit.

As he crossed the room to Duque, Jobert glanced briefly at Zenari. In a knot of bedclothes, Zenari had curled onto his knees with his forehead on his mattress. He whimpered though his panting, and, plastered to his back, his wet nightshirt trembled.

Zenari was hugging a leather satchel to his chest. His stolen satchel.

Jobert squared his shoulders at Dikaletus.

Dikaletus clicked his fingers. 'Marsden, examine the Hospodar's guest!'

Behind Dikaletus and Otal drifted a tall Caucasian man with a shaved head. His head and shoulders bowed over his long shift of soft grey. In either hand he carried stout-handled wooden boxes.

Settled into a comfortable couch, Dikaletus paused over a dripping peach. 'He speaks French. Do you not, Marsden? Jobert, this is my physician *kol.*'

Marsden oriented his bowed shoulders to Jobert. 'My French is poor, Master. Forgive me.'

Marsden placed the two boxes beside Zenari's bed. A sharp, acrid waft lifted from the chest as the lids were unlatched. The chests contained all manner of bottles and powder boxes, iron probes and clamps, tubes and rolls of linen bandages, and flat brass bowls with indented sides.

As he rolled his sleeves to his elbow, Marsden turned to Dikaletus. 'May I request, Master, assistance from a servant.'

Jobert stepped forward. 'I will assist.'

Kneeling beside the bed, Marsden and Jobert rolled Zenari onto his side. Marsden's slim fingers rippled in examination across Zenari's face and throat. Zenari remained unresponsive. With an ivory trumpet-mouthed tube Marsden listened to Zenari's chest and stomach. Marsden tilted his head to Jobert. 'May I ask questions of the gentleman's condition, Master?'

'Of course.'

'How long has he been overcome by these symptoms?'

'Two, perhaps three, weeks ago we became aware of his discomfort,' Jobert said. 'It has increased slowly over that time. We felt it might be the stresses of the journey.'

'Has the gentleman spoken of his concerns?'

Jobert looked to Duque. Duque shook his head. 'Not at all.'

Marsden nodded. 'Thank you, Master. I would like to examine

his abdomen. May I request your assistance in raising his night-shirt, please?'

Jobert gently folded up Zenari's nightshirt around his chest as Marsden drew one of the bedsheets across Zenari's loins. With his fingertips, Marsden palpated the top of Zenari's abdomen.

Zenari spasmed and cried out.

'Has the gentleman been vomiting?' Marsden asked.

Jobert looked to Duque. Duque shook his head.

Marsden inclined his head towards Duque. 'Forgive me, Master, are you acquainted with the medical arts?'

Duque folded his arms. 'I am a veterinarian.'

Marsden gave a bow of his head. 'Then you are ideally suited to patients who will not assist the diagnosis by describing their concerns.'

Duque snorted. 'Nor do my patients lie about their ailments.'

A smile flickered across Marsden's face. 'Has he had difficulty with his daily movements?'

'Yes,' Duque said.

Marsden opened his bag and produced a jar of ointment. He greased his fingers, drew back the bedsheet, lifted Zenari's testicles with the back of his left hand, and inserted two fingers into Zenari's anus.

Zenari groaned and gripped at the bedcovers.

Jobert winced.

Dikaletus' eyebrows arched in hope. 'Is the bowel obstructed?'

'Nothing untoward, Master.' Marsden removed his fingers.

Zenari wheezed with relief.

Marsden greased an iron speculum. 'Might you gentlemen take a firm grip on his knees, please?'

As Jobert and Duque held Zenari's bent knees in the air Marsden inserted the duck-billed probes into Zenari's rectum and wound them open with a screw shaft.

Zenari gargled incoherently through his fever, his eyes bulged, and he attempted to roll away but was pinned by Jobert's and Duque's weight.

Marsden raised his face from Zenari's buttocks and unscrewed the speculum before withdrawing it. 'It would appear an inconvenient constipation.' Marsden gave Jobert an odd side-eye glance. 'Most probably induced by the journey's difficulties. With your permission, Master, I wish to administer a laxative.'

Dikaletus sat up with a look of fascination. 'The welfare of the Hospodar's guest is of grave importance.'

Otal blew a long stream of spiced smoke to the plastered ceiling. 'In the meantime, we shall remain by his bed and provide any small comfort.' With a twist of his fingers, he indicated to servants by the door to fetch refreshments.

'Might you pin his shoulders, gentleman?' Marsden inserted a tube down Zenari's throat at which Zenari choked and gurgled. Through a brass funnel, Marsden tipped a measure of oily liquid which smelt strongly of aniseed and castor. 'An effect will be produced within the hour.'

Jobert and Duque withdrew to the window. 'If he was a horse with colic, what treatment would you prescribe?' Jobert asked.

'I too would dose him with castor oil.' Duque's muscular shoulders shrugged. 'Otherwise, cut his head off. What of your audience with the Hospodar?'

'The Hospodar's vizier has signed the deeds of sale. Raive's gold is now safe within the court. I still hold our gold for expenses during the herd's homeward movement.'

'Has the Hospodar's retinue departed? Has De Chabenac made good his escape?'

'De Chabenac now returns to Genoa with the remittance

advice. I have my copies.' A pat on the breast of Jobert's tailcoat gave a papery crinkle. 'It was my impression that De Chabenac was disappointed to be leaving. The bleating of Fazio and Moench to return home is irritating enough. And now what? Have you joined the doubters?'

'I do not doubt.' Duque looked Jobert in the eye. 'I know this is folly.'

Jobert planted a fist onto Duque's upper arm. 'With De Chabenac's departure, Duque, I need your strength to—'

Zenari began to moan and writhe.

Dikaletus smiled. '*Alham-dulillah*, the potion works. Soon all will be well.'

'If this gentleman has not had a bowel movement in some time,' Marsden said, as he greased a pair of forceps, 'I will need to break the stool.'

Otal sat up and placed down his porcelain coffee cup. 'Collect it so we may examine it.'

'Must we stay and watch him shit?' asked Jobert.

Marsden glanced at Jobert 'Master, might I seek your assistance again. Might one of you lift his thigh, please, and the other hold this chamber pot?'

Duque took a grip of Zenari's leg as Jobert lowered his scowling face uncomfortably close to Zenari's genitalia.

'The gentleman's manhood obstructs my view of proceedings. Might you ...' Marsden waved at Zenari's groin with the back of his hand.

'You bastard, Zenari.' With the back of his hand, Jobert swept up Zenari's testicles.

Duque smirked.

'Master, can you ...' With his lips close to Jobert's ear, Marsden whispered without moving his jaw, '... catch and conceal an egg?'

'An egg?'

Otal and Dikaletus rose from their cushions to peer over the activity.

Marsden inserted the forceps.

Zenari strained, arched and screamed.

'Ready?' Marsden breathed the words to Jobert. 'Catch!'

With a swift movement, Marsden withdrew the forceps and stood up obscuring Otal and Dikaletus' view of the proceedings.

Faecal material poured from Zenari, who groaned at the release.

As the shit emerged and coiled in the chamber pot, Jobert felt a hot, slimy egg fall into his palm. Jobert juggled the now-heavy chamber pot to maintain his grip on the slippery object.

'You may lower his leg, thank you,' said Marsden, 'and if I might relieve you of the chamber pot, please?'

Jobert whipped his hand to nudge Duque's knee.

Duque gave a start. He lowered Zenari's leg and his hand scooped the egg from Jobert's grasp.

Dikaletus' and Otal's scrutiny darted at the movement of Marsden, Jobert and the steaming pot. Marsden presented the ceramic bowl's vile contents to Dikaletus and Otal. Otal and Dikaletus scrutinised the putrid, bloody contents.

Once complete, Marsden placed down the pot, wiped Zenari's buttocks with a perfumed towel, slid down the hem of Zenari's nightshirt and then drew up the bedsheet. 'Shall I dispose of the contents, Master.'

'No!' Otal pointed to the table upon which the refreshments sat. 'Pour it on the table and scrape it flat with your hand.'

Without a twinge of reaction to his downcast mask, Marsden tipped the contents of the chamber pot onto the table and spread the faeces smooth across the surface.

Grimacing at the splashes of faecal material on his hands and forearms, Jobert held his hands away from his body with fingers splayed as he watched Otal's and Dikaletus' reaction to the lack of revelation. *They were expecting the egg.*

Dikaletus' face wrinkled with bitterness as he scrutinised the ghastly smear. 'Praise the Lord, I am pleased to see Zenari restored to health.' Dikaletus maintained a close inspection of how Marsden washed his hands and forearms and packed away his medical cases.

Otal's brows bunched in thought as he considered the dripping table. '*Alham-dulillah.*' Otal turned away, his hands writhing in frustration. With a flick of fingers to the servants by the door, 'Have the table removed and burnt.'

As Dikaletus, Otal and Marsden moved from the room, Jobert said, 'Thank you, Doctor.'

Marsden jerked in surprise. Dikaletus and Otal faces curled with bewilderment.

As the pungent table was removed by servants, Fazio entered with his knuckles to his nose. 'I have fresh coffee in the next room.' He peered at Zenari now splayed under the sheets asleep. 'What was wrong with him?'

Jobert glanced at Duque. 'The anxiety from the burglaries produced an inability to shit. Dikaletus' physician dosed him with oil. Dikaletus called the physician "kol". What is kol?'

'A slave.' Fazio shrugged. 'Common enough in these parts.'

'We need to sort Zenari before coffee.' Duque lathered his hands in the basin. 'Send for Moench. We will join you out of this stench in a few minutes. Jobert, come and wash your hands.'

Jobert shrugged his hands clear of his cuffs. 'I cannot believe I had to hold Zenari's balls so he could lay an egg. Do you still have it?'

'Lower your voice.' Duque watched Fazio leave the room. As Duque passed Jobert the bar of soap, Duque slipped a knobbly hard shape into Jobert's hand. Despite the soap's lavender fragrance, the egg still had an intestinal whiff.

'A ball of wax.' Jobert rolled the tallow ball in his palm. 'The candle he needed after someone raided his room in Diraç. Lock the door and keep watch.'

Placing the wax egg in a shaving basin, Jobert poured in the remainder of Otal's scalding coffee. As the wax softened, he broke down the wax until the contents of the egg were revealed. 'Fetch Zenari's toothbrush.'

Jobert scrubbed the object until it was recognisable. 'Look, Duque!'

In his palm, Jobert held a thick gold ring with a wide band, embedded diamonds on either side making it quite knobbly. On the ruby-encrusted square head, swirled an engraved device of crossed door keys. 'A ring! This is the keenly sought after jewellery.'

Duque slipped it on his finger. The ring slid loosely on his broad fingers. It even swivelled on his thumb. 'Whose fingers would fit this?'

'Dikaletus and Otal are competing for Zenari. For this ring.' Beside the open window, Jobert absorbed the lilting monastic melodies as well as the fresh July air. 'Was the ring destined for Otal? Zenari is the courier and Dikaletus is attempting to steal the ring from Otal?'

After the stench of the bedroom, Duque too inhaled the sweet air. 'On our first trip to Diraç, Dikaletus surprised Otal with his unexpected arrival. Dikaletus then attempted to capture Zenari.'

'Otal must be aware of Dikaletus' intent yet covered for him by executing the assailants in Diraç. Then once we returned with the gold, Dikaletus had Zenari's room searched.'

'He certainly took something then raced for Vidin.' Duque passed back the ring. 'Only for Otal to chase in pursuit. Yet Dikaletus set more thieves upon us in Vidin.'

Jobert slipped the oversized ring onto his own fingers. 'Whatever Dikaletus took, it was not this ring as Zenari then took the precaution of … but they are wealthy, powerful men, why would they risk so much for a gaudy ill-fitting ring?'

'They spread Zenari's shit thin to find it.'

'Then they will continue to search.' Jobert fist closed hard on the ring. 'Duque, hide it. Even if we were to be strip searched, and every item we own laid bare. It needs to move north with us. Find a place and do not tell me.'

Duque took the ring into his own closed grip. 'Then we are in more shit than that egg. Marsden has gripped us by the short and curlies. He knows we have what his master seeks. Our venture to buy horses is now madness. Do not proceed up the Prut.'

'If we leave now, they will know.' Jobert gripped Duque's shoulder. 'Our best way home is north into Moldavia.'

Chapter Eleven

Later that night, Jobert entered Zenari's bedchamber to find Marsden ministering to the fevered Zenari. The fetid air produced that morning was refreshed with scented candles, their flames wavering to the assured rhythms of the nearby monastery's choirs.

With Zenari's nightshirt tucked up about his chest and a bedsheet across his pelvis, Marsden massaged scented oil into Zenari's abdomen. A barely conscious Zenari winced at the touch.

At a rustle of fabric, Jobert looked up to see Otal entering the room.

Otal's face twitched with annoyance at Jobert. 'Tomorrow, we follow the Prut north, Jobert. Are you satisfied with the security of your gold?'

'The Hospodar has signed for the payment from France. De Chabenac has returned with the documents.'

'Have you not made provision for any unforeseen expenses?'

'I have a small sum still with me,' Jobert said. 'It is carried on our remaining pack-horse.'

'In gold?'

'Yes, ready to be converted into local currency. What is your interest in my money?'

'Be ready for an early start.' Otal puffed a derisive snort at the prone Zenari and swept from the room in a bloat of soft robes.

Jobert crossed the room to the washstand and poured water from the pitcher into the basin. When Marsden glanced up, Jobert nodded his head for Marsden to join him away from Zenari.

Marsden stepped closer and began to lather his hands with soap.

'Why did you sneak the obstruction to me?' Jobert whispered.

Marsden's eyes darted to the door. 'Dikaletus Pasha seeks something, Master. If the Pasha seeks it, then the Hospodar wants it. I suspect Otal Alaybey seeks that something. Men will suffer, perhaps die, until it is found.'

'Do Otal and the Dikaletus serve the same master?'

'No. As a commander of sipahi in Moldavia, Otal Alaybey serves the Hospodar, but Otal's loyalty is always to the Commander of the Faithful.'

Jobert passed Marsden a towel. 'Who?'

Marsden lowered his head in respect. 'Our imperial Majesty Sultan Selim the third — peace be upon him.' Marsden gathered his medicine chests.

'Stand fast, Marsden.' Jobert closed the engraved door softly. 'And you, a kol? A slave? Dikaletus' slave?'

Marsden stiffened momentarily before bowing. 'I am, Master.'

'Where are you from?'

Marsden averted his eyes. 'I was ... I am ... an American. Originally from Hinsdale, New Hampshire. I was the surgeon on a merchant ship. Barbary pirates took our ship in '95 and the crew was enslaved. I was purchased in Tunis before being sold in Constantinople. I now serve the vizier and his family.'

'I have seen slaves before ... but I have never spoken to one.'

'Where have you seen slaves?'

Twenty years earlier, from the deck of a French horse-laden collier standing in the roads off Port-au-Prince, Jobert had watched Africans, barefoot and in loose grey shirts, labouring along the length of the docks. Having encountered the babble of commands and curses in the wharves of Brest and Newport, Jobert had been struck by the lack of voices from those who laboured. 'In the Caribbean.'

Marsden nodded slowly as he considered Jobert. 'My master seeks a piece of exquisite jewellery. I see you have not yet revealed it to them. Dikaletus Pasha has commanded me to watch Colonel Zenari closely. Dikaletus and Otal will kill for what Zenari had hidden. For what you now hold. Do you not agree?'

'Then why have you placed yourself in danger by passing to me what ... your master seeks? I cannot imagine the consequences if your disobedience was revealed. Your silence invites threats. Your silence gives me leverage. What is your loyalty to Dikaletus?'

'I am treated very well. Christian to Christian. Others covet my position. Any transgression, and I would lose an eye, my tongue and a foot, and be chained to a galley's oar.'

'Surely not.'

'I have no need to imagine unendurable pain. I know it well, for I have performed these operations on others.' Marsden's lips trembled, before he lifted his chin to steady his mask. 'If it was revealed you had it, Colonel Jobert, you would lose your eyes, your tongue and your feet and spend your remaining days as a galley slave. I would be forced to remove your body parts, before I would be forced to remove my own.'

Jobert's dentures dug deep into his gum as he clenched his jaw.

Marsden smoothed the air in front of his waist. 'But I am no threat to you, Master. Your secret is safe—.'

'Our secret! What recompense do you pursue for your disloyalty?'

Marsden pressed his fingertips together in supplication. 'Indeed, I can be your eyes and ears as to what Dikaletus and Otal intend. Your journey north confounds them.'

'For what price, Marsden?'

Marsden levelled his steady gaze at Jobert. 'Once in northern Moldavia, smuggle me into the Austrian Empire. I will protect your life and the jewel. You deliver me my freedom.'

Jobert stepped back from the washstand. His thoughts took in Zenari askew in his sheets. Zenari mumbled in his sleep. 'Zenari knows the jewel is missing. He is a threat to us both. Should Zenari be tortured, as he surely must be, you will be revealed. And you, in turn, will uncover me. Since the jewel is of no interest to me, perhaps I should just pass it in.'

Marsden eyes tightened in concern. 'Can you not reason with Zenari?'

'Reason with the man who inserted that lump inside himself? Reason against torture? If I raise the topic with Zenari, then my knowledge of the object is affirmed.' Jobert held up a straight finger between them. 'Then let us keep each other alive, Marsden.'

Marsden eyes flashed.

'You attend to Zenari,' Jobert said. 'Administer him something. Keep him well enough to travel north, but ill enough that he requires you to attend him on behalf of Dikaletus.'

Marsden nodded. 'Leeches.'

Zenari stirred with a moan. 'Water.'

'Now go, Marsden,' Jobert said, 'and let me deal with Zenari.'

As Jobert poured a glass of lemon water, Marsden packed his chests and departed.

Jobert sat on the edge of Zenari's bed and pulled cushions towards Zenari. 'Your water, Zenari. Sit up.'

As Zenari shuffled under his covers, a ripe waft was released. Zenari gripped Jobert's sleeve. 'Where is the Key?'

'What key?'

Zenari's sunken eyes darted in his pallid face. 'Give it to me. I have been entrusted with it. Is it safe?'

'You passed only shards of wax.' Jobert's face creased in confusion. 'Did you insert a key inside yourself?'

Zenari snuffled as he gulped the water. 'There was nothing within me? Nothing?'

'You probably shat it out. What did you expect? Shitting a key. I am surprised you have not ruptured your bowel.'

'But I removed it each time.'

'Even when you lay in fever?' Jobert asked.

'What fever?'

'Do you not remember the barge down the Danube? Duque certainly does. You shat all over him.'

'I do not ... then Duque must have it?'

Jobert took the glass and refilled it. 'Can you imagine Duque diving into your turds to fish out a key?'

'It is not a key.'

'You said it was. Whatever it is now lies on the bottom of the Danube.'

Zenari groaned.

'Is it, or is it not, a key?' Jobert asked. 'What was the object?'

Zenari turned his head to the wall and sipped his water.

'Someone entrusted this ... key to you? Who, Zenari? Otal and Dikaletus have been hunting this key. You have placed us all in danger. We have been robbed and attacked due to your stupidity. Is this the reason you wish us to travel together?

Zenari, you idiot, I need to know your secret to keep us all alive.'

Zenari handed back his glass and sat back against his pillows. 'Before war came to Lombardy in '96, I studied antiquities in Rome. I became aware of the myth of Justinian's Key. Over twelve hundred years ago, with this Key, Justinian, Emperor of the Eastern Roman Empire, locked the eastern and western empires together. He who commands the Key is God's ordination as Caesar of the East and binds the empire of the east with the empire of the west. In variations of the myth, it opens the crypt of the Mother Mary. The eastern empire is now the Ottoman empire. The western empire is now the Holy Roman Empire ruled by Emperor Francis in Vienna.'

'But this Key cannot do these things. Surely?'

'It can in the eyes of those who believe. As a symbol of power, it bestows supreme authority on the man who wields it.'

Jobert twisted to sit more comfortably on the side of the bed. 'How has your involvement risen from student of a myth to buggering yourself with something more substantial?'

'Any references in ancient manuscripts describe the Key as a door key. The Ottomans never found the Key within Constantinople when they sacked it. Over the last three hundred years, there has been intriguing speculation by Genoese and Venetian merchants, as both republics maintained their trading colonies on the Black Sea coast. Just prior to us meeting in Mantua, when Venice fell in June 1797, I accompanied French forces in the sacking of Venice. I searched and found the provenance for the Key.'

Jobert's eyes narrowed. 'Provenance?'

'Documents that prove the authenticity of the Key.'

'The contents of your satchel?' Jobert noticed the leather case under Zenari's pillow. 'What Dikaletus stole in Diraç, forcing us into the Serbian mountains?'

'Yes.' Zenari gripped the buckled briefcase. 'From the provenance, I learnt the Key was a ring.'

Jobert frowned. 'A ring?'

'A bejewelled ring,' Zenari tapped his finger, 'not a door key. I learnt that the Key was secured in Rome. When Rome was pillaged in February 1798, and we—'

'And we did not get off on the best of terms in the back lanes.'

'I remember well enough, Jobert.'

'On that occasion your stupidity had you dunked in a gutter of piss. Now you have both of us neck deep in shit. Continue your story.'

'In Rome, I found the Key among the papal treasures—'

'The night you were absent from collecting the city's title deeds.'

'Do you wish to discuss our shared past, or our current predicament?'

'Continue.'

Zenari rolled his eyes to resume the thread of his story. 'In Rome, yes … I was unsure what to do, how I might use its power.'

'In the meantime, you became the silent emperor of east and west. I remember your hubris. But you have been travelling since, have you not?'

Zenari gave a sharp look at Jobert.

'De Chabenac commented on you being seen in Paris last Christmas.'

Zenari's shoulders drooped. 'Bonaparte's coup in late 1799 gave me an idea. This time last year, I approached Bonaparte himself in Milan after Marengo. I presented the provenance. Proof the Key existed as a ring, not a door key. Bonaparte promoted me colonel and appointed me his emissary to the Sultan. Bonaparte wished it gifted to Sultan Selim, a gift to mollify

Bonaparte's transgressions in Egypt and Syria and open a way for re-establishing cordial relations. It was for the Sultan to declare that he had discovered the Key and claim its mythical power. I departed Milan for Constantinople in August with the provenance and a secret entreaty to re-establish cordial relations between the two powers.'

'All the while Bonaparte's army rotted in Egypt. Where do Otal and Dikaletus fit in?'

'Following the victory at Hohenlinden last December, and imminent peace between France and Austria, Selim was aware of the prevailing strategic winds. Selim received me privately and, after his scholars studied my documents at length, accepted the provenance, and bid me return to Bonaparte with his warmest felicitations. Otal was my appointed conduit. His loyalty to Selim was assured. I returned to Bonaparte in January with Selim's reply.'

'When De Chabenac saw you in Paris.'

'Indeed. It was then that I presented the Key to Bonaparte. He even placed it upon his finger. For a moment he was the Caesar of the East and the West. It was all quite strange.'

With his thumb, Jobert rubbed his fingers upon which he had placed the Key. *I too have been Caesar of East and West.* 'I am sure for Bonaparte just a passing fancy.'

'Nevertheless, Bonaparte sent me to deliver the Key to the Sultan. In April, I had arranged to meet Otal in Diraç, through the guise of trading horses from Moldavia.'

'And Dikaletus? Why is he at odds with Otal?'

'The Phanariot Greeks are a powerful enclave within Selim's court. They were the officials who investigated the provenance of the Key against the evidence buried within Constantinople's vast library. When you and I arrived in Diraç in April, I was approached by Dikaletus.' Zenari leant close and dropped his voice to a whisper. 'Dikaletus represents the Greek desire to secure the Key and usurp the throne. The Hospodar would be their preferred candidate for the return of a Christian Caesar to the throne in Constantinople.'

Jobert shook his head. 'And you thought you could thwart Otal and the Sultan.'

'I thought if I could pass the Key to the Hospodar and deliver a Christian Caesar allied to Bonaparte, there might be favour shown toward me. Perhaps ... the King of a unified Italy?'

'The King of Italy? If the Greeks knew of the Key, why did Dikaletus steal the provenance in Diraç?'

'I imagine he hoped to secure the Key as well, but his thieves did not find it. At least with the provenance, the Hospodar would be convinced of the Key's existence and emboldened to assume the mantle of Caesar. In Vidin, Dikaletus told me to continue as ringbearer under Otal's protection. He would see me delivered to the Hospodar here in Bucharest. Upon the theft in Diraç, I ... concealed the Key before we travelled into the mountains.'

'And now, fittingly, the Danube locks east to west.'

Zenari's hand curled into a trembling fist. 'Otal grills me constantly on the Key's whereabouts. He reinforces his intent to present me at the Sublime Porte.'

Jobert tapped the satchel tangled in Zenari's bedsheets. 'Has Dikaletus returned the provenance?'

Zenari clutched the case's leather flap. 'Yes.'

'Then, the Hospodar, or his vizier, knows the Key is close at hand. What excuse have you given for your failure to deliver the Key to the Hospodar?'

Zenari pummelled the satchel with a balled fist. 'I lied to Dikaletus that the Key went missing when the provenance was stolen. I believe Dikaletus is keeping the Hospodar at bay until he can present the Key. Perhaps Dikaletus has returned the papers as a demonstration of ... I am not sure, but with the loss of the Key, the only value of the provenance documents is to light the morning fire.'

'Destroying those documents is a declaration that you have lost the Key.' With a shrug of his hands, Jobert stood. 'This ring is a distraction. It is of no importance to me. I have delivered two hundred kilograms of gold. Now I need to take the remaining fifty kilograms to collect four hundred horses. Two items I am unable to stick up my arse. You, on the other hand, are free to go home. You could sail for Italy. Take Fazio and Moench as your escort as they no longer have a heart for the venture. Perhaps catch up with De Chabenac in Constantinople.'

Zenari's grabbed a knot of Jobert's trouser leg. 'Wait, Jobert, I cannot suddenly depart for home. That would raise immediate suspicion. I must travel with you. Dikaletus may have been thwarted, but Otal needs to be convinced he will deliver the Key to the Sultan. They need to think I still have the Key, thus I remain of value to them.'

Jobert lowered his face to Zenari's grip on his pants. 'They could just as well have you tortured. You would then reveal me.'

Zenari opened his hand with a jolt. 'They would never lay a finger upon an emissary of France.'

'Most worthy emissary,' Jobert performed a courtly bow, 'have you forgotten the iron tongs our benevolent hosts rammed up your arse?'

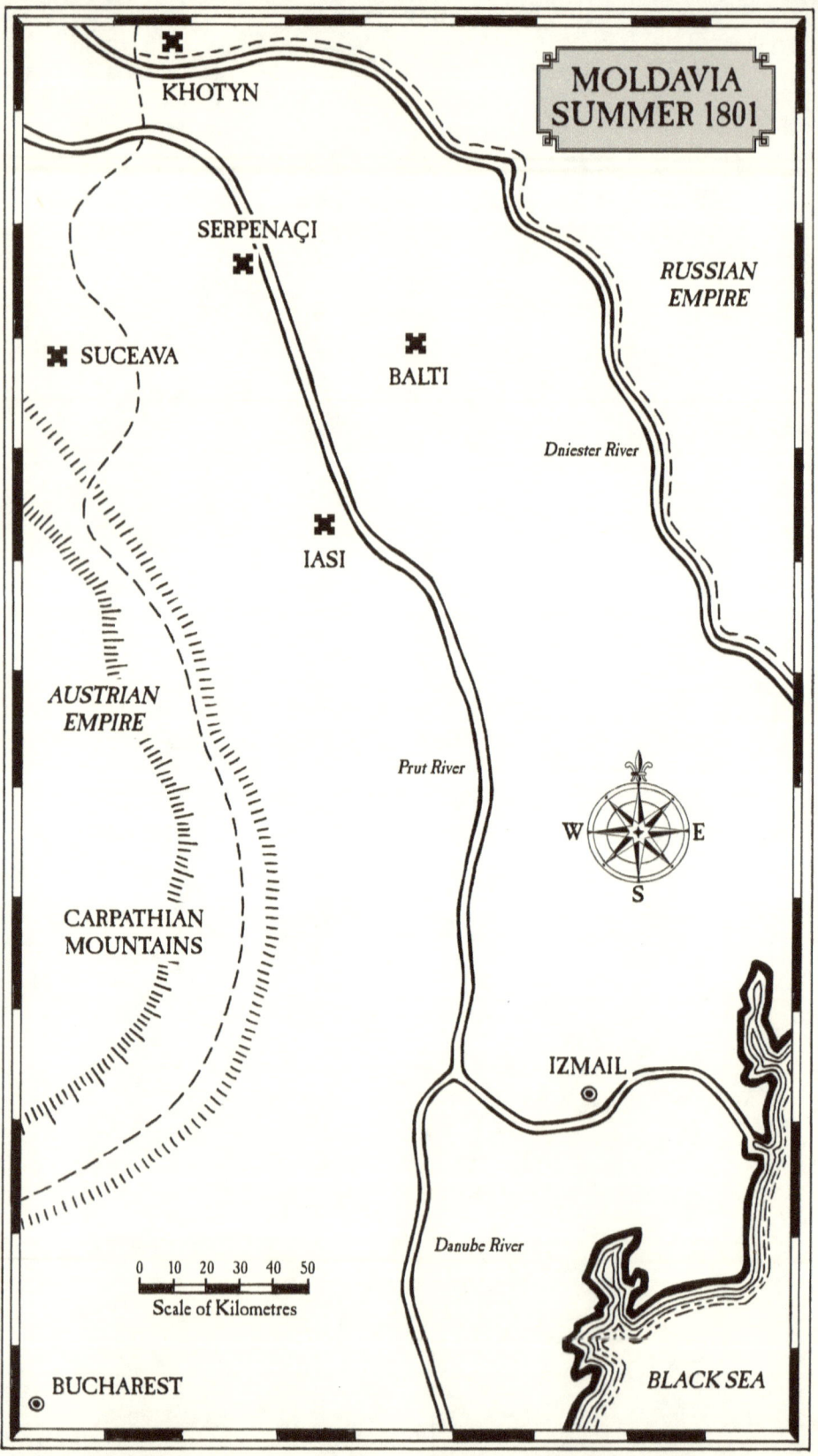

MOLDAVIA
SUMMER 1801

KHOTYN

SERPENAÇI

SUCEAVA

BALTI

RUSSIAN
EMPIRE

Dniester River

IASI

AUSTRIAN
EMPIRE

Prut River

W   E

S

CARPATHIAN
MOUNTAINS

IZMAIL

Danube River

0   10 20 30 40 50

Scale of Kilometres

BUCHAREST

BLACK SEA

Chapter Twelve
July 1801, Prut River, Moldavia

Jobert slowed his breathing as he aimed. A July southerly brought an Asian warmth that buffeted his foresight. Dancing grass tickled the hands that held the Turkish rifle.

Jobert lay on his belly, lifted above the plain on an ancient structure, taller than a man mounted. This frozen wave of earth ran in a straight line from horizon to horizon on either side of his firing position. Zenari had thought to ask its origins. A Roman wall, Otal had replied. Defence against the hordes from the wilderness beyond.

The breeze slackened. The dried seed heads between Jobert and his target paused.

Jobert breathed out and, as the foresight paused, he fired.

The sizzle of powder in the pan seared his face.

His ball struck. The *saiga* buck staggered.

Two more shots cracked beside Jobert. The saiga herd sprang.

Jobert's stag crumpled to its knees before its bloated nostrils thumped into the dirt.

Wild cheers erupted as sipahi and djelli horsemen leapt their horses down the embankment, lances lowered in pursuit.

Jobert refocused his gaze to the intricate, colourful designs embedded in the woodwork of his borrowed rifle. The smell of expended gunpowder and the feel of rocks jutting into his ribs reminded him of hunting mouflon with his grandfather. Those were treasured afternoons. The technical exactness of the old artilleryman as he guided the process of marksmanship. Jobert's boyish senses dizzy with the multitude of considerations in the shot. 'Only a heart shot?' His father would sour the prize. 'At that range, surely a head shot.' Never good enough.

'A fine shot, my friend.' Otal slapped Jobert's shoulder. 'And now, *alham-dulillah*, we feast.'

'*Alham-dulillah*,' Jobert passed the rifle back to Otal.

'Hah! Our thanks to God. You like this expression?'

It was one week since Jobert had departed Bucharest. They had travelled by barges along the Danube to the fortress port of Izmail. After receiving resupply in Izmail, they were now two days into a ten-day journey to the river stronghold of Iasi, along the western banks of the south-flowing Prut River, angry with snow melt from the menacing Carpathians. Their destination of horses in summer pasture lay just beyond Iasi.

But first, the consumption of Jobert's saiga for lunch.

Jobert half-squatted, half-knelt on the saiga's yellow hide. The antelope's severed head, mounted with long ringed horns, dripped on a lance behind and above him. Despite having taken meals with Otal's men for nearly five weeks, Jobert was still far from comfortable eating cross-legged.

Lunch was delicious. The buck's meat had been roasted, cut into strips, mixed with boiled rice and yoghurt before being drizzled with a fragrant chickpea sauce. Cups of thick, sharp coffee and smoky raki were gulped and swiftly refilled.

Behind Dikaletus, Otal, the senior sipahi commanders and Jobert's party, djelli musicians played lively tunes on the long-necked *saz* and the multi-stringed *bandura*, accompanied by the beat of a wide, shallow drum and the clapping of the Ottoman warriors.

Moench would want to contribute to this outdoor orchestra, but he was too busy scoffing dripping, bread-wrapped rice. As Jobert glanced at Moench, he noticed Marsden whisper in Dikaletus' ear.

Dikaletus nodded to Otal.

Otal wiggled a yoghurt-smeared finger at the musicians. 'They sing of Mamay, the great Cossack hunter.' Otal passed a large portion of spiced meat onto Jobert's flap of hot bread. 'We take our food from the plate directly in front of us. When we find we are blessed with a piece of good meat, we confer honour on our friends beside us by passing it to them.'

The lunch blankets had been set in the shade of the treelined Prut. On the grassy banks in front of the diners, sipahi soldiers laid out an arc of six individual blankets upon which they placed a leather war shield face down. Above the shields a tripod of lances was erected.

Jobert's fingers and teeth tore the succulent morsel apart. 'More entertainment, my friend?'

Otal flicked his fingers. The musicians fell quiet and withdrew.

'Dear Jobert,' Otal said, wiping his moustache with a cloth, 'my choices this afternoon will strain our friendship. A sacred object of great importance to the Sultan has entered our care.' He raised his finger. 'Let us not sully our mutual esteem by declaring you are unaware of the object.'

Jobert's guts rumbled at the mention of the Key of Justinian. He glared at Zenari across the luncheon feast.

'The object has gone missing. As loyal subjects of his Majesty, we are deeply distressed.' Otal's expressive fingers swayed as if they played an ominous tune. 'Our search to recover the object must know no limits. I beg your forgiveness if our search intrudes upon your person and that of your party.'

A wall of sipahi closed in behind Jobert and his men, their lances gripped in two hands.

Jobert's sabre, which he had removed for lunch, was no longer behind him. Jobert's bowel reverberated and filled. 'We are here for horses, Otal. We have been attacked in the street and burgled twice for this object. Zenari's object is not my concern.'

Koschak's hand slid to his cuff.

Otal stood, as did his senior commanders. 'You are becoming uncomfortable.' Otal's hand made a circular motion near his belly. 'Do not deny this for I can see it. I ask that you undress completely and sit upon the carpet.' He extended an inviting hand toward the tripods. 'Please let us not waste time in showing your umbrage. I am fully aware that my request is undignified and unreasonable.'

Moench grabbed at his stomach. He began to rise 'Excuse me, sir, I need to ...'

'I have chosen to inflict upon you a monstrous indignity for which only a saint could forgive,' Otal said. 'You have been administered a powerful laxative.' Marsden's head remained bowed. 'Your bowels will open soon. I insist you take your place naked upon the carpet before that occurs. I request you partake of your own volition before my duty to my Sultan compels me to ensure my requests by force.'

'This abuse is unpardonable.' Despite the pressing pangs in his gut, Jobert walked to the closest carpet and began to undress. 'You will pay, Otal. As will you, Zenari.' The wind bit into Jobert's bare skin. His hands gripped his hips as his belly spasmed. 'Quick lads, before we disgrace ourselves. This obscene ordeal will be over soon enough.'

'Such an example to your men is commendable,' Otal said.

One by one, Koschak, Duque, Fazio, Moench and Zenari stripped beside the lances on the blankets.

Fazio swore as he doubled over in discomfort. 'What is going on? What is happening?'

Jobert spat at Zenari. 'This is between Zenari and the Sultan. Ask him.'

'Gentlemen,' Otal said, 'should the urgency to defecate come over you, squat over the shield so the contents may be collected.'

Koschak seethed between clamped jaws. 'Once I shit, Zenari, I will force you to drink it.'

Zenari was forlorn. 'Maintain your professional etiquette in the face of hardship, Koschak. I will force you to drink my shit … sir.'

'Another obscene impost but an unfortunate necessity, Jobert,' Otal said. 'Would you offer my men your wrists?

Jobert noticed a greenhide loop at the crossover of the three lances. 'Fuck off, Otal. You have my parole.'

Otal held up a long finger. 'It is not sufficient, my friend. The search demands you be tethered to the lances, your movement anchored. The thoroughness of the search will prove conclusive to the Hospodar's satisfaction in his claims before the Sultan. I swear upon the holy book — praise be to the word of God — no further harm will come to you due to this object.'

Soldiers bound Jobert's wrists to the point where the stakes were lashed. The shield was shoved between his ankles. Hot pain tore through Jobert's groin as his bowel released. Jobert groaned and his body convulsed as his anus vomited a hot load. 'You bastard, Marsden! How much laxative did you feed us?'

Otal's men were sombre and systematic in their search.

Clothing was laid out on one end of the blanket. Every pocket emptied. Every fold turned out. Every stitch squeezed.

Marsden's hands squeezed through the human faeces in the shields.

Their saddle and packhorses were led out on the slope below

the lance tripods and unsaddled. The animal's hind feet were roped to the base of their necks, so as to conduct anal examinations. Boluses of dung were removed and squeezed between fingers. Portmanteaus and saddles were stripped and examined as closely as the clothing. Pack-saddles were dismantled.

Squatting with his arms stretched above him, Jobert was utterly drained. Before him, Otal's trusted sipahi commanders searched the purses of gold from within Jobert's pannier.

Observing closely, Otal and Dikaletus prowled among the blankets spread with their inventories and the pungent brimming shields.

With a slice, the six Europeans were released from their bondage.

Otal clapped his hands. 'This obscenity is concluded. Jobert. Will you join me for dinner?'

'Otal!' Jobert flexed his swollen wrists before he could wipe his arse, thighs and calves with a rag. 'Erect tents. Arrange baths. Bring soup. Now! Lads, on me! Fuck off, Zenari!' Jobert spat. 'You are not welcome here.'

Zenari staggered backwards, as if hit by a blow, sadness crimping his face.

Naked on the open steppe, Koschak, Duque, Fazio and Moench shivered around Jobert. The faces pulsed between anger and confusion. 'What was that all about? Why did that happen?'

Jobert looked each man in the eye. 'Fucking Zenari!'
Duque looked over the backs of the horses towards the lightly wooded plain, sucked his teeth, turned slowly to Jobert and gave a sly reassuring wink.

A week later, Jobert and the entire column of Turks stood rigid as the village they had just entered was alive with movement.

Jackals scampered. Rats scurried. Dogs wrestled. Crows hopped. Kites flapped.

All feasted on the dead.

Dead people.

Dead cattle.

Dead pigs.

After resupplying in Iasi, the Turkish column had continued north on the road to Balti, arriving at this village, which was a ferry crossing across the Prut. It was here Dikaletus would continue, under escort, to Balti, while Otal and Jobert maintained their course towards Jobert's horses.

In the village square, lance tripods supported five impaled men. The shafts had been inserted in through the anus and out through the sternum. The lances continued to thread through the lower jaw and out through the cheek under the eye. Each man's genitals were held in their mouth by an arrow embedded in their throats.

In front of the butchered, lay six decapitated women, bloated and green. The wounds to their groins were as severe as the men's. Their chests were flensed where their breasts had been removed.

The Moldavian djelli crossed themselves.

Otal mumbled as he dismounted.

Jobert glanced at Dikaletus for clarification.

'There is no God but Allah,' Dikaletus crossed himself as he translated, 'and Muhammed is the Messenger of God.'

Otal drew an arrow out of one corpse. The slim shaft came free with a sucking noise. The wound in the distended abdomen farted the build-up of gases of decomposition. Otal wiped the arrowhead of black slime on the corpse's hair which raised a cloud of fat flies.

'Who?' Jobert asked. 'Cossacks?'

'No.' Dikaletus held his fingers to his nose. 'Cossacks might cross the Dniester, but they would never cross to this side of the Prut. This is the work of uhlans.' Dikaletus thrust his chin west at the brooding face of the Carpathians. 'From Transylvania.'

'Uhlans!' For a moment, pelting rain filled Jobert's vision of Croatian lances pinning his friend Fergnes in the Caldiero mud.

'No, your excellency,' Otal wiggled the arrow in his fingers, 'this is not the work of uhlans. Yes, the hoofprints are unshod. The hindquarters have been removed from the cattle, but not the pigs. There are neither sheep not goat carcasses, as they have all been taken.' Otal pointed to burnt structures around the square. 'The church has been razed, but not the mosque. The ferry has been cut adrift on the eastern bank, not the western. The villagers have been slaughtered, not captured.' Otal's face bent with memories of past obscenities as much as the vision of the current disgrace. 'This is Begnzarov.'

'Begnzarov?' Jobert asked.

'Khan of the Crimean Tartars.' Otal waved the flies from his face with the arrow's black fletching. 'Cossacks!'

Otal led the column a further two days north to a hamlet which nestled by a ford over the Prut.

Cautious advance patrols circling the approaches to the crossing had found a trail of many hoofprints. Now, in predawn twilight, Jobert crept, with Otal and his sipahi scouts, to a point of observation outside the hamlet.

Under the hamlet's fruit groves where the fog was thinnest, Jobert observed horses hitched to branches. Lances were slung over saddle bows. Packhorses drooped under large dark bundles. Around a central fire shuffled a few sheepskin-clad figures.

'Who are they?' Jobert asked. 'Cossacks?'

'No, uhlans from Transylvania.' Otal jerked his chin towards the western Carpathian range. 'Bear hides and see there,' he indicated a line of hunched lumps bracketed by a pair of horsemen, 'slaves for the Carpathian mines.' Otal shook his head. 'But they are too few—'

A long note from a low-pitched horn droned through the morning air.

A crackle of musketry to the south, in the direction of Otal's djelli encampment.

'Our camp!' Otal shouted, as he raced to remount the Cricket. 'Swiftly!'

Galloping south, Jobert and Fazio, with Otal's sipahis, reined to a stop on a ridge south of the hamlet.

Beneath them in a valley a creek ran towards the Prut. A ford across the creek was nestled in a copse of elms. Within the broken ground of the embankments, on either side of the ford, a dozen dismounted djelli skirmished. Within the shelter of the copse, another dozen djelli, mounted as a reserve, milled amongst the lines of clustered packhorses.

The pops and puffs of their intermittent Turkish musket fire was aimed at two bands of around twenty horsemen. On either slope above the ford, bearded lancers in sheepskin coats and lumpy hats prowled well out of musket range. Overlooking the engagement a few hundred metres down the slope from Jobert, a knot of stationary riders under a rough-cloth banner guarded a few loaded packhorses and a straggle of roped captives.

Horns and whistles blew from the ford and beyond.

The djelli's mounted reserve disgorged from the ford to assail the provocative band of uhlans on the far slope.

'Tétény!' Otal drew his scimitar. '*Allahu Akbar!* Charge!'

'*Allahu Akbar!*' cried his sipahi as they wafted their blades aloft and lifted their horses to a canter.

Abandoning their loot and prisoners, the uhlans fled along the slopes. The sipahi attempted to chase individuals. On the ridge where Jobert and Fazio had first observed the scene, another twenty uhlans arrived from the hamlet. The dispersed spearmen that Otal's sipahi chased reassembled on their newly arrived reinforcements.

'Otal orders us to return to the ford,' Fazio interpreted Otal's shouts.

As Otal's scouting sipahi entered the tree line, the raiding djelli returned from the opposite slope. Moench led a scruffy pony carrying the meanest of saddle pads swaddled in skins and rags. Behind his horse, Koschak dragged a rangy youth with a rope around his captive's neck.

The boy tore at the slip knot choking him. Once loose, he screamed at Koschak.

Koschak responded with a solid wallop with the butt end of his lance.

Collapsed in the creek's mud, the young man snarled behind a veil of lank, matted blond hair and rocked with pain.

'Are these the raiders who massacred the village?' Jobert asked Otal.

'No.'

'How can you tell uhlans and Cossacks apart?'

'Although they both ride unshod horses,' Otal pointed at the youth struggling to stand and his wary mount, 'the uhlan ride with European stirrups. They have long hair, beards, and being Christian, they do not bathe. Uhlan gather under cloth flags. Cossacks under horsehair tugs. Those who have crossed the

Dniester are believers of the true faith.' Otal grinned. 'You will know them when you see them. As much as I despise them, they are magnificent horsemen.' Otal glanced at the riders under their mottled banner on the slope above them. 'Time to trade.'

With ropes fastened to the boy's wrists, two djelli shifted their horses outwards and stretched his arms. With a spear tip at the base of the boy's skull, Otal rode behind his hostage, and led a small delegation out of the ford towards the mob of bearded horsemen.

'Is he your blood, Tétény?' Otal asked. 'I propose an exchange, Tétény.' Otal slid the iron tip from ear to ear over the boy's scalp. 'This one for those you captured.'

The chieftain Tétény had the pale eyes of a wolf, simmering with a ferocity ready to burst through the restraint of their leathery eyelids. A ropey moustache extended beyond his scraggly beard. Under the brim of his fur hat hung four thick plaits.

Jobert was surprised that Otal spoke German to the Transylvanian.

Otal jabbed his chin at the uhlan chieftain. 'For Tétény and I to speak to Austrian officers, we need to speak the tongue of that empire.' Otal's face crimped with bitterness. 'Tétény plundered these lands after the Austrians invaded in '88.'

With a jerk of the chieftain's head, bows were lowered, and pressure released from bowstrings. Tétény's lips flattened doglike against clenched teeth. 'Who is this?' Tétény's voice rasped. 'He is neither German nor Russian.'

'Colonel Jobert of the French Army.'

'A Frenchman in northern Moldavia?' Tétény considered the other Frenchmen and their packhorses. Seeing his eyes sizzling and his nostrils flaring, Jobert knew Tétény was testing the air for potential spoils. 'You ride with your enemies, France. You draw your blade against your friends. Are you not at peace with my emperor and at war with his?'

'Your decision to raid will bring the wrath of your emperor upon you,' Otal said, 'when France and Turkey bring war to Vienna.'

Tétény spat towards the Cricket's feet. He jarred the bit in his own horse's mouth to turn the animal for the hamlet where his slaves and pelts were stashed.

The Turks followed the straggle of uhlans back to the hamlet by the Prut.

Once there, over twenty captured villagers shuffled forward in their thick rope bonds. Beneath their filth and the whip wounds across their faces, their ages were difficult to determine. Blood smeared the seat of their pants and skirts. Women gripped shawls and rags across their faces and chests where their blouses ought to have been.

As the prisoners were exchanged, the boy spat at his guards when he was released from his bonds.

Tétény's wolf eyes tightened. 'And my son's horse?'

'Payment for the bear skins.'

'Huh!' Tétény sneered. 'My gift to France.'

'Tétény,' Otal asked, 'have you encountered Cossacks on your incursion?'

Tétény's wild eyes rolled as he evaluated options. 'We have crossed their sign. Amongst the remains of a village to the south. We observed a patrol of one hundred to the north. We have no fight with the Crimeans. They hunt like bears. We avoid them.'

'And you scavenge like jackals.' Otal gave a dismissive wave. 'Now, take the hides and return to your caves.'

Once the uhlans had departed, Dikaletus and half the djelli escort forded the Prut and continued northeast to Balti.

Dikaletus bade Jobert and Zenari an effusive farewell, then he said to Marsden, 'Your task is set. Fail me, and I will have you amputate your right hand with your left.'

Marsden knelt to bow and no reaction registered on his face. 'Be assured, Master, I will not fail.'

As they rode north, Jobert and Koschak watched the dwindling column of uhlans and loaded pack-animals trek westward.

Koschak halted beside Jobert. 'How will we sneak four hundred horses past those bastards?'

Jobert winced. 'Otal, will Tétény return to his mountains?'

'No,' Otal said. 'Finding Frenchmen so far from Constantinople will arouse his interest. His uhlans will trail us like jackals.'

'Where next?' Jobert asked.

'Three days to our destination. Serpenaçi,' Otal said as he flicked his reins to a point on the vast forested horizon beyond the Cricket's ears, 'and your mares.'

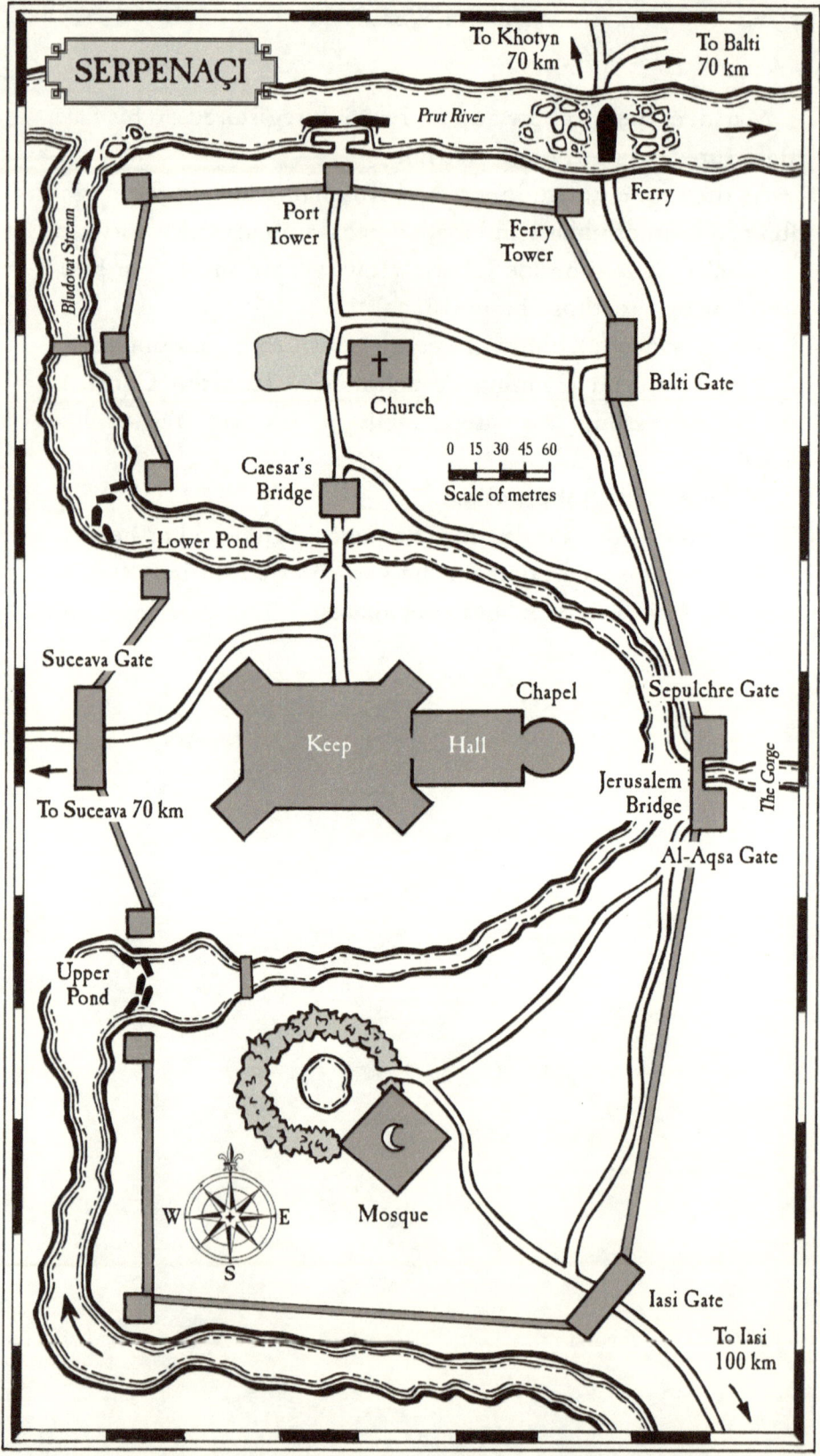

Chapter Thirteen
July 1801, Serpenaçi, Moldavia

On the last day of July, Jobert stood high in a stone tower and stared down on the town of Serpenaçi. As the Prut River slithered south through the Moldavian steppe, one of its reaches flowed east-west. Into this section of the Prut, the Bludovaţ Stream wove north among the riverside knolls.

On three such promontories by the banks of the Prut, nestled the *palanka* of Serpenaçi, where each spur contained the three sections of the town: the northern Christian quarter, the central Boyar's quarter and the southern Muslim quarter.

The most dominating building of Serpenaçi — where Jobert stood — was the three-storey, Byzantine stone Keep in the heart of the Boyar's quarter. From the Keep ran the only cobbled road in the town, north across Caesar's Bridge, into the Christian quarter, past the church of Saint Andrew the Apostle to the Port Tower perched above the Prut.

Amongst the cram of timber homes and sheds in the Christian quarter, the only stone buildings were the church, the gate house of the Caesar's Bridge and the Port Tower. The northeast facing Balti Gate was a timber arch flanked by timber walls.

Within the narrow streets of the Muslim quarter, a brick mosque faced south-southeast towards Mecca. From the Muslim quarter, a dirt road crossed the bridge across the ramparts from the Iasi Gate to its namesake town.

The external gates of Balti, Suceava and Iasi, were connected by high earthen ramparts, topped with timber palisades. On the outer side of the ramparts, sharpened stakes and thorny bushes were planted. A deep ditch ran along the foot of the mound. Timber towers stood at regular intervals along the walls. Even the Bludovaṭ Stream was dammed in two places, the Upper and Lower Ponds, and covered by towers to strengthen the defence.

The Christian and Muslim quarters were linked by the Jerusalem Bridge over a deep chasm, known locally as the Gorge. At each end of the Jerusalem Bridge were two timber arched battlements. The Sepulchre Gate stood on the Christian bank of the Gorge and faced the Al-Aqsa Gate on the Muslim side.

Jobert observed that, despite the centuries of effort to create a permanent defence, the walls showed signs of recent damage and repair. 'One piece of artillery of any calibre, Sevalnev, and this ancient structure would fold,' Jobert said, in German, to the leader of the Serpenaçi community beside him.

'*Inshallah*,' said Boyar Sevalnev. 'The one hundred muskets of the town's militia guard maintain the structure. In a time of war, Serpenaçi would be garrisoned by imperial troops. The damage you see was when we held the Russians in '87, if only for a short time.'

Jobert considered his host. 'Surrounded by enemies, no?'

Boyar Sevalnev was a stooped, rangy man, perhaps in his fifties. A stringy moustache outlined oddly feminine lips. Sevalnev spoke sufficient German to communicate with Austrian authorities in Suceava, as befitted his rank of prince. His clothing, of an embroidered shift, leather boots and an enamelled scimitar hanging from his woven waist sash, hinted at his regional authority. Despite being a prince of a town that smelt of pig shit, Jobert did not doubt Sevalnev's inherent wiliness was born of the imperative to survive.

Sevalnev swept his hand wide across the view of the town. 'We Moldavians are Orthodox Christian. Oppressed by the Muslim Turk. Taxed and conscripted by the Phanariot Greeks. We cling to our beloved river, trade our timber and bear pelts, threatened by all. *Alham-dulillah.*'

'*Alham-dulillah?* You thank God for your situation.'

'*Alham-dulillah* is more "everything is as God wishes it to be". It can be a response to a joyous occasion, or it can be an acceptance of how things are.'

'As a Christian, you use this Muslim expression?'

'It works.' Sevalnev shrugged. 'And what of you, Jobert, your family is well?'

Jobert groaned inwardly at the need to exchange family information. 'I am married with two sons. All is well.'

'*Alham-dulillah.*' Sevalnev smiled warmly. 'My sons—'

'On our journey north, we crossed paths with Transylvanian raiders.'

Sevalnev's eyes widened in surprise. 'Tétény's uhlans. We are threatened by raids from the Transylvania, but we maintain a trade in bearskins with Suceava.'

'And the Cossacks who have crossed the Dniester?'

'We have faith in the Christian Russians in Khotyn to keep a tight leash on their barbarous Muslim hordes.'

'How far are we from ...?'

'Anyone? The Ottoman outposts are Balti four days east and Iasi eight days south. The Austrians hold the fortress in Suceava four days march to the west. The Russian garrison is in Khotyn four days march to the north.'

Jobert searched beyond the walls for farms. Vegetable gardens and orchards grew at a two-hundred metre bow range beyond the walls. Between the walls and the orchards lay a wide, cleared space, with small sets of stock yards clustered near the gates for pack-animals or holding stock for market. All he could discern was rolling woodland, no hint of roofs or wisps of smoke to indicate habitation. All the human bustle appeared contained to the streets of the town, the banks of the river and the surrounding groves. 'And the horses we have purchased, where are they?'

'The herd?' Sevalnev flicked his fingers across the Prut. 'The herd is held in valleys to the north. Have you paid for these horses? They are quite vulnerable.'

'Yes, directly to the Hospodar. I have the bills of remittance as a statement of ownership of four hundred head. Vulnerable to what?'

'Vulnerable to being stolen. Then Otal has brought money with him? We watch over the herd, yet Otal has not paid us.'

'Stolen by whom?' Jobert asked.

Sevalnev's eyes strayed to the pewter brooch adorning Jobert's hatband. 'Where will you drive the horses to?'

'Dikaletus says he will ship them from the port of Izmail. What do you mean drive them? One man can lead four horses.'

'And which two hundred men will lead these horses? And where and how and with what will you train them to lead?'

Jobert's face creased with concern. 'Are they not trained to lead?'

'Trained? They are barely domesticated, Jobert. They are essentially wild.'

'I will speak with Otal. We will find a way.'

Sevalnev snorted. '*Inshallah.*'

In the bright sunshine of the next day Otal and an escort of twenty sipahi, with Jobert and his men, departed Serpenaçi through the Balti Gate. Beyond the walls, amongst the vegetable gardens and fruit trees in the final weeks before harvest, bees droned, townsfolk chatted, and children and dogs scampered.

The column of horsemen swam their horses across the Prut beside a hand-drawn hawser-ferry. On the far bank, where the Balti road turned east, Otal's column continued north along the Khotyn road.

In the rolling woodland meadows, men and women bent to till the ground amongst the green wheat or hunched to lug bundles of firewood.

Otal viewed Jobert's chestnut pack-horse carrying the gold-laden panniers with a disdainful eye. 'Must you bring your gold, Jobert?'

'Sadly, I must, since there is no one in this land I can trust,' Jobert said.

'As your host, you offend my honour, Jobert.'

'But a minor offence compared to my honourable host trussing me naked to purge my guts.'

'Where is Zenari?' Otal asked.

'He is not well.'

'Still not recovered?'

'He remains under Marsden's watchful eye.'

'Perhaps that is best.' Otal swept out his hand with a flourish. '*Alham-dulillah*, we are here.'

From the crest of a ridge, Jobert stared down at a wide valley full of hundreds and hundreds of horses. Jobert reached for his telescope within his tailcoat. In its absence, he remembered he was not in uniform and the instrument safe in his chest in Genoa. Why would anyone need a telescope to buy horses?

The air was full of their dust and sweat, with only an occasional neighed response from a mother to her lost foal's squeal. Mature horses grazed or rolled to itch their backs. Foals scampered between their dams, their sleek young bodies stretched as they raced. Gangly colts wielded their bared teeth to improve their fighting skills, but their half-hearted bouts of bravado were soon dispersed by the charge of more senior horses. Fillies in season mounted each other in a frenzy of sapphic squeals and bucks. Small groups of young stallions would burst from the herd at a focused trot, only to stop and lower their heads when thick clumps of grass appeared more inviting.

'You seem surprised, Jobert,' Otal said. 'What were you expecting?'

'I do not know, but not a valley of four hundred horses.'

'There are more than that here,' Otal said. 'Over six hundred. There are smaller groups of young males. Some mature stallions. But at least four hundred mares. You were not expecting a herd?' Otal twisted his head to comprehend. 'If I was to buy four hundred mares from France, how would I find them?'

'In stables.'

'No!' Otal's eyes widened in awe. 'You have breeding stables that can accommodate four hundred horses?'

'No, smaller stables spread across the many farms of a region.'

'Pah! There are no farms here. Just fortified towns clinging like burrs to the blanket of the steppe. Even villages are vulnerable.'

The memory of villagers butchered or shackled stained Jobert's thoughts. 'As I have seen.'

'Are there uncut colts within the herd, sir?' Duque asked. 'Have these horses not been handled? If they are unhandled, how do you separate them?'

Otal shrugged. 'Until now there has been no reason to do so.'

Duque threw his reins onto his horse's neck. 'We have purchased four hundred wild horses.'

'They are not wild horses.' Otal shrugged his shoulders. 'They are domesticated horses, just ... unhandled.'

Jobert scoured the scene. 'Where are the herdsmen?'

'You can see some, here and there. Youths from Serpenaçi. They are unable to control the herd. They are boatmen and timbermen, not horsemen.'

Jobert counted two or three pairs of riders across the vast scene. 'Never started. Never handled. Therefore unapproachable. How did you collect six hundred unbroken horses, Otal?'

'They were found grazing in a valley.'

'Found?'

'Who are they?' Koschak pointed across the valley. 'I see they are certainly horsemen.'

On the far side of the valley, the herd swirled as horses broke into the canter at a disturbance.

A column of lance-armed riders, in lumpy fur hats, trotted out of the wood line, through the parting horses and towards the Turks and their French guests.

'Who are they?' Jobert asked. 'Uhlans? Cossacks?'

Otal gathered his reins and urged his horse forward. 'Poles.'

'Poles?' Jobert asked as he trotted to follow Otal towards the approaching column.

'With the final absorption of Poland and Lithuania in 1795 into the realms of Austria and Russia,' Otal called over his shoulder, 'those seeking refuge have drifted south. The Sultan in his immense generosity gives these Poles sanctuary. They watch our northern border where our lands connect with the junction of the Austrian and Russian empires.'

A man on a broad-chested roan stallion led a twenty-warrior escort. Several of the trailing warriors carried severed heads impaled upon their lances. Pale grey heads with clotted beards and matted, braided hair. Uhlans. One slack-jawed head with blood-stiffened blond plaits was the unmistakable son of Tétény. *His impetuosity has finally undone him*, Jobert thought.

The chieftain who led the escort was heavily built, a thick moustache wedged beneath a bulbous nose, dividing his pockmarked cheek, and a thick lower lip underlined by a chin beard.

The Polish warriors faced off against Otal's sipahi in a wide ring of lance tips.

Without any emotion in his face, Otal greeted the chieftain with a touch to his head and heart. 'Hetman Koranski.'

Koranski's head hung to one side, face impassive, causing him to look up under his bushy brows. 'Otal Alaybey.' Koranski's face shifted to Jobert.

'You Poles speak a little German, do you not, Koranski?' Otal said. 'This is Colonel Jobert of France. He is here to buy the horses.'

Koranski indicated the herd around them. 'You like what you see, Jobert?' Koranski appeared tired, bored, as if the sunlight pained his sunken black eyes. 'Make me an offer?'

'The sale has already been agreed,' Jobert said. 'France has paid the Hospodar.'

Koranski's heavy head swung back to Otal. 'You sold my horses? When will I be paid, Otal?'

Otal shifted uncomfortably in his saddle. 'Do you not agree, Koranski, the Hospodar is owed the horses. A reasonable payment for living in the land of our beneficent Sultan.'

Koranski spluttered a laugh. 'River levels are low in the summer. I could take my herd to the Governor of Suceava.'

'Be at peace, my friend,' Otal said, 'I have brought cash with me.'

Jobert's attention jerked towards Otal. 'That is my money, Otal. Your gold from the sale sits in Bucharest.'

'Gold?' Koranski nodded slowly. 'These are my horses. I have not received that payment.'

'Have you stolen horses from him, Otal, or have stolen gold from me?' Jobert asked. 'You heap dishonour upon dishonour.'

'Jobert, do you want the horses or not.' Otal opened his expressive fingers.

'France entered into this sale in good faith.'

'Good faith? Here?' Koranski scanned the horizons. 'There is no good faith here, France. Here you take with the sword, and you keep with the sword.'

'Where did your sword acquire these horses?' Jobert asked.

Koranski shrugged. 'The east.'

'From whom? The Cossacks?'

Koranski spat. 'Fuck those heathen bastards.' Koranski peered at Koschak, Fazio, Duque and Moench. His eyes lingered on the chestnut pack-horse before his gaze returned to Jobert. 'Something of value kept close? How many Frenchmen did you bring, Jobert?'

'Six.'

'Six?' Koranski snorted. 'Enough to bring your money, but not enough to take six hundred horses.' Koranski glanced at the man on his right who held Tétény's son's head. The warrior shortened his reins.

A tension of readiness rippled around the Polish escort. The sipahi escort couched their javelins between elbow and ribs. Horses threw their heads as leg pressure increased in stirrups.

Jobert and Koschak shortened their reins and touched their sabre pommels with their fingertips.

Otal raised a finger. 'Koranski! Do not make a foolish choice.'

'What? To cut the head off a snake? Perhaps the Transylvanians caught you.' Koranski pointed to Jobert's panniers. 'Is that my money, Otal, or are these my horses? Wolf packs from the east and the west have the spoor.' He jerked a fat thumb at the severed heads. 'They close rapidly on you, Otal.'

'Perhaps Koranski is right,' Jobert said. 'Perhaps we should cut the head off the snake.'

Otal arched one eyebrow. 'You are a long way from home to make such threats, Jobert.'

'Right now, so are you, Otal.'

Koranski chortled, and with a head flick, his Polish horsemen rode away.

Jobert chose his own way. He ran his eye over the horses as he rode though the herd. The horses were fat and sleek on ripening summer grasses. Of the many black mares, and the few black foals that would stand still long enough, Jobert evaluated the angles of their conformation and the reach in their strides. He judged their character from their eyes as they responded to his plodding amongst them. Jobert was pleased with the quality of swirling horseflesh.

When Jobert sank to a halt, his friends reined in beside. 'We have bought some fine horses here, lads.' Jobert turned his horse to face them all.

Duque faced Jobert square on. 'Yes, without doubt, this is good stock, but we cannot catch and train four hundred horses to lead. Four hundred horses will require one hundred men to walk them for four weeks to the Danube ports. Have you forgotten the bandits in the Serbian hills? With the steppe crawling with Cossacks and uhlans, add another one hundred men to protect the convoy, plus surgeon, farrier, vet, twenty packhorses for gear, and at least ten packhorses for ammunition. This will be impossible.'

Jobert turned to Koschak with a wink. 'Was it not "if not us pricks, then who?"'

'Then no one, André,' Duque said. 'This is bullshit. We need to accept our dire situation and leave.'

Jobert shook his head. 'We do not leave, Duque. We stay. We make this work.'

'How?' Duque asked.

'We find a way.'

Koschak sat comfortably in the saddle, just behind Jobert's right shoulder, packing his pipe with tobacco. Koschak's green eyes evinced assuredness. 'If we do this, we need to have it done before the Cossacks find them.'

Beside Duque, Fazio sat slumped with his arms folded. 'How do we get them away from these Polish pricks?'

Moench's face and shoulders were bowed as he inspected the buckle on his reins. 'How do we get them past the uhlans?'

'Fuck getting the horses home.' Fazio shouted as he threw his hands in the air. 'How do we get ourselves home?'

Moench's moustache twisted with anxiety. 'Will we lose all our money?'

Duque raised a hand to halt the descent. 'André,' he said quietly, 'we need to leave.'

'We should have gone long before now,' Fazio said.

Moench looked scared. 'What are you going to do, sir?'

Jobert backed his horse out of the circle before turning away.

He rode aimlessly amongst the grazing horses. *I have horses I cannot move. I am surrounded by enemies. I have squandered my annuity. I have endangered my grandfather's legacy.*

Walking a wide arc, Jobert returned to the group.

Koschak was calm. Duque agitated. Fazio and Moench morose.

I have imperilled my friends. 'You are right, Duque,' Jobert said, 'it all appears grim. We will split the money so you can depart for home tomorrow.' Jobert drew back his shoulders. 'But I am staying.'

Duque shook his head. 'You cannot stay.'

I have gambled and lost. 'I must. I have no choice.'

'Of course, you have a choice. You always have a choice.'

Jobert leant back in his saddle. 'I do not.'

'If you stay, sir, so will I.' Koschak exhaled a plume of blue smoke. 'What will you do?'

I have failed. 'Make it work.'

Duque held up his hands. 'This situation is irretrievable. How can you make any of this work?'

Is this who I have become? Jobert shrugged. '*Inshallah.*'

Chapter Fourteen
August 1801, Serpenaçi, Moldavia

Each cool summer morning, a breakfast table was set under a marquee on the uppermost level of the Keep. On the second morning since visiting the herd, the breakfast conversation between Otal and Sevalnev was, as far as Jobert could understand, about the threat of rain. The only clouds on this heron-grey morning rose on Carpathian thermals to the west.

Duque flicked an orienting finger north beyond the Balti Gate. 'Here they come.'

As Jobert concentrated on juggling his rip of *pide* full of spiced vegetables and *hummus*, he raised his eyes to look over the Keep's stone parapet.

Sevalnev stood and observed the lead Polish riders disembark the Prut ferry. The guard called for the Balti Gates to open.

'You summoned Koranski, Jobert.' Otal sipped at his coffee and puffed at his shisha. Smoke and coffee was all Otal appeared to consume, apart from an occasional square of baclava. 'Should you not greet him?'

Jobert wiped his fingers on a serviette. 'I shall take a moment to finalise my thoughts.'

With an arch of his eyebrows, Otal followed Sevalnev and descended the stairs into the bowels of the Keep.

I am desperate. Jobert turned back to find his friends arranged by the parapet wall. 'I have a plan.'

'Of course, you do.' Duque leant over the parapet and snorted. Duque had followed Jobert from the farm into regimental service out of curiosity for the wider world. 'You always do.'

'A plan to get home with four hundred wild horses from the edge of the world?' Moench asked. Moench had ever suppressed his fears of the fight for a dice-rolled chance of a drink, a song and a woman once sabres were sheathed.

'I have asked Otal to summon Koranski,' Jobert said. 'I need Koranski and Sevalnev to supply their men for starting these horses under halter.'

Moench squinted. 'So, if they do not agree ... there is no plan?'

Koschak's neck twitched as he stared hard at Moench.

'I am just saying ...' Moench held up his hands. 'No plan ... we go home?'

Jobert nodded slowly. 'I have a simple plan. If it is accepted, I would need your help. If not accepted, then we leave.'

Moench chewed his lip and looked to Fazio.

Fazio shuffled and ground his teeth. Although they had met as adversaries, Jobert admired Fazio's audacity. 'I think we are in deep shit.' Fazio looked up under his thick eyebrows at Jobert. 'You wagered high in Italy, sir, but this stake ...' Fazio shook his head, then with a nod to the others. 'I will watch how these lads play their hands.'

Zenari, flexing his forearm from his morning leeching by Marsden, stood beyond Fazio's shoulder. *The fool who has nowhere else to go.* Zenari slowly became aware everybody was looking at him, waiting for his opinion. 'Oh, wonderful. Another Jobert plan.' Zenari tugged at his cuffs. 'In this place without decent sport, I await Jobert's next spin of the roulette with barely contained excitement.'

Standing three steps behind Zenari's breakfast chair stood Marsden, the desperate shadow. His hands clasped in front of his soft black-and-green coat. Marsden dared to raise his eyes.

Jobert beheld a look of trepidation. Jobert responded with a wink before his gaze passed to Koschak.

Koschak drew back his thick shoulders and looked directly at Jobert. Their friendship forged from the shared burden of leadership in battle. 'We need to get these horses past the post. Colonel Jobert will give orders. Each man will do his duty.' Ever the sergeant major.

All eyes were upon Jobert.

Jobert raised his chin and slipped on the mask of grim belief that we will all survive the next charge.

I must make this gamble work.

Downstairs, in the Keep's Hall, Jobert joined Otal and Sevalnev.

Koranski entered through the great oak doors flanked by six Polish spearmen. The crowns of their fur caps were dyed scarlet. The hems and cuffs of their yellow shifts were embroidered with intricate floral designs. The forearms which gripped their spears were adorned with silver bracelets. A sword and two daggers per man hung from their woven-cord sashes.

Sevalnev opened his arms in greeting. 'Welcome to my hall, Hetman Koranski.'

With his meaty hand on the hilt of his polished sword,

Koranski took a long moment to regard Otal and Jobert. 'Before we speak, I seek comfort in prayer. Boyar Sevalnev, might you guide me to your chapel?'

'These neighbours are colluding.' Otal scoffed and slid his eyes sideways to Jobert. 'Whatever your plan, Jobert, expect to be undermined.'

Jobert inclined his head towards Otal. 'I have learnt that harsh lesson from the master.'

'A man's sin is a matter between himself and God. Do not the prophets of our faiths — peace be upon them — extol the virtue of forgiveness?' Otal dismissed Jobert's grievance with a flick of his expressive fingers. 'Many ventures fail, Jobert. This wager is such a one.' Otal extended his bony hand like a fan towards the exit. 'Is it not an exquisite coincidence that the French buckle under our siege in Cairo, while here you are beset in Moldavia. Perhaps you should attend chapel also. For guidance. Or solace.'

Once Sevalnev returned to the Hall with Koranski, his hands swept from fur cuffs towards a large square table, at which a brocaded chair waited on each side. 'Please sit.'

Sevalnev sat at the head of the table, with his back to the hearth and beneath a tapestry emblazoned with his ducal coat-of-arms. Jobert took his place on Sevalnev's right. Koranski on Sevalnev's left. Otal sat at the base of the table angled slightly away.

Servants wheeled a squat brass samovar towards the table and poured tea into thick tapering glass cups. Copper platters of honey-fragrant baclava were placed beside each elbow. As he had requested, Jobert saw a blue glass decanter of raki on the table, accompanied by the Boyar's best silver cups.

Once the tea was raised in a steaming salute each to the other, Sevalnev said, 'I welcome you all to my hall, and call upon Jobert to address us.'

Jobert placed down his cup. 'Is German the common tongue at the table? Will that suffice?'

Acceptance was confirmed by the rolling of eyes.

'You all have a problem.' Jobert sat in a neutral position, his forearms on the table, his fingers lightly interlaced. 'Over six hundred horses devour your summer pastures and attract the attentions of your enemies — the wolves across the Dniester and the jackals in the Carpathians.' Jobert maintained eye contact with each leader. 'These horses must be shifted away from your communities to remove the threat of murderous raids.'

Koranski leant forward, his elbow on his knee, his head tilted to one side as his bovine jaw ground a square of baclava.

'France has paid the Hospodar for four hundred mares to move to Izmail,' Jobert said, 'and then shipped to Italy. I have a simple plan to move these mares in less than ten days. A simple plan which promises mutual benefit to all. May I share it with you?'

Otal looked to Sevalnev and Sevalnev nodded.

Across the table, Koranski stared with unblinking suspicion at Jobert.

Jobert looked at Koranski. 'I assume you are on the verge of stealing the entire herd, driving it to Suceava to sell to the Austrians.'

Koranski looked towards Otal and gave an uncommitted shrug.

'A move of desperation,' Jobert said. 'A move that will bring the anger of your Ottoman hosts. A move that will remove the Sultan's gracious protection of your families from the Cossacks.' Jobert's fingers unwound and pointed at Koranski. 'You would also steal from France who has purchased four hundred mares from that herd.'

Koranski rolled a thick wrist, palm upwards. 'Then pay me what I am owed.'

'France has paid the Hospodar for what you are owed.' Jobert thrust his chin at Otal. 'Take your grievance to him. Not me.'

Koranski remained motionless, but Jobert saw his eyes harden, if that was possible, and his nostrils flare.

Jobert drew his notebook from an inner pocket of his coat and smoothed open a page. 'Let us speak about how I might create an opportunity of benefit to you and your Polish community. France is in the market for your services. Would you be willing to be paid by France for one hundred of your warriors to catch and train to lead and tie, then lead the four hundred mares to Izmail.'

Koranski's pockmarked face creased with a squint.

Jobert held up a finger for emphasis. 'For which France will pay one hundred horses that remain from the herd — one hundred stallions and colts.'

Otal rumbled with warning. 'My friend, these horses — horses that are in excess of your four hundred mares — are not yours to give away.'

'Then, my friend, we shall speak with Dikaletus Pasha. I am sure the Hospodar will be happy to deduct the one hundred horses from the heavy debt already owed to Koranski's warriors.'

Koranski slid his reptilian gaze to Otal, and his heavy cheeks twitched into momentary delight. He swivelled his large head towards Jobert. 'One hundred men leading four hundred horses for four weeks to Izmail.' Koranski raised a fleshy paw in defeat. 'With hands full of lead ropes, while being hunted by Cossacks and uhlans, I cannot guarantee delivery. Taking horses to Izmail is worth more than one horse per man.'

'Lead the horses south.' Jobert folded his arms. 'Or remain here and explain yourself to the Cossacks.'

Koranski stared hard at Jobert, then raised his finger. 'I will accept one hundred horses for my one hundred men to … at-

tempt to deliver your four hundred mares to Izmail, only ...'
he aimed his thick finger at Otal, 'only if the Turks provide an
escort of at least two hundred djelli.'

Otal leant back and flared his bony fingers. 'And who will
pay for that?'

Jobert raised a conspiratorial eyebrow to Koranski. 'On the
word of his dragoman, the Hospodar is already obligated that
the horses will reach Izmail and then Ravenna safely.' Jobert
looked to Otal. 'All you must do is obey the commands of your
prince.'

Otal seethed.

'It will take two weeks to train four hundred horses to be
led from the saddle,' Koranski said. 'For this, I will only accept
that my men are paid in coin. Which I know you have.'

'It will take two days to prepare the herd, then two days to
draft the herd. It will only take two days to train the herd. Six
days total.'

Koranski's eyes narrowed. 'Allowing two days for summer
showers. Eight days.'

'Nine days,' Otal said, 'Salah al-Jamu'a must be observed.'

Jobert frowned at the comment.

'Friday is the Muslim day of prayer,' Sevalnev said, 'so add
another day for worship on the Sabbath.'

'As I said, ten days.' Jobert glanced at his notebook. 'Based
on the pay of a French cavalry trooper for ten days ... twenty
pieces of French gold would be divided amongst your men.'
From his inner pocket, Jobert produced a purse and pushed a
gold louis coin across the table to Koranski.

All the eyes around the table widened as the shimmering
coin slid across the timber surface.

Koranski glanced at the coin but made no attempt to reach
for it. 'How do I divide a gold coin between five men? Better
if it is one coin per man.'

Jobert's face creased in a humourless smile. 'At one gold coin per man, I would want your men to lead the herd to Italy. You can exchange the coins for Ottoman *kurus* here in Serpenaçi, and...' Jobert emphasised his point by raising his finger off the coin, 'another twenty pieces, a gift from France to you, in recognition of the inconvenience to your good self.'

As the tip of his thick tongue flicked at his lips beneath his moustache, Koranski looked from the gold piece to the purse and then to Jobert. 'Half now. Half on arrival in Izmail.'

'Why not?' Jobert poured two small cups of raki. 'Half paid here in Serpenaçi once the horses are trained, then half on arrival in Izmail. Shall we formalise our agreement with a toast?'

Koranski lifted the glass in salute and swallowed the contents in a gulp.

The mouthful of alcohol caused the embers of Jobert's confidence to glow in his stomach.

'I have a question,' Otal said. 'Four hundred mares require four hundred halters and lead ropes. Where is all this equipment?'

'Gentlemen, another opportunity of mutual benefit.' Jobert smiled and looked to Sevalnev. 'I wish to engage the services of the town.' Jobert drew another coin with care from his purse and slid it towards the Boyar. 'I wish to buy every blanket and hide in the town and have them cut and plaited into halters and two-metre lead ropes. Despite the halters being plaited and hand knotted, I will pay the French rate for a sewn leather headstall with buckles. One gold coin for every twenty sets of equipment tested suitable for the journey to Izmail. Twenty gold pieces total, and ...' again Jobert raised his finger from the coin to emphasise, 'an administration fee of five coins to yourself for any inconvenience caused. Are you able to provide?'

Transfixed by the gold, Sevalnev's pasty cheeks quivered with calculation. 'Why not?'

'My women can also produce such hand-plaited halters,' Koranski said.

'Here I am with gold desiring to purchase.' Jobert gave the purse a tinkling shake. 'Who will sell to me?'

Otal leant back, his thin face taut in consideration.

Jobert raised a finger. 'My purchases are not yet complete. I wish to lease Serpenaçi for ten days.'

Sevalnev raised his eyes from the coin. 'Lease the town?'

'The entire town. I wish to convert the town into a set of horse yards, to draft, separate and secure the different sub-herds.'

Sevalnev blinked in alarm. 'Six hundred horses enclosed in the town for ten days?'

'Not quite, but certainly an inconvenience. Shall we agree an additional administration fee of ten gold coins to alleviate that burden?' Jobert entwined his fingers lightly around the bulging leather sack of coins. 'My shopping list is long, Sevalnev. The horses need to become accustomed to tying up each evening if they are to travel to Izmail. Four fifty-metre lines pegged through the town to which the mares will be tied. So, another ten coins for rope.' Jobert tilted his head towards Koranski. 'Again, Koranski, you are welcome to contribute?'

Sevalnev's and Koranski's face were frozen in calculation.

Jobert glanced down at his open notebook. 'In addition, I wish to engage a workforce of one hundred townsmen to establish the rails, gates and troughs in the two days before the herd arrives the morning after tomorrow. Once the herd is within the town, I shall pay for forage to be cut and horses to be fed and watered. Ten days. One hundred men. The same daily wage as I am offering to the Poles. Twenty more coins. Again, with an appropriate administrative fee of five gold coins.'

Boyar Sevalnev licked his lips. 'I have not yet been paid for maintaining a watch over the herd these last few months.'

'Again, a matter between you and your Hospodar. Why not forego your annual taxes to Bucharest while the debt remains outstanding?'

Otal straightened with a jerk. 'Jobert!'

Jobert and Sevalnev exchanged a smile.

'Once Koranski has taken his pick of the best one hundred stallions and colts,' Jobert said, 'the remainder of the Hospodar's horses pass to you. I have a sergeant-veterinarian who can castrate without losing a horse. Is that acceptable?'

Sevalnev's vision slid between Jobert and Otal.

Jobert checked his notebook, then looked enquiringly at Sevalnev. 'Do we have a deal? Twenty coins for four hundred halters and leads. Twenty to engage the workforce. Ten for the horse lines. To you, ten coins to hire your town, and another twenty to offset any inconvenience to your good self. Eighty pieces of French gold, and around one hundred geldings to be distributed through the town for services rendered so far. Yes?'

Sevalnev beamed. 'Why not toast our contract?'

Raki was poured and quaffed.

The flame of confidence in Jobert's belly flared with the ingestion of additional spirits.

Otal tapped the table with a knuckle. 'What if there is insufficient blankets and skins to make four hundred halters and leads?'

'A good question for which I have an answer,' Jobert said. 'I shall draft a herd of up to fifty culls — lame, sick, old and blind — to be skinned. Each horse hide should yield sufficient green hide for the halters and leads we need.'

Sevalnev placed down his raki cup, a dribble of liquor on his pouting lips. 'Fifty carcasses in the town in summer?'

'Both your townsfolk and the Poles need to eat over the next ten days.'

Otal leant forward and placed his hands flat down on the table. 'Jobert, these horses are not yours to kill, skin and eat.'

'You are correct, Otal. For I am only willing to pay for halters and leads. The horses belong to the Hospodar, who would be willing — I am sure Dikaletus Pasha will agree — to provide as a down payment on services Serpenaçi has already rendered to the herd on the Hospodar's behalf.'

Baring his clenched front teeth, Otal took his hands from the table and placed them in his lap.

Sevalnev disguised his smile as he wiped the raki from his lips.

'Gentlemen,' Jobert said, 'if we are in agreement, then ... Koranski, you have today and tomorrow to gather your people and the herd and be outside the Balti Gate at dawn the day after tomorrow.'

Koranski remained immobile, his small black eyes sliding across each face at the table.

'Sevalnev,' Jobert said, 'you and I have today and tomorrow to build these yards internal to the streets of the town. Then two days of drafting horses, by which time all the halters need to be completed.'

Sevalnev nodded.

Otal leant back in the chair and folded his arms. 'And what of me?'

Jobert gave Otal a considered look. 'As we deliberate, the Cossacks descend upon their herd ... and our throats. As the most senior representative of their majesties, the Sultan — peace be upon him — and the Hospodar, might we prevail upon you to ensure our security. You have a force of twenty sipahi. Set vedettes at all points of the compass a day's ride from Serpenaçi's walls. Perhaps you would consider sending immediately for,' Jobert gave a curt nod to Koranski, 'a two hundred strong escort from Balti.'

Otal inclined his head in a feline manner. 'And my payment for these tasks?'

'Otal, your prince has already been paid. Your dragoman has already promised your services.' Jobert's face hardened. 'Now, is your moment to do your duty. Or do I need to force a shield between your ankles, as you did to me, to determine your honour?'

Otal's lips curled beneath his moustache as if Jobert had slid a turd towards him.

Jobert's face softened as he checked Sevalnev and Koranski. 'Then are we all committed to success?'
Koranski's cheeks cracked into a smile which did not extend to his eyes. '*Inshallah.*'

Chapter Fifteen

That very day, work began.

Otal tasked his sipahi with forming four patrols. After morning prayer, Jobert watched the patrols depart Serpenaçi. Turkish horsemen rode west on the Suceava road, south on the Iasi road, and, across the ferry, one patrol joined Koranski and his escort who rode to their village somewhere to the north, and Otal's patrol turned east on the Balti road, the most likely direction of the Cossack threat. With Otal, a courier rode with a message for Dikaletus in Balti.

With Otal's cavalry departed, Jobert and Sevalnev toured the town and discussed its use as a set of stockyards.

The herd would be brought across the Prut and through the Balti Gate into the Christian quarter. From there, with the streets barricaded to form a race, horses would be herded down into the church square, around which a stout wooden-railed fence would be erected. Dependent on their drafted status, the horses would be sent down fenced streets to either the Boyar's quarter via Caesar's Bridge, or the Muslim quarter via Jerusalem Bridge.

The morning was warming fast. To wipe the irritating beads of sweat, Jobert removed his brown, felt hat with its tall, rounded crown. With his hat in his hand, he reflected on the pewter çelenk, awarded in the Serbian hills a month prior, adorning the modest side-bow on the encircling broad, brown ribbon. *How far have I come since?* The memory draped a shawl of weariness about him. With a glance at the bustle he had created, and rub of the brooch for luck, Jobert shrugged off his concerns.

Jobert crossed the Jerusalem Bridge where he met Koschak moving between the church square and the mosque's fore-court supervising the gathering of timber for rails and rope for tethering lines. It was Koschak's distinct iron-grey bicorne of regimental origin, its initial black dyes dulled by the sun and its peak worn and stained by touch, that marked him out from the crowd. Koschak wore the hat slightly off-centre and low over his right eye.

'These horses will not take well to walking through the gates and over timber decking,' Koscak said. 'The gates and under the arches will be lined with branches and the bridge decking will be laid with grass and sand.'

'Well done.' Jobert gripped Koschak's upper arm. 'Press on.'

Seated in the shade by the cool pool in the mosque's fore-court, Fazio stockpiled blankets and hides, and instructed a large group of women in the rigging of a rope halter. Fazio wore a soft grey cap, which may have been mid-blue a long time ago. Whether pushed back from his forehead or pulled down firm, its baggy folds always fell to the right, the seem-ingly invisible restraining anchor for his right cheek and the cause of his preference for speaking out of the right side of his mouth.

'How are your recruits, Sergeant?' Jobert asked. 'Will we achieve the numbers of halters we need?'

'Like pushing shit uphill through briar thorns with your cock, sir.'

'A piece of piss for a trained trooper.' Jobert squeezed Fazio's shoulder. 'Have the new halters and leads rubbed into the sweaty coats of our horses to improve their smell to the new horses in the days to come. Where is Moench?'

'Down in the Bludovaṭ sorting water.' Fazio gave a wink. 'The silly prick is already swooning for a local woman.'

Jobert found Moench directing the placement of water troughs near to paths which descended to the Bludovaṭ Stream, and mangers close to the gates through which those tasked with gathering fodder would arrive. Moench wore a straw hat with a tall, dented crown. A new emerald ribbon, the tails of its bow just overhanging the handsomely rolled brim, was adorned with a canary-yellow feather. 'In town two days, and you are already claiming a prize?'

'Our laundress.' A wicked sparkle lit Moench's eyes. 'She is pretty enough.'

'Enough?' Jobert folded his arms. 'Do not have your cock jeopardise our enterprise. I will cut your balls off at the throat.'

'It is nothing, sir.' Moench held up his palms. 'Just a bit of fun. She brings me peaches. We have a laugh.'

Jobert pumped a stiff finger into Moench's chest. 'Moench, do not exchange your carrot for her peach.'

In a smithy by the Iasi Gate, Jobert met Duque working with the blacksmith creating two sets of hoof brands, each brand a numeral to be scorched into the toe of the hoof wall.

Jobert nodded towards the lithe smith with thick, ropy fore-arms. 'How goes the task? Is the language a bother?'

The smith's hammer paused above a glowing-red bar. 'I speak a little German, my lord.'

To wipe his brow, Duque pushed back his low-crowned felt hat, its brim curled up higher on the right. Its dull sea-green felt was girt with an ancient pink ribbon, the original scarlet mottled from fading and stains. 'The brands will be complete by sundown,' Duque said, 'I will return to the Christian quarter to establish the carcass frames within the meat market. What of you?'

'A quick check on Zenari.'

'Marsden, the slimy shit, is slowing killing Zenari with all this bullshit leeching. We do not bleed horses to heal them, so why do we do it to people? Zenari needs the leeching to cease to improve, not more quackery.'

Jobert pumped Duque a grim nod. 'I will speak to Marsden.'

As Jobert returned to the Keep, he spotted Zenari, identifiable in the crowd by his grey, felt hat with a tall, flat crown that increased in diameter towards the top, set off with a black, velvet ribbon with a generous rear-bow, shuffling across the Caesar's Bridge. 'Marsden, where is Zenari going?'

Marsden's downcast face showed his simple brushed black fez, tipped to the back of his shaved skull. 'Master Zenari has found the day too warm for his liking. I have arranged for some boys to take him to the river to bathe. And, Master?'

Jobert glanced at the slim man with his hands clasped in front of his soft black-and-green coat. 'Yes?'

'You will be aware of our proximity to Suceava, in order to make good your part of our arrangement.'

Jobert pierced Marsden with an angry stare. 'I am more aware of the proximity of uhlans and Cossacks that impede my options in that regard.'

The next day, Jobert accompanied Otal in his inspection of the eastern patrols.

Disembarking the flatboat ferry on the northern bank of the Prut, Jobert and Otal watched the Poles arrive with their carts, families, packs of dogs and herds of goats and cattle. They established their camp of spar and hide tents north of the ferry in a V-formation that narrowed to the cut in the embankment that led to the crossing.

As Jobert and Otal set off for the first vedette in the north-east, the lead horses of the herd were mustered into the neck of the V and then swum across the Prut.

'Their first step south,' Jobert said. 'Our scheme will work, Otal.'

'*Inshallah*. Come now, we have far to go.'

Thirty kilometres at the trot took two hours along the Khotyn road to the northeast. With the softness of an old quilt, the rumpled earth bulged from forested ridges to meadows in the dales. In the gentle creases, smoke would indicate the occasional tiny hamlets, their woven walls and thatched roofs blending amongst the boughs of their orchards and the ripening grain in their fields.

Once Otal confirmed that the sipahi patrol had nothing to report, they proceeded a further forty-five kilometres south at the trot, over three hours, to the south-east vedette on the Balti Road.

While they took a quick meal of dried chickpeas and apples with the southeast sentries, Jobert said, 'Five hours at the trot, Otal. These horses are superbly fit.'

'They are bred for this country. Similar to your France, no?'

'The rolling nature of the terrain, yes. The complete lack of population, no.' Jobert fed his apple core to his horse. 'With a three-hour ride between your posts, are you concerned with Cossack patrols bypassing your vedettes?'

'Perhaps not ideal, yet with such few men in such a wide country, we were still able to find the Russians when they invaded ten years ago.'

'But Serpenaçi's scars show that you could not stop them then.'

'*Alham-dulillah.*' Otal rinsed his fingers in a brass bowl proffered by one of his sipahi. 'We should head back now if you wish to convene your evening meeting.'

After a final ride of two hours at the trot, Jobert's lower back and thighs were stiff on return to Boyar Sevalnev's hall. Yet he did not reveal his discomfort as he addressed the conference. 'I see that the herd is assembled outside the Balti Gate, Koranski.'

Sevalnev threw up his hands. 'And are devastating our orchards.'

'Are yards built?' Jobert asked. 'Horse lines pegged?'

Koschak. 'Yes, sir.'

'Troughs for feed and water erected?'

Moench. 'Yes, sir.'

'Then, Sevalnev, any overnight damage to your orchards will be slight.' Jobert looked to Duque. 'Hoof brands? Ready to butcher the culls?'

Duque. 'All ready, sir.'

Jobert looked to Fazio. 'Two hundred halters ready for two hundred horses the day after tomorrow?'

Fazio's unshaven jaw twisted in distress. 'I have sixty that have passed muster, sir.'

'Shit!' Jobert's aching lower back spasmed. 'I planned on one hundred halters a day in the first four days. I expected two hundred by this evening. What is happening, Fazio?'

'The halters the women are making are pulling apart. I want to go home so badly, sir, I will not sleep until I have rigged the bastards myself.'

On the third day of Jobert's programme, the herd was mustered in through the Balti Gate then, in small groups, pressed into the church square.

Around the square, the rails had gates that allowed stallions and colts to be sent across the Caesar's Gate into the Boyar's quarter. Koschak stood on a raised platform on the church steps and tallied the horses as they were drafted though each gate. Fazio, Moench and teams of Poles remained in the saddle through the day, within the pens and races, to encourage the wild horses to follow their mounts to their destinations.

Foals rubbed hard against their mothers in the press of swirling dust. Separated foals screamed. The fear seeped through their coats and smelt like piss. Any identifiable colts were weaned right there and then. When any colt attempted to turn back towards the mares, a stallion would bite a chunk of flesh from its shoulder to keep it moving. Koschak smirked to Jobert. 'Some little boys are going to grow up fast tonight.'

Fillies and mares with foals at foot, or any other separated foals, were sent across the Jerusalem Bridge into the Muslim quarter. The horses were reluctant to step onto the timber decks that spanned the Gorge, and, snorting at the suspicious surface, they would leap over the threshold like sheep.

At the end of the sweaty and dirty day, the male herd was brought back into the Christian quarter, ready for further drafting on the morrow.

That evening, the horses packed the streets of the Christian and Muslim quarter. Townsfolk chased the hungry animals from their thatched roofs, their garden vines and their drying laundry. Poles moved, by foot and by horse, through the herds, mumbling and singing. Sidestepping puddles of horse urine, Moench contributed to the calming of both unsettled horses and townsfolk by playing his violin.

On the fourth day, all the male horses were redrafted in the church square. Those males selected by the Poles were sent out the Balti Gate and north across the Prut.

Duque's culls were sent out a gate to a side pen beside the Port Tower, known as the 'butcher's yard'. As it was the pen of animals designated for slaughter, it did not contain food or water. As each horse squeezed through the gate, swipes of whitewash were applied down their sides as identification.

The remaining sound males, to be distributed between the people of Serpenaçi, were moved through the Boyar's quarter and out the Suceava Gate to holding yards beyond the walls.

The day ended with the over four hundred strong female herd being evenly yarded in the Christian and Muslim quarters.

That evening, as the attendees assembled for the coordination meeting under the marquee on the Keep's battlements, Jobert looked down upon the dull, dark mass of horses within the circle of flames, smoke and dogs of the encircling Polish camp.

Otal, who had returned from his western vedettes, peered at the summer fruits available on copper platters. 'You misplace your trust, Jobert, to pay the Poles in horseflesh so soon?'

'In good faith.' Jobert held up a hand. 'And do not say "*inshallah*". Any news?'

'A courier from Balti.' Otal bit into a fat strawberry. 'A large Cossack warband raids the southeast.'

'Where is our escort from Balti?'

'Our courier to Dikaletus Pasha would only have arrived in Balti today. I would not expect the djelli for another five days.'

'We leave in three.'

Otal shrugged as his fingers lingered in their hunt over the fruit bowl.

Pushing aside apprehension for the unknown, Jobert called the meeting to order. 'Hetman Koranski, I see that you have received your distribution of stallions and colts. I have paid in good faith to secure your services for the movement of my mares to Izmail.'

'There is word of Cossacks, Jobert.' Koranski slowly twisted his cup of raki with his meaty fingertips. 'There is no word of djelli.'

Jobert held up his hand to quieten the murmurs. 'The djelli are closer than the Cossacks. Have you received your herd as payment, Boyar Sevalnev?'

'I have.' Sevalnev's eyes darted to refocus after the rumours of raiders. 'And Duque will castrate these horses?'

'Duque is a graduate of France's Alfort veterinary academy, and, for the last two years, a sergeant-veterinarian on the headquarters of France's Army of Italy. No finer surgeon at Serpenaçi's service.' Jobert produced a purse of gold louis, pocketed ten coins and slid the purse towards Sevalnev. 'Here is half payment. Forty coins. For the purchase of the labour and the halters. The balance on completion of training in two days' time.'

Sevalnev drew the calfskin purse into his lap.

'Where is my gold, Jobert?' Koranski asked.

'You have been paid in horseflesh for escorting the mares to Izmail, Koranski, a service you have not yet provided.' Jobert's tone was harsh, his eyes locked on Koranski. 'Your men will earn their gold once the herd is trained to lead.'

The assembly froze in anticipation of Koranski's response.

'I am not satisfied.' Koranski gave a slight flick of his thick fingers.

Jobert tugged the confrontation out of his shoulders and throat. 'Tomorrow, our goal is to train two hundred horses to lead and tie.'

Otal leant back with his arms folded. 'Ambitious.'

'Not at all. In both the Christian and Muslim quarters, I foresee two Poles catching, haltering and training to lead one mare per hour. Then a townsman leads that mare for hoof branding and ties her to the horse lines. Are horse lines established, Moench?'

'Ropes and pegs are assembled ready in both Muslim and Christian quarters,' Moench said.

'There we are,' Jobert said. 'With all one hundred Poles and fifty townsmen involved, we should have tied fifty horse per hour. Dependent on halters, we should have the task complete in four to six hours. Fazio, do we have two hundred halters for tomorrow?'

Fazio's thick moustache curled in embarrassment. 'One hundred and fifty, sir.'

'Then I will join you and we will work through the night,' Jobert said. 'Culls, Duque?'

Duque nodded. 'Over forty penned and ready for slaughter.'

'There we are.' Jobert planted his palms down on the table. 'Sevalnev, the remainder of the townsmen will kill, skin and scrape twenty-five culls and plait green hide halters for the day after. Tomorrow night, we feast on fresh roast.'

Later, in their stone-walled chamber within the Keep, Jobert watched his men slump onto thick-legged chairs around a small communal table. 'Come on, lads. Pinned as we are between storm clouds and warbands, we are undaunted. In three days, we depart for home.'

'What of the health of these mares?' Duque asked. 'Feet? Teeth? Worms? Ovaries?

'We will purchase hoof rasps in Iasi. We will drench for worms on arrival in Ravenna. Their teeth will be floated on the road to the Loire. Ovaries we can examine once stabled in the Loire.'

Moench had his forehead on his forearms on the table. 'If you could stable me in the Loire tonight, I would drop my pants right now and you could examine my fucking ovaries.'

The drooped shoulders around the table rippled with laughter.

Duque's tired eyes squinted through the candle flicker. 'You spoke of castrating one hundred colts for the town. To castrate, those horses also need to be started in halter and trained to lead. That requires another one hundred halters. Which men are available to assist me?'

'Not every horse needs a halter,' Fazio said. 'Why not just rope them and throw them?'

Duque winced. 'A little barbaric, no?'

Jobert's fingers twitched in support of Fazio. 'These are not our horses we are cutting. We are committed to paying the town in one hundred geldings. What they do with those horses is their business.'

Moench lifted his head. 'Teach the town's midwives. I imagine they will relish the task.'

Fazio snorted. 'If the women castrate as well as they braid halters, the horses will decorate this town with their guts by dinnertime.'

'Lads, stay focused' Jobert said. 'We need to tie ten halters each before we retire.'

Duque tapped Fazio. 'We will do a final check of the horses and gather the blankets we need to tie halters. Come, Moench.'

'Lads, I will join you on your rounds,' Jobert said as Duque, Fazio and Moench departed. 'If you would stay a moment, Koschak, I need to refill my purse.'

In the adjoining six-bed dormitory corner by Jobert's cot, Koschak knelt beside Jobert and unbuckled the panniers.

The iron doorlatch, between the main room and the bedroom, rasped open.

Koranski and six spearmen stood across the entrance.

Jobert and Koschak looked up from the pannier's purses. 'You have no business in our sleeping quarters, Koranski. Out!

I will speak with you in the main room.'

Koranski's jowls flexed as he spotted the contents of the open pannier. 'Jobert, I am not content with our arrangement.'

Jobert and Koschak stood and moved between the panniers and the Poles. 'Move out into the main room.' Jobert jabbed an emphatic flat hand towards Koranski. 'As promised, Koranski, you have received your pick of one hundred stallions and colts. With each horse valued at fifty gold coins, you have more than sufficient.'

'We had agreed to more. My … our fees?'

'Your greed is unbecoming.' Jobert gave Koranski a withering look. 'You have done nothing to earn any of your fees yet. You have driven the horses to Serpenaçi to draft out your share. The one hundred horses that you have taken into your herd is payment for the escort to Izmail. Half of what we agreed—'

'Piss on what we agreed.' Koranski's pocked jowls quivered. 'My people and horses are threatened by Cossacks.' Koranski's black gaze settled on the open panniers and their purses of gold. 'The Turks have no force here to protect my families. I am returning to our hills.'

'You are breaking our agreement.'

'Any agreement with you, Jobert, is of little consequence.' Koranski shrugged before he nodded to his spearmen. 'But I will take that gold.'

'Stand fast, Koranski.' Jobert's and Koschak's scabbard hissed steel as their sabres were drawn.

With a grunt from Koranski, the Poles converged on Jobert and Koschak flailing their lances in reverse. With the warriors' hands well down their shafts, the butts whipped up and down. In the confines of the small room cluttered with cots, Jobert and Koschak were unable to parry the assault and cut at their opponents' fingers.

Forcing them backwards, the long wooden shafts soon beat

Jobert's and Koschak's blades aside, then cracked against their extended wrists and forearms.

A sweep of spear cracked against Koshak's ankle as the base of another spear jabbed forward and thumped into his face. With a grunt, Koschak crumpled to one knee clutching his bloodied cheek. He raised his arm to protect his nose when a lance butt smacked into his unguarded ribs. Koschak scrabbled to draw his dagger from his cuff. A hard smack from a lance knocked the small blade clear.

Jobert dropped his sabre from a jarring blow to his wrist. A rapid thrust was aimed at his face and caught his left eye. Coloured stars exploded in Jobert's vision. Two blows corked Jobert's thigh. He tripped on the panniers under his feet and crashed heavily onto an upturned cot leg. Sprawled under the advancing Poles, Jobert struggled with his right arm hanging limp.

'Stay down, Jobert,' Koranski said, as his Poles swept up the French sabres and threw them across the room.

By sliding lance hafts through the panniers' flaps, the Poles lifted both panniers.

Koranski's fleshy skull hung to one side as he considered Jobert. 'Consider the horses paid in full, Jobert. They are all yours.'

'That is not Turkish gold.' Jobert shuffled on side and cradled his throbbing right wrist. 'That is French gold. You are stealing from me, Koranski.'

'You are nobody, Jobert, and this ...' Koranski said as he slapped the leather saddle bags, 'this is money lying on the ground.'

Chapter Sixteen

Jobert struggled to his knees, as Koranski and his spearmen vacated the apartment. Jobert's face ached and his left eyelid would not open. He probed his mouth with his fingers and removed his dentures.

Across the bedroom, Koschak lay on his back, his face smeared with blood.

Jobert crawled to Koschak's side. 'Do you want to sit or lie on your cot?' Jobert's hand hovered over Koschak's left ear. 'You have a scalp laceration. I will fetch Marsden.'

Koschak writhed. 'Not that poisonous prick. Duque. Fetch Duque.'

The door creaked open and Zenari entered, supported on Marsden's arm. Both Zenari and Marsden mouth's hung slack at the state of the overturned beds and the injured Jobert and Koschak.

'Excuse me, gentlemen,' Marsden spoke to others in the main dining room, 'your assistance is needed.'

Duque, Fazio and Moench entered the dormitory and froze.

'What happened?' Duque asked.

Koschak looked bitter. 'Those bastard Poles.'

Jobert hung his head. 'We have been robbed.'

'Did they take—' Duque rushed from the room.

'Duque, wait!' Jobert called. 'Where is he going?'

Marsden lowered Zenari onto his cot, unlatched one of his medicine chests besides Zenari's bed and turned to Koschak. 'May I attend to you, Master?'

Koschak looked at Jobert in resignation. 'It is not so much my head, as my ribs. I think they are broken.'

Placing a cotton dressing over the laceration, Marsden turned to Moench. 'Would you put pressure on the wound, please, Master?' As Moench knelt beside Koschak and held the dressing firm, Marsden lifted Koschak's arms above his head and began to palpate Koschak's chest.

Moench was ashen. 'Have we lost all our money, sir?'

Fazio seethed. 'How do we pay to get home?'

Koschak lifted his head so Marsden could strap it. 'Prepare for a long walk.'

Moench slumped back. 'A hungry walk.'

Koschak nudged Moench. 'Our journey home will be paid by you, lad, satisfying the ladies of Moldavia, Wallacia and Serbia.'

Moench turned to Jobert. 'Do we leave tomorrow, sir?'

'After a flogging with spear staffs, Moench,' Koschak winced, 'perhaps one day's rest.'

Jobert sat on the edge of his cot nursing his left arm. 'Now is not the time for rest. I must retrieve this situation.'

'Retrieve?' Fazio coughed. 'We have lost our gold, sir.'

'How much do you have in your purse?' Moench asked.

'Ten louis,' Jobert said. 'I did not have a chance to take another purse. Do not tell anyone of the theft. The town is only half paid.'

Fazio pressed his fingertips together under his nose. 'How will we pay?'

Colour flooded Moench's cheeks. 'Our first concern is not Sevalnev. Our first concern is ourselves.'

'No, lads,' Jobert held up a palm, 'our first concern is our mares. Sevalnev's goodwill is key to our safe departure. I have paid forty coins so far, which covers labour and halters. I have ten coins remaining which will pay for rope. What remains outstanding is thirty louis for Sevalnev's fee and the fee to lease the town.'

Koschak groaned as Marsden rolled him onto his cot. 'Perhaps Sevalnev goes without.'

'Perhaps,' Jobert said.

'Master?' Marsden looked towards the door then peered intently at Jobert. 'Suceava, Master, is just four days away and costs nothing. Place yourselves at the mercy of the Austrian Governor there. A European and a gentleman.'

Moench glanced at Fazio. 'Why not, sir?'

'You gave your word, Master.' Marsden's lips barely moved as he whispered. 'I have kept mine.'

Koschak glowered from under the bandages wrapping his hairline. 'Sir, what have you promised this slimy prick? He poisoned us on the ride north. He is an Ottoman spy. Why is he here?'

'Lads, stay sharp.' Jobert grunted to sit comfortably on the edge of his cot. 'Possibly summer storms, and the consequent mud, will soon be upon us. We remain fixed on preparing these mares to march south. Marsden, Zenari looks pale. Would you attend to him? Gentlemen, let us give Zenari his peace.'

Entering the main room, Jobert closed the dormitory door behind him. 'Moench and Fazio, a quiet meal in our rooms is in order.' Jobert waved a finger towards Koschak's bandages. 'Would you collect some dinner for us all, please?'

Duque entered as Moench and Fazio departed.

'Where did you go?' Jobert asked.

Duque gave a rare enigmatic smile. 'All is good.'

Jobert leant over the table and motioned for Koschak and Duque to come closer. 'Koschak, I have need of you.' Jobert glanced at the closed bedroom door. 'I need you take Marsden to Suceava. And then onto Paris.'

Koschak's face contorted with anger. 'You want me to save the prick who poisoned us to the point our arses bled? Fuck off … sir.'

Duque inserted a stiff hand in front of Koschak. 'Aid Marsden's escape? You cannot be serious, André. There is already a long list of reasons to have us executed. Why add aiding a dragoman's slave to escape to the score?'

'This is not an act of honour, Duque.' Koschak's lips crimped as he forced himself to whisper. 'There has been an exchange. Is this your bond to Marsden, sir?' Koschak looked at Duque. 'Did you know of this?'

'No.' Duque could not disguise his guilt.

'Then you can fuck off too.' Koschak flexed his aching knuckles. 'Just Marsden and I? When?'

'Under the cover of these coming storms?' Duque said.

'Soon.' Jobert laid his hand on Koschak's shoulder. 'Very soon. Duque, prepare at least four of our horses and portmanteaus in the Keep's stables.'

Koschak slanted his cheek to Duque. 'Is that why you are always dashing to check something in the stables?'

'I have a further request, old friend.' Jobert grinned at Koschak's murderous look. 'Tomorrow, Otal will check his vedettes to the west towards Suceava. I need you to ride with him as a reconnaissance.'

'I can barely put weight on my ankle, and you want—'

Jobert winked. 'You do not need an ankle to ride.'

'This day just gets better and better.' Koschak's mouth hung slack. 'Tomorrow?'

Jobert nodded. 'Otal's patrol is a day's ride from Serpenaçi. When you depart with Marsden, the sipahi will not expect riders approaching them from behind. Then you have three days clear ride for Austrian territory.'

'Take my horse,' Duque said, 'so that yours stays rested until needed.'

Jobert smiled. 'You can always practice your jumping and lance techniques.'

Koschak's face soured. 'With a split loaf, broken ribs and a busted ankle. Piss off.'

Jobert gave Koschak's shoulder a gentle squeeze. 'If a prick like you cannot do it, who can?'

Koschak snorted. 'I am going to regret that fucking comment.'

The next morning, the fifth day of Jobert's plan, from the river mist enclosing the town in the twilight before the dawn, waterfowl nesting within the Bludovaţ's upper and lower ponds awoke with squeaks and honks.

In that half-light, as women threw armfuls of fodder into the mangers for the loose mares, Jobert, Duque, Fazio and Moench staked out two horse lines. One line along the street that ran from the Balti Gate to the Sepulchre Gate, and one running from the Iasi Gate to the mosque.

Through the nickering mares, Otal and Koschak arrived.

Jobert inspected the Cricket's high head and extended stride. 'Despite seven hours at the trot for four days in a row, and yet he prances to undertake today's journey.' Jobert nodded at Duque. 'We need this bloodstock in our army.'

Otal frowned at Jobert's black eye. 'You, too. Who?'

'No one.'

'Koranski?'

Jobert shuffled. 'No.'

'He has taken your gold.'

'Sevalnev does not know yet.'

Otal downturned mouth caused the tips of his moustache to poke far beyond his chin. 'The prophet — peace be upon him — teaches us that God does not burden a man with more than he can bear.'

'I would appreciate if God might lighten the load ever so slightly.'

'God did not place the load upon you, Jobert. You did. It is for you to relieve yourself of your burden.' Otal gathered his reins. 'Do you not need Koschak for training horses?'

'We are both exhausted. I need him to take a day's rest?'

Otal peered at Koschak. 'Hard riding for six hours? Why not a hot bath, a good lunch and a long sleep.'

Koschak straightened stiffly in the saddle. 'I would prefer fresh air and a little exercise, sir.'

'You are aware, Jobert,' Otal said, 'today only the Christians are available to assist with horses.'

'What? Why?'

'This morning the imam will be blessing the culls to be slaughtered and then from midday the faithful will attend congregation.' Otal shrugged and rode on.

Koschak grimaced at Jobert's farewell nod before following Otal.

At breakfast on the Keep's upper ramparts, Jobert rolled his wrist gingerly as he washed the horse-rope grime from his hands. If only he could rinse the ache from his battered forearms.

Sevalnev frowned at Jobert's welts. 'I have just been told the Poles have gone. I heard that they attacked you. Why?'

'I need to adjust the plan,' Jobert spooned a fried egg onto his hummus. 'Each day for the next four days we will train one hundred mares a day. As we train so we demonstrate to the best horsemen, amongst your townsmen, how we wish the horses to be handled. Ten of the culls will be slaughtered today for both fresh meat this evening and hides for plaiting further halters and leads tomorrow.'

Sevalnev's pinks lips squeezed in consternation. 'The last four days have been too much. Another four is intolerable. Great anger ferments in the town, Jobert, at how the horses devour our forage, the constant need to fetch water is draining the ponds. Our ruined gardens. The smell. The noise.'

Jobert looked to the dull western sky. 'The coming storm will sluice the town of horse piss.'

'Impact of rain is water, yes, but it is also but mud and no work.'

'Come now, Sevalnev. Twelve hours of daylight to tie up one hundred horses in the Muslim quarter by tonight. We are so close to completing and departing. And you being paid.'

Through the long day, eight mares were driven into the octagonal enclosure erected within the church's forecourt.

Jobert, Fazio and Moench would lift their energies and encourage the trapped mares to trot around the enclosure in a clockwise direction. As they flowed past his central position, Duque swung a lasso noose and swept it onto a passing head. As Duque looped each mare's neck, Jobert smirked at an earlier comment of Otal's. 'Lasso is an Arabic word, gifted by the Moors of Spain to Europe.'

Upon the noose slipping fast around the neck, the horse would immediately gallop forward and kick-out. Three Moldavian offsiders would anchor the rope with Duque. In not more than half the enclosure the horse would choke on the fastening noose and be pulled to face Duque.

So as not to present a threat, Jobert stepped slowly towards the nervous horse, along the rope line, with his energy diminished, his shoulders hunched, and head lowered. Once beside the quivering horse, as he crooned a soothing mumble, he offered his knuckles for the horse to sniff. Taking his time, Jobert rubbed the horse's neck and cheek and loosened the quick-slip noose around the throat. He offered the lead rope and halter for the mare to smell. The horse arched its neck to observe, listen to and scent the plaited tangles. Jobert rubbed the lead rope over the horse's mane, the noseband over the nostrils and the pollband behind the ears, before fastening the halter with a simple knot fastened behind the left, or nearside, eye. Jobert then removed the lasso loop over the ears and down the face.

With a final rub, Jobert passed the lead rope to Moench. As Jobert did so, Duque lassoed another mare, and Jobert took a halter from a Moldavian assistant and, without fuss, dust or turmoil, repeated the haltering process.

With the same non-threatening slouched posture, Moench squeezed gentle pressure down the lead rope, which transferred into the halter, to turn the mare's head and neck. With pressure-release encouragement, the horse would yield its hindquarters away from Moench. With the hind feet having stepped away from Moench, the fore feet could step tentatively towards him. Moench rewarded the horse's bravery with a rub, before repeating the dance. Once the horse found it could make Moench's energies subside by stepping towards him, the horse took more confident steps to win the game. Following a rub and muttered encouragement, Moench swapped to the offside and repeated the process. Once the horse demonstrated it could follow the suggestion of the lead rope, Moench passed the lead to Fazio before taking the next haltered horse from Jobert.

Fazio, also stooped and crooning, would lead the mare to the side of the enclosure where the Serpenaçi farrier waited with the hoof brands. As the numerals of the hoof brand was burnt into the hoof wall of the nearside forehoof, although feeling no pain at the procedure, the horse would recoil in surprise at the smoke and sizzle.

Fazio then led the mare to an erect post within the enclosure. A dally of lead rope was slipped around the pole to simulate being tied to a fixed point. While Fazio rubbed the horse's neck and back, a Moldavian offsider monitored the lead rope. If the horse pulled back suddenly, the lead rope's loop tightened around the post, but the loop around the post slid slightly so the tightening was not jarring. Reacting against the discomfort of the halter's pressure behind its ears, the horse stepped forward. In that moment, the horse found the halter loosen and rubbing resume.

With a nod and final rub, Fazio allowed a pair of Moldavians to lead the mare out of the enclosure, before taking another horse from Moench.

The mare and her handlers would then walk the streets for the next hour, mumbling and rubbing as they went, only stopping to tie to posts for short time, before securing the mare to the horse line, alongside the seven other mares with whom she started the hour within the enclosure.

Each and every hour, at eight horses an hour, for twelve hours without break, Jobert, Duque, Moench and Fazio repeated the process. Jobert's body baulked with pain from the beating he had received the evening before. Jobert coughed on the pall of dust in the church forecourt, pulverised by three days of drumming hooves. At sunset, Jobert handed his one hundredth mare for the day to Moench.

That evening, the mosque's lilting call blended with the chirps of frogs and the streaks of orange sunset.

As Jobert hobbled along the horse lines, those horses that had been led to the water troughs, whinnied as they returned to their mates. Each mare, drooping with sleep following an intense day of emotional exhaustion, lay down on her belly with her front feet tucked under her chest.

Jobert tested the quick-release slip knots on the horse line, where one end of the knotted lead rope leading to the halter remained firm, while the other end, if pulled by a horseman, would easily slide undone. Working his way quietly between each mare, rubbing gently along the ribs and rumps of each horse, he admired the hard work of the day and the quality of the horses. The first of his one hundred pretty mares ready for their journey to the unimaginably distant Loire valley.

As the humid evening air pressed down upon dinner in the Keep's Hall, Jobert sniffed at the shift from horse dust to pungent smoke. 'Apart from evening cooking fires, Sevalnev, what else is burning?'

'Tonight, Jobert, the whole town roasts. The slaughter of ten culls today has yielded over three thousand kilograms of horse meat. That is five kilograms of meat for every man, woman and child in Serpenaçi. People are roasting for the coming week and smoking the excess. It will be too much for the town to bear to butcher another ten culls tomorrow.'

'Ten carcasses will yield me fifty rawhide halters. If you want me and my horses to leave your town, then start eating.' Jobert turned to Fazio gnawing on his roast horse steak. 'How many halters do we need to plait tonight?'

Fazio grimaced. 'Another fifty.'

Moench moaned.

Having returned from Otal's inspection of the western patrols,

Koschak arched his back in discomfort, as he poked at his meat and rice.

Jobert toecap nudged Koschak's boot. 'Satisfied with what you saw?'

Koschak's gaze roamed for nearby eavesdroppers. 'If I had to do it at night ...' He nodded, before his red-rimmed eyes slid to Jobert. 'And you? You good?'

No. 'Yes.'

'Bullshit.'

'Yes, I am sore.' Jobert took a hunk of meat from the central platter and placed it on Koschak's flatbread. 'But, to walk along tonight's horse lines felt so good. We are so close to going home.'

Chapter Seventeen

The morning was distinctly cold. A dirty wind raced through the lanes and rattled the shutters, informing the populace of the coming storm. Tipping his hat brim at the stinging grit, Jobert limped amongst the horses on the horse line. Ears flicked and eyes rolled back to him as each mare monitored his slow hand slide along their skin.

A week had passed since Jobert first rode through these horses in the wide valley. *So close now.* To roll his shoulder and caress the horses flared his injuries from the beating received the night before last and the fatigue from the gruelling twelve-hour day yesterday. As their fur quivered at his touch in the wind, the mares' warmth bolstered Jobert as he considered the daunting effort required to complete the herd's training. *How badly do I want this?*

A smart walking rhythm announced Otal, astride the Cricket, on his way to the sipahi screen. 'According to your original plan, Jobert, today would have been the last day of training.'

'The townsfolk are not horsemen. They are too slow. Too rough.' Jobert indicated the tethered mares with pride. 'We have one hundred mares secured. With available halters, we should tie up another one hundred by this evening.'

'*Inshallah*.' Otal patted his gelding's neck. 'This is not a blessing that these horses are here. That you are here. When do you now plan to depart?'

'Tomorrow and the day after will complete the training. We would depart for Iasi three days from today. Your djelli from Balti must be close. Any news?'

'The earliest they could arrive is tomorrow evening. Why? Do Cossacks haunt your dreams?'

Jobert sniffed. 'I have fought them. They were not that impressive.'

Otal recoiled. 'You genuinely surprise me, Jobert. Where have you fought Cossacks?'

'Does it matter?'

'You claim you have crossed blades with Cossacks. Where?'

'Italy,' Jobert said.

'Italy?'

'When Suvorov marched a Russian army across the Alps two years ago.'

'Hah!' Otal flicked up his fingers. 'You think the Tsar would waste his best cavalry on Switzerland? Cossacks come in many different forms. You probably fought Christian Latvians. Koranski and his Poles are Christian Cossacks from Ukraine. Those they stole the horses from are Muslim Cossacks from Crimea.' Otal leant forward on his pommel. 'They would find the hills and gardens of Italy unfamiliar. Not so here. This is their country. While we Turks are tied to our mountains, our farms and villages, a Cossack's country is his horse. He is rooted to his saddle as a tree is to the earth.' Otal sneered, evidently pleased with his rebuttal of Jobert's prowess. 'Anyway, who will lead your horses south? The men of Serpenaçi? This week alone impacts on their summer harvest.'

'I do not know.' Jobert's face twisted with the conundrum. 'Perhaps negotiate with Sevalnev—'

Otal shot Jobert a withering look. 'Negotiate with what? You have lost all your—'

A shout.

Metal alarms clanged from the ramparts above the gates.

A scream.

'To the Keep, Jobert,' Otal shouted. 'Get up behind!'

Doubling Otal and Jobert, the Cricket trotted from the horse lines, across the Caesars Bridge and into the Keep. Dismounting stiffly, Jobert pressed his hurting body to follow Otal and climb the three storeys of stairs to join Sevalnev on the Keep's battlements. As they scanned the orchard perimeter, the westerly breeze tugged on banners and capes.

Jobert tipped his head to not lose his hat. 'Sevalnev, do you expect a storm today?'

'A Carpathian wind announces a Crimean threat.' Sevalnev turned to the cloud-covered sunrise. 'The storm will engulf us from the east.'

A horn blew from beyond the Suceava Gate.

From the gloom, the outlines of sheepskin-wrapped horsemen appeared at every gate.

'Cossacks?' Sevalnev asked.

'No, look.' Otal pointed. 'Banners.'

Bitterness rose in Jobert's throat. 'What do those bastard Poles want now?'

'Not Poles, Jobert,' Otal said. 'Uhlans. Look! There is the jackal, Tétény, under his banner.'

Jobert lifted an eyebrow in inquiry. 'How did Tétény's hundred horsemen slip by your screen?'

Otal's shoulders slouched. 'They must have ... found my patrols.'

Some of the horsemen emerged from the groves, dismounted and erected lance tripods. Lashed to mounted guards stumbled three hunched Turks. Two corpses were thrown down behind Tétény's mount.

Otal gripped the stone battlements.

'Which of your patrols?' Jobert asked.

'The southwest patrol. Koschak and I were with them yesterday morning.'

Jobert took hold of Otal's elbow. 'Then we should speak to the jackal before he tears into his catch.'

Jobert, Otal and Sevalnev descended, mounted and rode out through the Suceava Gate towards Tétény, his raiders and his prisoners.

The skin around Tétény's mad eyes rippled, as if he perceived something hellish. 'Give me Koranski, Otal Alaybey.'

'I do not have Koranski.' Otal's cheeks warped into a heartless smile. 'But I see Koranski cooled your son's hot head.'

Tétény's throat tightened into sinewy cords. 'Do not provoke my vengeance, Turk.'

Jobert held up his hand and nodded towards the prisoners. 'Tétény, do these Turks no further harm.'

Tétény's eyes rolled to focus on Jobert. 'Otal is my enemy, France. He understands how things are here.'

'There is an opportunity for trade.' Jobert raised both palms in placation. 'Let us talk.'

'What do you have to bargain with, France? Gold?'

Jobert's posture softened. 'Something of greater value to you. Cossack brood mares. Each mare worth fifty pieces of gold.'

Tétény bared his teeth. 'Speak, France.'

Otal pivoted to Jobert. 'Cease your negotiations, Jobert. These dogs are not entering Serpenaçi.'

'If I employ them, they are.'

'No, they will not enter,' Sevalnev said. 'They can train your horses outside my walls.'

'Wake up! Both of you.' Jobert leant in his saddle to address both Sevalnev and Otal. 'Otal, do you want your men returned? Do you want me gone?' Otal crept his thoughts to the kneeling sipahi. 'Sevalnev, do you want those horses gone? Do you want to be paid? Then allow Tétény's men entry today, and we can all depart tomorrow.'

Otal glowered as he shifted in the saddle and gritted his teeth.

'Tétény, I have four hundred Crimean brood mares within Serpenaçi,' Jobert said. 'I need to lead them to the port of Izmail. One hundred have been started under halter. I will pay one hundred mares for one hundred of your men to spend one day starting the remainder under halter and six days leading the mares as far as Iasi.'

Tétény squeezed his reins. 'One hundred and fifty mares.'

'Hah! I will only pay one hundred and fifty mares if you lead the herd all the way to Izmail.'

'I will need men to secure the mares I have earned,' Tétény said. 'Sixty men for the seven days to Iasi.'

Jobert sniffed at the counteroffer. 'Leave your mares here and pick them up on your return. Eighty men to take three hundred mares to Iasi. A week's work will earn you one hundred brood mares. Train two hundred today. I have fresh kills for greenhide and tonight a feast of fresh roast horse meat. Depart tomorrow and I shall cut out one hundred mares and run them out the Iasi Gate to your men.'

'No, send them through the Suceava Gate.'

'No. The Iasi Gate. Once my horses are caught, haltered and tethered.'

Tétény's jaw bunched in calculation. 'Perhaps I might take all the horses.'

Otal flicked his reins onto the Cricket's withers. 'Ah, his true colours emerge. You are truly an idiot, Jobert, to enter into an agreement with this maggot. You will lose your life and your herd before Iasi.'

Jobert folded his arms. 'You know Begnzarov has crossed the Dniester.' Tétény winced at the name. 'He hunts for the herd. To be clear of Begnzarov, you would have a five-day ride to drive a herd of four hundred horses.'

'What protects us from Begnzarov on the road to Iasi?' Tétény asked.

Jobert rolled his head with indifference. 'Tomorrow we are expecting an escort of djelli from Balti to escort the herd to Iasi.'

'Two hundred horses in one day?' Tétény looked upward to the roiling clouds. 'I do not think so, Jobert.'

'Eighty men in ten hours? A team of four men to rope, halter and lead one horse every hour. I think so, Tétény.'

Tétény looked at the Turkish dead and prisoners and then to Otal. 'So, I have your word, Otal Alaybey, that I enter Serpenaçi under a truce?'

Sevalnev raised a stiff finger. 'It is my word that matters here, Tétény. Otal and Jobert have no troops here. My militia obey me. Enter dismounted, wearing only your swords. No bows, firearms or lances.' Sevalnev checked for any opposition from Otal. 'Perhaps bring your men into the sanctity of the true church and receive the Lord's blessing on your work. Your men will be accommodated in the church. You, Tétény, will be my guest in my hall. You will not be harmed. You have my word.'

Otal sighed in agitation then formalised the arrangement with a slow bow of his head.

With a guffaw, Tétény turned back to address his warriors.

The prisoners were unlashed from the uhlans' saddle bows and kicked towards the corpses.

Otal nodded to his wounded men. 'I must depart now for the eastern screen.'

'I will fetch Marsden for your wounded,' Jobert said.

'And I will fetch the imam for your fallen martyrs,' Sevalnev said.

With a grunt and a nod to his sipahi, Otal trotted the Cricket to Suceava Gate.

Sevalnev's hand shot out and grasped Jobert's sleeve. 'I am outraged Tétény's worms are within my walls.' Sevalnev tugged at Jobert's arm for emphasis. 'But I will pay this price, Jobert, to rid my town of you and your cursed horses.'

Jobert returned to the Keep and entered the rooms allotted to him and his men.

Marsden squatted by Zenari's bed, placing engorged leeches into a ceramic bowl with a pair of forceps. Zenari lay on his back, his eyes shut, his face taut as if concentrating.

'The uhlans are at the Suceava Gate,' Jobert said. 'They have three of Otal's sipahi. The Turks are wounded and require your immediate attention.'

'Yes, Master.' Marsden began to re-stock his medical chest.

Jobert motioned Marsden aside. 'With the uhlans here, the road to the west is open.' Jobert reached into his tailcoat and passed an envelope to Marsden. 'The storm this evening may provide cover.'

'Tonight!' Marsden gawped in surprise. 'How do I ...' He sought an explanation from the envelope.

'Duque has horses, capes and portmanteaus ready. Koschak will escort you to Paris.'

Marsden face buckled to comprehend. 'That explains his choice to ride in such pain yesterday.' To stabilise his fear, Marsden gripped the envelope with two hands. 'I have not sat a horse in six years. Who is Mademoiselle Chauvel?'

'My cousin.'

Marsden panted through trembling lips.

'Once we are together in Paris ...' Jobert gripped Masden's shoulder. 'Come, now. You have wounded and I have three hundred horses to catch.'

With twenty men minding the uhlans' horses outside the Suceava Gate, Tétény and eighty of his disarmed warriors gathered at the round yard set up on the church forecourt.

Jobert, Duque, Fazio and Moench demonstrated their method from yesterday to the assembled uhlans. Duque, supported by a few Moldavians, roped a mare. Jobert fitted her halter. Moench yielded her to follow. Fazio introduced her to tying to a post and led her to have her hoof branded. A pair of Moldavians then led her away to walk around the town before attaching her to the horse line.

'All this slouching, rubbing and mumbling.' Tétény shuffled with unease. 'You treat your horses too gently, Jobert.'

'To treat a horse harshly only teaches it to fear you. In the heat of battle, such a terrified mount would baulk at each command in terror of punishment. Surely, you would not reward your enemy such an advantage. For in that moment of resistance by the horse, you enemy seizes the advantage and lands his blow. Every warrior relies on a partner that immediately complies.'

Tétény sneered. 'The French cavalry must be mounted on lambs.'

With his hands on his hips, Jobert faced Tétény. 'It was upon those lambs, we French emptied uhlan saddles in Lombardy with ease.'

'Croatian saddles.' Tétény spat. 'Not Transylvanian.'

The wind had increased through the day, whipping dust and dried horse dung along the lanes of Serpenaçi. The uhlans' and Moldavians' work with the mares raced against the gathering storm. Dividing into twenty teams of four, the uhlans caught, haltered and branded one mare every half-hour.

The four horse lines were established around the major streets of Serpenaçi. Two led from Sepulchre Gate to Balti Gate and to Caesar Gate. Another two lines were strung from the Mosque to Al-Aqsa Gate and towards Iasi Gate. The one hundred mares trained the previous day, and had spent the night tethered, were distributed along all the lines. They proved to be settled companions to the new arrivals.

With uhlan assistance, by late afternoon, three hundred horses stood captive.

As was Serpenaçi captive to the approaching storm. The town cowered, pinned beneath a back-green volcano of cloud within which lightning flared in its guts.

The gusts brought fat rain drops as Jobert, Koschak, Duque, Fazio and Moench walked the horse lines. They checked the security of halter leads, as well as how the lines themselves were anchored to posts, cart axles and bracing beams that supported the fortress' walls.

As they moved, the men rubbed the horses' shoulders, backs and rumps. Hunkering against the wind, the mares tucked their tails, lowered the heads and touched each other's nostrils for reassurance.

Close to the Sepulchre Gate, a woman sailed on the gusts towards Moench, her skirt and shawl tight against her thighs and shoulders. She reached under her flapping shawl and passed Moench a bundle, before her billowing clothes sailed her away down a lane.

'Peaches tonight, gentlemen.' Moench grinned at his arms full of fruit, as Jobert and the others huddled about him. 'Home tomorrow.'

'Tonight, lads, we will run a piquet on the horse lines,' Jobert said, shielding his bitten peach from the dust eddies, 'as we need to do until we reach Izmail.'

'How far to Izmail, sir?' Fazio asked.

'One week to Iasi, and then two more until the port.'

Fazio beamed his juice-flecked moustache. 'Last night of a full belly and a dry bed.'

'Yes, lads,' Jobert said, 'this time tomorrow night we will camp on the Iasi road. But now, Fazio and Moench, return to the Keep, find us all dinner and fetch out your capes for your shift tonight. Koschak, Duque and I will walk the horses in the Muslim quarter.'

As Fazio and Moench returned towards the Caesars Gate, Jobert pulled his tailcoat tight about him and faced Koschak and Duque. 'The road west is clear of uhlans and covered by this storm.' Jobert cocked his hat brim towards Koschak. 'Did you rest today?'

Koschak squinted up at the monstrous thunderhead and gave a quick nod.

'You go tonight?' Duque raised his eyebrows. 'Then I should check your horses.'

'And you tomorrow, my friend.' Koschak gave Duque's back a solid slap of thanks as Duque too departed for the Keep.

Koschak's green eyes pierced Jobert. 'What will you do to stop the uhlans stealing the mares on your three-week walk south?'

'Fill the pricks hands with lead ropes, and they will be too exhausted to steal.' Jobert gripped Koschak's shoulder. 'That is my challenge. Your challenge is to steal a day's march by night in a storm.'

Koschak winced as he straightened. 'If pricks like us ... eh?'

Chapter Eighteen

That evening, curtains of rain lashed Jobert and Koschak from the darkness above. From the blackness beneath Caesars Bridge's trestles, the Bludovaţ Stream gargled and spat white foam. The bridge's planking was scraped by unseen branches and slapped by clumps of spinning leaf litter. Lightening flared grey over the morose shingled roofs. Between the groans of thunder, the melodic call to prayer rose and fell.

In the Caesars Bridge gatehouse, a number of caped sipahi, of which Otal was one, peered into the splattering glooms to assess the weather's intensity.

Jobert pinched at the tip of his flapping cape in the wind. 'We are inspecting the horse lines. You?'

'Evening prayer, of course,' Otal said.

'I will press on and check the mares in the Muslim quarter,' Koschak said, and followed Otal skipping the rivulets in the downpour.

In the torrential rain, from Caesars Gate to the Sepulchre Gate, and then around the corner to the Balti Gate, one hundred and fifty mares slumped with their heads hanging low. They were exhausted from their training and being underfed for four days locked in the town. Jobert took his time walking down the line, mumbling assurances as he tested the quick-release slip knots on the central line and halter knots on each horses' cheek with rain-numb fingers. He stepped slowly around the hindquarters of each horse, rubbing its back and loins, feeling for any sudden tension in the muscles to indicate a forthcoming kick.

The night sky exploded as lightning struck the Ferry Tower.

The horses screamed and reared.

The central horse line surged.

The jolt pitched Jobert headlong into the mud. He tucked into a ball as front hooves thrashed around him.

Animals tugged and slipped, tripped and rolled.

Halters snapped.

The wooden end piquets tugged loose.

Pressure from both ends of the line caused the horses to pull back and forward.

Jobert attempted to cross through the mashing horse bodies away from the sawing central line to the side of the street.

The tug-of-war was being won by those horses closest to the Balti Gate.

Snagged in the line, Jobert grabbed at the straining lead ropes as horses' heads yielded to the direction of travel towards the Balti Gate. He gripped the mane of a horse beside him to pull him forward. If she stopped, he would duck under her neck to the outside of the throng.

The light of the spluttering torches of the Balti Gate raced nearer. Guards bellowed at the horses.

Jobert dug his heels into the squelch beneath. 'Close the fucking gates!'

Horses on the outside of the right-bending central line raced for the opening. Horses on the left, rammed into the sides of the gatehouse. In terror, the mares' eyes rolled white in the lightening.

Jobert was crushed amongst their bodies. He felt his ribs buckling.

He fell to his knees.

Battered by hooves, he scrambled for the gap of the opened gate against the wall.

Cringing in a crevice, Jobert watched in dismay as horses stumbled and raced into the darkness beyond the gate. He scrambled towards the guards on the street level who had raised the internal locking bar. 'Why was the gate opened?' Jobert screamed against the rain filling his mouth.

'*Dikaletus Pasha vine!*' The guardsmen grabbed and reefed Jobert aside, as a group of six spear-armed men pushed into the entrance.

One caped figure started yelling at the guards. 'Is that you, my dear Jobert?' Dikaletus slapped Jobert's aching chest. 'Where is Otal Alaybey?'

Under the shelter of the gate's arch, the rain thrashed against the timber walls. 'In the mosque,' Jobert said. 'Where are the two hundred djelli?'

'I have only an escort of twenty,' Dikaletus said. 'No more can be spared. The ferry cable is broken. The Prut cannot be swum by horse. My men shelter on the north bank.'

On the way to the mosque, Jobert found Koschak shielded from the rain within the Al-Aqsa Gate. Jobert gripped Koschak's lapels as Dikaletus shouldered his way through the rain to the mosque. 'Lightening has spooked the mares in the Christian quarter. They have pulled out their piquets and bolted through the Balti Gate.'

'Ah, fuck!' Koschak put his fingertips to his temples. 'Find them? Bring them in? Cut them loose?'

'No,' Jobert said, 'Come with me to the mosque and find out what news Dikaletus brings.'

Jobert and Koschak caught up with Dikaletus at the entry foyer to the mosque.

'Remove your boots and stockings.' Dikaletus wiggled his fingers towards stacks of capes and neatly paired shoes. 'Your wet jacket. Wash your hands and feet.'

Jobert looked down at his saturated clothing and wrinkled fingertips. 'I am already washed.'

Jobert swept back his dripping hair as he entered the spacious room. Above, timber beams, carved with geometric patterns, lifted the mosque's ceiling. Below, lattice screens separated areas within the room. Candles, clustered like fruit on summer's boughs, spread a calm warmth. Between the regular spacing of worn patches, Jobert's bare feet sank into the intricate weave of the carpet-lined floor. A tall finely turned pulpit rose at the front of the rectangular room.

Otal bowed to Dikaletus, touching his fingers to his forehead and heart. '*Assalamu alaykum*, Dikaletus Pasha.'

'*Wai alaykum assalam*, Otal Alaybey,' Dikaletus performed the elegant greeting. 'Begnzarov is upon us.'

'How long do we have?' Jobert asked.

'Begnzarov's main column has been identified east of Balti,' Dikaletus said. 'The bulk of the djelli have been sent to engage them. Otal, as the Hospodar's most senior cavalry officer, you are recalled from here to take command of the force. Recall your sipahi. Gather in Hetman Koranski's warriors. You return with me at dawn.'

Otal glanced with derision at the puddle soaking the carpet beneath Dikaletus, Jobert and Koschak. 'I am unaware of Koranski's location. He has caused an incident here in Serpenaçi and withdrawn, I can only assume, north. But Tétény is here.'

'Tétény!' Dikaletus' moustache flared. 'Here?'

'At the request of the Hospodar's esteemed French guest, I currently accommodate one hundred uhlans within the walls of Serpenaçi, barracked in the church and gorging on the Hospodar's horses?'

Dikaletus squinted in confusion. 'Eating horses?'

'Jobert has taken it upon himself to trade the Hospodar's stock.'

Dikaletus' bare feet squelched as he turned to Jobert. 'What? How? You have started a war, Jobert.'

'Jobert has taken it upon himself to divide the herd.' Otal inclined his head and clasped his hands in front of his waist. 'The French will accept three hundred mares. Jobert has lavished one hundred horses each upon Koranski, Sevalnev and Tétény, and ordered fifty to be butchered for meat and hides.'

Jobert's cold clothing scraped at his stampede-bruised skin. A weariness buried him as he contemplated explaining himself to Dikaletus. 'I have an arrangement for Tétény's men to lead the horses to Iasi at dawn.'

Dikaletus searched the carpet for clarity. 'Jobert, you have no authority to distribute ... and you believe that barbarian will honour your agreement. You are a fool, Jobert. I must speak to Sevalnev.'

Otal made a soft clap. 'And I must recall my western patrol.'

Jobert jerked at the opportunity within Otal's handclap. 'Allow Koschak to take your message. He rode out to them yesterday.'

'Good.' Dikaletus' finger swept up to regain supremacy. 'Koschak, before you depart, fetch Boyar Sevalnev, the Tétény creature ... and Zenari ... and my Marsden. We shall meet in the Boyar's Hall.'

Jobert retreated across the carpet with Koschak towards the mosque's entry. 'Tonight is the night to fly. Are you ...'

Koschak grimaced. 'I feel confident as far as the sipahi patrol.'

'Which Tétény has … place Marsden on my horse.' Jobert poked Koschak's chest. 'You take the Cricket.'

Koschak whistled. 'It will make my end swift if I am caught.'

'On the contrary. All the greater incentive to ride hard. It is a few short weeks to Michelle's. I will be back soon. Leave word. In Paris, at the farm, and with Raive in Italy.'

Both men gritted their jaws at this farewell. A curt nod was exchanged between them both, then they bound each other in a tight hug, fingers gripping deep into muscle. 'Now go!'

Within the hour, in a dry jacket, Jobert entered the hall with Zenari, arriving just behind Tétény and an escort of six Moldavian militiamen.

Dikaletus raised his nose to the doorway behind. 'Ah, my dear Zenari, you are well?'

Zenari wobbled in uncertainty. He was pale, wasted and dishevelled. He stammered an incomprehensible response.

Within the hall, Sevalnev threw his fur-clad arms in the air. 'Must this abomination be displayed in my hall?'

On the lance from Dikaletus' djelli escort, rocked the twisted grey face of a once-handsome youth. The long thick lashes. His feathery moustache. Topknot plastered with blood. The sinews and blue veins trailed from a slim tanned throat.

Tétény's wild eyes rolled at the grotesque head, then spat onto the hall's flagstones. 'Cossack.'

With his little finger extended Dikaletus swished a black arrow with tattered fletches. 'Begnzarov comes.'

Jobert peered with interest as the slim projectile. 'It is the same as we found in the massacred village?'

'It is. Where is my kol, Jobert?'

'He was not with Zenari,' Jobert said. 'He must be with the wounded sipahi. I have sent one of my men to fetch him.'

'Wounded sipahi? Who wounded them?'

Jobert glanced at Tétény.

Dikaletus drew himself up. 'And Otal has not removed your head?'

Otal stabbed his fingers at the decapitated head. 'That will soon be you, Tétény.'

'What is your plan, Otal Alaybey?' Sevalnev asked.

Otal breathed deeply. 'Begnzarov's warband lies southeast of Balti. The djelli are concentrating there. I ride east at dawn to command them in battle.'

Sevalnev pink lips squeezed together. 'You will leave us without early warning?'

Otal sniffed. 'There is nothing here worth my protection.' Otal flicked the back of his hand at Jobert. 'If you crave security, place your trust in Jobert's uhlans.'

Tétény's clawed fingers raked at his beard. 'I am not waiting for Begnzarov. I will take my horses south and cross the Bludovaț. We are better out there than in here.'

'Are you sure, Tétény?' Jobert asked. 'Driving one hundred horses to Suceava will take five days.'

'I will take my chances on the open steppe. Release the mares I am owed at dawn.'

'Keep your horses safe in Serpenaçi.' Jobert lifted his palms and pushed against Tétény's expanding desperation. 'Lead my horses to the garrison at Iasi. In the meantime, Otal Alaybey will have dealt with Begnzarov. You then return home to your mountains with your mares in safety. Sleep on it. We shall speak further at breakfast.'

With a snarl at the Cossack boy on the lance, Tétény departed with his militia escort.

'Otal, I smell a ruse,' Jobert said. 'We know Begnzarov has swept south to intercept the movement of his herd. He would have massacred enough villages to know the herd lies to the north. He would know of your Ottoman garrisons in Balti and

Iasi. His main body lies between both garrisons to lure you away from the north. This herd is what Begnzarov desires. Here is where he will come.'

'Not if I find the dog first.' Otal raised his finger to someone behind Jobert.

A waiting messenger dashed from the door to bow and whisper at Otal's side.

Otal stiffened and bared his teeth at Jobert. 'Curse you, Jobert! Koschak has stolen the Cricket. Marsden convinced my groom that Koschak needed the horse to take a message to recall the western patrols. Suceava Gate's commander reports the departure of two riders, leading two horses. One rider was Koschak.'

Jobert appeared confounded. 'Just as you requested in the mosque, I dispatched Koschak to the western patrol.'

'In this storm?' Otal hissed. 'On my horse?'

'The other rider?' Dikaletus asked.

'Marsden!' Otal scoffed. 'Your kol conspired to have the Cricket stolen.'

Dikaletus' mouth formed a perfect O under his red moustache. 'My Marsden? Escaped? For where?'

'Austria, obviously,' Otal said. 'The ferry is damaged, and the Prut runs too high to be swum at night. Khotyn is not their destination.'

Dikaletus' head traversed in small twitches. 'Have men been dispatched to apprehend them?'

'Who?' Otal asked. 'I have no faith in these Moldavian militiamen. Only djelli could track them on a night like this.'

Dikaletus blinked. 'But my djelli are on the other side of the Prut. They rode all day, and they must escort us both to Balti tomorrow.' Dikaletus' red moustached quivered. 'Jobert, this is unconscionable that you have stolen such property. You shall pay.'

'I was unaware of the plot.' Jobert shrugged. 'My men are

aggrieved at how we have been deceived and treated.'

'Your treatment?' Dikaletus trembled with outrage. 'Have you not been fed and accommodated? All at my personal direction.'

'As we have been robbed, assaulted and purged, all at your personal direction.'

Zenari coughed. 'Perhaps they have the Key.'

Otal and Dikaletus jerked at Zenari's hoarse whisper.

Dikaletus waved his arrow at the commanders and servants around the hall. 'Sevalnev! All of you! Leave us.'

Otal strode towards Zenari with his hands clawed to rip. 'What do you know of the Key, Zenari?'

Jobert stepped between Otal and Zenari, his finger raised in warning. 'I know Marsden rifles through our belongings on your command, Otal. Still, the Key has not been found. I deduce Dikaletus does not have it. He arranges attacks upon Zenari and me in the streets of Diraç. Our rooms are ransacked in Diraç and Vidin. We are strip searched and purged. Yet he still does not present it to the Hospodar in Bucharest. If Dikaletus does not have it, then you must, Otal Alaybey.'

'You know of the ...' Otal blinked at Zenari then back to Jobert. 'If I had the Key, I would present it to my sovereign. I do not have it.' Otal spun and threw an accusatory finger at Dikaletus. 'I shall declare that Dikaletus has stolen it and plans a coup with the Hospodar. The Hospodar will renounce any such claim. Tortured on his whereabouts of the Key, Dikaletus will be executed for his conspirations against the Sultan,' Otal swivelled to the cowering Zenari, 'and then the eye of the Sultan — peace be upon him — will be upon you, Zenari.'

Zenari stared gobsmacked at Jobert. 'I do not have the Key.'

Dikaletus poked the arrowhead at Zenari. 'But you did conceal it within yourself, did you not?'

'Not at all.' The cords in Zenari's neck strained as he struggled to speak. 'You disturbed its concealment when you stole the provenance. I have been unable to find it since Diraç. You will attest it was not present when Marsden examined me.'

Otal sneered. 'Are you saying, Zenari, you have lost the Key? How will your new King of the French express his displeasure at the loss of such an antiquity?'

Dikaletus waved his arrow like a baton. 'I suspect Jobert's hand in this. You, Jobert, have conspired to steal property of great value from not only myself and Otal Alaybey, but the Sultan himself — peace be upon him.'

Jobert's jaw trembled. With cold. With injury. With exhaustion. With anger. 'You trussed me naked and poisoned me. You have searched every crease and crevice I have. You, Dikaletus Pasha, have lost the Key, and the Sultan — peace be upon him — will learn of your name.'

Otal's eyebrows and moustache curled into menace. 'The Key has been hidden for twelve hundred years. If you die, Jobert, and it remains lost, no one will be any the poorer.'

Jobert bared his teeth in anger. 'I have lost everything. My gold. Half my horses wander the night. Soon my head will decorate a barbarian's lance. If I coveted such a treasure that is desired by the Sultan himself, why would I remain here?'

Otal's moustache twisted with derision. 'Your commitment to the purchase of these mares is pathetic.'

Dikaletus swished the Cossack arrow. 'My dear Jobert, any arrangement concerning these horses is null and void. I shall review my thoughts on any support to move horses to Ravenna.'

'Then I shall return to Bucharest and receive back France's gold from the Hospodar.'

'I doubt you will ever leave the walls of Serpenaçi, Jobert,' Otal said. 'The loss of my horse and his slave, albeit both of great value, is one matter. But the opportunity to secure the Key is another. Dikaletus, I shall summon your escort, and I will—'

With a flick of the arrow shaft, Dikaletus created silence. 'That most vital of endeavours, our humble service to the Sultan — peace be upon him — is ever at the forefront of our minds. You, Otal Alaybey, are his most gifted hunter. Which prey would the Commander of the Faithful be most eager to unleash you upon? The Key ... or Begnzarov.'

Dikaletus' fiery eyebrows arched as he tapped the severed Cossack head with the arrowpoint.

Chapter Nineteen

The thick grey clouds scudded across the morning sky, their curling tendrils of mist threatening to hook the tallest roofs of Serpenaçi. The chill breeze removed any warmth from the dull day.

On the Keep's battlements, Jobert — wrapped tight in his cape, with Duque, Fazio and Moench by his side — observed the inhabitants of the town emerge into the street-long puddles of slop created by dried dung and powered dust of horse movement blended with last night's downpour.

Those in the Christian quarter responded to Sunday's tolling church bell. Sevalnev, Zenari, Tétény and the uhlans trudged through the muddy slime of the converted horse-yard forecourt to attend the Prime service with the Christian community.

South of the Keep, with morning prayer well finished, the Muslim citizens picked their way through the gluggy silt and surveyed the storm's damage. Collapsed roofs, broken branches, torn awnings, torrent-ripped gardens and dead chickens filled the scene of destruction. The people were greeted with agitated neighing from the hungry one hundred and fifty mares tethered evenly along the horse lines, and the fifty loose horses among them.

To the west outside the Suceava Gate, two dozen uhlans gathered snapped branches for smoky fires as they maintained a watch over the roaming Transylvanian herd.

Across the writhing brown Prut, Otal, Dikaletus and the dismounted djelli escort departed Serpenaçi through the Port Gate, and, taking a river barge, crossed to the djelli camp on the northern shore before pressing on to Balti.

Beyond the eastern walls, amongst the orchards facing the Balti Gate, lay long strings of exhausted tethered mares, anchored by those horses that had tripped on the ropes and broken their necks. Groups of untethered horses, either those allocated to the uhlans or those with broken leads, drooped their heads under each other's bellies.

Jobert's scrutinies were interrupted when Moench asked, 'Where is Lieutenant Koschak, sir?'

'During the night, Otal Alaybey has sent Koschak to Suceava.' Jobert avoided Moench's enquiring eye. 'A warning to the Austrians about the Cossack raid.'

'Koschak took Marsden,' Duque said, 'and three of our horses.'

Fazio and Moench blinked at the unexpected absence.

'Of greater importance,' Jobert grinned and slapped Moench's shoulder, 'we go home today.'

Fazio's moustache curled with suspicion. 'Five men on three saddle horses?'

'The saddle horses will go to you two and Zenari,' Jobert said. 'I will walk the first few days and start mares under saddle for Duque and I. But first, you all go out to the orchard and inspect those who escaped last night. Once Tétény returns from Mass, I will discuss the arrangements to have us on the road this afternoon. This evening, we will camp amongst the groves and set a routine with the uhlans and the mares. We take our first step home—'

A horn blast bawled from the uhlan camp.

Metal alarms clanged from the western towers.

From the orchards opposite the Suceava Gate, mounted and dismounted uhlans and their loose horses streamed towards the gatehouse. The militiamen manning the tower bellowed to close the gates. Capstans groaned to raise the drawbridge. The racing uhlans screamed at the closing gateway.

Jobert watched as some sheepskin-clad horsemen raced to head off the herd, or galloped for the closing gate with scimitars drawn, or ran down fleeing uhlans with either lance tips or their mounts' hooves.

'There is not more than thirty of them. But who?' Jobert frowned as he scanned the confusion. 'Poles or Cossacks?'

A knot of steadier horsemen caught Jobert's eye. They rode on a tight rein, in rectangular oriental-styled stirrups and under a tufted black-and-red tug. A tufted horsehair battle-standard similar to Otal's.

'Cossacks!'

Within Serpenaçi, the alarms summoned the militia to the walls. The uhlans streamed from the church, across the Caesars Bridge, to have a screaming match with the Suceava Gate guards about access through the gates.

Jobert strode to the steps that led from the Keep's battlements to the ground level of the Boyars quarter. There, outside the Keep, he found Sevalnev and Tétény coming from church.

Musketry crackled from the battlements of the Suceava Gate. sUhlans had climbed to the highest platform from where they directed Moldavian musket fire at the raiders. This allowed desperate uhlans to squeeze through the slimmest opening of the wooden barricades.

'Begnzarov is here.' The ferocity in Tétény's eyes jabbed at Jobert. 'I need to leave.'

'You have no horses.'

'What of the horse earnt yesterday?'

'Half are in the Muslim quarter. Half are out in the groves. None are started under saddle.' Jobert raised placating palms. 'Stay and fight, Tétény. Think of the loot. Each Cossack will bring horses, coin, coats, weapons, saddlery. There is your prize.'

Tétény's unkempt beard jiggled as he twitched in fear. 'I cannot wait. They will surround the town.'

'The Cossacks cannot swim the Bludovaţ,' Jobert said. 'It is in flood.'

'That will not stop them.' Sevalnev hugged his fur-lined robes to his ribs. 'The Cossacks will melt into the mud and reappear on the other bank. They are impervious to heat, cold or any discomfort.'

Jobert clenched his teeth at Sevalnev's and Tétény's dissembling. 'There is only a patrol of about thirty. Climb the gate and see. Not enough to surround us. Not enough to take the horses on the outside of the walls. We need to speak with Begnzarov to understand his intentions.'

Sevalnev clutched at his fur-trimmed coat as if Begnzarov might climb inside. 'His intentions are abundantly clear, Jobert. Begnzarov will kill us and take what he wants.'

An hour later, on the drawbridge in front of the shut Suceava Gate, a large carpet was laid. Upon the rug were set four cushions, a samovar, and the same tapering glass tea service that had graced Jobert's initial negotiations at this time one week ago.

'Begnzarov, the Khan of the western Tartars.' Sevalnev's cheeks blushed in admiration at Begnzarov's approach on a magnificent stallion. 'The horse and the rider are renown. The horse is Al-Anfas. The Breath of God.'

As Al-Anfas accentuated each stride, thick muscle rippled across his black chest and along his rump. The elegance of each footfall caught Jobert's attention. 'That is an impressive horse.'

Behind Begnzarov rode an escort. Each Cossack wore a domed iron helmet, chain mail, and carried bows and full quivers. Handles of daggers rose from sashes and scimitars hung from hips. Long-barrelled muskets were slung over shoulders or tucked under saddle straps. Each man rode a tall black horse. Jobert acknowledged any guard, French or not, would appear fearsome on such horses.

This has to work.

Behind the escort, prisoners stumbled, and corpses were dragged. A bound Turk was distinct among the bearded Carpathians. Neither Koschak nor Marsden were among them.

Begnzarov swung lightly down from his arched-necked mount.

Sevalnev indicated cushions on which they might sit.

Jobert lowered himself stiffly to perch with his back to the gate.

Tétény sat behind his right shoulder, his breathing sharp and restless.

Sevalnev, on Jobert's left, poured tea. 'Great Begnzarov Khan,' Sevalnev translated his Moldavian conversation into German, 'it is with shame that foreign oppressors forbid me from welcoming esteemed guests into my hall.'

Begnzarov sat opposite Jobert.

Begnzarov face was carved from timber. The top knot on his bald skull stood proud in bangles of gold. His ice-blue eyes were deep set and moved slowly across each of the tea party. His moustache was pencil-thin across his thin lips. Begnzarov's tanned and lean upper body was clad with an embroidered waistcoat. The muscles in his forearms rippled as his gnarly fingers twisted a string of prayer beads.

Begnzarov touched the teacup rim to his top lip and then placed it down. Begnzarov was neither seething nor sullen. He was not attempting to intimidate. He appeared a man resigned to the unpleasant task of picking up fresh dog shit with his fingers. 'Where is my old adversary, Otal Alaybey?'

Sevalnev pursed his full lips. 'He descends upon you as you take tea.'

Confusion registered as a wrinkle in Begnzarov's eyelids. 'Who represents the Turks? You, Boyar Sevalnev?'

Sevalnev looked down at the samovar

Jobert calmed his breathing. 'I am Lieutenant Colonel André Jobert. I am a representative of France. In the absence of Otal Alaybey, I represent his Majesty Sultan Selim, the Commander of the Faithful — peace be upon him.'

Begnzarov nodded. 'Peace be upon him.'

On the signal of the Khan's nod, the Turkish prisoner was shoved forward of Al-Anfas. In full view of the audience on the walls of the Balti gatehouse, the Turk was "shirted". Lifting the prisoner's arms, Cossacks ran a knife slit around his abdomen and back. A skirt of blood seeped down the Turk's waist, as he wept '*Allahu Akbar.*' Using the same tearing movement as Otal had inflicted on the Bosnian bandits, the Cossacks lifted the flap of skin up to the man's armpits and throat. With his arm pinned by his own skin, the Turk fell to his knees, his muffled gasps as he struggled to breathe.

Begnzarov slid his hard gaze to see the impact on Jobert and Sevalnev, before he took another sip of tea. 'These horses are my horses.'

'No,' Jobert shook his head. 'These are the horses of France. These horses have been purchased from the Hospodar of Moldavia.'

'These horses were stolen from me.' Begnzarov considered Jobert. 'The thieves were not Turkish. Who were they?'

'Poles,' Jobert said.

'Koranski?'

Jobert nodded.

'Where are the Poles?'

Boyar Sevalnev jerked his chin north. 'Towards Khotyn.'

Begnzarov curled his lip in disgust. 'And these?' He flicked his prayer beards at the captive uhlans. 'Are they Poles?'

Tétény coughed. 'They are not. They are my people.'

Begnzarov's eyes wandered across Tétény's matted hair and grimy coat. 'Are you Koranski? Or one his Poles?'

Tétény's lips spasmed to conceal his clenched teeth. 'I am not. I am Tétény. I am Transylvanian.'

Begnzarov raised his chin towards the Carpathians over his shoulder. 'Are you in the service of the Ottomans?'

'I am not.'

'What are you doing here?'

Tétény nodded to Jobert. 'I have been engaged by France to take the horses south.'

'Do you have a claim on my horses?'

Tétény looked at Jobert. 'I do not.' Tétény eyes rolled in calculation. 'Return my horses, Great Khan, and I will quit the lands of the Turks this day.'

Begnzarov rocked his head to indicate an internal conclusion had been reached. He nodded over his shoulder and flicked his prayer beads.

The prisoners were shoved forward.

Begnzarov lowered his face to the teacups on the carpet, before he raised his eyes to pierce Jobert. 'As this country yields little in way of payment, France, I must be paid in full for my horses. Or my horses must be returned.' Begnzarov looked at Boyar Sevalnev. 'I do not care by whom.' Boyar Sevalnev cringed. 'Or … I take them back.' Begnzarov's head tilted for emphasis. 'All of them.'

Sevalnev's fingers stoked the air in agitation. 'I have received one hundred colts as payment. Allow me to undo this wrong against you, Great Khan, and return them.'

'I accept, Boyar Sevalnev. For now, keep them safe for me, as I must depart to gather my warbands and return.'

'You honour me with such responsibility, Great Khan. I ask that you might spare a little kindness to Serpenaçi when we welcome your return.'

'If your gates are open when I return, then I will be inclined to forgiveness, Boyar Sevalnev. Perhaps we shall take tea together in your hall.'

The rising notes of the midday call to prayer lifted over the town's defences.

Begnzarov looked towards the mosque behind the walls.

Boyar Sevalnev stood and, sweeping his hands towards the closed Suceava Gate, invited Begnzarov to prayer.

'No!' Jobert stood and thrust a rigid hand towards Begnzarov. 'No. You have massacred and razed the towns of the Sultan. As his representative, you will not enter this town. Not to pray. Not for any other reason.'

Begnzarov's thin lips pressed tight, and he gave Jobert a slight inclination of his tanned and weathered face to indicate they were now enemies. 'If as you say, France, they are your horses, then I shall take your horses.'

Jobert clenched his jaw. '*Inshallah.*'

Begnzarov passionless eyes swept to Jobert's sabre. 'When I return, France, look for me. I will seek you.'

'I am at your service.'

By mid-morning the sun's warmth bore down on the Moldavian steppe. From the ground rose clouds of humidity and midges, from which no-one in Serpenaçi was spared. Begnzarov and his warriors squatted under the orchard's shade and watched the Suceava Gate.

'We are trapped.' Tétény lips warped around his clenched teeth. 'Begnzarov will gather his warbands.' Tétény's snout jabbed at Jobert. 'The loose mares in the Boyars quarter are mine.'

Jobert folded his arms and cocked his head. 'No, they are not. They were payment for leading the herd to Izmail. If you leave, Tétény, you leave having improved your skills in catching and haltering brood mares.'

Tétény spat at Jobert's boots.

Soon after, Tétény's one hundred uhlans mounted and trotted west.

With the departure of the Transylvanians, Begnzarov's advance guard withdrew south.

Jobert clicked his fingers. 'I need to get a message to Otal.'

Fazio stepped forward. 'I am your man, sir. I will do it.' Jobert scowled at Fazio. 'I speak Turkish. It will be easy enough to track the djelli in the mud.'

'How will you cross the Prut?' Jobert asked.

Sevalnev flapped his hands. 'There is a ford further down the river, south of Serpenaçi, it may be flooded but it will be a better place to swim a horse.'

'I will lead a second horse to this ford.' Duque cleared his throat and clamped Fazio's shoulder. 'To make sure he … just in case he loses …'

Jobert grasped Fazio's upper arm and squeezed. 'Ride swiftly, my friend.'

With an axe, a musket and a cartridge box, Jobert and Moench then spent the morning destroying thirty mares severely injured in last night's flight and recording their hoof brands.

Jobert and Moench entered back through the Iasi Gate to inspect the tethered mares within the Muslim quarter.

Within the gate, at the end of the horse lines, stood Sevalnev with his feet planted, his arms tucked tight across his chest, his eyes wide and his cheeks red.

Behind Sevalnev lurked Zenari, half-turned away with his head bowed.

Around the horse lines a muttering crowd gathered.

Sevalnev clenched his quivering pink lips. 'Zenari tells me Koranski stole your gold.'

Zenari shrugged to no-one in particular.

Jobert's shoulders slumped. 'Koranski has stolen from us both. You are owed thirty pieces of gold. This is all I have left.' Jobert held out the last ten coins.

The crowd pressed closer and craned their necks to observe the exchange.

Sevalnev stared at the offered coins. 'You have rolled all your dice, Jobert. You have wagered all your coin. You are in my debt for forty gold coins. Our doom is upon us. I want you and your horses gone. Outside the walls, you may claim to Begnzarov you represent the Sultan. But you hold no such authority within the walls. My town is destroyed. Loss of gardens, loss of water, no payment.'

Jobert curled his fingers around the gold. 'Sevalnev, you know I have gold vouchsafed by Otal Alaybey. For you, an extra purse of fifty gold coins.' Jobert waved a stiff palm at the horse lines. 'There are three hundred head of horses ready to lead south, once Otal Alaybey defeats Begnzarov. I seek one hundred men to lead them. I need another fifty men to support the convoy. Just to Iasi. The men will be returned to you in two weeks.'

Sevalnev's looked exhausted. 'How will we be paid?'

'I will sell fifty in Iasi and pay each man the proceeds.

You will receive a twenty per cent tax.'

Sevalnev held up his hands. 'We are not horsemen, Jobert. Your grooms and your escort will move by foot. What will they eat? How will they be paid? I have a counterproposal.'

'Yes?'

'Release the horses.'

Jobert jerked backwards. 'What? Drive them to the Danube as a herd? On foot?'

'No.' Sevalnev's voice was barely a whisper. 'Release them onto the steppe. And you, Jobert, depart never to return. I am happy to escort your party as far as Balti, where you can rejoin Dikaletus.'

'Those horses are my horses. Leave me those that are tethered.'

'I am not denying you any of your horses, Jobert. Simply, take them outside my walls.'

In the shadow of the battlement's arch and with his back to the barred fortress gate, Jobert rocked into a fighting stance and calmly drew his sabre.

The threat of Jobert's extended sabre fixed everyone's attention.

Moench and Zenari hastened to his side and drew their blades.

'Can the three of you control my gates forever?' Sevalnev's arms drooped to his sides. 'My people are on the verge of being raped and butchered, by any one of a number of barbaric hordes, including our reviled overlords. We sought inspiration from your newly won liberty, equality and fraternity. Yet you have inflicted suffering upon us, and now threaten us with death. What do we have to lose? We have no gardens, no flocks, no water, no blankets. What else can you take, Jobert?'

Jobert looked upon the Serpenaçi's crowd, each face seething with anger and bitter with resentment.

Moench's and Zenari's sabre tips dipped with their wavering spirit.

Jobert's heart pounded against his ribs. Not with fear.

I have failed.

Jobert lowered his blade.

They have won.

With flowing smoothness, Jobert sheathed his sabre.

Moench and Zenari beside him twitched at his capitulation. The crowd hissed with exhaled relief.

With shoulders heavy with sadness, Jobert turned his back on the crowd. He willed his leaden knees to bend as he walked towards the brooding gate. He heaved to lift the locking bar. He strained to pivot one of the gates inwards.

As he walked past Moench and Zenari, Jobert croaked, 'We go home today.'

The crowd stepped back as Jobert walked to the closest tethered horse and undid the throat knot on the halter. The freed mare stood still.

Moench stepped in.

Jobert lifted his hand. 'Stand back. These are my horses. This is my problem.'

Zenari dropped his head, turned and walked away.

Across the horse line, Moench ran his palm down the back of a quivering mare until he stood by her eye and the halter knot. 'Untie them from the line with leads trailing? Or remove the halters completely?'

Jobert removed the halters one-by-one. 'It is over, Moench. This is as close as we ever got to winning.' His numb fingers fumbled with the knots. 'Do not untie the last dozen. Those we can lead home.'

'When? Tomorrow?'

'No. Today. When Duque returns.'

Loose mares shuffled together. In twos and threes, they drifted towards the open gate. As more were freed, their trotting urged others to trot out of the gate. Suddenly horses leant on their lead ropes awaiting untying, before leaping to the canter. The mud of the quarter's roads soon became hoof-splattered flecks. Flecks soon pounded to dust. Heads high, snorting, pressing, nipping, eyes rolling, ears twitching. A blur of brown, black, chestnut and grey fur raced out the Iasi Gate.

The crowd flapped half-heartedly as they shooed the horses out of their town. Consternation gripped their faces, as two of the agents of the town's destruction, flood and a herd of horses, were now to be replaced by tribal brutality.

Jobert followed the last of the released mares out of the gate.

I am a failure.

I lost my regiment.

I lost Gianna.

I have lost my annuity.

And now I have lost a half million francs in gold and a vast herd of vital brood mares.

I am destitute in a foreign land.

Koschak is gone.

Fazio is gone.

I am about to have my friends impaled, eviscerated and decapitated.

If we stay, we die.

If we go, we die.

Whatever happens, we will die.

I must die.

Fuck Begnzarov!

I cannot be taken alive.

Chapter Twenty

Jobert entered the main room of their two-room apartment. The stone-walled room smelt of mildewed hessian. The thick timber shutter was latched across the arrow slit in the outer wall. Light trickled in from the outside as if an afterthought. The hearth was cold, and a mound of kindling sat awaiting a spark. Stark timber chairs were square to the bare table.

Jobert touched the empty bench against the damp wall. How long was it since he had dined at Raive's Genoan home? Would carpets, glassware and candelabra be so frivolous? Beyond the hearth stood the closed door to the shared sleeping quarters. What if that door led to a well-stocked pantry? A deep bath? A soft bed with clean sheets?

Jobert opened the door to the bedchamber. A pulse of acrid smoke and sweat pushed at his throat.

Zenari leant against the obliquely narrowing sill of the chamber's arrow loop. Smoking a simple tin shisha, he exhaled east over the hall's tiled roofline. Zenari did not acknowledge Jobert's entry.

Around the lit hearth in the bedchamber, six timber and

rope-net cots lined the wall, with the foot of each cot extending towards the room's centre. In the centre of the straw-filled pail-lasses that served as mattresses, each man's portmanteau lay on top of their folded blankets. Jobert removed his hat, coat and sword belt and hung them from an iron hook.

Placing his portmanteau on the floor and bunching the fold-ed grey blankets as a pillow, Jobert collapsed on his cot without removing his boots. He folded his forearms across his face to confine his swirling thoughts.

How much have I lost?

Jobert imagined leaning back into Bleu's warmth as he had last summer.

He ached for Gianna's consoling embrace.

Rolling to face the stone wall, his nose sought her soft, scented curls within the stale body odours of the rough woven blankets.

'Where is Justinian's Key, Jobert?' Zenari asked.

'Piss off, Zenari.'

'Marsden has it, does he not?'

Jobert shook his head.

'While I had the Key, I had dreams ...' Zenari exhaled his tobacco breath. 'When I lost it ...'

'I doubt you are the first to succumb to the power of the ring,' Jobert said. 'I expect that it has corrupted other men's minds down through the centuries.'

'Why not yours?'

'A piece of jewellery? If I had it, I would probably use it as a bribe.'

'But we do not have it. Do we?'

Jobert rolled onto his back and stared at the rough-hewn timber ceiling. 'No. It is gone.'

'And I am purged of its allure.'

'After this trip, I am not sure purge is a word I would ever choose again.'

Zenari blew a long stream of tobacco smoke out of the arrow slit. 'Koschak may have financial gain as a motive, but it is more likely, knowing both of you as I do, that you ordered Koschak to escape with Marsden and the Key.'

Jobert flopped his arms across his face once more and groaned. 'I do not know who has the Key. I do not know where the Key is. I do not care.' Jobert raised himself onto his elbow. 'I truly do not fucking care about the Key, Zenari.'

'Now you know what it is like to lose everything.' Zenari waggled the shisha's mouthpiece out of the slit. 'I watched you release the horses. That must have hurt. A personal loss to you of one hundred thousand francs, Jobert.. Over thirty years wages as a colonel. Ouch!'

Jobert shook out a blanket, draped it over his shoulders and rolled back towards the wall.

The door to the main room squeaked open. Scabbards clanked as they were hung on the wall.

'Hungry, lad?' Duque's growl hummed from the main room.

'Certainly not for more horse meat,' Moench said.

Chairs by the dining table scraped.

I cannot avoid them, Jobert thought. He rolled over to find Zenari squatting by the bedroom hearth, scrabbling at the straps of his satchel. 'What are you doing?'

'If the Key is lost, then there is no little need to keep my copy of the provenance.'

'Stop, Zenari, keep your provenance. If only as a fine memento of your time attempting to re-unite two empires.'

Zenari's fingers caressed the papers backlit by the flames. 'Then the Key—'

'I know nothing of the Key.' Jobert rose from his cot to slump against the doorframe that separated the bedchamber from the main room.

Moench's head was cradled in his folded arms upon the table.

With absent minded strokes of his steel, Duque flicked lint sparks at the kindling. 'We have saved a dozen mares into the Boyar's stables. Are you still thinking of departing for home tomorrow?'

Jobert watched the sparks fail to catch alight. 'I do know what to think. Everything I thought so far has been wrong.' Jobert shook his head at the floor. 'I doubt ...'

Moench raised his head from his arms. Concern pinched his eyes.

'You are tired. We are all tired.' Duque harumphed as he poked twigs into a pop of infant flames. 'We are at the mercy of these vicious bastards. Earlier in the year, you spoke of dreading your return to Milan. How do you feel about being in Milan right now?'

'To think we hesitated to travel beyond Naples.' Moench's chin rested on his folded arms. 'What a merry romp that would have been compared to the shit we are now in.'

'I am responsible ...' Jobert's hands groped in the air. 'I am responsible for losing all our money. I will repay—'

'Let us get safe home first.' Duque dismissed Jobert's comments with a wave of his three-fingered right hand. 'Would you consider remaining here in Serpenaçi until the Turks have defeated—'

The Keep boomed with muffled shouting.

A pounding rap struck the door, before it swung open.

A Moldavian guard thrust his head into the room. '*Unde este Boyar Sevalnev?*'

'Boyar Sevalnev? No.' Jobert shook his head and sought the Moldavian word for "why". '*De ce?*'

'*Polonezii,*' said the Moldavian guard. '*Koranski este la Poarta Balti.*'

'Koranski!' Strapping on his sword belt, Jobert strode from the room. 'What does that bastard want to steal now?'

Crossing the Caesar Bridge, Jobert walked through the streets of the Christian quarter. Townsfolk were busy enclosing goats and chickens for the evening, repairing garden fences and vines trellises, and toting split firewood and pails of water into their kitchens. Yet they still had energy to slide Jobert a scowl as he passed.

As he entered the Balti gatehouse, Jobert looked each guardsman in the eye. A few smirked. Most gave sharp nods of begrudging respect, their lips pursed in embarrassment or condolence.

Mounting the upper reaches of the Balti gatehouse to join Sevalnev, Jobert winced at his loose mares across in the orchards nibbling low hanging fruit leaves. Some horses had followed their mates down into the ferry crossing to drink at the edge of the Prut.

'By the Grace of God, what will we now receive?' Sevalnev jerked his chin north, where the orange dusk melted to mauve.

Beyond the Prut, along the Khotyn road, a convoy of lumpy wagons, bowed people, straining bullocks and dashing hounds emerged from the gassed steppe. The Poles had returned with herds and families.

In the twilight, a dozen horsemen, Koranski's heavy form distinct amongst them, scattering mares as they emerged from the cutting that ascended from the ferry.

Jobert spat over log wall of the deck. 'The thief returns for more.'

Sevalnev spoke sharply in Moldavian. From the upper deck, the guards barked down to those manning the gate's bars and the drawbridge capstan.

'I will not speak with him.' Sevalnev sniffed and drew his fur-trimmed cloak about him. 'He has stolen from me. We are reliant on our allegiances to survive. He has broken trust. He has revealed himself to be no more than all the rest. My people are at the mercy of the great powers, but I am not intimidated by Koranski. My walls and my militia are more than a match for his rag-tag Poles.' Sevalnev looked at the dark shapes of horses roaming the groves beyond bow ranges. 'What are your plans now, Jobert?'

'I will await the return of Otal Alaybey and then I shall depart with as many horses as I can lead.'

'Then I shall continue to extend to you every courtesy as my guest.'

Jobert snorted. 'Piss off, Sevalnev. For the money that France has paid the Hospodar, in lieu of promised horses, I own your miserable town. You remain as an extension of my courtesy. I have provided fifty carcasses and gifted three hundred halters, worth fifteen gold louis, to the town. You will be able to salvage my stray horses at your leisure.'

Koranski and his flanking spearmen halted their dripping horses well out from the sharpened stakes embedded in the ditch that lined the base of the timber walls.

Koranski raised a few fingers in greeting. 'Boyar Sevalnev, perhaps we can pray together.'

'Your sins are too much for our small church, Koranski.' Sevalnev raised his chin. 'You are not welcome in Serpenaçi.'

Koranski nodded his head. 'Are you aware the Cossacks are somewhere south of the town.'

'Like a crow,' Jobert said quietly to Sevalnev, 'Koranski watches and waits to pick at our corpses once the wolves have killed, eaten and gone.'

Sevalnev crossed himself. 'We know, Koranski. Begnzarov took tea at the Suceava Gate.' Koranski jerked towards the western gate over the walls beyond his horse's ears. 'I spoke at length to Begnzarov at midday.' Jobert raised an eyebrow of surprise at Sevalnev's comment. 'I made him aware of your theft from him. Begnzarov now gathers his warbands. Expect to meet with him soon, Koranski.'

'You crossed paths with the Cossacks?' Jobert asked.

For a moment, Koranski remained motionless. Only the flick of his rein-ends betrayed his consideration of Jobert. 'Their trail led to the banks of the Prut. They are west of the river.'

'And the sipahi patrols to the west?'

Koranski shook his tilted jowls. 'All impaled and eviscerated. No survivors. Have you sent a message to Balti?'

If Fazio evaded the Cossacks, Otal will be aware by morning. 'Yes.'

Koranski looked to the horses nipping at the lower boughs within the orchards. 'The mares have been released. Why?'

Jobert shoulders slumped, his face downcast.

Koranski snorted with pleasure. 'Sevalnev, this Frenchman is nothing. He draws breath only at your convenience.'

'I am a guest,' Jobert growled to Sevalnev, 'at the Hospodar's pleasure.'

'Hah!' Koranski coughed. 'The Hospodar is far from here, Jobert. This is a land of unfortunate accidents.' Koranski adjusted his seat in the saddle. 'Sevalnev, I can regather these horses which strip your fruit trees. Allow me to use the town to sort and sell. We will become rich together. I will pay you what Jobert owes you.'

'There, Sevalnev,' Jobert clicked his fingers, 'the bastard reveals his need. To gain the shelter of the town.'

'The horses are a curse,' Sevalnev called down to Koranski. 'Let Begnzarov have them. I want nothing that threatens the security of the town. The Turks will learn of your theft, and your people will be hunted and flayed alive. Sell to Suceava. Live under the protection of Vienna. Are they not who stole your homeland in the first place?'

'Come now, Sevalnev. I have French gold. We can share it.'

'Keep it. Do not bring it within my walls. You may need the gold to bargain with the Cossacks for your life. Jobert has told Begnzarov of the gold.'

'Jobert has proven himself incapable.' There was anger in Koranski's voice. 'I have the power to regather what we have both worked hard to maintain these past months.' Koranski opened conciliatory palms. 'If I gather the horses and place them under guard, will you let my women and children shelter within the walls.'

'No,' Sevalnev said. 'You have stolen from me. You have broken our bond of trust.'

Koranski's gaze travelled along the fortified walls from the Ferry Tower to the Sepulchre Tower. 'Perhaps you are correct, my wise friend. I have offended you and now must regain your trust. I shall not impose. In the morning, I will lead my people to Iasi and call upon the mercy of the Hospodar to protect my families. I shall place my warriors at the service of Otal Alaybey.'

Sevalnev's shoulders drooped with relief.

Koranski's band turned in the sodden road and pressed their horses for the swift-flowing ferry crossing and their camp beyond.

'It is a ruse, Sevalnev.' Jobert squeezed Sevalnev's elbow. 'He is coming for Serpenaçi. I feel for certain Koranski will cut his way into the town to save his people.'

Sevalnev shrugged off Jobert's grip. 'He would not choose that.'

'It is a significant tactical option.' Jobert poked a rigid finger at Sevalnev. 'You cannot risk it occurring. Double your guard tonight.'

'No, Jobert, if I did that every time a band of scruffy horsemen rode past, the townsfolk would mutiny due to onerous guard duty. I have just averted an insurrection of your making, Jobert. Do not incite another.'

Koranski recrossed the ferry to his waiting horsemen and their families, wagons, and flocks. The convoy dissolved to set camp and gather riverside flotsam for evening fires. Children's laughter pierced above the bleating of the goats they herded. Yoked oxen lowed as they were led to the banks of the Prut. As pots settled above cooking embers, stringed banduras trilled amongst the cowhide tents. The hum of human chatter and song, barking of dogs, neighing of horses and the bells on goats set a consistent rhythm before and after sunset.

Once dark, without light or noise, seventy of Koranski's one hundred warriors led their horses two hundred metres beyond the orchard belt. They mounted and trotted to a ford on the Prut a few kilometres south.

Once they had swum their horses across onto the river's right bank, the Polish horsemen made their way north again towards Serpenaçi. Their horses were greeted with the neighs of the loose mares grazing in the moonlight.

With the dark smudge of the town's groves well north of them, the Poles stepped down from their saddles and squatted amongst the shadows of the boughs of the riverside willows. Knives slid from leather sheaths to carve apples and smoked-dried beef.

From under the boughs, ten Poles departed on foot. Crossing the grasslands between the Prut and the Bludovaț, they kept clear of the abandoned herdsmen's huts. The swampy grass from the recent rain squelched under their soft leather boots.

On the eastern bank of the swollen Bludovaț, five men stripped to their breeches and knife belts. Horn bows and full quivers were slung across their shoulders. Gripping inflated goat's bladders, their colleagues slid in the Bludovaţ's mud and draped them with branches, so the swimmers would appear as flood debris. Other bladders were camouflaged with broad-leafed waterweeds as deception should they be inspected by the Moldavian patrols.

Once disguised, the swimmers paddled out into the stream's black water and drifted north towards the sleeping town.

The clear summer sky allowed the light of a half-moon to bathe the land, but as the moon fell swiftly to the western horizon, its shadows were long on the reaches of the Bludovaţ Stream. The Polish infiltrators drifted under the Moldavian sentries in the towers of the Iasi Gate

Undetected, the swimmers floated between the two towers that dominated either side of the Upper Pond. Here, one at a time, they abandoned their disguised bladders and dove under the pond's barriers.

Controlling their breathing, they froze in the shadows as a three-man Moldavian patrol from the Boyar's quarter inspected the dam's edges. As the patrol's torches reclimbed the Bludovaţ's paths, the Poles slithered out of the shallows and squelched up the steps of the steep paths into the Muslim quarter.

Blending from shadow to shadow with bows half-drawn, and keenly aware of dogs and the militia patrol within the Muslim quarter, three of the swimmers moved through the streets to hide near the gatehouse door of the Iasi Gate. Near the Al-Aqsa Gate, two others squatted out of the reach of the starlight.

Here, in the shadows, they waited.

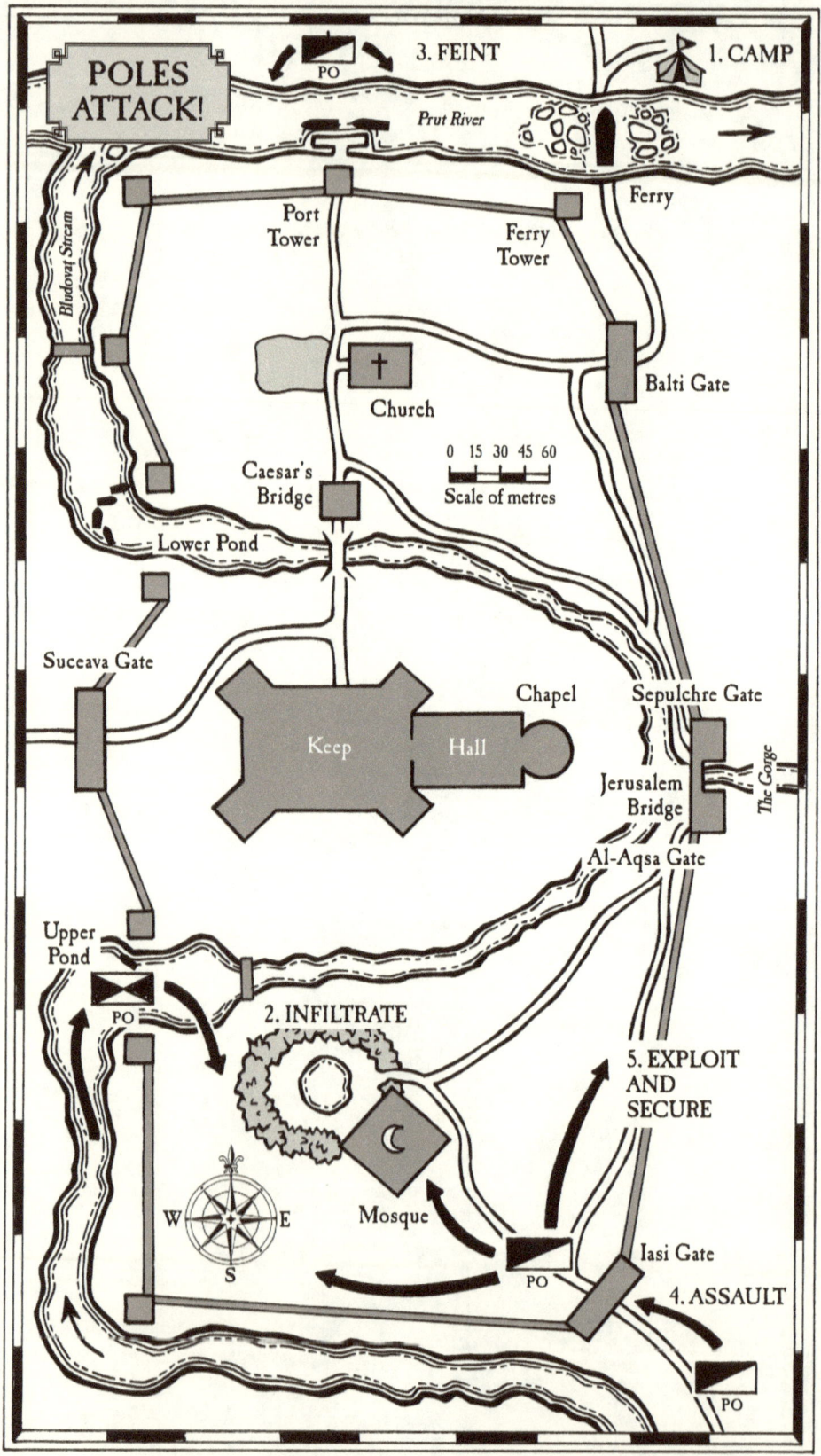

Chapter Twenty-One

When Jobert emerged from the Keep's stairs onto its upper level, there was not yet any hint of grey on the eastern horizon. Not yet birdsong from the surrounding orchards and the river-banks, much less any dawn. Only dull stars and weary guardsmen blinked sleepily, awaiting the end of their shifts.

Jobert exchanged grunts with the Moldavian sentries as he warmed himself by their brazier.

The call to morning prayer was sung from the towers above the mosque. One hour until dawn.

Jobert's wakefulness on any morning was a combination of long habit of speaking with the sentries, the disturbance of nightmares and the need to think with a clear head. Last night he had not slept well. He hoped to gain clarity that a fresh dawn might bestow.

'Those bastard Poles.' Jobert muttered as he peered north in-to the grey glow. Bracket mounted torches on the gatehouses and towers blurred by the blanket of river mist hindered any clear sight of activity amongst the dark, silent lumps of the Polish camp.

Jobert looked south as mares called to each other. Under the moderate warmth of the grove's canopy lay the outlines of exhausted horses, their front feet tucked under their chests.

Beyond the southern ring of fruit trees, out of the fog bank, three streaks of flame soared through the air.

'Look!' Jobert jabbed a pointing hand for the guard to orient. 'Signal arrows.'

The sentry nodded and made the action of drawing and loosing a bow.

Across the river from the Port Tower, horns bawled.

'We are under attack.' Jobert pointed to the iron ring in the centre of the Keep's battlement. 'Stand to arms. The alarm!'

As the guard sprinted to the Keep's alarm, a frantic metallic beat sounded from the towers along the north wall.

Throughout Serpenaçi, each tower took up the clanging.

Men raced from the gatehouses either side of the Jerusalem Bridge to their posts. Soon after other men, armed with muskets and swords, raced from homes within the town. They formed in ranks in the forecourts of both the church and the mosque.

From beyond the river, a flock of arrows arced through the sky.

Across the river.

Over the walls.

'Jobert!' Duque, Moench and Zenari ran onto the upper deck of the Keep.

Jobert searched for any activity in the vicinity of the Balti or Suceava Gates to support such an assault. 'The attack from the north started after signal arrows were sighted in the south. It is coordinated with some other activity.'

'Why assault across a river?' Duque asked.

'Exactly!' Jobert waved his hand at the frantic action on the northern towers. 'This is bullshit. Horsemen do not assault across a river in open boats against a fortified wall. The action against the Port Tower is a feint. A distraction.'

'While the gates hold,' Zenari said, 'we are safe, yes?'

Jobert raced to the southern wall of the Keep's upper deck. 'They plan on breaching the gates. From the inside.' Jobert stiffened. 'They are already inside the walls.'

Jobert's eyes raked the gatehouses that pinned the ends of the Jerusalem Bridge and the embankments of the Bludovaţ.

Despite the cries and shouts throughout the Serpenaçi, all the tower alarms were silent.

Except one.

'They have breached the Iasi Gate.' Jobert stabbed his flat palm towards alarms in the Muslim quarter. 'Duque and Zenari, prepare to leave. Moench, with me.'

'Leave?' Zenari asked.

'Just in case.'

Duque saluted. 'Find us in the Boyar's stables.'

Moench looked down, open mouthed, at the chaos in the Muslim quarter. 'Why not—'

Jobert strode for the inner ramp. 'On me, Moench!'

Jobert and Moench descended to ground level and ran across Caesar's Bridge.

In the church forecourt, militiamen, dressed in long sheepskin coats and tight sheepskin hats, and armed with muskets and long knives, gathered as a crowd. An officer, in a cylindrical red felt hat and wearing a knee-length leather jacket over which his cartridge box and sword baldric were crossed, cried to his assembly of men and waved to the northern walls.

Jobert gripped the man's sleeve and tugged. 'No. Jerusalem! Jerusalem!' Jobert shouted in German hoping someone might understand. One soldier stepped to the militia commander, beseeched him and waved in agitation at Jobert. The soldier was the wiry blacksmith Duque had worked with to make hoof brands.

'Do you speak German?' Jobert asked.

'A little, my lord,' the smith said.

'Tell this commander the Iasi Gate is breached.' Jobert tapped a knuckle against the smith's chest with each order he gave. 'All men to the Jerusalem Bridge. You stay with me. Translate what I say.'

Jobert and Moench raced towards the Sepulchre Gate. The noise of the assault was muffled by the tight-packed timber buildings of the Christian quarter. A dozen militia men shuffled behind with muskets rattling against the long knives thrust through their belts and cartridge boxes clattering against their hips.

Jobert entered the Sepulchre Gatehouse, a log blockhouse with two pairs of inward opening gates. One set faced into the Christian quarter and the other set closed the northern end of the Jerusalem Bridge. There were around ten guards in the gatehouse, and they immediately began arguing with the militia commander upon his entry behind Jobert.

Jobert and Moench heaved the bar of the closed Sepulchre Gate, squeezed through the opening gate and crossed the Gorge over the narrow Jerusalem Bridge. The bridge was composed of two short ten-metre drawbridges, one from either gatehouse, which met in the middle of the Gorge. A thick, frayed looped rope threaded through bollards served as a loose guard rail.

Jobert entered the Al-Aqsa Gatehouse to find another ten guards. Four manning the gate on the lower level and around five or six men shouting, firing muskets from the deck above. The outer Al-Aqsa Gate was being pounded with fists by bellowing men outside.

Jobert pointed at the gate. 'Open!'

The militia's faces were full of fear. '*Nu!*'

Jobert lunged to the gate's bar. The guards grabbed at his jacket. Their hands fell away once the militia commander and a dozen militia men crowded into the gatehouse.

With the help of the incoming militia, the gate opened.

People from the Muslim quarter scrabbled to get inside. Jobert and Moench were forced back by the crush of dozens of terrified townspeople dragging goats on lead ropes. The sounds of musket fire beyond the gate were overwhelmed by bellowed arguments by those moving in opposite directions in the confined log structure.

Jobert grabbed at Moench's lapels to pull him close. 'Moench, support me from the upper deck.'

Moench's face twisted in anguish. 'Support you with what?'

Jobert shoved his way out into the lane from the Al-Aqsa Gate and into the Muslim quarter.

Beyond the Al-Aqsa Gates, a twenty-metre space was cleared before the windowless walls of the first buildings of the Muslim quarter. Within the space, where vegetable gardens had been pillaged by Jobert's ravenous horses, a single rank of ten Moldavian militia men were falling back as a ragged line. The men were screaming at each other in Moldavian.

Within the morning shadows of the buildings beyond the gates, over a dozen Poles maintained their cover from Al-Aqsa's musketry, firing their muskets and bows at the retreating Moldavians. Should Koranski's warriors emerge in the lanes between the buildings, Moldavian crossfire would erupt from the chapel directly across the Bludovaț.

Arrows and musket balls zipped by.

As the gaggle of Moldavians reached the gatehouse, Jobert flapped his arms wide to indicate one rank. 'Two ranks. On me!'

The smith relayed the order.

The officer drew his sword and prepared his men to fire. As he raised his sword, two Polish arrows thunked into his chest. He moaned as his red hat plopped to the mud. He fumbled his sword. He sank onto his bottom to sprawl at his men's feet.

Jobert raised his sabre. 'Fire!'

The smith screamed and fired.

A crackling explosion of smoke and flame engulfed the space between gates and walls.

Jobert lowered his sabre horizontally. 'Charge!'

The militia dropped their muskets, drew their knives and sprinted after Jobert towards the Poles.

Emerging from the enclosed gun smoke in the tight space between the rough-cut timber buildings, a solid line of Poles formed a shield wall. From over the front ranks' shoulder, a few muskets and arrows were fired, and lances were thrown.

With cries and moans, a few in the lead of the militia stumbled onto the gravelled road.

On a shouted command, the front rank took a step forward and thrust out their lances at the closing Moldavians.

Jobert grabbed an extended shaft. The Pole dropped his shield to protect his belly.

Jobert ran his sabre down the man's inside thigh, slicing open the massive arteries that lay between groin and knee. The man shuddered and hissed at the cut.

Before the Pole could kneel in the growing puddle of his own blood, Jobert had already delivered a neat right thrust at the neck of the warrior next in line. The Pole dropped his lance to grab at his spurting throat.

From behind him, a muzzle protruded directly at Jobert. With a roll of his wrist, Jobert parried the musket upwards as it fired, sliding his blade under the barrel and removed the first two fingers of the musketeer's left hand.

A rough tug on his jacket from behind stopped Jobert stepping into the Polish second rank.

The smith puffed hard over Jobert's shoulder. 'Come back, my lord. We go.'

The militia had broken in front of the Poles and now

streamed back to the Al-Aqsa Gate. Other militia in the upper ramparts bellowed and waved at their comrades in the street.

The Poles screamed to follow.

Musket balls whizzed.

Arrows sizzled in flight.

Jobert sprinted for the gate. With gun smoke burning his lungs and sweat blurring his vision, Jobert screamed to summon his draining strength.

Ahead of Jobert, half an arrow appeared in the back of another racing Moldavian. The man grunted at the missile's impact and then whimpered as he realised his fate and fell. Jobert and the smith stumbled over his shuddering body.

'Jobert!' Moench waved his sabre from the upper ramparts.

The Al-Aqsa's gates were closing.

Polish musket balls splintered the timber around him.

The smith and Jobert shoved at the backs of a half-dozen men barging their way into the narrowing channel.

Jobert tripped.

He stared down at a criss-cross of dropped muskets.

Jobert gripped the crossbelt of the smith with his left hand and twisted outwards to present his sabre to any oncoming Poles.

Out of respect from the crossfire from Al-Aqsa and the Boyar's chapel, the Poles maintained their fire of arrows, musketry and thrown lances from the safety of the buildings.

The smith was sucked into the shadowy interior of Al-Aqsa.

'Jobert!' Moench screamed, reaching out an arm for Jobert.

A thrown lance arced above Jobert.

A simple wrist twist parried the missile just to his right.

As the spear thudded into the timber deck, Moench screamed and hauled on Jobert's shoulder.

The lance had embedded in Moench's left boot and pinned his foot to the decking.

Moench's mouth formed a perfect O of surprise.

Jobert dropped his sabre onto his sword knot and yanked at the embedded lance shaft. The lance came free, as Moench and Jobert were hauled clear of the closing gate.

The gate's bar clunked into its iron brackets.

Moldavian militiamen shoved and shouted to escape through the inward opening gate to the Jerusalem Bridge.

'Stand fast, Serpenaçi!' Jobert bellowed, searching for the smith. 'Hold the Al-Aqsa!' No one around him understood his German.

The Poles pounded and roared from beyond the outer gate.

Musket balls from the chapel cracked into the gatehouse's log walls.

'Jobert!' Moench cried.

Men continued to race over the bridge above the Gorge to the Sepulchre Gate.

Jobert could not even mount the ladder due to the men descending in haste.

The smith appeared in front of Jobert. 'We must go now, my lord.'

'Stop these men,' Jobert shouted. 'Take your wounded.'

The smith yelled and shoved with his musket at those attempting to slip across the bridge. They grabbed at wounded comrades and dragged them out into the sunshine towards the Sepulchre Gate.

Jobert ascended the ladder that led to the upper ramparts of the Al-Aqsa. As his head emerged through the upper deck, two Polish warriors had scrambled over the wall. Jobert spat an expletive and descended to the dark lower bridge deck.

In the sunshine on the Jerusalem Bridge, the smith, supporting a wounded militiaman, entered the Sepulchre Gate. Halfway across the bridge, Moench crawled on his hands and knees painting a blood-wet trail in the crusted mud behind his left foot.

Jobert gripped Moench's shoulders. 'Up, Moench, up!' Jobert heaved to lift Moench, as Moench clung to the front of Jobert's tailcoat. 'Now, lad. Hop, hop, hop.'

'My lord, quickly,' shouted the smith from the barely open gate at the end of the bridge.

The deck beneath Jobert's feet heaved.

Jobert dropped Moench and fell heavily to his hands and knees. Holding his sabre, his knuckles punched into the rising timber deck. In Jobert's giddy peripheral vision, the Gorge beneath appeared to subside away.

Moench cried out, as his feet seemed to rise above his head.

Jobert lunged and grabbed Moench so he would not plummet into the Gorge.

Only as Jobert and Moench slid backwards into the gate's dark maw, did Jobert realise the Sepulchre Gate's drawbridge was being raised.

At the bottom of the slide, rough hands dragged them both aside to close the gate.

Crumpled on his elbows and knees, Jobert choked and sneezed in the dust.

A hand slapped Jobert's panting ribcage. 'We are safe from those Polish horse-fuckers now, my lord.'

After midday, from the vantage point of the three-storeyed Keep, Jobert assessed the battle damage.

The Polish convoy had disappeared in the morning fog from north of the ferry, and now emerged through the orchards south of the Iasi Gate to snake its way into the Muslim quarter. Despite the height of the Prut from the recent rain, Jobert mused, Fazio, the Polish raid and now the Polish wagons have crossed the southern ford.

The families of the Muslim quarter were now hostages. Horrified townsfolk scampered the tight lanes of the suburb to avoid Polish marauders. Tugging goats and bent with sacks and pots, they abandoned their homes for the sanctuary of the mosque.

Koranski kept most of his warriors busy with manning the Iasi Gate, building a barrier of horse yard rails in front of the Al-Aqsa Gate, and lugging sheepskin-clad wounded, thus making Polish and Moldavian indistinguishable, into the mosque.

Ten Moldavian dead were dumped on the rim of the Bludovaț's embankment across from the Keep. Thrown head first, the fluids from their wounds drained into mud collars about their ears.

A cough from Duque broke Jobert's examination. 'André, Sevalnev seeks you.'

'How is Moench?'

'He will live, but he is not fit to travel.'

'Look!' Jobert shook a balled fist as Polish warriors carried heavy leather saddlebags suspended from lances across their shoulders into the mosque. 'Our gold.'

Duque gripped Jobert's elbow. 'André, Sevalnev awaits you below.'

In the hall below, Jobert entered a snarl of argument, which only grew sharper with his arrival. The urgent hands of Sevalnev's militia leaders were thrust towards Jobert and then were flung up into the air in despair.

Jobert sank back and folded his arms. 'They can piss off if I am to be blamed for this.'

With upraised palms, Sevalnev sought to push a cloud of

conciliation at the embossed leather jerkins of his lieutenants. Sevalnev's face drooped with exhaustion when he espied Jobert. 'Jobert, we seek the pleasure of your company. We seek your advice as to our defence.'

'No, my lord, we do not want France's advice!' the wiry blacksmith bellowed in German. He thrust his arms wide. His comrades fell silent. The smith held up placating palms to Sevalnev. 'That is not our demand, my lord.'

Sevalnev bowed his head over his wringing hands. 'They … I … request that you, Jobert, might … command our defence.'

'What?' Jobert's face crimped with offence. 'After the town forced me to turn my horses out? Piss off, Sevalnev.'

'The Poles can focus their attack. To defend we must spread thin to determine the direction of their thrust.' Sevalnev swept a palm towards the gathered militia leaders. 'They would appreciate a professional soldier to command the defence.'

Jobert expanded his chest as he inhaled the opportunity. His jaw hardened to rock, as his gaze pierced each man.

The militia lieutenants drew themselves up in silent response. Their eyes and lips tightened as they indicated their willingness to obey.

With a glance at Sevalnev, the blacksmith took a step towards Jobert. 'My lord, the Poles hold Muslim families hostage in the mosque.' The smith's broad knuckles squeezed the pommel of his sword. 'With no hope of securing the Keep, I believe the Poles will attempt to take the Christian quarter to give themselves more room to bring in their families.'

Jobert acknowledged the assessment with a nod. 'What is your current strength, Sevalnev?'

Sevalnev asked the gathered commanders in Moldavian.

'How can you not know?' Jobert's bark startled the gathering. 'No wonder you need replacing.'

'Around eighty muskets, my lord.'

'Why did you drop your muskets when we charged the Poles?'

'To free our hands for our blades, my lord.'

'Do you not have bayonets?'

The smith drew himself up. 'Bayonets are a coward's weapon.'

'How many muskets did you gift the Poles at the Al-Aqsa Gate?'

'A dozen, my lord.' Under Jobert's withering stare, the mail links in the smith's leather chest armour shivered. 'What would you advise for our defence?'

'I would not advise a defence.' Jobert's fist punched a whip-snap from his palm. 'I am ordering an immediate counterattack.

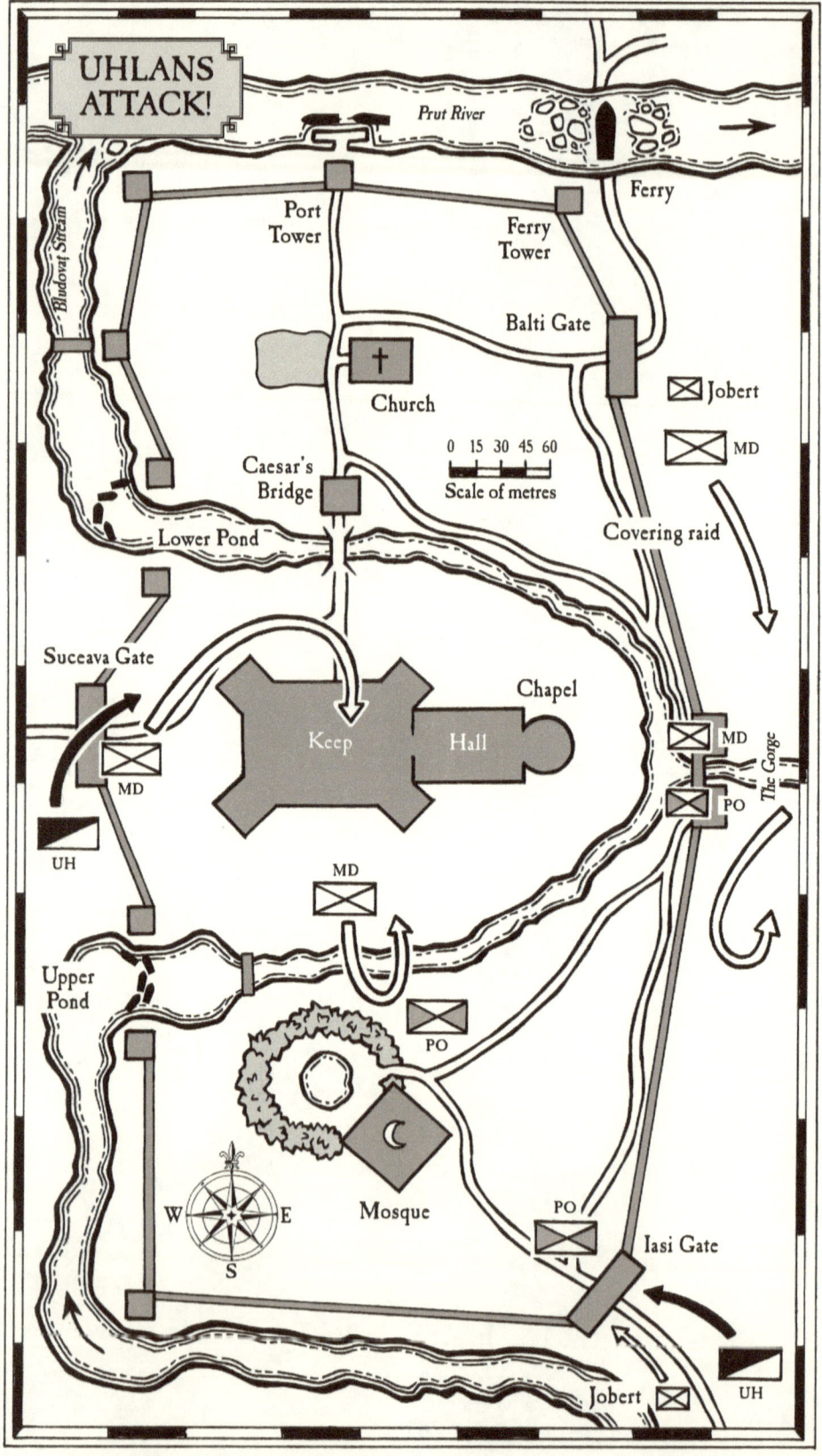

Chapter Twenty-Two

Jobert entered their allocated chamber, his arms full of two short duelling pistols, a cartridge box without a crossbelt, and a musty sheepskin coat.

Duque screwed up his face at the woolly coat. 'How long was the beast dead before you skinned its fleece?' Duque took the cartridge box and opened the flap. 'No crossbelt? I will rig it with my sword belt.'

'Thank you.' Jobert's face soured as he wiggled the flints in the jaws of the pistols' hammers. 'How are you, Moench?'

Moench propped on blankets against the wall, his bandaged foot raised on an upturned basin. He swallowed hard against his shivering. 'I am fucked, I suppose.'

'I have a job for you, my lad.' Jobert drew the dagger from his left sleeve to scratch at the flint's surface. 'You must rest. If we need to ride hard to escape here, that wound needs to be in best shape.'

Moench's pallid face squeezed with panic.

'Here, André, put your arm through.' Duque slung the cartridge box over Jobert's left shoulder, then removed it to adjust the straps. 'If we need to go, I have provisions packed onto our remaining three horses. To avoid descending the stairs in haste, I might tuck Moench snug in some corner of the stables.'

'How does that sound, Moench?' Jobert asked.

Moench searched Jobert's face for hope. 'Good, sir.'

Zenari gripped the back of a chair. 'Colonel Jobert, how may I be of service?'

Jobert stripped off his tailcoat and wound a Turkish sash tight about his abdomen, before evaluating Zenari with an impassive face. 'I need you in the front rank.'

Zenari straightened. 'Then I shall strap on my sabre.'

'Before you stand to arms, I would have you wear my jacket and hat.' Jobert passed his clothing to Zenari. 'Might you take post beside Sevalnev today.'

'My goodness.' With a mischievous smile, Zenari inspected Jobert's battered hat with its dull metal decoration for bravery. 'Masquerading as a French officer on a foreign field. Alas, should I fall today, I shall be bereft of all honour.'

'Should you fall, Zenari, do not tear the coat.' Jobert squatted beside Moench and squeezed his shoulder. 'Stable hay will be more comfortable than those miserable cots, lads. I will see you tomorrow evening to assess the improvements of your dance steps.'

Receiving a bleak nod from Moench, Jobert departed the apartment for the counterattack preparations in the Keep below.

With the Muslim quarter secured that morning, the vulnerable Polish camp, having completed the circuitous journey to ford the Prut, compressed itself within the Muslim quarter.

As the Poles manned the walls and ravaged the homes of the Muslim quarter, three Serpenaçi militia groups assembled to enact Jobert's plan.

Twenty men maintained an annoying sting of fire from the

Sepulchre Gate and the Boyar's chapel onto the Poles holding the Al-Aqsa Gate.

Another team of forty Moldavians, led by Sevalnev and Zenari, in Jobert's hat and jacket, streamed from the Balti Gate and, as a fire line, assaulted the Iasi Gate. Following an exchange of musket balls and arrows, the Poles gathered their horsemen to charge. In the face of such a threat, the Moldavians slunk back to the safety of the Balti Gate, leaving crows and kites to circle the smouldering Muslim quarter.

Yet, with the closing of the Balti Gates, an initial success had been achieved. For Jobert had selected around twenty men of the remaining Muslim militia of the Serpenaçi garrison and the best hunters. The noisy advance of the hasty raid, once around the head of the Gorge in the orchard belt, covered the movement of Jobert's squad. Once within the leafy groves, Jobert's squad melted into the roots and culverts.

Night fell.

Under the stars, Jobert's raiders snuck down the right bank of the Prut arriving at the crossing point the Poles had utilised twenty-four hours earlier. Well south of the town, they prowled across the grasslands to the left bank of the Bludovaț, conscious to not disturb the wandering mares. Then having followed the Bludovaț Stream north, settled into the gloom beneath the boughs of the fruit groves two hundred metres from the walls and ditches of Serpenaçi.

'And now we wait,' Jobert whispered to the grim Moldavians squatting around him. 'At dawn, the Poles will release their herds to graze. During the day, our comrades will appear busy preparing to assault across the Bludovaț. Once the flocks are brought in for the evening, we will storm the gate. Our rush will be supported by an assault across the Upper Pond.'

Jobert pulled his sheepskin coat around him, bit off a plug of dried horse meat and wriggled into the cooling earth.

Serpenaçi's pre-dawn call to prayer woke Jobert. He rolled onto his elbow and knees to force himself awake.

'My lord?' A hand was laid on his back. 'My lord, horsemen are on the Iasi road.'

The report jolted Jobert's heart to racing. 'Cossacks?'

The smith mumbled to a few squatting Moldavians. 'Possibly, my lord. Their scouts are entering the groves.' There was fear in the smith's whisper. 'They are very near.'

'How many and where?'

'Our sentries count around one hundred at a camp further south along the Bludovaṭ.'

'Assemble the men in silence.' Jobert placed a hand on the smith's shoulder. 'Then show me these Cossack scouts.'

Jobert, the smith and two Moldavian hunters crept carefully from orchard trunk to trunk, until Jobert identified gesticulating hunched figures by the roadside. As roosting waterfowl woke to chirp and honk in the branches around them, one bulky form stood up, put his hands on his hips and spat.

'Tétény!' Jobert withdrew the Moldavians deeper into the shadows of the vine trellises. 'Not Cossacks, but uhlans.'

In the grey light, the smith's eyes bulged and his breathing was shallow. 'What would you have us do, my lord?'

'It is nearly dawn. The Poles will open the Iasi Gate to release their flocks to graze. The Polish sentries will find the uhlans. We had best rush the gates as the herds are being brought out.'

'But Boyar Sevalnev is expecting us to rush the gates this evening. We will have no support.'

'Indeed, none. Except for the uhlans. We had best run faster than they can charge.'

Jobert and his scouts returned to the waiting Moldavians nestled in the embankment above the Bludovaṭ.

Two hundred metres from Jobert and his men, the screech of iron hinges, the clip-clop of hooves and the tinkling of goat bells heralded the discharge of the Polish flocks from the Iasi Gate. As a few pairs of mounted sentries dispersed toward the edges of the orchard, so the herd of bleating goats fanned out onto the grassy plain beyond the walls. Children tending their animals called and whistled as they ran to contain the flanks of the ambling flood.

A thunder of hooves from the south.

A shout from a Polish sentry.

A scream from a young herdsman.

The metal alarm ring on the Iasi Gate began to clang.

'Now, lads!' Jobert hissed, hoisting his scabbard. 'Run!'

Ahead of the labouring Moldavians, children ran towards cries of sentries on Iasi's ramparts.

Around them, alarmed goats scattered, causing the runners to weave and trip.

The hoof falls sounded immediately behind Jobert. The gate did not seem to be coming any nearer. He had no breath to exhort the men. The pain from his beating by Koranski's guards cramped his knees. Jobert tore at his sheepskin jacket's lapels to remove it, only to find his sword belt was fastened around it. The pistol barrels punched into his belly as he ran. He drew one and twisted the other for greater comfort.

Muskets exploded from Iasi's parapet.

Their aim was high. The balls zipped above.

Uhlans cried out just behind.

A dozen Polish spearmen shuffled into line at the drawbridge. The Polish line danced around the screaming children and braced for the charging Moldavians.

Jobert drew his sabre, locked his elbows to extend both pistol and sabre and bellowed. 'On me!'

He fired the pistol at the shield to his front and tore through the resultant smoke cloud. Jobert's sabre tip slid a lance shaft off the centreline between him and his closing opponent, and the sabre stabbed straight through the Pole's throat.

Jobert wheezed as he tugged the sabre from the collapsing man.

Around him, the militia, in their rage, hacked down the remaining Poles.

Polish warriors were streaming from the streets leading deeper into the Muslim quarter to the gatehouse.

Jobert glanced back for the uhlans. *Can we close the gates?*

Only strides away, screaming Carpathian war cries urged on a wall of galloping horse flesh. Square nostrils led by lance tips.

The smith wrenched Jobert amongst the Moldavians struggling to close one of the wooden gates.

Horsemen burst through the remaining open space.

Polish muskets emptied the saddles that made it through.

Polish shoulders rammed the gates beside the struggling Moldavians.

Dismounted Transylvanians speared and hacked to maintain the breach.

Wounded horses, dragging their riders by their stirrups, lurched amongst the wrestling, grunting men.

The air beneath the gate arch reeked of sweat, dust, blood and piss.

Jobert stuffed his discharged pistol into his sash and withdrew the other. He grabbed the smith and shook him. 'To the mosque!'

About a dozen Moldavians ran from the gatehouse down the stall-lined street towards the blank brick backwall of the mosque. Groups of Polish warriors ran past them. Since both groups wore either simple shirts or lambswool jackets, carried knives and muskets, they passed without comment.

Bursting from the shade trees around the mosque's fountain pool, the Moldavians raced for the entrance to the mosque. The two Polish spearmen who emerged from the entry were cut down in an instant.

The cold interior of the mosque smelled of wet carpet, sheep and souring wounds. Against the far wall, terrified women and elderly cringed and clung to their children and goats. On the carpet strewn floor lay about thirty wounded, Polish and Moldavian, from yesterday's combat.

Beside the pulpit squatted heavy pack-horse panniers.

Jobert gripped the smith's shoulder and pointed his pistol at the timber pulpit. 'Barricade the door with that. Is there access to the roof? I need to understand what is happening.'

'Why not the minaret, my lord?' the smith asked. 'The tower from where the call to prayer is sung.'

Jobert ascended the minaret stairs and found a tight shallow balcony to view Serpenaçi. He instinctively reached for his telescope to find it absent from the inside of his borrowed sheepskin coat.

Fighting sounded on all sides of the Muslim quarter. Muskets fired, blades thudded and arrows hissed, amongst the constant screaming and shouting. Muslim families streamed towards the mosque with bundles, children and goats.

Tétény's banner flapping above the Iasi Gate confirmed the uhlans had secured the entrance to the Muslim quarter. Yet the Poles, with muskets and bows, held the streets against any Transylvanian movement beyond the gatehouse. Between the standoff were strewn limp dead who sprouted a crop of rigid arrow shafts.

Beside Jobert on the balcony, the smith blew an ascending series of notes on his hunting bugle. Supported by rousing cheers, an identical riff was repeated from the vicinity of the Jerusalem Bridge.

Jobert grunted with satisfaction. Koranski's strength was stretched as his Poles in the Al-Aqsa Gate traded shots across the Jerusalem Bridge with the Moldavian militia within the Sepulchre Gate.

Jobert's comfort soured to shock. Across the Bludovaţ within the Boyar's quarter, Tétény's banners hung on the Suceava Gate. 'How have horsemen breached a gate?' Lance-wielding uhlans bundled Moldavian militia back into the Keep and the hall.

On the Keep's upper level, Jobert saw Duque, distinctive in his green hat with its brim curled up higher on the right. Jobert scanned the parapet for his double but could not see Zenari. Of greater disappointment was the realisation that Duque and Moench, surrounded by uhlans, were now trapped in the Keep.

Below in the streets approaching the mosque, Jobert spied Koranski flanked by his guardian spearmen. 'Koranski!' Jobert bellowed.

'Jobert?' Koranski looked up to the minaret with a start.

'I have something you need, Koranski. Join me here alone.'

'I do not answer to you, Jobert. Where is Sevalnev?'

'Fuck Sevalnev!' Jobert flicked his fingers. 'Sevalnev's pathetic efforts allowed your attack to succeed. I was elected by the militia to lead the counterattack. I am this town's commander, not Sevalnev. Before you speak to Tétény, you need to speak to me. Join me. Keep your sword but come alone. No harm will come to you. You have my word. Enjoy the view.'

Soon after, Koranski squeezed into the minaret platform and viewed the smoking wreckage of the Iasi Gate and the pall of dust over the town.

'You are stretched thin, Koranski.' Jobert smoothed his hand across the vista of Serpenaçi. 'You face Moldavians at the Al-Aqsa and from within the mosque. You face uhlans at the Iasi and across the Upper Pond. Your families and your herds are crushed into this quarter. You have lost your gold and your hostages. You are in a bad way, Koranski.'

Koranski continued to view the town, but his black, beady eyes flickered in calculation.

Jobert stabbed a rigid finger to the kites riding the smoky

thermals above. 'Koranski, you could not have sent a clearer signal to Begnzarov. Begnzarov is now coming. It is within my power to give you to Begnzarov. Or ...'

Koranski. 'Or?'

'To protect your community from Begnzarov, you need the Iasi Gate from Tétény, and you need the Sepulchre Gate to cease being a threat and become a dependable flank. Only I can give you those. The survival of your people is dependent on me.'

Koranski winced, his head swivelling over his shoulder towards the Suceava Gate and the Keep.

'Tétény is not a patient man,' Jobert said. 'His blades press hard upon your children's throats.'

'You have the gold?' Koranski squinted at Jobert. 'Then you ensure I receive the Sepulchre Tower and the Iasi Gate.'

'Piss off, Koranski. My gold is my gold. You still must pay for the safety of your people. And you must pay me.'

Koranski looked suspiciously at Jobert. 'What price?'

'My men, my families and my gold all move in perfect safety from the mosque and across the Jerusalem Bridge.'

Koranski breathed out and jerked his head in agreement.

'Good. Then let us descend and speak to Tétény.'

In the chamber of the mosque, Jobert beckoned the blacksmith. 'Koranski has assured clear passage to the Sepulchre Tower. Move everyone now.'

'Stop!' Koranski clenched his fist in the air. 'No movement until negotiations with Tétény are completed.'

Jobert stabbed two rigid fingers into Koranski's chest. 'My people move now, Koranski, while your people enjoy their last sunset. Any hopes of their future sunsets are at my convenience.'

Koranski glared in simmering resentment.

Jobert snarled at the smith. 'Do as I command. Also ...' Jobert stabbed a pistol barrel at the leather panniers of gold.

'Those saddlebags are ... the property of Boyar Sevalnev and Otal Alaybey.' The smith viewed the panniers with trepidation. 'Take them. Otal Alaybey will reward your service for their safe keeping.'

As the smith and another militiaman hefted the heavy sacks onto their shoulders, Jobert turned to Koranski. 'Accompany me, now, to Tétény at the Iasi Gate.'

Polish warriors muttered to each other at the spectacle of Koranski and Jobert, flanked by Koranski's bodyguard, proceeding along the road from the mosque to the foot of the Iasi Gate.

Tétény and four Carpathian bowmen rose from behind the parapet of the Iasi gatehouse. 'Come any closer, you Polish bastard, and I will cut you down.'

Jobert stepped forward with his hands on his hips. 'Get down here now, Tétény.'

The uhlans released the pressures from their bowstrings as Tétény descended to the roadway.

On his arrival in front of Jobert and Koranski, Tétény's face contorted as if he had stepped in dogshit. 'What are you doing here, Jobert?'

'I command the town's defence.'

Tétény rasped a throaty cough. 'You speak to Cossacks on behalf of the Sultan. Now you are one of his generals?' Tétény looked about him. 'You are not doing a very good job, general. Where is Sevalnev?'

Jobert shrugged. 'You are interrupting Koranski's and my combined counterattack against the Isai Gate, Tétény. What do you want?'

Tétény sneered. 'Piss off, Jobert.' Indicating Koranski, he said, 'The men need to speak. Koranski, I have all the horses, and I have these,' Tétény jerked his thumb to the upper reaches of the Iasi's towers where six Polish horsemen had Transylvanian blades pressed against their throats. 'You, Koranski, owe me the life of my son.'

Koranski shrugged. 'He chose to draw his sword against the loyal subjects of the Sultan on the land of the Sultan. He accepted a warrior's death.'

'Fuck you, Koranski. I will open these throats myself. The only way they live is if you pass me the French gold.'

Koranski's beady eyes twitched in calculation.

'Piss on you, Tétény.' Jobert smiled. 'I have the gold.'

'Bullshit!' Tétény said, and both he and Jobert looked at Koranski for confirmation.

Koranski lowered his eyes. 'Jobert has the gold.'

Jobert waggled his finger. 'No gold for you, Tétény. Murder your hostages, steal my horses and ride fast.' Jobert pointed south over the Iasi Gate. 'Begnzarov is somewhere behind you and closing.'

Tétény rolled his wild eyes in calculation. 'Then you, Jobert, buy the lives of these people. I have Moldavian prisoners as well.'

'I do not care for their lives.' Jobert shrugged. 'Murder them,' he said as Koranski bared his teeth, 'and you will start a war, Tétény. Suceava is the first place Otal Alaybey will turn to rubble. And your name will be known in Vienna.'

Tétény sneered.

Jobert turned to Koranski. 'What else do you have to trade, Koranski? Your goats?'

Koranski glared.

'The Pole has nothing.' Jobert pointed a finger at the uhlan chieftain. 'Yet I can give you, Tétény, something you need.'

Tétény's eyes narrowed.

'I can give you sanctuary from the Cossacks within these walls. Begnzarov will come and you and your men will be safe. Otal will arrive soon and see Begnzarov off.'

Tétény's wild eyes scanned for a trap. 'You cannot give something I have taken with my sword. I have the Boyar's quarter.'

'Yes?' Jobert folded his arms and rocked back on his heels. 'And will you muster five hundred horses across the Bludovaţ before sunset? Will the Boyar's quarter hold all these horses as well as your own mounts? You have nothing more than the shadows of the Suceava Gate to cower within while I tower above you from the Keep.'

Tétény snarled.

'Begnzarov hunts Koranski for stealing his horses. I will declare to Begnzarov that the town is held by us Moldavians,' Jobert patted Koranski on the shoulder, 'and all the Poles Begnzarov seeks are contained within the Boyar's quarters. Begnzarov cannot tell the difference between Christians. You will be attacked from the Keep from my Moldavians, and across the Bludovaţ by Koranski, while the Cossacks breach the Suceava Gate.'

Tétény shuffled as his fists clenched.

Jobert. 'Or …'

Koranski shook his head at Jobert with disdain.

Tétény's face twitched to bare his teeth. 'Or?'

Jobert shrugged. 'You release all Polish and Moldavian hostages unharmed. You return the Iasi Gate to Koranski. You muster all horses back within the Christian and Muslim sector by sunset. You retire within the walls of the Boyar's quarter and prepare your defence,' Jobert said as he winked at Tétény, 'knowing your flanks are secured by your allies.'

Tétény bared his teeth and spat into the dust.

'I will take that as your wholehearted agreement.'

Tétény jabbed a claw-like finger at the Polish hetman. 'You still have a blood debt to me, Koranski.'

Jobert scoffed. 'Piss off, Tétény, attend to the tasks I have set you. The men need to speak.' Jobert slapped Koranski's shoulder before steering him away. 'I have delivered the survival of your families, Koranski. Now prepare your defence and prepare to receive a few hundred of my horses. Care for them as well as you cared for my gold.'

Jobert turned down the street that ran from Iasi to Al-Aqsa to join the families and wounded from the mosque.

'What seals our pact, Jobert?' Koranski asked.

Jobert pivoted back. 'If you were a man of honour whose integrity I could trust I would shake your hand.' Koranski stepped forward and offered his hand. 'But since you are not ...'

Jobert turned on his heel and departed the Muslim quarter over the Jerusalem Bridge.

Chapter Twenty-Three

Jobert gripped tight the timberwork of the Caesar's Gate parapet against the utter bone-melting weariness which threatened to erode him. Beneath him, loose mares swirled and snorted in the streets of the Christian quarter, calling to each other in the moonlight-infused dusk. Tétény's uhlans had mustered in all the horses through both the Balti and the Iasi Gates. Now, above the Caesar's Bridge, Jobert awaited Tétény.

Jobert turned to Zenari. 'This noise would be perfect cover for a Cossack approach.'

'Speak of the Devil,' Zenari jutted his chin, 'and he shall appear.'

Tétény halted his horse on Caesar's Bridge. 'I have sentries that are missing, Jobert.' He fought the impulse to look up to Jobert's superior position on the gatehouse. 'They have not returned.'

'Do you not have a horn call to which they will return?' Jobert asked.

'Sound the horn and alert the Cossacks?'

'What Cossacks?'

'They are out there.' Tétény's lupine neck swivelled towards the Suceava Gate. 'I can feel them.'

'It is good you can feel them, Tétény, because your scouts will not see them.'

'Hah!' Tétény snorted. 'Cossack stealth is a myth. They are not that good.'

'No, they are not. But your men are woeful. They are bandits, not warriors. Last night your scouts entered the orchard with the intent of spying on the town and failed to notice the thirty Moldavians lying in wait to rush the gate.'

'Get fucked, Jobert.' Tétény flapped his reins in frustration. 'If I need to be insulted further, where will I find you?'

'I will stand post on the Sepulchre Gate. My Italian … friend, Colonel Zenari,' Jobert said as he slapped Zenari's shoulder, 'will remain here at Caesar's Gate at your service.' Tétény began to back his horse off the bridge. 'Wait, Tétény, join me in the Keep. I wish to speak with Sevalnev.'

'If we cannot cross this bridge to our allies,' Tétény said, 'then our allies cannot cross to us.'

'Let us observe that arrangement, Tétény, while allowing either you or I to pass unimpeded.'

Jobert descended the gatehouse and followed Tétény into the Keep. 'Why not avail yourself of Sevalnev's wise counsel in chapel, Tétény, while I fetch a blanket.'

Upon entry to their stone-walled rooms, Jobert found Duque at the table fussing in his portmanteau.

Jobert raised his eyebrows in enquiry. 'Moench?'

'Asleep with fever.' Duque glanced at the closed bedroom door. 'Do not fret.' Duque passed Jobert a platter of dried horse meat, half-cooked rice and a fat orange peach. 'He will be prancing the *gavotte* by Christmas.'

'Fresh peaches?' Jobert mumbled juice down his unshaven chin.

'Moench's laundress.'

'How does she pass the uhlan sentries?'

'She shares her Moldavian peaches on the way in, and her Moldavian profits on the way out.'

'How enterprising. No wonder Moench admires her.'

Duque smiled without humour. 'If I need to find you, where ...'

'The Sepulchre Gate.' Jobert ground his teeth on the unyielding meat. 'A vantage point where I can watch both bags of vipers, the Poles and the uhlans. I have posted Zenari on the Caesar's Gate to remain in contact with Tétény. Why?'

'André ...' Duque pushed at his rice with his spoon, 'do you want the ring?'

'The Key?' Jobert's brow furrowed in confusion. 'For what purpose?'

'I do not know, but since no one is searching for it ... is now not the best time to keep it close? It will be better in your pocket, than where it is now. In the battle to come we could easily be separated from its hiding place.'

'Why? Where in hell did you hide it?'

Duque shot Jobert a wink over a rare smile.

Jobert snorted. 'Your little packhorse?'

'Do you not remember your study of equine anatomy in Genoa?'

'I flicked through some pages about the bones of the spine ...'

'Yes, but what part of the spine?' Duque picked up a lantern. 'Come and see.'

Down in the stables, the mare blinked at Duque's lantern and continued to munch on her hay in the timber manger. Duque placed the lantern on a post by her face.

Duque waggled a hoof pick. 'I will clean her feet.' Duque flicked Jobert a horse-brush. 'You can get busy on the other side.'

Jobert ran the stiff straw strands of the brush along her neck and down her mane. He peered into the shadows of adjoining stables and confirmed they were occupied by only animals. 'It has been with her since Bucharest?'

Duque lowered her nearside fore and slid his fingers down her nearside hock. 'Yes.'

Jobert watched under her belly expecting a cavity in her foot to be revealed. 'And it evaded the sipahis' search when we were abused on the plains?'

'Yes. Swap sides and keep brushing.'

Duque placed down the last hoof and tucked his hoof pick into his pocket. 'You have done a shoddy job on her coat. Not concentrating on the task? Do better on her tail.'

Duque slid his fingers into her mouth and wiped the chewed hay from her teeth. He then, with one hand, rolled her tongue out of the side of her lips, and with the other, reached into her mouth to inspect her back teeth with his fingertips.

In his mind, Jobert compared the size of the Key to the size of a horse's molar. *Surely, the Key would be bigger?*

Duque closed her mouth.

'Where is it?' Jobert asked.

'Keep brushing, Trooper Jobert. I want to see that tail glow like a maiden's locks.'

Jobert changed his brush strokes from downwards to grasping the tail bones and flaring the tail hair into a cascade. 'I do not have to stick my hand up her arse, do I?'

'Of course not. She would shit it out soon after it was inserted—'

'Hah! Unless she was Zenari.'

Duque shrugged with resignation. 'And what a surprise the

Hospodar's gardener would find at the base of his tomato trellis a few days later.'

'So, if not her arse …' Jobert slumped as he inspected the dual orifices under the mare's tail. 'I have foregone the pleasure of a vagina for some months. Is this to be the reward for my abstinence?'

'No. Anything inserted in the womb would induce septicaemia and kill her. Besides, once deep in the uterus, it could only be retrieved by opening her up. Stay focused, keep brushing.'

As Jobert shifted his grasp, his hand froze at an unexpected touch. His fingertips prodded at a bulge on the end of her tail. He tucked the brush under his armpit and drew his dagger from his left cuff. 'The last bone of the coccyx. You clever prick.'

As Duque fussed with her eyelids to inspect her eyes, he spoke quietly. 'Make your slices discreet.'

Jobert scraped the blade against a ball of wax and hair. 'I would not have thought it would fit over the last bone of the coccyx.'

'Not any normal ring, but it would when it is designed for an emperor's finger wearing a ceremonial leather glove.'

The hairy wax egg soon plopped into Jobert's hand. With the Key gripped tight, Jobert slipped away his dagger and continued to brush her tail. He stepped back to admire his handiwork with his hands on his hips. 'You clever little girl. Enjoy your dinner.' With a surreptitious movement Jobert tucked the wax ball into a fob pocket on the inside seam of his trousers.

Of what value to me is a key that connects empires?

'*Allahu Akbar.*'

The opening phrase of the Islamic call to prayer shook Jobert from his slumber. The direction of the prayer disoriented him, until Jobert remembered the imam now received his faithful in the church's forecourt.

Jobert gripped his cape around his shoulders, moaning as he straightened, and looked over the Sepulchre Tower's parapet.

From the dawn mist in the orchards, other calls to prayer were raised.

Jobert's guts turned to ice as he spun to peer outwards.

'Cossacks!' Besides Jobert, the smith gripped his knuckles in supplication. 'They are here.'

Shoulder to shoulder in front of the groves' trunks, dark figures bent and swayed in prayer. Nearly one hundred Cossacks out from the Balti Gate and a similar number beyond the Iasi Gate.

Within moments, alarms clanged from the Keep and all along the walls.

Polish horns droned throughout the Muslim quarter.

The church bell drowned out the imam's summons.

Zenari appeared at the base of the Sepulchre Gate. 'There is about one hundred of them beyond the Suceava Gate and about half that north of the river opposite the Port Tower. Tétény is at Caesar's Gate. He seeks your plan?'

'Tétény's orders are clear. Keep the Cossacks on the outside of the walls.'

Zenari turned in small hesitant circles before shuffling back into the Christian quarter.

'Jobert!' From Al-Aqsa's ramparts, Koranski's squat form shouted over the Gorge. 'We are surrounded. Where will Begnzarov thrust?'

Jobert closed his eyes and breathed deeply.

He opened his eyes. 'I expect Begnzarov to attack the Christian quarter. That immediately separates the Muslim quarter from the Boyar's quarter.' Koranski dipped his head in tacit assent. 'Begnzarov will distract first. I expect he would attack the damaged Iasi Gate, rather than the solid Suceava Gate. Apart from uhlan mounts, the Boyar's quarter does not contain—'

A Cossack whistle shrieked.

Jobert reheard the sound of bone whistles from fighting Cossacks in Lombardy two years before. He shielded his eyes against the low red sun.

'There is Begnzarov.' Koranski pointed to a rider on a surging black stallion on the plain in front of the Balti Gate.

From the orchards' shadows, four prisoners were shoved forward by their captors. Prisoners were thrust onto their knees. Their wrists were lashed to their ankles. Cossacks jabbed lances through one of their bent knees pinning the prisoners to the dirt. The doomed rocked their heads in pain. Their misery was heard by the audience on the walls.

The Cossack guards withdrew to the flanks, bows ready, arrows notched. Begnzarov remained immobile mounted on his magnificent war-stallion. Behind Begnzarov, a standard bearer held Begnzarov's personal tug aloft. Tufts of red, white and blue horsehair, with trailing plaits of black, adorned the carved and painted shaft.

Begnzarov sprang down from the saddle and strode well forward of the row of rocking captives. He raised his arms wide in expectation of someone from within the walls to join him.

Koranski extended a palm of invitation from Jobert towards the waiting Khan.

Jobert mumbled to the smith. 'I suppose that would be me. But I cannot speak his tongue. Fetch Tétény—'

'My lord, the Crimean will speak Moldavian.' The smith bowed his head. 'I will attend you.'

Jobert descended the Sepulchre Gate, walked between the

silent, crowded streets of the Christian quarter and exited the Balti Gate.

He walked out onto the plain. Any hopeful grass shoots had been mowed by loose mares. Jobert's stride crunched on the baked mud.

Begnzarov awaited Jobert's arrival in a wide stance. He was bare-chested, apart from an open sheepskin vest. His skin was scarred, brown and taut over lean muscle. A long ivory-handled knife was tucked into his waist sash. A scimitar hung low on his left hip.

Behind Begnzarov, stripped to their waists, three men and a woman sobbed their respective prayers. The faces of the prisoners were smeared with caked blood, yet their representation was obvious.

A sipahi whose bloodied topknot was plastered to his skull.

A Pole, scalped of his blond plaits, bore black bruising across his abdomen.

An uhlan whose fractured cheekbones and broken nose swelled above his spittle-matted beard.

A black-haired Moldavian woman whose face and breasts were mottled with yellow and purple bruises. The female prisoner was Moench's laundress who had brought them fresh peaches.

Jobert's words struggled from his trembling throat. 'How is she outside the walls?'

The smith was spasming in fear. 'Probably snuck out to gather fruit.'

Jobert's heart sank to his bowels. *This is not about to end well.* He turned to the smith. 'Can you see what is about to happen to them?'

Against his frozen neck, the smith's eyes bulged towards Jobert.

'A battle is to be fought this day,' Jobert said. 'Many will die.

Where will you and I best give our lives for Serpenaçi this day? Being cut down out here by these pricks?' Jobert nodded at the flanking Cossack archers. 'Or directing the fighting inside the walls? Where?'

The man struggled against shrinking within his leather battle-jerkin. 'Inside the walls, my lord.'

Jobert turned to face the smith. 'We are the first gate this bastard faces. If he breaches you and I, he will breach the Balti Gate. He must not pass. He must not pass us.'

The smith squinted at an emerging potential. He slid his crimped fearful face to Jobert. 'He will not pass, my lord.'

Jobert returned his steady gaze to Begnzarov and slowed his breathing.

Begnzarov's eyes were calm, his features emotionless as if Jobert had demanded this regretful inconvenience. When he spoke, his voice was steady.

'He asks if you now command the town, my lord.' Beside Jobert, the smith looked from Begnzarov to Jobert, then licked his lips and nodded. 'Do you still represent the Sultan — peace be upon him?'

Jobert gave a curt nod.

'Why you, France?' Begnzarov asked. 'Is there no one left?'

Jobert did not answer.

Begnzarov prodded with his booted toe a pillow of lambs-wool courier satchels. 'Your messages have not been received. You are quite alone.'

Jobert's face spasmed as if slapped. *Did Fazio carry a satchel?* 'Is this your negotiation, Begnzarov? These peoples' lives for the return of your horses?'

'I do not negotiate for the return of my horses, France.' Begnzarov gave a slight shake of his head. 'I have already asked. It was you who denied me.' He smoothed his palm wide. 'Here is my reply.'

Nausea rose in Jobert's throat. *This is not a negotiation. This is a declaration of combat.*

Begnzarov stood behind the sipahi. He drew the broad-bladed knife from his sash.

The sipahi's face was blank as he stared at the middle distance, intoning '*Allahu Akbar*' over and over.

Begnzarov cupped the young man's chin and whispered the blessing '*Allahu Akbar, siddiqui*', before swiftly cutting deep into the sipahi's throat. In a harsh gurgle, blood gushed down the man's chest and Begnzarov's baggy trousers. Begnzarov continued to saw through sinew and bone to separate the head from the shoulders.

Begnzarov dropped the decapitated head in the dirt.

The sipahi toppled sideways, for his spewing neck to cushion on the lambswool satchels.

Begnzarov levelled his eyes at Jobert as he stepped behind the Pole. 'Do you harbour those who stole from me?'

The Pole's jaw spasmed as he attempted to stem his tears and repeat his prayers. Like the Turk, the Pole was a slender boy. Perhaps not as good a rider as others in his patrol. Or not mounted on a fast enough horse. Or chose the wrong turn in the melee. Or hesitated.

'Koranski is his hetman.' Begnzarov lifted the Pole's chin. Flies buzzed from the matted scalp wound. 'Koranski is my thief. Tell Koranski his people will suffer for their insult.'

The young man looked into Jobert's eyes.

With the blessing of '*Allahu Akbar*', Begnzarov buried his knife beneath the Pole's sternum and drove it towards the boy's pelvis.

The Pole's intestines emptied, writhing white, blue and green, onto the fog-moist turf. He squealed and panted. Black flies settled on the viscera pooling around his knees. He looked up to Jobert for direction.

The smith gripped his knees and vomited.

Jobert swallowed the bile that had risen in his throat and clenched his jaw. *There are no consequences for these actions.*

'Do the Transylvanians stand with you?' Begnzarov stepped behind the uhlan and squinted to the western mountains. The low morning sun chased puffs of valley fog up their dawn-washed slopes. 'If they do not oppose me, I shall set this man free.'

Jobert's nostrils flared as he held Begnzarov's weary stare.

'Do they, France?'

Jobert willed his face to remain calm.

Begnzarov's lips twitched with regret. 'Then they have chosen unwisely.'

The smith spat a stream of saliva to mutter the translation.

The uhlan braced his shoulders as his bladder emptied. His lips beseeched the wings of circling crows blending the pinks, greys and mauves of the morning sky.

Gripping the uhlan's beard, Begnzarov slid his blade lightly across the man's windpipe.

Bright-red bubbles surged and popped.

For long minutes, the uhlan writhed for breath.

As his last gasps spasmed his throat, Begnzarov dug his blade tip deep into the warrior's cervical vertebrae severing the spinal cord.

The man went limp. His eyes rolling at the loss of sensation through his body. His frothy coughs became less.

With a final swipe, Begnzarov removed the head.

Jobert fought against lowering his eyes. He looked to the summer clouds with their promise of a scorching day.

The Moldavian woman croaked a phrase. Jobert recognised her Moldavian. 'Please, my lord.'

Begnzarov asked the smith, 'Do you know her?'

The spasming smith twitched a nod.

Begnzarov waved his blade towards the walls of Serpenaçi and addressed the smith. 'Do you have a wife, a mother, daughters, waiting?'

'Can you do anything to stop him, my lord?' the smith rasped to Jobert.

'Stand fast!' Jobert's curled fingernails sliced into the palms of his balled fists. 'Not a fucking move, soldier. Our time to avenge has not yet come.'

The smith slumped.

Jobert held the woman's eyes. 'And we will avenge them.' His voice wavered. 'You have my word.'

Begnzarov winced, as if him being here, doing this, was an unfortunate necessity not of his making. 'French mercenaries can do nothing.' He tightened his fingers in her hair. 'Tell Serpenaçi to fight like tigers and die with pride. There will be no quarter for any we find alive. Their departure to their God will not be as sweet as hers.'

The smith sobbed.

In two swift movements, Begnzarov opened her throat and cut through bone to remove her head. He wiped his blade along her matted tresses. 'Here.' He offered Jobert her slack-jawed head. 'Take her. Return her to her people.'

Jobert stood motionless.

The smell of blood and piss.

The buzz of flies. The screams of kites.

Begnzarov shrugged and dropped her head.

He moved backed to his thick-chested stallion and vaulted into the saddle with a light spring. From there, Begnzarov watched Jobert, his head tilted in curiosity.

The Pole coughed at Jobert's feet. Having sank back onto his restraining lance, the mortally wounded man trembled with shock. His intestines shuddered. 'France. Please.'

Jobert's mind raced with emotion.

He could not think of a suitable blessing.

Jobert drew his sabre.

The smith sobbed.

Jobert thrust through the base of the throat and cut the young Pole's aorta.

The youth toppled sideways into the puddle of his urine.

Jobert pointed his dripping sabre at Begnzarov. 'Begnzarov, I swear I shall neither clean my blade nor sheath it, until it has drunk deep from the blood of your people.'

'Tell him!' Jobert screamed at the smith.

Begnzarov nodded his understanding. '*Inshallah*, France.'

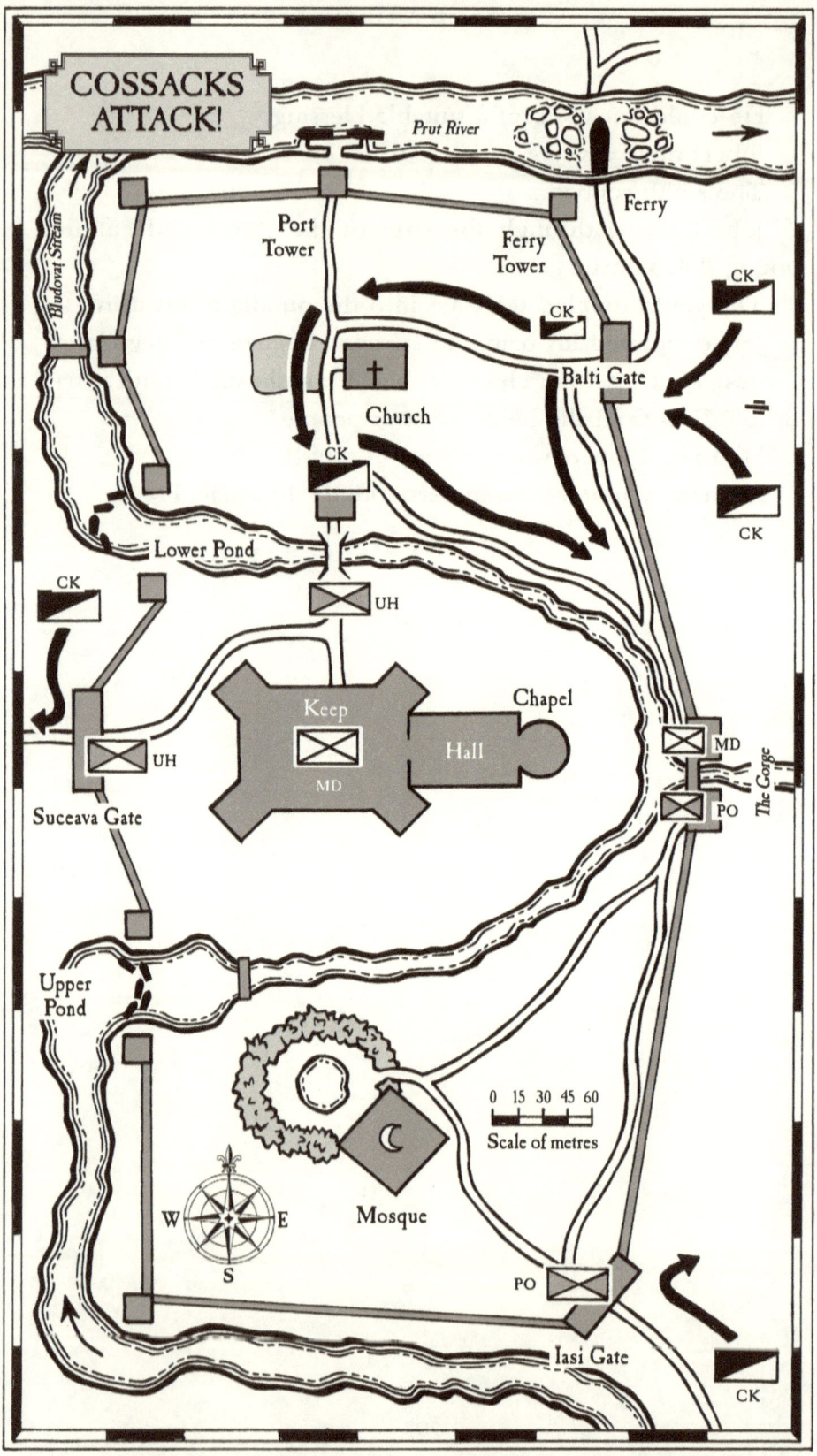

COSSACKS ATTACK!

Prut River

Ferry

Bludovaţ Stream

Port Tower

Ferry Tower

CK

CK

Balti Gate

CK

CK

Church

CK

Lower Pond

CK

UH

Keep

Chapel

Hall

MD

MD

UH

PO

The Gorge

Suceava Gate

MD

Upper Pond

0 15 30 45 60
Scale of metres

W   E
S

Mosque

PO

Iasi Gate

CK

Chapter Twenty-Four

Jobert strode rigidly back to the Balti Gate. No one knows we are here. The smith shuffled behind. *There are no consequences for Begnzarov's brutality.*

Atop the walls and along the embankments around the gate the silent faces of Serpenaçi watched Jobert. Tétény and a handful of his Transylvanians observed from the heights of the Balti Gate. Zenari stood in the open gateway. Koranski and his Poles also sought a sign from the observation point on the Al-Aqsa Tower. On the Keep, Jobert sought Duque on the crowded battlements.

The flap of Serpenaçi's standards stirred on the morning breeze.

Crows squabbled on the beheaded corpses.

Kites flapped to circle the day's early thermals.

Jobert looked at the blood of the Pole on his sabre. *What would I say even if I spoke their language?*

Anger at the appalling brutality clawed a path out of his chest.

'Fuck them!' Jobert thrust his fist in the air, the blade over his head pointing to his left. 'They shall not pass!'

The smith thrust his own weapon in the air and screamed. '*Nu trece!*'

The audience of over two hundred voices thrust their blades in the air and screamed back at him. '*Nu trece!*'

Jobert held his sabre tip further into the morning blue. 'They shall not pass!'

Those on the wall roared back and shifted their weapons to reflect his. '*Nu trece!*'

Jobert turned around towards the Cossacks under the orchard boughs beyond the green shoots of summer. He lengthened his arm forward, flattening his blade at the enemy. '*Nu trece!*'

The men on the wall bellowed and cheered.

Jobert gripped the smith's shoulder. 'Close the gates. Commanders to me.'

Inside the gates, the crowd shoved around him. The smith bellowed for order. Zenari, Tétény and recognised Moldavian lieutenants gathered close.

Cossack horns wailed. Cossack arrows began to rain down on the Port and Ferry Towers from the far bank of the Prut.

Jobert jabbed the smith's chest. 'Here we are strong. Now is our time. Yes?'

The Moldavians bellowed at the translation.

'Every Moldavian warrior to the Balti Gate,' Jobert said. 'Evacuate all families out of the Christian quarter into the Keep. Reset the timber race that will channel the horsemen, if a few of them should enter, to the far side of the church and into the round yard within the church's forecourt. Zenari, take a ten-man reserve to the Sepulchre Gate.'

Tétény's wild eyes rolled as he bared his teeth. 'My men, they are ... they—'

Jobert held up his flat palm. 'Your men are not soldiers. You are nothing but murderers and thieves. You do not know how to stand firm and protect a community. You only understand how to rape it.'

In an attempt to spit at Jobert, Tétény could only fleck his cracked lips with white spittle. 'Piss off, Jobert.'

Jobert lifted his sabre into the space between them. 'You saw what Begnzarov thinks of your Transylvanians. For you there is nothing but death outside these walls. If you want to live you will do as I say.'

Tétény intense stare focused on Jobert. 'And do what, you French turd?'

'Leave fifty of your men to hold the Suceava Gate and the towers above the ponds. You and thirty of your men will man the towers along Prut. My Moldavians—'

'Your Moldavians?'

'My Moldavians will hold the Balti Gate. Should it be breached, we shall withdraw to the Sepulchre Tower. You withdraw your men through the Caesar's Gate. Hold Caesar's Gate, Tétény. Do not lose it. While you hold Caesar's and Suceava Gates you will be safe. Go now and hold the Prut wall.'

Jobert grabbed the lapels of Tétény's grimy sheepskin coat. 'They shall not pass!'

'*Nu trece!*' roared the Moldavians.

Tétény's eyes sought escape.

The dull thud of an explosion caused all to jerk.

Jobert's mind raced. 'Artillery?'

A crack of stone.

'The bastard! He has brought a cannon.'

Screams.

The smith's gnarled fingertips wafted towards Jobert's sleeve. 'A three-pounder gun is laid on the Iasi Gate.'

'On me!' Jobert ran to the Jerusalem Bridge and demanded to be let through.

The smith relayed the garbled reports from within the Sepulchre Tower. 'The Cossacks are attacking the Suceava Gate.'

'A feint.' Jobert heaved on the locking bar on the gate over the Gorge. 'They are evaluating our strength around our three external gates.'

Jobert strode onto the Jerusalem Bridge. Looking up at the Al-Aqsa Tower, he shielded his eyes from the summer sun with his sabre arm. 'Koranski?'

The Polish guards looked at the dark stain of Polish blood on his blade, cried the order to open the gate, and pointed into the Muslim quarter. '*Poarta Iasi.*'

A muffled detonation of gunpowder from beyond the Iasi Gate.

One thick timber door puffed into a shower of spinning shards.

The breath of a spinning iron ball.

Jobert dropped to his belly, his knuckles punching his gripped sabre hilt into the gravel.

A black blur skipped through the opening and drilled a hole in the mosque wall.

Jobert stood as Koranski lumbered towards him.

Koranski rolled his jaws on something distasteful. 'A three-pounder pack-gun.'

'Then limited ammunition.'

'Enough to smash my gate and soon yours.' Bone whistles sounded through the shattered gate. 'Here they come.'

Jobert stood in the ruptured gate and observed the assault. A swarm of Cossacks charged at the gallop. Three horses carried six men. Five dismounted and ran at the breech, leaving one mounted man to lead the horses clear.

Yanked by the collar, Jobert stumbled backwards to the sound of Koranski's voice. 'Return to the Balti Gate, Jobert. We will hold them here.' Koranski spun away and roared in Polish, as Polish spearmen and musketeers filled the void.

Jobert and the smith ran back across the Jerusalem Bridge and up onto the Sepulchre Tower, from where he watched the three-pounder be dragged around the head of the Gorge. 'They are shifting the gun to breach the Balti Gate.'

Jobert scrambled out of the tower and into the streets of the Christian quarter. 'Open the gates. Lower the drawbridge. Stand clear of the gateway. Incoming shot.' Militia men raced at the smith's translated commands. Jobert pointed to the rails which had guided the horse herd to the church forecourt. 'Form line behind the rails. Be prepared to close the gate on my command.'

An agitated Tétény accosted Jobert in the open gate. 'A gun! They will breach the walls. I cannot stand here.'

'You have no choice but to stand, Tétény. They are not through yet. Await my word to withdraw to the Caesar's Gate. It is there you must stand.'

The gun fired.

Jobert shoved Tétény sideways.

A ball came whizzing through the empty gateway, cracked on the packed gravel and smashed through the timberwork of shops lining the road from gate to church.

Jobert smirked at the gun's crew frozen in puzzlement. *I have given you nothing to fire on, you prick Begnzarov. What now?*

A horn blast.

A howl from one hundred throats.

Cossacks thundered forward out from the orchard foliage.

Jobert sneered. 'Their charge has obscured their gun. Close the gates.' The Moldavians on the walls whooped as they fired their muskets into the packed target. 'Kill three Cossacks each.'

The Cossacks milled and cantered away from the barred entry.

Under his tufted battle-standard, Begnzarov sat immobile on his black stallion and fifty warriors mounted behind him. *He maintains a reserve against this gate. This is what he wants.*

The reloaded gun was hauled forward by ropes.

'Converge your fire.' Jobert swept his arms wide then brought his fingertips together, his blackened blade extended. 'Kill the gun crew.'

The small cannon fired canister at the Balti Gates' embrasures. Pellets zipped past. Men reeled backwards.

The gun fired again.

Stone cracked.

Tortured metal screamed.

The ball spun up into the air and thudded into the embankment.

Cossacks cheered from the shade of the boughs.

Jobert leant over the parapet. 'What did it hit?'

'The hinge is lost,' the smith said.

One of the gates swung out on its lower hinge and snapped under its weight to hang askew.

Jobert shoved through the militiamen. 'To the breach!'

Fire arrows struck the gate that had remained closed.

'Why, my lord?' the smith said. 'They cannot burn the gate?'

Smoke filled the arch.

'They advance beyond the smoke.' Jobert signalled towards the stock rails. 'Retire. Form line behind the rails. Front rank spearmen. Second rank musketeers.'

From behind the V-shaped rails, the militia were mesmerised by the pitch smoke in the gateway. A spell only broken by a call from the upper ramparts of the Balti Gate. 'The gun is coming forward.'

'Lie down!' Jobert bellowed.

Canister tore through the shattered gate frame.

A few of the slower defenders folded backwards.

Fifty-odd Cossacks charged on foot through the smoky breach. Some raced up the ladders into the upper reaches of the Balti Gate.

Moldavian muskets fired.

The Cossacks rushed the rails, only for Moldavian blade and spear tips to strike deep.

Jobert scrambled though the rails and slashed at the wounded and floundering Cossacks.

The Cossack assault staggered backwards.

More whistles.

Cossacks aloft on the Balti Gates' ramparts sniped with arrow and musket ball. Under the protective hail, Cossacks tore down the rails on the far side of the race.

The remaining gate swung inwards, but only halfway due to the corpses strewn under the arch. Horsemen poured through the entrance. Horses tripped or leapt over the crawling wounded.

Another Moldavian fusillade collapsed the initial wave of horseflesh.

Men crawled to get clear.

Another wall of horses and lances erupted from the smoke-choked portal, Begnzarov leading, only to be funnelled down the raceway around the church.

'They will circle the church and be slowed by the herd beyond.' Jobert stood tall and waved his dripping sabre towards the Jerusalem Bridge. 'Withdraw to the Sepulchre Gate!'

Jobert, the smith and Moldavians shuffled to the Sepulchre Tower, where twenty lances of the Moldavians were covered by Zenari and ten militiamen up in the ramparts.

'They shall not pass!' Jobert shouted from the base of the gate.

'*Nu trece!*' the militia roared back.

'Where are your muskets?' Jobert asked the smith.

'We dropped them to close with our enemy with the blade, my lord.'

Jobert groaned at the utter stupidity of such ill-discipline.

The rumble of hooves alerted Jobert to the enemy activity beyond the curtain of smoke billowing from the burning Christian quarter.

Zenari pointed from the parapet. 'They are herding the mares out of the quarter.'

When the rumble of hooves subsided, over twenty Cossacks emerged from the smoke to be silhouetted.

A ripple of Moldavian muskets exploded.

A deep horn blasted.

The advancing Cossacks began to back up.

Begnzarov loomed from behind his line. 'France!'

Jobert stepped forward.

With his scimitar in his right hand and the long ivory knife in his left, Begnzarov rode his horse with his seat and his legs, the reins drooped over the withers.

Jobert shrugged out of his jacket, unbuckled his sword belt and adjusted his sabre hand within his glove.

He evaluated his opponent.

Without any pressure on the bit, the stallion skipped lightly, collected over his hocks. Begnzarov achieved a deadly lightness through the horse with just his heels. The horse had been schooled by German-influenced masters. Or it has been stolen from a Russian nobleman.

Begnzarov's charger sprang towards Jobert, skipping its canter leads as it came.

Jobert threw himself to avoid the flashing hooves. He rolled in the dust and coughed at the smoke.

Begnzarov stood between Jobert and the safety of the Sepulchre Gate.

Begnzarov's purpose was serious and clear.

Kill me, rob the Moldavians of leadership, and inspire his men. Then I must attack his strength. Jobert raced at Begnzarov. *Attack the stallion!*

Begnzarov flexed his horse's right, or blade-side, towards Jobert's rush.

Jobert cut at Begnzarov's thigh to draw his blade wide, then swept under the scimitar to aim a reverse cut at the horse's hocks.

For Begnzarov, an easy parry and a yield of his mount's hindquarters.

Just as Jobert had predicted, for with his own blade sweeping to the right as a result of the missed cut, and with Begnzarov's blade beginning an arc that was aimed at Jobert's shoulder, Jobert swept his sabre up, over and down onto the horse's nostrils.

Begnzarov yielded the horse's face away by shifting its shoulders. He spat abuse as his scimitar slid wide with the shift of the horse.

Taking advantage of Begnzarov's exposed back, Jobert stepped to the horse's rump and, swinging his sabre like an axe, aimed at Begnzarov's spine just above his sash.

In the moment of Jobert's cut, with a touch of sharp-edged oriental stirrup from Begnzarov, the horse lowered his head and kicked out.

Jobert was too close to receive the full force of the offside hindfoot. The muscular leg surged along his left forearm.

The brushing force sprawled him in the dirt. Jobert rolled awkwardly into a crouch.

Twirling to recollect its power following the vicious kick, Begnzarov's horse now presented it nearside. And, gripped in his rein hand, Begnzarov's ivory knife.

The gap to make it to the safety of the Sepulchre Gate was closing.

Jobert sprinted for the horse's rump.

The horse was not flexed in a way that would allow a kick but did deny Begnzarov bringing his scimitar to play.

Jobert thrust his blade at Begnzarov's left kidney.

As Jobert expected, Begnzarov parried the strike with the knife. Jobert punched his sabre guard into Begnzarov's elbow.

Begnzarov dropped his knife between the skipping hooves, yet swung his scimitar up, over and down at Jobert.

Jobert dropped backward to the ground, the arcing blade tip just missing his chin. Jobert rolled, rose clutching Begnzarov's knife and stumbled towards the black hindquarters.

Begnzarov continued to pivot his horse to bring his scimitar to bear on his dismounted opponent. Then Begnzarov reversed his horse's spin.

Jobert saw the shift in Begnzarov's hips to initiate the silent command through the saddle.

In the moment he was threatened by blade and hooves, Jobert sprinted towards the gate.

Clear of Begnzarov, Jobert looked up to the men on the Sepulchre Gate and held the ivory knife aloft. 'I have the knife! Now for the throat!'

The Moldavians shook their weapons at the Cossacks and roared. '*Nu trece!*'

Begnzarov's face cracked the faintest of sneers.

You see me now, you bastard. Jobert rammed the Cossack knife up into the air to represent the universal sign of cock-and-balls, then screamed, 'They shall not pass!'

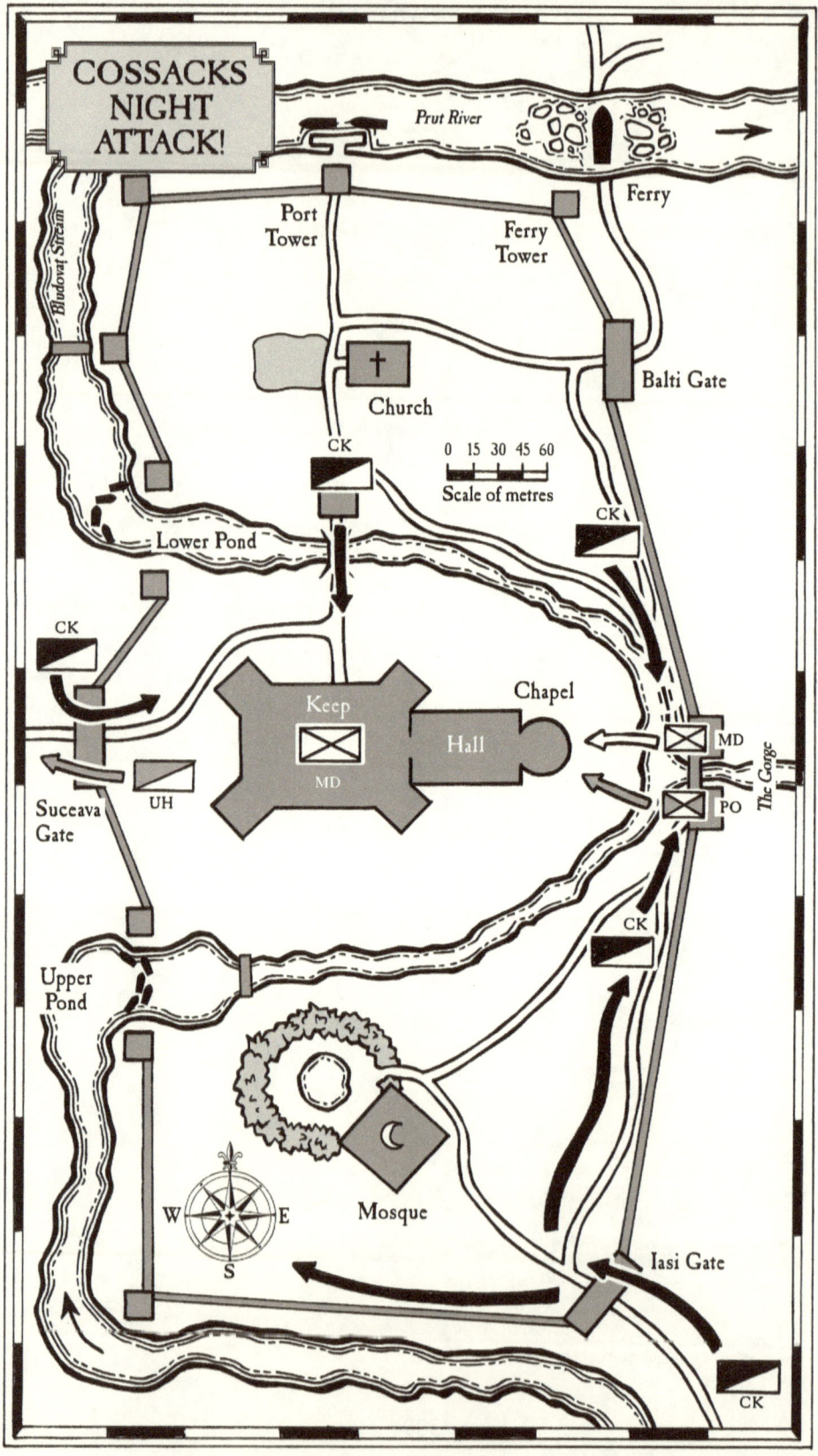

Chapter Twenty-Five

The afternoon brought a lull to the fighting. Each side prepared for the night.

A hasty council of war, of Jobert, Koranski, Sevalnev and
Tétény, met on the steep embankment paths beneath the Boyar's chapel, where a hastily erected three-rope bridge spanned
the confluence of the Bludovaţ and the Gorge.

When asked by Sevalnev for his assessment of the night
ahead, all eyes turned to Jobert.

Jobert pursed his lips and scratched his sabre tip in the dirt.
'I believe Begnzarov has less than one hundred and fifty men,
so he will not attack tonight, but consolidate his defence of
the Christian quarter before a dawn attack. Koranski's thirty
Poles will withdraw from the Iasi Gate and defend the mosque.
With less than twenty Moldavians in the Sepulchre Tower, I
will abandon it before dawn and withdraw to the mosque also.
I expect Otal Alaybey to arrive the day after tomorrow.'

Tétény squatted on the path leading up to the chapel. His
chewing of a stem of grass caused his beard to bounce across

his chest. 'Then our defence would be stronger if my seventy uhlans manned the Keep.'

Sevalnev's eyes widened at the suggestion and then flicked with alarm to Jobert.

'I would agree with such a sensible option, but ...' Jobert's warning finger held Sevalnev from expressing his thoughts. 'Otal Alaybey confided that he will encircle the town to enter through the Suceava Gate. Your defence of that gate, Tétény, is vital.'

With the conference ended, Sevalnev and Tétény ascended the thorny paths to the Keep, and Jobert and Koranski wobbled back over the rope bridge before their own ascent to the Jerusalem Bridge.

Pausing to catch his breath as Moldavian militia and Polish horsemen passed them lugging full buckets, Koranski's moustache and thick lower lip twitched in contemplation. 'Why would I defend the mosque with thirty men, when I told you I have fifty sabres available?'

'That entire plan and our strengths was a lie, because tonight, I expect Tétény will betray us,' Jobert said. 'He made no effort to hold the Caesar's Gate, and now Begnzarov has immediate access to the base of the Keep. Did you notice how calm Tétény appeared just now? At any other time, he is as jitery as a bag full of cats.' Koranski grunted his agreement. 'Thus, I shared lesser strengths than what we really have, and I expressed an underestimate of what Begnzarov could possibly achieve.'

'The revelation of our defence plan is the fee that Tétény must pay Begnzarov for freedom.' Koranski harumphed. 'So, you handed Tétény a turd. What then is our actual plan?'

'I calculate Begnzarov arrived with around three hundred warriors.' Jobert wiped the sweat of the climb from the three-day growth on his chin. 'Begnzarov will attack tonight. My thirty Moldavians will hold the Sepulchre Gate. Your fifty Poles will secure the Iasi Gate.' Jobert winked. 'And we pray that Otal Alaybey arrives tomorrow.'

'Can I evacuate my families from the mosque to the Keep?' Koranski asked.

'No.'

Koranski turned on the path and hung his heavy head to look down at Jobert. 'Why not?'

'The rape and massacre of your families is a consequence of your choices, Koranski.' Jobert rubbed his forearm of its dull ache administered by Koranski's spearmen. 'You purchased this dilemma with your greed. You chose to steal the mares from Begnzarov. You betrayed Sevalnev by attacking Serpenaçi. You betrayed me by stealing my gold. You chose to abandon me when we could be standing in Izmail right now with my mares on board their galleys and my gold in your pocket.'

Koranski's bulk blocked the upward path. 'Do not whimper, Jobert. I could easily have dealt you worse.' His black eyes maintained their consideration of Jobert. 'What do I have to pay?'

Jobert looked down at clumps of weeds twirling in the brown water beyond the thorny track. Jobert looked up and set his jaw. 'If we are to deny Begnzarov our heads on his lances, Koranski, then I demand full command of your warriors, and your total obedience to my orders.'

Koranski's pocked cheeks quivered.

'Your fifty Poles will deny Begnzarov the Iasi Gate,' Jobert said. 'If they press their assault, or they attack into the Muslim quarter along the Upper Pond, you are to withdraw back to the Al-Aqsa Gate. You know the streets. They do not. Make them pay for what they hope to plunder.'

'When can I move my families across the Bludovaţ?'

'My hostages?' Jobert cheek creased in a mirthless grin. 'I will send word to Sevalnev. Have your people cross the rope bridge after sunset.'

Koranski grunted a nod. 'You have not yet sheathed nor cleaned your blade.' Koranski flicked his finger towards Jobert's sabre. 'My thanks for ... young Volodymyr.'

'Who?'

'The boy who Begnzarov ...' Koranski jerked his chin towards those executed this morning.

Jobert scowled at the blood congealed on his steel and clenched his teeth at the memory of Begnzarov's depravity. *They all do it.* Otal decapitated thieves. Koranski impaled heads. Tétény enslaved a village. *If you are of no immediate value to me, then why are you alive?* 'They shall not pass.'

Koranski turned and trudged up the path.

'But as for you, Koranski,' Jobert said at which Koranski half-turned, 'if you do not obey me, I shall have your families thrown from the Keep's parapet.' Jobert raised a rigid finger. 'And I keep my word.'

A few hours later, the night air filled with a Cossack imam calling the faithful to stand shoulder to shoulder and praise the Almighty. The song-like prayer competed with the thirsty, restless animals — Jobert's two hundred mares and the hundreds of Polish mounts and herds — squeezed into the streets of the Muslim quarter.

From the Sepulchre Gate, Jobert had watched the Cossacks consolidate their defence, collect their dead and wounded and herd Jobert's two hundred mares and Serpenaçi's one hundred young stallions to join the uhlans' captured mounts outside the town. Also, fifty Cossack reinforcements — perhaps a screen, perhaps a rearguard against Otal — were observed arriving over the ferry crossing.

Zenari emerged through the hatch in the rampart's timber floor. 'Sevalnev took some convincing to accept the Polish families into the Keep.'

Jobert shook his head. 'How is Moench?'

'Weak. Scared. Duque has set up camp in the stables. He has two packhorses and a saddle horse for Moench ready to ...'

Jobert reached out and tugged at the strap of Zenari's satchel taut across Zenari's chest.

Zenari looked down at the leather case. 'The provenance. A memento of a five-year dream that became a nightmare.'

With dusk, the moon in its first quarter glowed low in the western sky. From his limited perspective in the Sepulchre Tower, Jobert knew Begnzarov would act before moonset in a few hours.

As predicted, the evening's assault began with Tétény's betrayal. The clanging alarms from the Polish-manned towers south of the Upper Pond announced the uhlans opening the Suceava Gate and the clamour of the dismounted Cossack charge.

Moldavian musketry from the embrasures of the Keep's multi-storeys spat illuminated smoke, as the uhlans slunk out and the Cossacks flooded the Boyar's quarter through the Suceava and Caesar's gates.

The commotion at the western end of the Keep covered the rumblings that accompanied the evacuation of Polish families from the Muslim quarter. Heavily laden women, children, elderly and wounded emitted murmurs of frustration and sobs of agitation, as a bunched line of miserable figures trailed through the Al-Aqsa Gate, groped down the steep embankment paths, swayed across the unsteady rope bridge at the confluence of Gorge and Bludovaṭ, and ascended to the Boyar's chapel.

In the shadows of the fruit groves at the eastern end of the Gorge, the sound of hooves, tinkling chains and creaking axles caught the attention of the Moldavians manning the Sepulchre Tower and the Poles in the upper reaches of the Al-Aqsa.

Zenari gripped the timber parapet. 'The gun is being relocated.'

'Or it is a deception.' Wary of Cossack snipers, Jobert pulled Zenari's shoulder lower than the parapet. 'That piece fired less than ten rounds today. Begnzarov will be low on powder and ball. His next bombardment matters.'

A few hours before midnight, Serpenaçi cringed in blackness. No moon, no braziers and no torches marked the antagonists' positions. Only stars and occasional musket fire pricked the gloom with light.

Through the dark hours, not within Jobert's influence, Cossacks and Poles skirmished continuously, and raged in outbursts of hand-to-hand combat, across the Upper Pond's dam and around the Iasi Gate.

Wrapped in a blanket against the groping river fog, Jobert slumped behind the Sepulchre's parapet with Zenari to avoid sniper fire. 'Continuous Cossack assaults, but no supporting artillery. Begnzarov is bringing the gun to bear on one of Jerusalem's gates.'

The hours passed.

The musketry around the Keep and through the Muslim quarter diminished. Jobert's last sensations before he succumbed to exhaustion was the neighs of the horses being mustered out of the Muslim quarter.

The call to prayer kicked Jobert awake.

As he blinked to orient his foggy brain, he realised the call was coming from the minaret.

'I have withdrawn my remaining thirty warriors to the Al-Aqsa.' In the darkness, the stench of Koranski's battle-filthy body alerted Jobert that the Polish hetman squatted beside him. 'Begnzarov has now drawn up his wolves to our gates. We can expect their final assault soon after their devotions.'

'Then we must strengthen the defences of the Keep,' Jobert said. 'Withdraw through the Sepulchre down to the rope bridge. Destroy the Jerusalem Bridge by cutting—'

The three-pounder exploded from the shadows of the Christian quarter.

The ball shredded through the outer gate of the Sepulchre Tower.

Screams of agony tore from the bridge deck below Jobert, Koranski and Zenari.

Koranski jumped up. 'The bastards are not at prayer. We need to move. Now!'

Jobert grasped Koranski's jacket sleeve. 'Give me ten of your best. I will cover your movement. I will lead a raid on the gun.'

Koranski coughed a laugh. 'Cheeky prick, Jobert. Very well, I will set my men towards the Keep and join you with my best.' With the howls of a Cossack assault emanating from the smouldering ruins of the Muslim quarter onto the Al-Aqsa Gate, Koranski disappeared through the floor-hatch to rejoin his warriors.

Jobert turned to the smith. 'Once the Poles are through, lead the Moldavians to the Keep.'

The Cossack three-pounder fired again.

Zenari jabbed at his finger over the parapet. 'The gun is in the lane to the Balti Gate.'

'We need to kill the gun.' Jobert punched Zenari's shoulder. 'Are you with me?'

'How?'

'Rob it of ammunition.'

In the darkness of the bridge deck, men grabbed a wounded mate between two and lugged the injured through the inner gates and down the paths. The wounded cried and groaned at the rough movement. The Polish and Moldavian bearers struggled to cross the rope bridge with their suffering burdens and clamber the banks of the other side.

Above the lane's gun smoke, an iron-grey sky greeted Jobert's sprinting raiders. With the tumult of Al-Aqsa assault behind them, Jobert's party dashed through the concealing haze.

With the snap of chains, the timber decking and spans of the Jerusalem Bridge's two drawbridges clattered into the Gorge.

The twenty Poles and Moldavians soon found themselves in the midst of exhausted Cossacks lounging around a labouring gun crew. The swiftness of their surprise and the drawn points of swords, knives and spears condemned the closest Cossacks to swift butchery. Shouting alarm, the survivors sprinted deeper into the dawn shadows of the Christian quarter.

Jobert peered about him in the gloom. 'Find the ammunition!' he cried to the Moldavian smith. 'Can anyone see packhorses? Or stacked boxes?'

No sooner were weapons withdrawn from their kills, than the squeal of bone whistles, hoarse roars of '*Allahu Akbar!*' and the drumming of trotting warhorses rebounded off the timber walls of the suburb. In the lane, Begnzarov led his warriors on a high-stepping Al-Anfas. The walls seemed to bend against the squeeze of Cossacks flooding towards them.

The Cossacks halted under Begnzarov's plaited tug. Like a hunting pack, they quietened as Begnzarov drew his scimitar before swinging down from the saddle.

'Withdraw to the Keep!' Koranski bellowed.

The Polish and Moldavian soldiers raced for the Sepulchre Gate.

The smith screeched utter hatred and dashed, with his sword outstretched, at the dismounting Begnzarov.

With a smooth slip step, Begnzarov parried the smith's

blade, rolled his wrist and slid his blade under the smith's ribs. Begnzarov's left hand never relinquished his reins.

The smith released a deep groan and folded to the ground, as an impaled offering, under Al-Anfas' jet-black muzzle.

Unfazed by the flashing weapons, the stallion arched his thick neck.

Zenari pointed at the cannon halfway between Jobert and Begnzarov. 'Spike the gun!'

Jobert patted his pockets. 'With what?'

Zenari tore Jobert's hat from his head and ran to the gun. Standing astride the cannon's trails, Zenari ripped the çelenk from Jobert's hat brim and plunged the clasp pin into the touchhole.

'Well done, Zenari!' Jobert cheered. 'That will certainly suffice.'

Beaming at Jobert, Zenari expanded with a flash of immense pride.

Begnzarov's face appeared just behind Zenari's ear.

Begnzarov's fingers gripped down on Zenari's left shoulder.

Begnzarov's blade slid out of the centre of Zenari's waist-coat, just below the satchel strap.

Zenari looked with confusion from the widening dark stain beneath the erupting scimitar to Jobert.

Zenari squatted astride the gun trails. He lowered his face onto his forearms folded on the breech, as if he kissed the pewter badge of bravery in the touchhole.

Begnzarov stepped clear of Zenari's slumped form and peered at both Jobert and Koranski. As the result of some internal decision, the muscles in Begnzarov's jawline softened and he raised his chin. 'Koranski!' With a sweep of his scimitar, Begnzarov invited Koranski to meet him.

Koranski stiffened. 'Spend my gold wisely, Jobert.'

Yelling across the Bludovaț tore Jobert's eyes from Zenari's immobility. A Moldavian counterattack spewed from the chapel to support the retreating Poles and Moldavians. Duque's green hat led the charge.

'No, Koranski,' Jobert said and shook his head, allowing his sabre to fall on its sword knot, 'if anyone will kick the shit out of you, it will not be him.' Jobert grabbed Koranski by the lapels and spun him off balance. 'It will be me.' With a wrestler's flip, Jobert threw Koranski over the edge of the embankment.

Koranski tumbled and rolled and grabbed at the rope bridges anchor points and halted any fall into the Bludovaț.

'Do not whimper, Koranski,' Jobert called down. 'I could easily have dealt you worse.'

With a glance to confirm Koranski was groping his way across the bridge, Jobert swept up his sabre and faced Begnzarov.

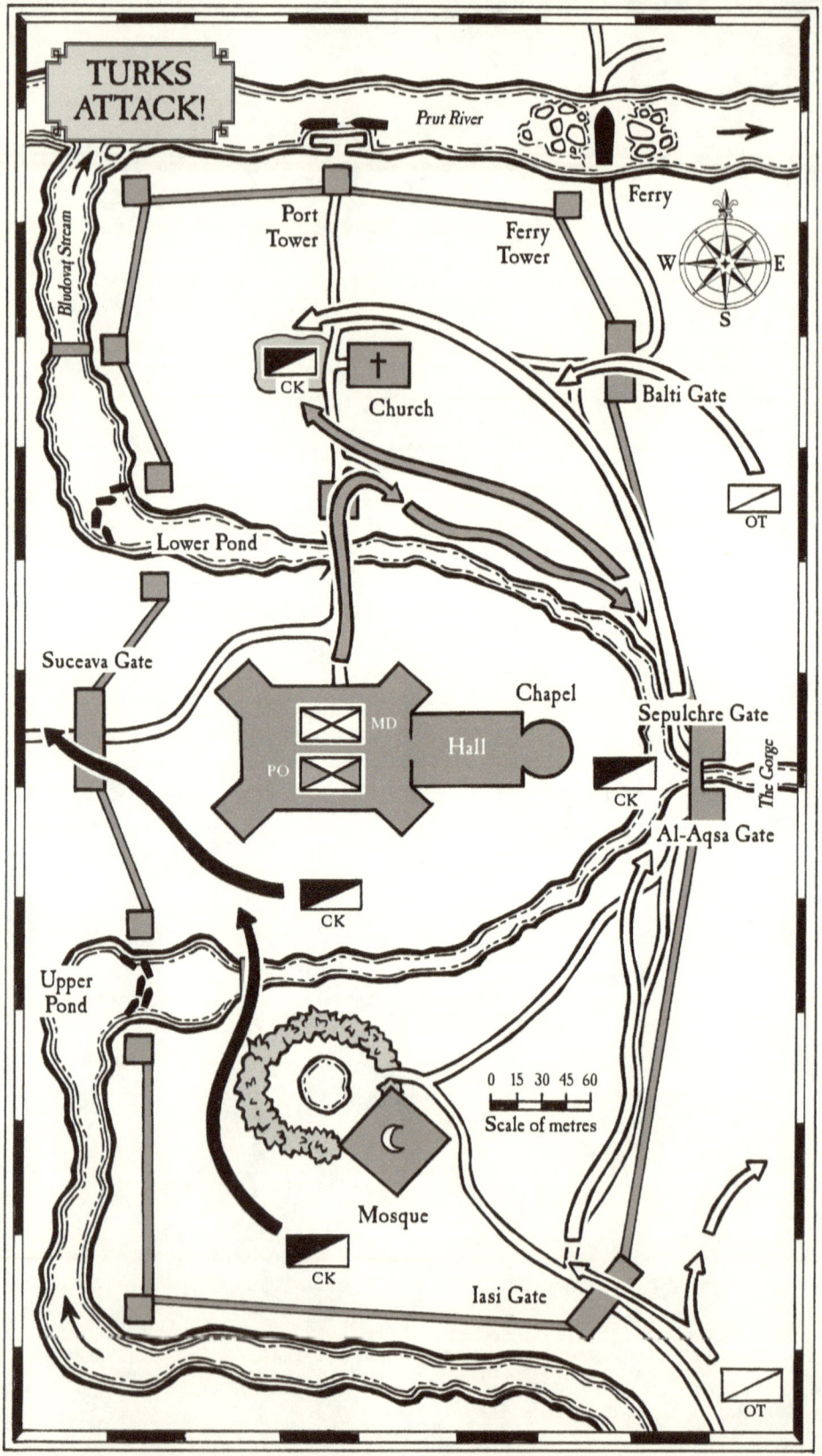

Chapter Twenty-Six

Jobert inhaled and expanded his aching body. He flexed his gloved knuckles within his hilt guard and adjusted the sword knot enclosing his wrist.

Begnzarov rolled his scimitar over his wrist as he evaluated Jobert.

The Cossacks, in the approaches to and the ramparts of the Sepulchre Gate, laughed as they craned to observe the spectacle.

If we dropped the drawbridges, how are they there? Jobert growled his focus back at Begnzarov.

Begnzarov stepped in an arc around Jobert.

Predicting Begnzarov's circling attempt to place himself between Jobert and the embankment, Jobert slid his balanced pose towards the path descending to the Bludovaţ.

Horns blew.

Hundreds of hooves thundered beyond the walls. *My mares?*

Begnzarov glanced at the Sepulchre's ramparts, now brimming with shaven, top-knotted Cossack heads.

A distant chorus of long, high-pitched, trilling caused Begnzarov to lower his guard and shout at those in the tower, whose attention was beyond the timber walls.

Clear ululations of '*Allahu Akbar!*'

Musketry crackled from the Muslim quarter.

A red-faced Cossack screamed from the Sepulchre's parapet. '*Begnzarov Khan! Turki zdes!*'

Begnzarov spun and barked orders at the surrounding men. *Now!*

Jobert spun, ran and stumbled down the paths to the Bludova's rope bridge by the junction with the Gorge. Over his laboured breath, he heard the hiss of arrows. Jobert tripped and tumbled into the riverside thorns. He slashed at the brambles with his sabre, only for their barbs to rip at his shoulders and thighs.

Musketry exploded from the base of the chapel across the stream.

The rope bridge lurched at his tread. Arrow fletches dotted the brown water around where he swung. Jobert flopped on-to the single footrope, and then clambered hand-over-hand, his sabre scraping against his belly, the Bludovaţ sucking at his thighs.

On the Boyar's bank, hands grabbed Jobert's tailcoat and hauled him up. Moldavian fists and stale breath buffeted Jobert, as he was lugged to the crest of the embankment beside the chapel's wall. Jobert heaved in lungsful of acrid air and gripped Duque's jacket as he fought to gain his bearings.

'André,' Duque cried, 'Otal has returned. The Turks are attacking through the Iasi. The Cossacks have abandoned the Boyar's quarter. Sevalnev has secured the Suceava Gate. Koranski's Poles are carrying the Caesar's Gate.'

Cossacks held both the Al-Aqsa and Sepulchre towers. Between them, a single rope stretched taut allowing lithe warriors to clamber across the Gorge.

Glimpsed through the smoke, turbaned djelli darted forward with muskets ready.

A fusillade erupted from the broken structures of the Muslim quarter facing Al-Aqsa.

The bald and wool-capped heads above Al-Aqsa's parapet disappeared.

Scimitar in hand, Otal Alaybey dashed towards the timber gates. A column of dismounted djelli surged behind him.

'What now, André?' Duque asked.

'Take me to Koranski and Caesar's Bridge.'

Hampered by wet trousers and squelching boots, Jobert leant on Duque as he trotted around the Keep to the Caesar's Gate. 'Moench?' Jobert wheezed to speak.

'He is fine.' Duque puffed as he took the weight of one of Jobert's elbow. 'Zenari?'

Jobert flashed a look of sadness. 'No.'

Duque grunted.

As Jobert, Duque and Koranski emerged from the Caesar's gatehouse, horns sounded from the church's bell tower. Cossacks flitted amongst the destruction of the homes within the Christian quarter, along the paved road to the church.

A rueful glance creased Koranski's pocked cheeks before he shrugged his thick shoulders. 'We await your orders, General Jobert.'

'To the Sepulchre Gate!' Jobert voice was hoarse from exhaustion. 'On me!'

There was little about the grime-smeared sheepskins that identified Pole from Moldavian as the angry band of over fifty men hurried behind Jobert and Koranski.

At the sight of Cossacks limping from the skirmish over the Jerusalem Bridge, Jobert bellowed, 'Charge!'

The Moldavians and Poles swept through the Sepulchre's outer gates. Their fury slaughtered any bald top-knotted foe who faced them. Men clambered to the upper deck. They wrenched open the inner gates, from which only a single rope line spanned the chasm. Cossacks were bundled over the side to join the broken drawbridges in the Gorge below. The roar of the Turkish attackers rumbled within the Al-Aqsa tower, which only rose to fever pitch as the outer gates were opened to the assaulting djelli.

Abandoned horse lines were soon put to service creating a two-rope bridge.

Jobert wobbled on the unwieldy structure to cross to the opposing gatehouse. He willed his trembling body to mount the ladder to the upper deck of the Al-Aqsa Gate. His shoulders and thighs burned to gain each rung. The faces and injuries of Begnzarov's execution victims yesterday morning obscured the cloudy sunlight from the hatch above.

The rampart was full of struggling Cossacks repelling djelli clambering over the parapet.

Otal was trapped in one corner.

Jobert's blade twirled, scoring the shoulders and faces of surprised Cossacks. Having wounded with the tip, he savoured each lunge to dispatch.

'I am now twice in your debt.' With a grim nod of thanks, Otal shoved Jobert towards the hatch that led to the bridge.

Soon Jobert and Otal joined Koranski at the Sepulchre's outer gates. Around them mingled Turkish djelli, Poles and Moldavians.

'Otal,' Jobert grabbed at Otal's chain mail, 'the man I sent ... Fazio ... is he ...'

'Ask him yourself.' Otal thrust his chin.

Duque and Fazio held each other by the elbows, their besmirched faces lit by exhilaration.

'How many does Begnzarov have with him?' Otal asked.

'Around two hundred,' Koranski said, 'but they are split. Half have abandoned the Boyar's quarter. Half are bottled up here in the Christian quarter. They are retreating to the church. Perhaps to escape via the Port Tower.'

'Then they have no escape.' Otal's dismissed the option with a flick of his long fingers. 'I have a force on the far side of the Prut.'

Jobert cocked his head. 'Otal, may I suggest …'

Otal slid his dark eyes to Jobert.

'Secure the Balti Gate,' Jobert said as he jabbed his sabre to the right, and then with a sweep of his left hand, 'Koranski and I have less than one hundred Moldavians and Poles. We will pursue them to the church. Why not meet you in the church forecourt?'

'A simple plan.' Otal shrugged. 'Why not?' Otal slapped Koranski on the shoulder as the troops moved deeper into the Christian quarter.

Jobert stepped back towards Duque and Fazio. 'Fazio, you slippery prick. You made it.' He crushed Fazio into a tight hug. 'You know of Moench? And Zenari?'

Fazio glanced at Duque. 'Only that Moench is wounded, and Zenari …'

'Where is Zenari?' Otal asked.

Jobert walked just out from the Sepulchre Gate to the Cossack cannon and the dead man who rested against its barrel. Jobert lifted Zenari's shoulders. His lips twitched in a sad grin.

With an inhaled breath, Otal drew himself up, as Duque and Fazio slumped.

Jobert removed Zenari's satchel and slid it over his shoulder. 'I have lost my mares, but I still have you lads. Today, we go home. Tonight, we camp somewhere south of Serpenaçi.'

'Come on,' Duque said, as Turkish troops surged forward around them, 'the sooner we finish this, the sooner we are home.'

'My dear Jobert!'

Jobert spun around at the imperious tone of Dikaletus Pasha.

Dikaletus' face was burnt deep pink from days of riding and the morning's fighting. As he took in Jobert's torn and filthy attire, he swished an elegant, engraved scimitar. 'Is Sevalnev alive?'

'Yes,' Jobert said, 'he is in the Keep.'

'Take me to him.'

'Find him yourself.'

'Your tone disappoints me, Jobert.' Dikaletus' pudgy fingers waggled from the hilt of his unblooded weapon. 'You are a long way from Paris now. I will make an exception for the exertions of battle. Speaking of disappointments, where is Zenari?'

Standing beside the gun, Jobert placed a gentle hand on the back of Zenari's head. 'Zenari gave his life protecting what belonged to his Sultanic Majesty — peace be upon him.'

'*Alham-dulillah.*' Dikaletus' eyes, lips and moustache quivered as he sought a point of advantage. He flicked a manicured finger at Otal. 'Otal Alaybey, the only way Jobert can save himself is to deliver to me the Key.'

'This fucking Key!' Jobert muttered and put his hands on his hips to support his fatigue. His fingertips brushed the lump in his trouser fob pocket. 'The Key is a gift from France to the Commander of the Faithful — peace be upon him. It is for the Sultan alone. Your claim, Dikaletus Pasha, or that of your Hospodar's, is no more.'

Wearied by the distraction, Otal looked at his dismounted djelli moving into the streets of the Christian quarter. 'Where is the Key, Jobert?'

'I have the Key.'

Otal jerked back, his moustache drooping even further.

Dikaletus snorted as if an assumption of his had been proven. 'Of course, you have it, and now you wear Zenari's satchel.

Your deception will be your undoing. Apart from your debt to me for what you stole, our arrangements are complete.'

'Far from it.' Jobert took a menacing step forward. 'The Hospodar received two hundred kilograms of gold in fair payment for four hundred mares landed in Ravenna. You have failed to deliver, Dikaletus. It is you who is in debt to me. I have taken partial compensation with the gift of your property, your kol Marsden, for the lies, the attacks, the robberies and the laxative.' Jobert swivelled to Otal. 'Otal, you will transport me and my party home to Ravenna in perfect safety. On arrival in Ravenna, I shall inform you, and only you, of the location of the Key.'

Otal squeezed Dikaletus' shoulder. 'You are a long way from Bucharest, Dikaletus Pasha. Why not join me at the Sublime Porte where we shall deliver it together. Now, we waste time, as I have a Crimean Khan to decapitate.'

Abandoning Dikaletus gawping where he stood, Jobert strode after Otal.

Oriented by the stone steeple above the haze and the shattered roofs, Jobert walked the mangled streets leading to the church. A town of timber, straw and fabric was now charred or ash. The smoke squatted in lanes carpeted with shattered pottery. Women hugging babies, children and elderly scrambled through the detritus of their homes. The moans, the sobs and the snarling of dogs now dominated over the coarse shouts and the clang of steel.

As the circular stone walls of the Byzantine church appeared, Jobert found himself at the back of a crowd of soldiers.

The fighting had stopped.

Except the clanging of two blades.

Jobert pushed his way through the crush of nearly five hundred Turks, Moldavians and Poles. Their bodies stank of smoke, sweat and blood. Soldiers cheered '*Nu trece!*' and made way for him.

Jobert stepped into the church's forecourt beyond the front rank of the crowd. How long had it been since the herd was drafted here? Since mares were roped and Jobert slipped their first halters on? *Less than a week ago?*

He could see on the steps of the church, around one hundred Cossacks hunkered in a solid spear line. Their demeanour showed they were unbowed and prepared for any assault.

In the centre of the church's forecourt, the two great champions, Begnzarov and Otal, circled each other.

Begnzarov thrust low.

Otal parried and stepped in close. In a swift levering movement, Otal grasped Begnzarov's scimitar pommel, pressed down on his blade and disarmed Begnzarov.

Begnzarov's free left hand lifted Otal's collar, before he threw Otal in a wrestler's leg sweep.

Otal fell heavily, releasing both combatant's blades in a clatter of steel on stone.

Begnzarov dropped his knees into Otal's ribs and trapped him.

Begnzarov's gnarled fist punched repeatedly into Otal's face.

Begnzarov rose and, as he collected his scimitar, spied Jobert standing clear of the front rank of the surrounding Turks, Poles and Moldavians.

Otal rolled to clear his throat of choking blood.

Begnzarov delivered a swift kick into Otal's abdomen, then lifting Otal's jaw, dragged Otal up on his knees. With his fingers digging into Otal's lower jaw, Begnzarov touched his scimitar's edge on Otal's throat.

Jobert stepped forward. 'Begnzarov, no!'

Expecting a new champion to best the enemy captain, the Moldavian and Polish soldiers hailed Jobert again with roars of '*Nu trece!*' Some of the djelli who had accompanied Jobert north along the Prut recognised him and spread their opinions of the Frenchman amongst the other Turks.

Jobert tipped his head in acknowledgement and held up a hand for silence.

Apart from the small breathing movement of his nostrils, Begnzarov's lean face showed no emotion at either the interruption or the reaction from the crowd.

Jobert walked into the forecourt. 'Koranski, translate for me.'

The tiniest flicker of amusement warped Begnzarov's cheek as Koranski stepped forward.

Jobert held up his palm. 'Koranski, speak to our men. In Moldavian, Polish and Turkish. Tell them to step back. Charge on my command. Only on my command, Koranski.'

Koranski's face drooped into a churlish pout.

'You are in my debt, Koranski,' Jobert spoke slowly and clearly, 'Do not betray me again.'

Koranski snarled his orders at which the gathered men did not respond. He then roared and swept his sword in a wide arc to rattle against their spear tips.

The crush of filthy men shuffled rearward.

Jobert hooked a thumb on Begnzarov's ivory-handled knife snugged in his waist sash. 'Begnzarov, once you have finished with Otal Alaybey it would give me great pleasure to open your throat with the knife I took from you.'

Begnzarov thumped Otal's throat with his scimitar's hilt.

Otal collapsed backward and writhed, gagging.

Three Cossacks pinned Otal's gasping form with their lances.

Begnzarov raised his blade *en garde* to Jobert. 'Otal Alaybey is a respected enemy whose death I have long sought. We shall both enter Paradise together, *alham-dulillah*. You, France, are nothing but a novelty.'

'Watching your blood soak into the earth is a pleasure I must forego, Begnzarov,' Jobert flicked his sabre tip at Otal, 'because I have not finished with him. He inflicted a great abuse upon me. Otal owes me a debt of suffering which must be repaid before he is lavished with eternal pleasures.'

He is my passage home.

Jobert raised a finger to Begnzarov's circling. 'I propose a trade.'

Begnzarov's, Otal's and Koranski's unblinking eyes locked on Jobert.

Jobert relaxed his attacking stance. 'It is within my power to exchange the lives of you and your men,' Jobert swished a disdainful finger towards Otal, 'for his. You may stand on the threshold of a blessed afterlife. But, once you depart, the fate of your families is misery and damnation. Only I can deliver them from this doom.'

The crowd surged with murmurs. The facade of the church amplified the muttering within the Cossack ranks.

'Begnzarov, reflect on the alternative.' Jobert's blade had lowered as he projected his voice to the crowd, via Koranski's translation. 'With the deaths of Begnzarov Khan and Otal Alaybey, the Lord Almighty would welcome such powerful warriors by his side. But the loss of such eminent persons will start a war. A war that would please the Tsar. His regiments will occupy your Crimean homelands. Your families will be helpless without their warriors, without their Khan, to protect them.'

A grumble swirled amongst the Cossacks once Koranski translated.

'Begnzarov,' Jobert said, 'I have the authority here to allow you to mount your warhorses and pass unhindered to the Dniester.'

A sway of Begnzarov's head indicated a likely rejection was forthcoming.

The comments among the Turks, Poles and Moldavians rumbled.

Jobert bristled. 'Koranski, command our men to silence.'
Koranski barked.

Begnzarov noticed the exchange.

'In a demonstration of good faith, I wish to add to my proposal.' Jobert twirled his sabre to keep his weary forearm from stiffening. 'France is willing to exchange five hundred horses—'

Begnzarov's shoulders bunched. 'My horses.'

'No, Begnzarov, my horses!' Jobert jerked his thumb at his chest. 'Koranski stole them. I bought them.' Jobert jabbed an accusatory finger at Begnzarov. 'Your herd is a novelty. You did not protect your herd. Will you repeat that offence by not protecting your families? Now is the time for you to defend what is most dear.'

Begnzarov shuffled in anger and looked to Otal's prostrate bleeding body.

'Is my offer of interest, Begnzarov?' Jobert asked. 'His life for your freedom. My horses for …'

'For what?'

'Al-Anfas.'

Begnzarov squinted at Jobert. 'All our lives for one life?' He swept his scimitar's tip towards Otal. 'All those horses for one horse?'

'Such is my power, yes.'

Otal raised himself on one elbow. 'It is not your power to grant this, Jobert.'

Jobert swung his disdainful gaze at Otal. 'Another great man willing to be welcomed into Paradise. Shame on you. You have known the predations of the Sultan's enemies.' Jobert extended his sabre towards the smoking destruction in the streets around them. 'Where every town in Moldavia will become Serpenaçi. Will this war please the Sultan? With Dikaletus and the Hospodar ready to blame you, what will happen to your lands and your family?'

Otal raised the back of his hand towards the lance tips as if he might brush them aside.

Begnzarov twitched his fingers and the Cossack guards withdrew.

Otal rolled over and rose on one knee. With much stiffness, he lifted his bloodied face to Begnzarov. He dropped his punch-swollen eyes to the forecourt's cobblestones and nodded.

Begnzarov gripped and regripped his scimitar's hilt. 'Perhaps you have the power, France, here and now. But you have no power once we have the herd between the Prut and the Dniester. Once there, Otal Alaybey will order our destruction.'

Jobert rested his sabre on his toecap and shook his head. 'Not if you travel with something of great value to the Sultan.'

Otal winced in alarm. 'Jobert, no!'

'Begnzarov,' Jobert said, 'you would receive something of such extraordinary value that would compel Otal to escort you, your men, your herd, unharmed and unimpeded to the Dniester to ensure this item's safety? Something Otal Alaybey would honour our arrangement to have returned.'

Begnzarov's thin lips separated as if his focused breathing might divine this shift in the negotiation. 'If I am safe across the Dniester, why would I not keep this thing of great value to the Sultan?'

'This thing that will safeguard you, your men and your families has no value to any mortal soul. Only the Commander of the Faithful — peace be upon him — cherishes it.'

'Silence, Jobert!' Otal's wiry hands formed extended claws towards Jobert. 'You must not speak of this.'

'Silence, Otal Alaybey!' Jobert flicked the back of a rigid hand at Otal. 'Are not all the people who will be consumed in this unnecessary war more important than something that has languished in an Italian vault for a millennium? Do you not want your name praised by the Sultan for averting conflict with his neighbours? Or would you rather be the courier of a ... novelty?' Jobert nodded to Begnzarov. 'Now, give him your word.'

Otal stood stiffly, looked Begnzarov in the eye and spoke.

Begnzarov was immobile.

The crowd was frozen.

Even the smoke from the razed homes stilled.

As the crowns of great trees topple slowly when felled, Otal and Begnzarov bent and bowed to each other, touching their fingers lightly to brow and heart.

Koranski snorted. 'It is as you command, Jobert.'

Tremors crept up Jobert's guts. He lifted his ribcage to quell them. 'Our contract is confirmed upon you passing Otal Alay-bey the reins of Al-Anfas. From there, Begnzarov, you are free to collect your herd and go.'

Begnzarov flicked his fingers for his horse to be brought to him. He stroked the stallion's forehead, cleaned the encrusted dust from the corners of Al-Anfas' eyes and straightened his forelock.

Begnzarov bent his ear to the stallion. 'France, Al-Anfas wishes to know what this thing is that guarantees our return to our families? This thing that is of immense value to the Commander of the Faithful — peace be upon him?'

Jobert arched his back, as if the warmth of Bleu's ribcage held him. 'Please pass my deepest respect to Al-Anfas and inform him that this ... thing which ensures your safety ...' Jobert smiled as he touched his heart, '... is me.'

Chapter Twenty-Seven
September 1801, Ravenna, Italy

On the first day of September, the low morning sun transformed the near-flat Adriatic into rippled gold leaf. The magical haze was framed by the dark green Italian coast either side of the Marina di Ravenna beneath the mauve dawn sky. With sails furled on the Ottoman corvette, barefoot Turkish sailors in baggy knee-length pants worked deftly to drop anchor and raise baled goods from the hold, as longboats rowed out from the marina's timber piers.

Three weeks ago, Jobert did not believe he would see a Serpenaçi sunset, let alone a Ravenna dawn.

Three weeks ago, Begnzarov had wasted no time setting out for the Dniester River. Upon being granted freedom in exchange for Otal and Al-Anfas, loose horses were mustered that afternoon, and the Cossacks pushed the herd north for the imperial border. Jobert rode to the rear of Begnzarov's guard and couriers. Less than one thousand metres from their flank, a column of Otal and his djelli shadowed the Cossack herd.

As they proceeded north that afternoon, Jobert watched a team of Cossacks rope a foal, and without stopping, let alone dismounting, butcher the foal in the saddle and distribute the hot, fresh meat for the journey. Such sustenance allowed the steppe warriors to drive the herd as far as the setting moon would allow.

After pre-dawn prayer the next morning, Begnzarov's men mounted and stepped off once more.

Horses, either the herd or mounts, grazed as they walked. A Cossack might make a small nick in the jugular of his horse, and men would ride alongside, lean out of their saddles and drink the hot, rich soup direct from the horse's throat. The slice would heal soon enough. Tomorrow another man would offer his horse's blood to sustain his comrades.

Jobert did not dismount until the time of the evening prayer. Following days of combat and now this extended ride, his body was racked in wooden excruciation.

On the afternoon of the next day, having travelled one hundred kilometres in forty-eight hours, the herd swam the Dniester and returned to Russia. Collapsed in painful exhaustion on the south bank of the Dniester, Jobert watched the setting sun mottle the Cossacks and their receding herd into shadows.

Now, under the sharp light of this Italian morning, Jobert grinned as Fazio and Moench jostled by the ship's bulwark with their meagre luggage and clamber down into the longboat.

'Coming, André?' Duque asked, as he hefted only a single saddlebag over his shoulders. The remaining purses tinkled as Duque descended the gangway.

Just as other purses clinked on Jobert's return to Serpenaçi, from the Dniester, some weeks previously. 'You all have a problem,' Jobert had said to Sevalnev and Koranski, 'both your communities have lost severely. Does Tétény remain a threat, Otal?'

'What has become of Tétény is not known,' Otal said, 'for it is God who ordains such things and God alone knows best.'

Sevalnev pursed his moist lips. 'We have discussed bringing the Polish families within the walls to rebuild.'

Koranski's deep-set eyes pinned Jobert. 'With the loss of so many men and horses, we need help to survive.'

Jobert upended one of his two panniers. Nearly forty purses rattled out between them. 'If divided equally, I have calculated each family, Polish and Moldavian, would receive the equivalent of one year's salary of a French cavalry sergeant.'

Sevalnev and Koranski froze at the pile of coins between them.

Otal's long fingers splayed fan-like across the pyramid of calfskin packets. 'It is written in the holy book — praise be to the word of God — that God provides a single seed from which grows a single stalk of many seeds. Should a man plant those many seeds so he will reap an abundance. As it is with grain, so it is with coin.'

'My dear Dikaletus Pasha,' Jobert cupped his hand around the dragoman's silk-clad upper arm, 'perhaps the gold can be converted into smaller local denominations for a reasonable fee?'

Dikaletus' red moustache trembled in agitation at Jobert's familiar grip. 'My dear Jobert, why ever would you do this?'

A sad smile bent Jobert's lips as he surveyed the wreckage of Serpenaçi. '*Alham-dulillah.*'

Jobert looked down the shifting gangway extending to the waiting longboat. How many boats had he boarded in these last few weeks?

Upon separating from Begnzarov on the Dniester, Otal and Jobert returned along the Prut's upper reaches to Serpenaçi on a fishing raft. Then an oared barge swept them all to the port of Izmail where Dikaletus took his leave. A swift galliot took

Jobert and his friends to Constantinople, where Otal attended an awkward imperial audience. Finally, the Ottoman naval corvette ploughed the waves to Athens, Diraç and, this morning, Ravenna.

At the ship's rail, Jobert said, 'Enjoy Al-Anfas, Otal.'

Otal cleared his throat. 'As you saved my life three times in combat, Jobert, for your theft of the Cricket, I forgive you. I live in hope that you might forgive my trespasses against you.' Otal's hooded gaze searched Jobert's face for possibility. 'As for your theft of an imperial treasure ... where is ... who has the Key?'

Jobert turned his face to the rising sun and smiled. 'Begnzarov.'

'Begnzarov?' Otal's drooping moustache twitched in confusion. 'Why him, Jobert?'

Jobert descended the gangway. 'Goodbye, Otal Alaybey.'

Two weeks later, the gentle waves of Handel's *Water Music* swept through Raive's candlelit dining room.

Jobert beamed at the joy on Moench's face as Moench played alongside a chamber quartet. As they had done in his sumptuous bath before dinner, Jobert felt his shoulders relax within the refuge of the Genoese apartment.

The same companions that had dined together in February, Raive, Marguerite, Camille and De Chabenac, now graced the table with companionable chatter.

Jobert sat back as his plate, smeared with *salsa di noci* and every morsel of *pansotti di Rapallo* devoured, was removed. 'And there are no repercussions on the failure of the enterprise? No diplomatic incident?'

Raive smothered a conspiratorial grin as he wiped his moustache with his serviette. 'We have signed documents of sale with the court of Bucharest. Moreover, a preliminary treaty of peace between ourselves and the Sublime Porte will soon be signed.' Raive squeezed Jobert's forearm. 'Nothing has been lost. The gradual transfer of mares can be gently pursued, for the Hospodar would not wish to disrupt the resumption of good relations by the Sultan.'

'Peace be upon him,' Jobert mumbled and stared beyond Raive's manicured touch to the brushed fabric of his own newly tailored coat. The scent from Jobert's *eau de parfum* lifted from his lapels. As Raive withdrew his hand, Jobert rolled his forearm within the tingling caress of his freshly laundered shirtsleeve.

'And what of Zenari's personal effects?' Jobert asked. 'His innumerable hatboxes?'

Raive reflected on the wild berry aroma of his *Rossese di Dolceacqua* and turned to De Chabenac on his left. 'Might you undertake that sad burden, De Chabenac, on your return to Milan?'

De Chabenac raised his crystal glass in toast. 'To Colonel Zenari.'

Marguerite's long nails stretched like kitten's claws towards Jobert's embroidered cuff. 'Were the Ottoman women very beautiful, darling?'

Jobert's mouthful of *tagliatelle verdi* soured.

In recent dreams, Jobert saw a woman's body lying at rest in her blood and urine, chest down amongst spilled peaches. Jobert held her decapitated head at arm's length by a scruff of her hair in his fist.

It was Gianna's head he held. 'Please, André,' her decapitated head asked through blue lips.

Jobert realised it was he who held Begnzarov's ivory-handled blade.

He twisted the engraved silver dinner fork in his fingers above his *manzo alla Genovese*. 'The Ottoman ladies were of such extraordinary beauty, madame, that their memory will remain with me for some time.'

Marguerite's nails retracted towards her smile.

Across the table, Camille's dark eyes considered Jobert. 'With this new peace with Britain, will you be coming to Paris with us?'

Jobert twitched towards Raive for clarification.

'Yes, negotiations have been ongoing for some time,' Raive said. 'Although far from any formal conclusion, probably early in the new year, an announcement is expected any time soon.'

'After Christmas in Avignon, darling Raive will be seeking suitable apartments in Paris,' Marguerite said. 'Camille and I shall be looking forward to making your cousin's,' Marguerite said, nodding to Jobert without eye contact, and then smiling at De Chabenac, 'and your sister's association before the season.'

Raive's cutlery paused in mid-cut. 'With peace, the generals now gather at our First Consul's side.' Raive's cheek curled with mischievousness. 'Now is the time to brush off our dress uniforms and reacquaint ourselves with old friends who will be in need of aides.'

Is that who I am? Jobert expelled a slight snort. '*Inshallah.*'

Raive flinched with confusion at the expression, while De Chabenac suppressed a grin.

Once the ladies had retired from the table, and Raive excused himself to administer kisses in the nursery, Jobert and De Chabenac retook their seats.

'Thank you for the return of my investment, Jobert.' De Chabenac glanced towards the door as the household staff withdrew having cleared the table. 'Such an unexpected gift.

Duque informs me you returned all our investment funds but kept nothing for yourself. Why? Were you unable to make use of Zenari's note of his assumption of responsibility for any losses?'

'That note applied to his decision to the passage of the gold through the Serbian mountains. Once the funds were receipted in Bucharest, Zenari's note was null and void. My movement north with our gold was my responsibility.'

'But no one had suffered — financially, at least — Raive and his investors have their hooks in Bucharest and we have been repaid our impetuous gamble. Though, by my calculations, you have lost in the vicinity of fifty thousand francs. Why?'

The weight and flavours of the dinner compelled Jobert's desire for the softness and warmth of this evening's bed. His mind swooned in anticipation of his fatigue seeping into his down-filled pillow.

'It was in their power — Otal's and Dikaletus' — to give me what I wanted.' Jobert's jaw clenched. 'Yet they chose not to.' Despite his hard stare at De Chabenac, Jobert's face flinched with emotion. 'It was in my power to give the people of Serpenaçi something they needed.' Jobert shrugged. 'So, I gave it.'

On the last warm day of October, having returned to the family farm, Jobert crawled on his hands and knees through the seed heads of yellowed grass towards Bleu.

Bleu lay on his belly in the Auvergne sunshine, knees tucked under his chest with ears alert to the approaching Jobert.

Conscious that he did not want to appear predatory to his warhorse, Jobert paused his creeping to inspect wilted wildflowers. Jobert made a crunching noise with his mouth as if he was sloppily eating something juicy.

The sound captured Bleu's full attention.

Not wishing Bleu to stand, Jobert extended himself to lie on his belly. He bit into an apple and spat the saliva-slicked segment into his hand as an offering to Bleu.

Following a confirmatory sniff of the gift, Bleu's lips and tongue took the juicy segment into his mouth, followed by the remaining fruit, and ground it between his teeth.

Jobert crawled past Bleu's brown head and shoulders and leant against Bleu's warm back.

Sandwiched between the gentle sun and Bleu's hot ribcage, Jobert looked up as a kite hovered overhead scanning for field mice. Beyond Bleu's drowsy head in the farm's lower pasture, this season's colts rolled on their backs in the long grass, then rose to chase each other, only to prance, tails flying, beyond the lunge of a playmate's nip.

Jobert took his notebook from his tailcoat pocket and withdrew Michelle's folded letter. He decided against rustling the paper and disturbing Bleu's slumber. He knew the message well enough. The Cossack lance made a dashing accessory, as the Cricket received compliments and Koschak accepted invitations, during their daily Parisian promenades. With the relaxation of the British naval blockade, Marsden had taken a passage from Brest to Boston.

Jobert's thumb rubbed over a page in the opened notebook.

Two months had passed since Jobert had stood on the banks of the Dniester with Begnzarov. As the sun set on that day, Jobert had read from this very page in his notebook. Jobert had asked Sevalnev and Koranski to translate the phrases he needed, in either Moldavian or whatever tongue Begnzarov spoke. Scribbling down the fragments phonetically, Jobert cobbled together a message which he haltingly read to Begnzarov on that steppe sunset.

'Give this to Tsar Alexander.' Jobert passed across Zenari's satchel. 'The papers describe a thing of immense value to the Tsar.' Jobert looked deep into Begnzarov's weary eyes. 'Immense value. Then trade this.' With the Key pinched by Jobert's thumb and forefinger, the stones in the gold caught the day's last rays. Jobert passed across the ring. 'This has vast power. Demand a high price. A very high price. Understand?'

Begnzarov raised his gaze from the Key to Jobert. For just a moment Jobert felt he saw a softening under the warrior's cheekbones, before Begnzarov gave a single nod with his reply, 'Understand.'

The rise and fall of Bleu's ribs under Jobert's shoulder blades induced drowsiness.

As Jobert tipped his brim to tilt his hat, his fingertips scraped across a nobbled metallic surface. He removed his hat to inspect the ornate çelenk pinned to the crown. The family of the Serpenaçi blacksmith had replaced the clasp pin in exchange for Duque's little chestnut pack-horse.

Flies crawled towards Bleu's half-closed eyes.

Jobert set his hat on his head. With a wave of his hand, the flies dispersed, and he whispered, 'They shall not pass.'

Jobert's adventures, in 1802, continue in
An Eye For Ground.

If you enjoyed Jobert's adventure, it would be
deeply appreciated if you would provide a review
in your favourite online bookstore.

Visit **www.jobert.site**

to discover more about the Jobert series.

Author's Note

In 2005, I served, as an Australian Army officer, on the Pakistan-Afghanistan border for twelve months. My service was in the immediate aftermath of the Western coalition's invasion of Afghanistan in 2002 and Iraq in 2003.

I was attached to the Pakistan Army and posted to the border city of Quetta. The tribal people of Quetta were poverty stricken, highly illiterate, culturally fragmented, fervently religious, deeply conservative and heavily armed. Three separate conflicts raged throughout the city at this time; one of which was an extension of the tribal conflict that overflowed from Afghanistan less than one hundred kilometres away.

On this battlefield, in full view of the declared enemies of my nation, I served alone and unarmed.

A distressing aspect of living and working in conflict zones — my experiences were in Timor Leste, Pakistan-Afghanistan border, Kashmir and Iraq — was that the local people I lived with and befriended remained and suffered under the ongoing calamities and injustices.

I was wounded during my service in Pakistan, but I remained at my post and completed my duty. My connection to that place remains with me, as I continue to manage daily the consequences of those injuries.

A wise and dear friend said to me of my writing journey, 'As you build Jobert, so you rebuild yourself.' The year 1801 was an opportune lull in the French Revolutionary and Napoleonic wars to whisk Jobert away to somewhere unexpected.

In *If God Wills It*, I hoped to convey from my time in an environment of extreme stress a sense of desperate vulnerability.

In one moment in a foreign land, all is as it is at home. In the next moment, aspects are bewildering, disorienting and threatening. Perhaps you have found the same.

Rob McLaren
Veresdale, Queensland
December 2024

Bibliography

Calvert, M., Young, P., *A Dictionary of Battles, 1715-1815,* New York, 1979

Dupuy, R.E., Dupuy T.N., *The Encyclopaedia of Military History,* London, 1970

Glover, G., *The Forgotten War Against Napoleon – Conflict in the Mediterranean 1793-1815,* London, 2017

Johnson, W.E., *The Crescent among the Eagles-The Ottoman Empire and the Napoleonic Wars,* Ocean Springs, 1994

Nicolle, D., *Armies of the Ottoman Empire 1775-1820,* London, 1998

I also acknowledge the insights and detail provided by the Wikipedia, Google Maps and YouTube websites.

Chronology of Events

The following chronology lists the historical events that are referred to within the story.

1800

14 Jun   Battle of Marengo. France, under Bonaparte, defeats Austria to reclaim Lombardy.

3 Dec   Battle of Hohenlinden. France, under Moreau, defeats Austria to end the War of the Second Coalition.

1801

9 Feb   Peace of Lunéville signed between France and Austria.

8 Mar   British landing near Aboukir Bay, Egypt.

21 Mar   French defeated at the Battle of Alexandria. The French Army, under Menou, digs in ready for the siege of Alexandria.

31 Mar   Ottoman army arrives at El-Arich.

19 Apr   British and Ottoman forces capture Fort Julien at Rosetta after a four-day bombardment opening access to the Nile River.

27 Jun   General Belliard surrenders French forces in Cairo.

31 Aug   Siege of Alexandria ends with Menou's surrender of all French forces in Egypt.

Ready Reference –
Military Organisations

A very quick and simple overview of military organisations:

Squad/File/Patrol – Cavalry soldiers were grouped together in threes or fours to patrol, cook and sleep together as well as ride together in larger formations.

Section – Twelve men, when at full-strength, or three squads/files, commanded by a corporal.

Platoon – Two sections, twenty-four men at full-strength, commanded by a sergeant.

Troop – Two platoons, fifty men at full strength, commanded by a second lieutenant.

Company – Two troops, one hundred men at full strength, commanded by a captain.

Squadron – Two companies, commanded by the senior captain of the two companies.

Regiment – Three or more squadrons, commanded by a colonel. The regimental commander had two chiefs of squadron who could assist him by commanding one to three squadrons on independent tasks.

Brigade – Two or more regiments of infantry or cavalry, with supporting artillery, engineers and logistic support, commanded by a brigadier (a rank of general).

Division – Two or more brigades, with associated support, commanded by a major general.

Corps – Two or more divisions, capable of significant independent operations, commanded by a lieutenant general.

Army, or Army Wing – Two or more corps, commanded by a general.

Ready Reference – Measurement Conversion

A very approximate conversion of metric measurements:

One inch is approximately two and a half centimetres.

One metre is approximately one yard, or three feet.

One thousand metres, or one kilometre, is approximately two-thirds of a mile (five-eighths).

One mile is approximately one and a half kilometres.

One kilogram is approximately two pounds.

One litre, or one kilogram of water, is approximately two pints.

Dramatis Personae

This story is a work of fiction within a historical setting. In the list of characters below, those with their names underlined actually <u>existed</u>, otherwise the character is a creation of the author's.

Army of Italy

Raive — Colonel, a staff officer on the headquarters of the French Army of Italy.

Zenari — Colonel, a staff officer on the headquarters of the Cisalpine Legion.

André Jobert — Lieutenant Colonel, a staff officer on the headquarters of the French Army of Italy.

De Chabenac — Lieutenant Colonel, a staff officer on the headquarters of the French Army of Italy.

Koschak — Lieutenant, a staff officer on the headquarters of the French Army of Italy.

Duque — A sergeant-veterinarian on the headquarters of the French Army of Italy.

Fazio — A sergeant on the headquarters of the Cisalpine Legion.

Moench — Jobert's trumpeter on the headquarters of the French Army of Italy.

Yann Chauvel — Jobert's uncle. Ex-sergeant-veterinarian Manages the family farm in the high country of the Auvergne.

Marguerite and Camille	Marguerite is Raive's wife and Camille is Marguerite's cousin and companion.

Ottoman Empire

<u>Hospodar Constantine Ypsilantis</u>	Prince of Wallachia and Moldavia, vassal states of the Ottoman Empire.
Otal Alaybey	Commander of Moldavia's cavalry.
Dikaletus Pasha	A dragoman/aide of the Hospodar.
Tétény	Chieftain of Transylvanian uhlans.
Boyar Sevalnev	Governor of the (fictitious) Moldavian town of Serpenaçi.
Hetman Koranski	Chieftain of refugee Polish Ukrainians in northern Moldavia.
Begnzarov Khan	Cossack Khan of the Crimean Tartars.